T-Shirt

Richard Asplin was born in 1972. He has been a stand-up comedian, guitarist, film critic, marketing assistant and underpant salesman. He lives in London with one girlfriend and two cats.

Richard Asplin

T-SHIRT AND GENES

ARROW

Published by Arrow Books in 2001

2 4 6 8 10 9 7 5 3 1

Copyright © Richard Asplin 2001

Richard Asplin has asserted his right under the
Copyright, Designs and Patents Act, 1988 to be
identified as the author of this work

First published in the United Kingdom in 2001 by Arrow Books

Arrow Books
The Random House Group Limited
20 Vauxhall Bridge Road, London SW1V 2SA

Random House Australia (Pty) Limited
20 Alfred Street, Milsons Point, Sydney,
New South Wales 2061, Australia

Random House New Zealand Limited
18 Poland Road, Glenfield,
Auckland 10, New Zealand

Random House South Africa (Pty) Limited
Endulini, 5a Jubilee Road, Parktown 2193, South Africa

The Random House Group Limited Reg. No. 954009

www.random.co.uk

A CIP catalogue record for this book
is available from the British Library

Papers used by Random House are natural, recyclable products made
from wood grown in sustainable forests. The manufacturing processes
conform to the environmental regulations of the country of origin

ISBN 0 09 941684 0

Set in 12/16PT Walbaum MT by SX Composing DTP, Rayleigh, Essex
Printed and bound in Great Britain by
Bookmarque Ltd, Croydon, Surrey

For Helen

'Traditional scientific method has always been at the very *best*, 20-20 hindsight. It's good for seeing where you've been. It's good at testing the truth of what you think you know, but it can't tell you where you *ought* to go.'

Robert M Pirsig

PART ONE

'Genitals are a great distraction to scholarship'
Malcolm Bradbury

'Okay but quick then,' she giggled. 'And not here because I've got a staple gun up my bottom.'

'Sorry, sorry. Howabout there, up against the year planner?'

'Yes, okay,' she grinned, kicking off her heels. 'If we go hard enough we can rub off Year Ten's field trip.'

A beginning for which I must proffer an apology. It would have been a tad more sophisticated, a touch more sultry and a whole urgent teenage pounce more bloody sexy to have started this off another way.

I mean. A staple gun up her bottom. I ask you.

But there was no stopping us now. I'd gone and

3

suggested it and after three *go ons,* a couple of *why nots* and a *you know you want to,* the larky buzz had got the better of her and we began to strip hastily.

Deborah, for 'tis she (colleague, crush, date, lover, girlfriend and finally fiancée in that order) sprung up from against the desk and frantically began to busy herself with tuggings at her jacket and a fiddly skirt zip. I fumbled shirt buttons urgently and concentrated hard on hard-ons.

'That door's locked, isn't it?' Deborah hiccuped with panic, attempting as business-like a tone as she could whilst hopping about behind the armchairs, her skirt snagged on her toes. 'Double check, quick double check.'

'It's okay okay, I've got it!' I hopped over the low table littered with crowded ashtrays and yellowing TES's to the heavy door. Deborah quickly crouched forward, gripping her unbuttoned blouse tight together and shushed closed the yellow curtains sending the room into a chalk-dust summer haze.

Truth is, the door wasn't locked. Well come on, that kind of defeats the object of public-place sex in my book. That thrill, that crafty-fag-behind-the-bike-sheds charge of naughtiness. That's why people bother, isn't it? I mean if you're going to lock doors and turn out lights and crouch down and *shhh* you may as well be at home. Believe me, if a knob's worth doing, it's worth doing right.

'Locked and bolted,' I lied, rattling the handle noisily.

Back into the room, I let my shirt fall to the floor as Deborah skipped forward gingerly but with a flash of Christmas morning eagerness. We leant up against the creaky pigeon holes and I slipped cold hands around her waist. Warm and squidgy where flesh met elastic.

'I can't believe I let you talk me into this,' Deborah whispered, hunching her shoulders coyly. 'Here of all places. And now. We *can't*.'

She had a point. The staffroom was cold (one radiator – broken), beige (one repaint – 1976) and smelly (one gargantuan dog-end containing Old Holborn and corduroy permanently smouldering behind something). This, coupled with the parents' evening going on above, and yes, perhaps my suggestion of a quickie was better kept locked behind closed pants.

But we touched noses Eskimo style and our eyebrows said *Oh yes we can* in sexual semaphore.

'I've been sitting in that hall upstairs for hours,' I said, fiddling nervously with Deborah's earring, 'and I've been thinking of nothing but you. Naked on this floor.' Deborah slipped herself out of her blouse with a crackle of static and I gulped hard. 'All the while that Mrs Tyler moaned on about her little Stuart and his bloody biology results I had that little slit in your skirt in the corner of my eye.'

'Did you see what she was wearing?' Deborah

laughed. 'Or almost wearing. Douglas couldn't take his eyes off her.'

'I wasn't watching,' I said. 'Something else on my mind,' and I ran a finger over the strap of her bra. 'Well, a couple of things.' Deborah's hands rummaged about my waist beneath me and there was the clink of hasty belt buckle followed by a loud zip.

'*Shhh!*' I winced.

'Get these trousers off,' she whispered close into my ear. Her tight hot breath caused a Presley wobble from my bare knees.

'Now in these stages,' I began, my twitching fingers wrestling urgently at her bra clips, 'that is the pre-copulatory stages of homosapien mating, the mouth will often concentrate on regions of the partner such as the ears, neck and genitalia . . .'

'Not now, Charlie, don't start,' Debs said. 'Leave it in the classroom.'

'Breathing will deepen and the pulse rate increase from 70 to 100 per minute.' We faced each other, my dopey grin exactly failing to mirror her coquettish smirk. Deborah bent to whisk her tights off, rolling the shiny fabric lower, and I resumed the lecture.

'As arousal intensifies . . .'

'Not at this rate, buster,' came the teasing interjection as she balled up the hose and tossed it over a foamless armchair.

'Thank you,' I parried, my arms around her waist

once again and breathing slowly into her ear. 'A sexual flush may appear over the upper abdomen and breasts.'

Oh, I should point out, I don't always do this. I wouldn't want you to get a bad impression of me. You'll have ample opportunity to get a bad impression of me later. But I sometimes do. It makes Debs smile and I don't come as quickly. Guys have their own little ways, don't pretend they don't. Times tables, footie commentators, whatever. This is mine. Okay?

I trailed my fingers a curve around her legs up to the waistband of her flowery knickers. She noted my momentary hesitation.

'What? They're my last clean pair, sod off. You with your fake Calvin cheapos,' and she twonged my waistband.

I looked down. True enough I was sporting in my wobbly fashion those button up Y-pants with legs, Deborah having *Mmmmed* at a similar pair in some fashion monthly. They didn't quite look the same on me, however, as I don't so much go in and out in the right places as out and then a bit further out in most places. No apologies, I like bacon butties as much as I loathe home multi-gyms.

So where was I? Oh yes.

'Well they'd better go then,' I said.

'With the greatest pleasure, Mr Ellis,' Deborah smirked and unhooked the offending pantwear, yanking them down to my knees.

'Now,' I said. I slipped my hands under her arms and pinged off her bra, the white elastic gave a sigh and relaxed around her shoulders. 'As we see, the female's ample visual stimuli affects the male's penis which, by means of vaso-congestion, modifies in dimension dramatically.'

'There you go, blowing your own trumpet again . . .'

We kissed quickly through toothy grins, my sweaty palms on her bottom, easing her hips towards mine. Deborah ran her index fingers down my torso, coming to rest with an expert cup, causing a Mexican wave from the home terraces.

'Similarly in the *fee-hee-hee*male, the *ahh vah vah vahh*ginal tubes will distend, extending the *oh oh ohh*verall length by up to ten centimetres.'

'Mmm, I wish you'd extend your oh-oh-ohverall length by ten centimetres.'

We kissed again, eyes closed this time, harder and deeper and longer – she tasted of Deborah. Our tongues did that tongue thing, twirling, curling, swirling and unfurling. She broke away, holding my stare and eased backwards onto the floor between two skeletal armchairs and I followed, definitely not uh-uh no way honest m'lud suddenly thinking about Stuart Tyler's mum. Honest.

Well honestish.

I knelt at her feet, leaving Mrs Tyler standing by the pigeon holes.

Look, it happens. Concentration nips off for a fag and

smack, you're shagging someone else. You either blink hard and promise to give your concentration a thorough dressing down a bit later for not taking its job seriously, or you go with the understudy and bite your lip during the screamy bit. I'm a blink hard kind of guy myself.

I looked down at Deborah and was suddenly aware of ourselves.

She was naked, save her flowery knicks, next to that nasty haemorrhoidal armchair, in the staffroom of the school in which we were both employed. I was, for the first time, seeing my two lives juxtaposed. Work and woman, life and love, home and away.

Lesson and, as it were, playtime.

Sliding my palms up her thighs, I crooked awkwardly forward and followed their trail with kisses.

'To fully appreciate the metamorphosis of the female's reproductive organs,' I resumed, my face now inches from the flowery fabric. Daisies I think. 'A close inspection of —'

'Would you stop talking to my fanny!' Deborah cut in. I grabbed the waistband in my fingers and, as Deborah arched herself up a smidge, I slid the undies to her ankles.

'*A-haa, here we see the clitoris at play.*'

'Charlie, I mean it . . .'

'*A shy and nocturnal species at heart, it prefers to spend its time in the safety and shade of the bush. Emerging only for sustenance at sunset, it is a rare and captivating —*'

'Captivating sight,' Deborah interrupted. 'We know, we know. Mr Attenborough, you'll be adding this one to the endangered species list if you don't get down and start paying it some attention. Now lie down,' Deborah said forcefully, shifting up onto her elbows. 'Lie down and shut up.'

I sank down onto the itchy, brogue-worn floor and she knelt over me. I lay my head back on the carpet and closed my eyes, Deborah taking my scrotum in her hand, the perfect touch sending the usual warm fuzziness around my jawline and then up around my brain, veering left to dispatch a load to the spine. A lazy smile appeared on my lips and I made an *Ooh-don't-stop* kind of noise, her hot thighs squeezing my ribcage.

Deborah had her eyelids softly closed at this point, her chest rising and falling in deeper and deeper breaths. She remained for a few aching moments astride me, holding me, when she knelt up and rested herself above my twitching groin. I raised three feet into the air, leaving the coarse carpeting far far away, suspended on a pillow of heartbeats and impending unbearableness. The staffroom ceiling shifted and swam and my eyes rolled back. I felt her warm breath on my face. My teeth gritted into one huge back tooth and I gazed a soft focus gaze into Deborah's eyes. Glancing down, her breasts hung quillimetres from my chest.

'Now?' she said, easing her hips backwards.

10

And then with a shriek she sat back fast, her fingernails biting into my shoulders.

'*What the hell's that?!*' she spat.

'*Ow ow!*' I squawked, throwing my arms wide, 'You're bending him ... *ow!*'

'*Shhh!*' Deborah hissed. 'I heard something outside.'

We froze, heartbeats pounding like Zulu drums, not daring to breathe.

Nothing.

Deborah looked down.

'I hope I didn't scare him?'

One blind eye stared back in timid innocence. Reaching down, Deborah gave him a prod and a gentle twang. Wee balls wobbled but they didn't fall down.

'Kiss him better?' I suggested hopefully.

'Nice try,' she smiled, lowering herself slowly. '*Niice try.*'

'Ohh, ohhh yes. My scrotal skin,' I panted. 'Is ... is it constricting?'

'Oh Charlie . . .' Deborah said. Which I think was more of an annoyed Oh Char*leyyy*, rather than a wildly passionate *Ohhh! Charlie.*

'*Ohhhh! Yes, Charlie!*' she gasped again. (Hmm, could've been wrong then.) Deborah's voice was throaty and cracked as she began to lose herself in the moment.

'Constricting?' I whimpered again. 'Red-red-reducing the *oh-oh-ohhhh*verall mobility of my testes?'

11

My buttocks clenched together and I began to writhe on the carpet. 'Ow fuhhhck, it burns.'

With ever increasing speed, Deborah began to move up and down and in circular motions around my hips.

'Ohhhh Christ!' I gasped, now lost and blinded with longing. Faster and faster she moved. 'Point eight of a second, point eight of a second,' I began to chant.

'Yes, *yesss,*' Deborah urged, building into a rapid bouncing rhythm, snatching in sharp high breaths on every beat.

'Yesss, it's it's it's the male species muscle contractions when approaching *or or or org*haaaasm,' I cried. The insane ramblings of the delirious I know. 'Point eight of *ahhhh* second.' I could feel the unmistakable spasms begin to groove their little reproductive booties down to the ground. Any second now, any second now . . .

And then Deborah screamed.

Fucking hell, I thought, snapping my eyes wide open. That's a first. Deborah isn't, by and large, what you'd call a screamer. There's been moaning. Oh yes. Lots of blue ticks in the moan ledger. Grunting even. Once. Parents' house. Thin walls. You've been there. Not to my parents' house, obviously. But in one of those don't-make-a-sound situations. But screaming. And I mean a real slasher-flick, hairs on the back of your neck type screams. This was a first.

I was allowed to dwell smugly on what was clearly a

9.0 performance from the young British squad for about a second.

Deborah sprung up, also a first, and hopped nimbly behind the nearest armchair.

'Charlie!' she half yelled, half stage-whispered through pursed angry lips.

'Debs, Debs,' I responded in my best caring, sharing tone. 'What's going on?'

'I think we'd all like to know that,' came a far, far too familiar voice.

I turned to face the source of the question.

Standing in the frame of the wide open door was a small boy. Eleven, maybe twelve years old. Brand new blazer, shiny buttons matching his even shinier cheeks. His grey V-necked sweater pulled down too far, so it was visible around the hem of his jacket. He was never going to grow into that one. But it wasn't his voice. He was Timothy Fraser. Year seven. I had spoken to his parents only an hour ago. His parents. Governors, if I recalled.

Yes. Governors. Both of them.

They stood behind him. As did it seemed the entire board. Plus Douglas. Year head. About eight or nine middle-aged faces glared at me. Well the women did. The men seemed more interested in Deborah, naked, her arms across her breasts with just an understuffed chair for her modesty.

The standard by-the-book parents' evening tour of

the school. Governors and heads of year cordially invited. I looked down at myself. Bare as my noughth birthday. Prostrate on the threadbare carpet. Pink, flabby, out of shape. But with one clear working part. A very clear working part. The voice thundered again.

'I demand to see the head.'

Hmmm.

Dear Tell Me How,

My teacher who has a beard called Mr Coulter said that before there was people in the world there was just monkeys and even before dinosaurs. Is this true? I aksed my mum and she said to aks my dad but he is asleep.

thankyou very much, when i grow up i want to find out where the dinosaurs went if they went to another planet because of the oxygen.

Master Charles Ellis age 7

Dear Charles,

Thank you for your lovely letter and the drawing of the chimpanzee fighting the Tyrannosaur. To answer your question, long before monkeys, and even before dinosaurs, about 4 billion years ago, the only living things on planet Earth were something we call microorganisms. These are very tiny living things, each made of a single cell, too small to see without a microscope. Everything that lives came originally from these tiny creatures. Imagine them as slimy bogeys or little fleas that live on your dog – but even smaller!

Thank you for your interest and keep reading!!!

Assist. Editor, Tell Me How.

TWO

*'Don't you call me a mindless philosopher, you
overweight glob of grease'*

C-3P0

Adrian jostled, elbowed, 'I'm sorried,' and 'Could I just,
thanksed,' his way from the heaving bar. A beer bottle
was clenched maternally between his arm and ribs,
another in his sweaty right hand. His left gripped a
straight glass of monochrome Guinness, its creamy
head lilting a gentle Oirish path down his knuckles.

'There we go, chaps.' He laid the drinks to rest on the
sticky table in our cramped booth. Brad shuffled along
and Adrian took his seat among the dreggy empties and
the white dandruff of picked-at beer labels.

'Sexual frustration,' he declared, dropping the papery

slivers one by one into the grimy ashtray. Brad chuckled. I glanced at his cheeky phizog and shook my head. Satisfied with his level of pleasure in my situation, I resumed my painstaking examination of the table in front of me.

Hmm. *Man Utd*. Lovingly carved. Beautiful crafts-manship that. A dedication to sport that is truly rare these days. Uplifting really. Oh look, another budding George Hepplewhite has penned a wee critique just beneath. *Are cuntz*. Lovely. I gave an internal sigh and rejoined planet Earth.

'So –' I began, after a frothy swig.

'*So?*' Brad yanked the conversation out of its chair by the earlobe impatiently. 'Have you heard any more? Can you go back? Are you fired, suspended, what?' He visibly caught his own sugar-rush salaciousness and relaxed suddenly into a trendy slouch. 'Y'know. Whassappnin'?'

Truth is, because I've known Brad long enough – as helpful and good-natured and splendid a chum as he is, he wanted all the goss, all the police-tape evidence so he could begin to solve my problems. So he could embark on sentences that featured the words 'your shoes', and 'big picture' and (brace yourself) 'ball-park' (vomito, vomitas, vomitat). Brad, like us all, calls it 'just trying to help'. But Brad, like us all, is merely a rubber-necker at the hard-shoulder pile-up of emotional misfortune. Life doesn't afford us the opportunity to feel really cosy that often. Not really warm-cockle satisfied. It's just not like that. So on the eighth day God created other people's problems. And lo, he saw that it was smug.

'Jury's still out,' I shrugged. 'Should be the end of the week.'

'Can't they just give you lines or something?' Adrian offered. 'Write out a hundred times *I will not filthy up art teachers in the staffroom during parents' evening*?'

I shook my head.

'And there's still no word from Debs?' Brad began mentally scrubbing up for the autopsy. 'She hasn't got back to you,' gloves please, nurse 'or popped round,' scalpel. 'Or . . . ?'

Or what? Dished out loving hugs and sworn allegiance to the soiled flag of lustful impetuousness? Held my hand and told the headmaster the staffroom was normally so full of clueless fucks she was surprised anyone noticed the difference? No. Nothing. Deborah, it seemed, had vanished. Her answerphone was whirring and bleeping with my apologies and repentance like R2D2 at a Prodigy gig. And it was currently a dead heat between me and her doorbell as to which had been depressed for longer.

But it was now a full week later. And nothing. Adrian attempted gallantly to jolly me up.

'But you're still getting married, though, right? I mean, that's all still on?' Like some chirpy cockney tailor, Adrian struggled feverishly to stitch a silver lining into my concrete overcoat of a mood.

'You tell me,' I offered feebly. My two bestest friends in the whole wide world sat opposite me. Ten years of vocational education, five years of vacational Friday nights and a graffitied wooden bar-table between us. I looked imploringly into their eyes for some kind of answer. Some kind of new and improved psychological detergent that killed all known predicaments dead, ideally leaving my heart with just a pine-fresh smell, flush after flush.

Adrian chewed his lip. Brad excused himself and nicked off to the bogs.

Adrian and I sloshed and gulped in silence for a moment, silence being quite spectacularly the wrong word.

The Prince Albert pub is, unsurprisingly, on Prince Albert Road, London NW1. On this particular Friday, the Albert, like all London pubs, heaved with the pre-club throng — sweaty posses of shiny young ladies, all attempting to look sixteen years old (except the sixteen year olds, all of whom were attempting to look twenty-five). And for every excitable female, three eager, hairy males strutted, boozed and sneered their labels about the bar. The PA system oofed out a bassy cardiometer of club anthems, vibrating the girls' cock-tales while threatening to upend the lads' gassy beers. Come ten-thirty the place would alchemize back into a pleasant little London boozer. As if there were gold in them there hills, the flocks and herds would beat retreat to their danceteria of choice. Everyone over the age of twenty-five could then breathe out, unclench sphincters and relax again. Unfortunately, this little ritual would invariably succeed in making the remaining few feel like Chelsea pensioners, with mutterings of 'Bloody kids,' and 'In my day . . .' eminating from the most liberal of booths.

'Bloody kids,' Brad tutted as he retook his seat. 'Why do we come here, can someone remind me? Can't hear a damn thing.'

You'll be pleased to note neither Adrian nor myself felt compelled to do the classic 'H-huh! *Pardon*?!' gag. Small mercies.

'You're cheering me up,' I reminded him as he drained his bottle o' Bud. 'Apparently.'

'Then cheer the fuck up. If anyone's got problems it's Daddy Cool here.'

We discussed Adrian's impending fatherhood with a mix of Gump-ish wisdom and guyish gaggery. Well, I say discussed but Adrian was being as off-hand and dismissive as ever. When you've known someone since they were twelve, as we all had, watching them metamorphose from short shuffling caterpillars into . . . well slightly hairier shuffling caterpillars, you have an invested interest in their sex life. We had staggered around a blurry pub-crawl to celebrate Brad's first blow job and all chipped in for champagne when I'd eventually lost my cherry. (We'd all needed fake I.D. for the former and used real I.D. for the latter – you do the maths.)

But on this occasion Adrian was playing the fatherhood cards very close to his Benetton knitwear indeed. Virtually all the info we had on his giant leap into maturity we'd had to pummel and squeeze out of him or get from Elizabeth. So more often than not these new-mannish round-table discussions just descended quickly into juvenile nonsense.

Brad lifted an empty beer glass to his lips and echoed 'Luke, I am your father' about sixty times and we laughed snotty bubbles into our drinks. There were two or three 'no worries' and the odd 'Heyyy, you'll be *fine*'. And we knew he would. We inquired about Elizabeth. She was fine too. Apparently, and this was news to me, all pregnant women don't look like Demi Moore. You're shocked, I know. Elizabeth had become, in these last stages, not so much Demi as Patrick. But with larger breasts. Which, we were comforted to hear, were also fine.

It was my round.

I chivvied along my seat in that half-standing, half-sitting way that booths insist on and started for the teeming bar. Brad moved the subject on to a colourful anecdote involving himself and some 'macho gorillas' that he'd encountered at the blow-hand dryer. I left them to it.

I loitered for about twelve years, finally securing a place at the bar. Biology teacher, not a *bad* job, I mused, dipping my elbows into two convenient puddles of lager froth and letting the woodwork take my weight.

Not a bad job at all really. Quite respectable. Power, prospects, pensions. Other cool stuff beginning with P. Not quite what a young, fired-up would-be radical (two Billy Bragg albums, mid-period) might have dreamed of. But never the less, *Playstation*. Knew there was another one.

'Ex'-biology teacher. Yes. Not quite the same ring, I fancied. The fraying denim remnants of my lofty, lefty youth may well beam with lad-done-well pride. But I needed more convincing. Not the most deafening call for people in my lack-of-position. And randy, tubby, back-on-the-shelf ex-biology teachers? God I needed a drink. If only to stimulate my receptor cells and send transmissions along my glossopharyngeal and lingual nerves.

Sorry, sorry. One thing we definitely *can* do. Have three too many and bore the dribbly arse off everybody with wanky shop talk.

Over my shoulder, Adrian and Bradley slumped contentedly. They picked at beer labels whilst no doubt competing for the funniest anecdote, the sickest joke, the best impersonation of Michael Caine. Our whole relationship was entirely founded on the shaky ground of one-upmanship and always had been. Who could do the filthiest burps and skiddiest BMX-ings had blossomed through GCSE results to who had the shittiest boss or (not kidding) who had the most remote controls in their house.

Last count it was Brad. Six. Don't ask me.

I pondered this one occasionally: would we still be sneering and bickering for the top spot on our death-beds? If the cold war hadn't been thawed out and defrosted, might we have found ourselves lying among charred desolation, our last human breaths whispering across the blackened wasteground? *What?! Call* that *radiation sickness? Get outta here! I've lost eight layers of skin. I look like ya momma!?*

Now competition among males in any species is industry standard. Everybody knows this. Being the best, the first − it's accepted. Like electric guitars, carburettors and limericks about people from Venus, it's just *what guys do.* Sometimes subtly −

'Oh really? *I* got the digitally remastered director's cut in widescreen with surround sound.'

Sometimes well, not.

'Yeah? *Yeah?* Outside. Now. C'mon! 'Kin wanker. *Wangarrr!*

Charming.

Now pretty much everything has been blamed for this. Poseable action figures in dappled fatigues; school grading systems; Saturday morning cartoons. But if anything is going to stand in the dock and raise its hands in responsibility, it's going to be our little chum, the Y chromosome. Maleness itself.

In virtually all species, it's the guys who have all the attitude. Alpha *females* in a chimp hierarchy are tricky to spot, more often than not age is the deciding factor. But spotting the guv' in the gang is easy peasy, pudding and, in the most part, pie. He'll be strutting about, chest out, mouthy and victorious. Other chimps sometimes even bowing to kiss his feet. Same is true in some ways, believe it or not, for chickens.

The term *pecking order* was coined by a Norwegian biologist back in the squawking twenties when he noted distinct behavioural patterns in our eggy friends. Chickens in new groups solved disputes by simply jabbing anyone who got in their way so everyone quickly learned their place. By the end, the winner – big bird, one mean clucker – was the guy who'd won the most bouts. And so it went on down the line. Those with the biggest peckers, as it were, getting the most seed.

In the animal kingdom, it's definitely worthwhile climbing that corporate ladder. Major perks await. Alpha male chimps get the best of everything available – best home, best food and best women. This makes the top rung a productive but precarious place. They will spend a lot of time looking out for challengers to their throne. Holding court as top chimp, top chicken or top cat (the indisputable leader of the gang) – it's a position worth fighting for. It's the only place that guarantees an abundant lineage.

*

Back at the bar.

'Yes, mate?' I yelled my drinks at the wet-look, waistcoated barkeep. The music thudded about. The bar-room crush barred all room and crushed, Brad's gorillas taking up most of the space — folded tenners and twenties clamped between hairy digits, their dark eyes flicking between the harried staff, eyebrows bouncing for attention. Roars of primeval, chummy laughter burst sporadically from surrounding tables. It was about a quarter to ten. Gear sticks and fan-belts were being lubricated in the noisy pitstop, ready for the first few laps of *dancing and romancing*.

'Gorillas'. Not quite. In a way, Brad's middle-class metaphor was spot on. Gorillas are polygamous as a species. And these fellas didn't look like one-woman-men to me. As they spoke, you could see their hungry eyes darting about, like Ronco Bare-Flesh-Detectors set on demo.

But gorillas have very low relative testes weights. Small balls to you and me. Now I'm no Jane Goodall, but from their volume and confidence, this lot had to be packing some serious testicles. All whipped out at once, they could probably affect the tides.

Ho-hum. I paid for the drinks and made my way boothwards. Maybe lifting spirits would lift my spirits.

THREE

'I'm tired and I want to go to bed'

Richard Dreyfuss

I retook my seat. Brad and Adrian were laughing. I seemed to have interrupted them telling each other they only wanted the bloody doors blown off.

'Obliged,' Adrian nodded. We clinked glasses for no better reason than we all had glasses and it made a nice noise.

'Was that broad at your parents do, then?' Brad asked.

'Broad . . . ?'

'Jezus, listen to this guy. That one you kept going on about.'

'Mrs Tyler? Yes.'

'Heh-*heyyy!*' they both said in unison.

Look I should explain. I've only met this woman a couple of times. Me (Mr Ellis), her, her satanic offspring Stuart and Douglas, the head of year. Little meetings after school to do with lack of effort, lack of homework — a general lack of pretty well everything I require from my biology class. Not that I'm some Dickensian Bumble, understand. I merely require, if not 180 IQ points, then at least 100 keeping-the-noise-down-and-not-pissing-me-off points.

Stuart scored minus 40 on both scales.

I pretty much wanted to have sex with her the moment she marched into Douglas's office in a leather and leopardskin hipsway of pouty cleavaged humpability. Although I was seeing Deborah at this point, Mrs Tyler and her long-lashed, gravelly voiced curves was to star in most of my imaginary nocturnal dalliances from then on.

Which in some twist of logic way, convinced me that Debs was the girl for me.

I've had this theory out with Brad and Adrian and they both concede, so I feel confident in slicing up this gateau of wisdom for you to wrap in your party bag and take home.

When Adrian first met his wife, Elizabeth, he wanted to marry her. Out of everyone I had ever met through my educational years, Adrian was the romantic one, the one for wine and roses and chocolates and support and respect and treating girls properly. Which of course meant in his teens, he didn't get to treat girls at all. He would sit in his room listening to The Smiths and writing bad poems. Or perch on kitchen chairs watching sporty kids do all the snogging at parties.

Brad, mostly.

So when he did finally meet Elizabeth, the woman he chose to share his beloved Tom Hanks movies with, he wanted to marry her and do what married people do. Not have sex as often as they used to and bicker about soft furnishings. And he confided in us about her continued lack of attendance in his five-fingered fantasies. As much as he loved her, she just refused to turn up. I shared my Mrs Tyler anecdote and we nodded, like three wise old Yodas, into our beer. *Hmm, two women you have. Choice you must make, hmm? Use the sauce, Luke.*

Somehow our stomach churney sixth-form-poetry feelings were stopping us using these women as sexy pervo material. Not that we didn't have numerous alternatives in our mental wings, it's just these were all Ann Summers bedecked leggy model types − vacuous page three lovelies. Not women we wanted to hold, laugh with and share Keatsian summer evenings with.

Not women like Deborah.

*

'So you gonna make your move on her?' Brad asked. 'Get her in for another meeting? Show her your *syllabus*?'

'No,' I said.

'How come? She sounds like just what you need. You gone off her? Leather miniskirts and stockings not do it for you any more?'

'He's got a point,' Adrian piped up. 'You don't have to marry the woman. Just, y'know?' And he gave a whistle and a chicken-wing elbow twitch.

It's the Madonna–Whore dichotomy.

In the lamb-chopped days of Victorian sexual morality, there were two kinds of dames. The future spouse with which to talk, and the casual shag with which to pork, this behaviour being deeply rooted in male mental and genetic make-up.

Natural selection has designed us to be as prolific and perfect gene-machines as society allows. Get your genes into the next generation or woe betide your species. Which essentially means, guys, have lots of healthy babies and bring them up as strong, sexy, confident people. i.e. as good gene-machines. And so it goes on.

Now on average, one's children are made up of 50% the mother's genes and 50% the father's. So for guys choosing their mattress mate, it isn't just about who's got the longest legs, or curviest butt etc. You have to consider things like fidelity.

Yes this gal might be a spectacular lay, taking more positions than a *Guardian* reader on the abortion issue. But what if she's taking these positions with others? You don't want to be spending valuable hunter-gatherer time rearing children that aren't yours.

In fact, biologists by the name of Baker and Bellis showed back in 1984 that the quality of a man's sperm is based, not on how often he lets it out, but on how long it's been since he last saw his partner. The longer she's been out of sight, the more opportunity she's had to take delivery of another man's consignment.

So by all means, guys, your body says, have some fun, sow those seeds. But. If you're looking for a long-term quality investment with good dividends and high interest rates, that quiet girl in the corner may be a better stock in which to make your deposit.

Which is why Mrs Tyler is at home, chain smoking and tugging her leopardskin leggings from the Hotpoint. And I'm engaged to marry a sweet, secondary school art teacher whom I love.

Sorry, I mean I *was* engaged to be married.

Was.

'We've just been discussing your situ, vis-a-vis work 'n' stuff.' Placing his bottle gently down with great care, Brad linked his fingers and began to gesture in a *Late Review* sort of fashion. 'Let's look worst case.

Debs is outta here, hasta la vista, baby. The school heads, governors or whatever, go total mondo freakoid. Come next term, it's P45 time, ten-four, good buddy.'

I should point out, Brad is not actually from the Upper East Side of New York. He's from Ruislip. He's just always talked like this. It comes from a misspent youth, late nights, experimenting with VHS. *Try some of this, man*, someone will whisper, passing a taped-from-TV copy of *Die Hard* around the room. Innocent enough. But then *Die Hard* stops doing it for you. Six months later you're shaking, pale-skinned, bleary-eyed, wandering round Blockbuster looking for that one quick fix of Tommy Lee Jones to get you through the weekend. Tragic really.

'Yeah. Cheers, mate,' I sighed. I knew all this of course. I'd spent the last seven days thinking of little else. But I didn't need it drawled out in bad cop-drama-ese at me. 'So what am I going to do?'

'Hmm, it's a toughie, no doubt about it.'

'Yep,' Adrian agreed.

Big pause. Not a big help. Just a big pause.

'Well, young Chucky m'boy, what you ain't gonna do is get anywhere by rushing in all guns blazing, shooting your mouth off to this Douglas character or getting all antsy with Debs. Be cool, be calm, don't rush anything, take your time. Things will sort themselves out.'

'You are actually The Fonz, aren't you, Bradley?'

31

'Heyyy.' He thumbs-upped and we all kicked him under the table.

'What you're *going* to do,' Adrian stepped in wearing his logic hat, 'is kick around your flat for another week, realphabetising your books and feeling sorry for yourself.'

'Fair point,' I shrugged. 'So what *should* I do?'

'If I was in your shoes,' (told you) Brad offered matter-of-factly, 'I'd just apologise.'

'Tried it. She's not listening.'

'Well try a bit bloody harder. It's the only way. Sorry to Debs for ruining her career and reputation and stuff. Sorry to the school for ruining . . .' Brad searched for the words. 'I dunno. Ruining their carpet, I guess.'

He was enjoying this and who could blame him. A juicy little problem to solve and one that made him look alpha-male superior. Brad mismanaged a West End bookshop for his monthly crust. No heavy-gowned traditions or chalky mottos for him to kowtow to. He led a simple life of promotions, sales targets and hardback bestseller lists. He had never understood my early engagement – women were to him a weekend distraction, bit of sport when there was nothing on at the local Cineplex. A handsome enough fellow and one time President of the university Film Soc, he had spent his late teens loading B movies into projectors and leading first years into his bedroom. And in my teaching post, he was convinced I was selling myself short, that I was on the road to nowhere, that I had sold out my hopes.

Competitive as we were, we still wanted each other to be happy. Earning noticeably less than ourselves, but happy.

'About all you can do,' Adrian agreed through a milky mustache of real Dublin smoothness.

I stared into my vodka, dancing the clinky ice around the glass for a bit.

'And if I don't want them back?'

'Then you're a knobwit.'

'No I mean it. Why can't this be the best thing that ever happened to me?'

'Losing your job, prospects, career and, oh yes, fiancée, all on the same day?' Adrian inquired. Quite understandably. He wasn't privy to the desperate mental salvage job I had contracted out to my inner homunculi.

I sat back in my seat. The pub was beginning to empty now. Every so often, a sharp wind would sneak its way past the doorman and mingle unwelcomely as jackets were passed around and pints downed in one-one-one-one-yayyyyy. From the copious amounts of 'See yas' and 'Laters' that were being bandied aggressively about it looked like everyone was off to the same club. They would all reconvene in a forty-minute queue and eight-quid door fee later to continue where they left off. Debating the Premier League, rating supermodels and leering boisterously at passing totty. And the men likewise. If they could get their gargantuan bollocks through the doors, that is.

I chucked back the last finger of fiery liquid.

'Maybe this is the kick up the arse that you're always telling me I need? I could jack in the teaching. Do something else. Start afresh or, well, y'know, do —' I was floundering — 'other things . . .'

'Yeah. Right. Like what, pray tell O Jack o' no trades, master of less?' Brad inquired.

'Oh I dunno.' And I didn't. Here's where my new five-year plan fell short. By about four years and three hundred and sixty-four days. My life was dead frogs and red biros. Had been for nigh on five years. That was me.

I hadn't always wanted to teach biology. Hadn't always wanted to teach at all. When I was a wee laddie I wanted to grow up to be Steve Austin. Then as an oily teenager, I kind of fancied — well, pretty much everyone really. Girls and the impressing thereof took priority over little things like career objectives and breathing. All I had known was that I wouldn't be happy until I was something big in science. I wanted my name on the weighty tomes that one can't take out of the library without a note signed in triplicate by the head of Cambridge University. I wanted to do something of value, something I'd be remembered for.

Now everyone goes through this brief affair of ideological passion at some point, I guess. Nuns, missionaries.

My mum.

She was a local G.P., which I suppose explains where my interest in biology appeared from. She, like all medical students, had spent her twenties learning and studying and pushing beds down high streets for Rag Week and crikey just having so much revision on at the moment. Because she cared, because she too had wanted to make that all important difference.

Sadly, my smug idealistic tirade had dissolved about two years into university. The moment reality came a-knocking, I panicked. My dreams of becoming the next Charles Darwin, having libraries and theories named after me – they heated up, bubbled and evaporated into the laboratory air. I just sort of pulled in at the most convenient parking space. One that didn't involve tricky reverse manoeuvres or frantic hand gestures. And there I was. Twenty-two years old. Enjoying ten weeks' holiday and forty-two weeks' yelling per annum. As I said. Not a *bad* job.

But this? This I hadn't bargained for. All of a sudden, my meter had run out. Tow trucks were juddering into my rear-view. My hazards began to blink nervously.

'Maybe I'll get something part-time over the summer. Just in case, y'know? Just while I sort myself out.' The guys nodded. A light bulb of occupational opportunity clicked into illumination above my head. 'Either of you got anything where you are?'

A pause. A pause just big enough to squeeze the phrase *A-ha-ha-haa, dream on, buster* into if you trimmed the edges and squashed it up a bit. Adrian stood up sharply, reaching for his wallet.

'You need another one of those,' he said, pointing at my empty glass.

It wasn't a question.

Twenty to eleven. *Twenty to eleven and all's a bit crap.* Too many ones-for-the-road, not enough to eat. Well, not enough to eat that didn't taste of cheese and onion. The pub was considerably emptier now. Replacing the clubbers, clean air and dirty jokes now fought for a place at the foul, fuggy tables. I had lost count of how many I'd had. But my pockets now sleigh-belled with coppers instead of rattling with quids. My eyes hurt. Some upper-class squatters from the Royal College had begun rehearsing a tricky Shostakovich timpanii part in my frontal lobes. And the bloody pub quiz machine wasn't helping.

'Fuck! Of course. I fuckin' knew that one.' Brad jabbed and punched the flashing buttons. Our drinks, only half attempted, wobbled on the top of the strobing screen.

'Then why didn't you press it?' Adrian countered.

'Coz . . .' Brad's no doubt intelligent and logical response hung in the air. 'Fuck. What does E.C.G. stand for?' The three of us peered glassily at the options.

'That one.' I pointed at the screen. 'B. Electrocardiogram.'

'Sure?'

'Poz,' I lied.

Brad punched the button violently, as if to scare the machine into giving us some easy ones or else. It made a congratulatory *bleepity bleeep*.

'*Yesss*,' Brad hissed. 'Good one, Charlie.'

Total guess of course.

The Albert's quiz machine was another ritual in the game show that was our relationship. As if competing abstractly over status and achievement wasn't enough, just before closing, someone, well Brad, would insist on a few goes.

If we were chimpanzees, we'd just stop drinking and have a fight.

'Pop Music or Nature?' Adrian was at the helm. 'Nature, I think,' and he selected with a prod. 'Who discovered penicillin? Oh easy.' He thumbed the button with a 'Puh-leeese' sigh. The machine moved on to the next question. I gave my aching head a twitch.

'Do you think Debs will call then or what?' I asked no one in particular. 'Bound to, isn't she? I mean eventually. Isn't she? Bound to.'

'Shhhhh,' Adrian hissed. '*Palmiped*. Hmm,' he muttered. 'What's that, Charlie? Like an extra hand or something?'

'No no, that one. No thumbs,' I corrected. The machine gave a *nurrrgh*.

'You bastard. It was *webbed feet.*' He gave the machine a threatening thump on its faux mahogany finish and went to the toilet. Brad took his bottle from the top and swigged.

'Of course she'll call, you dope. She's just cooling off, having some time to herself 'n' shit. Trust me, I know women.'

'Yeah? Yeah, you think?'

'Fuckin' A. And don't you worry about work neither, they'll have you back. And if they don't, I'll get you something for a few . . . Oh goddam it! *Ovaries.* I fuckin' *knew* that one. Go on, Chucky, you're up.'

I squinted hard at the screen. I really hoped he was right. Although I'd moved on to maudlin drunk at this point, so even if he was right, he was probably wrong.

I gave *Pop Music* a jab and rattled my way through three easy ones. Bucks Fizz, 1979, and 'Shaddap Your Face'.

'Four thousand to beat my score,' Adrian piped up, now back from the loo and eager to hold onto his title.

'Well haven't you got a big penis,' I snapped, punching the neon buttons. Totally unprovoked, I know.

'Sexual frustration,' Adrian repeated, smugly.

The machine gave an unwelcome encore of its nasal buzz and I kicked it.

'Arse. *Galápagos Islands.* Bloody knew that one.'

I was angry. Angry with myself for risking my job.

Angry with Deborah for being angry with me. Angry with Brad for forcing me into a battle of blurred wits and small change. Angry with Adrian for having a loving wife and child on the way. I was angry. Oh, and I was very pissed. And I was going home.

South American Islands visited by Darwin. *Galápagos.*

Bloody *knew* that one.

Dear Tell Me How,

You know lots of things. When people were just micro-organisms how did they get legs and hair so they could walk? i aksed my mum and she said to aks my dad but he is in the shed potting the lettice.

thankyou very much. where you work is there cavemen to tell you all about dinosaurs or do you pretend?

Master Charles Ellis age 7

i don't have a dog i have too rabbits.

Dear Charles,

Thank you for you letter and the lovely drawing of your rabbits having a fight. What a lot of blood! You forgot to tell me their names.

The micro-organisms eventually 'evolved' into other animals. This is a way of saying that they changed very slowly.

In nature, things change for two reasons. 1. Because where they live has changed and they have to adapt to survive, and 2. Because of what we call 'mutation' which has to do with tiny things called 'genes'. Ask your mum to look these words up for you. It took a long time and a lot of changes to get from slime to monkeys! About 3,960 million years!

Many thanks for your letter. Keep reading!!!

Assist. Editor, Tell Me How

FOUR

'Waste of trees,' he had once said. *'Stupid clumsy ugly heavy things.*
The sooner technology comes up with a reliable alternative the better.'

Stephen Fry

My thoughts, that which they were that brusque and chilly London night, could have been spellchecked, formatted, saved and printed under the document title *Wankitypooflaps*. The slow soft-focus throb of a fresh headache was my travelling companion as I trailed my sozzled self flatwards through the sultry city darkness. It was one of those London evenings when you become aware once again of the air's grey weight. But I was comfy enough – my body sweating out excess liquor through every greasy pore while the snappy breeze slapped some sobriety into me. Efficient. Good cop, bad cop.

My head, however, was not much cop at all, my cloudy grey matter having prescheduled the evening's viewing — Deborah. Repeats on all channels.

I could replay with Maxell videotape clarity her face from the humiliating Friday previous. The Governors had *Harumphed* and *Well-Reallyed* for upwards of a day and a half before backing out through the heavy door and leaving us alone. Deborah had uttered only three words to me since.

I blame my 'Oops!'

She didn't want an *oops*. Fuck alone knows what she did want. But it wasn't *oops!*. She briskly yanked on a skirt, threw on a blouse and struggled to locate discarded court shoes, all with nasal huffs and puffs that would have more suited Thomas the Tank Engine, while I stood, naked, cold feet on the scratchy floor, the *Debrett's* in my head flipping frantically for the socially correct behaviour. After taking far far too long cross-referencing its index, it came up with *Oops*. I can only imagine it's a very old edition.

Deborah wobbled her shoes on, brow furrowed into a corrugated sheet of fury and stormed to the door, grabbing her jacket from the back of a chair. 'Don't call me.' A bookcase-teetering slam. And that, as it were, was that.

I scuffed and stumbled over the Wellington Road where the Jarvis International Hotel squats in all its Trusthouse Fawlty veneered pomposity, stubbornly ignoring the impatient squirt of a black cab horn. Oh to go back, I thought wearily. The past is indeed, as the man said, a foreign country. A country with very strict extradition laws and armed, mustachioed police at every checkpoint. They do things differently there. Stupid things mostly. They don't lock staffroom doors for one. They also usually neglect to insist their girlfriends just wait up a second for heaven's sake so they can travel home together and start the patching-up process.

I clumped into the kitchen, the fluorescent bulbs strobing into life. To my utter astonishment, Deborah lay full length on the greasy worktop. She wore white virginal underwear, stockings and white stilettos — she gazed at me with forgiving, alluring eyes.

Oh no, my mistake. It was the toaster.

I let the cold tap run noisily for a moment. She would call back. Surely. Of course she would. Brad was right, we were engaged, for fuck's sake, that had to mean something. There would be a message from her on the machine. Bound to be. I mean, that's what engaged is, isn't it? Well isn't it? It's an agreement, a carbon-papered triplicate of the heart. I, the undersigned, hereby referred to as *The Engagee*, agree to abide by the rules and conditions here stated. See page 5, paragraph 7, clause xxi:

I will not bugger off home (hereby referred to as The Chintzident Room) to mother (hitherto to be referred to as The Quaintiff) at the first whiff of rocky-boatatiousness.

My head buzzed behind tired eyes and I filled a smeary pint glass with *Vin de Thames*, vaguely recalling something about water and hangovers. Or was it milk? Or was that before drinking? Or was that raw eggs? My brain was in no mood for a late-night round-table debate on the subject. So I gulped down two mouthfuls and threw the rest down my shirt. Much better. Rattling briefly through cupboards of empty Coco-Pops packets and dusty Cupasoups, I settled finally on some Tesco Value bourbon biscuits, decked out in their handsome QPR livery of cheapness, and munched them half-heartedly into the lounge.

Collapsing with a sigh into an armchair, I gave my fizzing scalp a thorough scratch. Yes, the past may be a foreign country but I had enough fading holiday souvenirs to keep the memories alive.

I cohabited my poky hovel with Mr Bruce Willis and Master Michael J. Fox, and fine compadres they were too. Deborah had never really gotten on with them, something to do with primeval gunghoism or latent homoeroticism — whichever *ism* that week's *Observer* had a supplement on. But they brightened up the woodchip and never hogged the bathroom.

The tiny flat, while I had been pushed, nudged and finally dragged wailing and howling into adulthood, was my Dorian Gray. A portrait of a time past conjured not from ice and rock, but from brittle coloured plastic and pulpy fading paper. Aside from the tattered *Back to the Future* and *Die Hard* posters, adolescent albums, stocking fillas, photographs and toys littered the landscape.

Oh, and the books.

Books upon books upon books, a few of which were on more books but, well, you get the idea. Like a palaeontologist examining fragments of time through the layers of deep rock, so my past could be tracked and traced through the changing spines and pages of musty paperbacks.

I scanned the shelves idly, shameless delay tactics, I'll admit, letting my problems beep away on hold awhile. Familiar surroundings punched me on the arm with chummy bonhomie. *Hey buddy, hang with us, we won't judge ya, howzabout we drinks to da old times?* Thanks, boys, mine's an Alka Seltzer, no ice.

I can't remember if my interest in all things sciencey had lead me to choose certain books or if, inversely, my interest in certain books had lead me to a career in sciencey stuff but either way, guilty or not, there they were. *The Know-How Book of Experiments; 101 Things to Make & Do.* There, second one along, no spine. That was a jumble sale *Tell Me How* from 1978. Ten thousand years of knowledge reduced to a moreish finger-nibble buffet of facts for my eager young appetite.

Moving on, ladies and gentlemen, follow me, here on your left you'll see a bookcase devoted to early teendom. Notice the smattering of obligatory James Herberts and Stephen Kings, the spines cracked at the rudey bits; the self-conscious posing period of adolescence – Rye Catchers, Mockingbird Killers.

Those on our tour with sharp hearing will make out IKEA shelving bowing and groaning in a noticeable Scandinavian accent.

The rest of the room, some of the hall and a healthy swathe of kitchen were striped with what Sunday supplements would glossily refer to as Popular Science. (Could never quite work this out. Is there an *Unpopular Science*? Phycology maybe – the in-depth study of algae? Myrmecology perhaps – the close-up look at ants? Gynaecology – a probing study of . . . No. Probably not that last one.)

It's about now, I suppose, I should reveal that my parents divorced when I was nine. That the confusion and resultant feelings of panic, loss, rage and alienation in a cruel, godless universe neatly explain my obsession with scientific law and a desire to bring order into a world of chaos.

But they didn't. It was just a natural progression. Feed a child enough *Tell Me How*s or *Show Me What*s or *Ask Me Nicely*s, they'll either grow into frustrated young psychopaths intent on dissecting social workers just to see what makes them tic . . .

. . . or secondary school science teachers.

The *Puffin Book of Inventors* had begat *A Not Quite Brief* Enough *History of Time* and I had never looked back. Or rather, if you want to be smart about it, I had done nothing but look back. The work of bearded men, two hundred years dead, became my passion. They sat in still, silent congress in front of me.

I knelt down with a beery groan, crunching bourbon crumbs into the thin carpet, and shuffled all-foursly over to the bookcase. For company. For comfort. For exercise, for . . . God's sake I don't know.

My eyes pulled focus slowly on a slim gap in the ordered regiment of spineage. A slivery inch of space, but a gap none the less.

Now. If you got home to find a book missing, or a CD, or a ceramic fucking hedgehog or whatever it is you like, could you immediately tell which one was absent? An instantaneous register call – *Here sir, here sir, off sick sir, tummy bug?* No. Exactly. Of course you couldn't.

Well I could. Because I'm irritating like that. AWOL was an old hardback of *The Naked Ape*. Petty? Yes. Picky? Quite possibly. So painfully and childishly Why-Don't-I-Just-Build-A-Fucking-Library-Up-My-Arse-And-Be-Done-With-It? Well perhaps.

But you're in my house, so shush.

It wasn't missing, of course. Burglars in North London may be choosy, but they're not that choosy. Deborah had it.

I pictured it for a second on her shelves. Her sturdy lemony pine shelves that I had put together in a sweaty, bad-tempered display of machismo one couply Sunday. Among her kitschy cat ornaments and elaborate candle-sticks. The last seven days had stuck little mental yellow Post-It's Hers-Mine-Hers-Mine on everything in the flat. Every knick-knack a twinge of nostalgia.

And then I thought . . . actually I wasn't going to tell you this bit. It was one recollection of that night I was going to keep balled up and stuffed right down. But in for a penny I suppose. I caught myself hoping Deborah was in her flat thoughtfully clutching a naked ape tightly to her chest (so to speak), fighting back hot tears of regret and loss. Maybe staring into her mobile phone and beginning tentatively to scroll down to *'Ellis, C'* on the phone book.

I looked over at the answerphone. A red zero sat flatly

in the display. Zero. No calls, it said. No calls, no friends, no future for you, sonny boy. Just go to bed. Stop crying and go to bed.

I only managed the latter.

Dear Tell Me How,

My mum said that mutation means that when things go wrong. Say you were born really small so you were not good at putting toys away in the cupboard then your babies would all be short and not put their toys away. My mum is a doctor in her work. She says that genes have DNA in them but she forgot what that means and is tired now. I asked my dad but he was washing the lawn. Did we mutated into gibbons and all our hair fell off so we were nude and had to invent clothes?

Master Charles Ellis age 7

(my rabbits are called steve austin and ears-ears)

Dear Charles,

Thank you for your letter and your lovely drawing. I think the monkeys look very smart in their new school shoes.

DNA stands for Deoxyribonucleic Acid! They are the tiny tiny bits of your body that have all the information about you in them, like a little recipe. You got your genes from your parents, half from Dad and half from Mum. Which is why you are the way you are!

I am sending you a chart for your bedroom wall so you can follow the path of human 'evolution'. (Can you remember what that word means?)

Thank you for your letter. Keep reading!!!

Assist. Editor, Tell Me How

I enclose a Tell Me How badge as well. Wear it with pride!

FIVE

'Scientists are rarely to be counted among the fun people. Awkward at parties. Shy with strangers, deficient in irony'

Fran Lebowitz

Welcome back. You join me about ten days later, give or take a week. Without the grown-up regime of toast, bus, school, bus, pizza, bath, teeth and bed, time began to get all Dali on me. Hours began to ooze over the edges of the day like spilt treacle, or else whole afternoons would vanish over sepia horizons before I'd even daubed toothpaste on the brush.

I'd spent the first few miserable days rehearsing and performing to empty stalls my one-man show: *The Trick is to Keep Busy* or *Don't Be Re-recording None of*

51

Those Old Answerphone Messages Again, Ma. Just killing time, or at least getting a good firm grip on its collar. I went to the movies in the afternoons to take my mind off things my mind really should have been taking on, having no one's hand to grab during *Hannibal* and no one to wake me up after *Bridget Jones's Diary*, doing my best to disguise the pungent, sour odour of Calvin Klein's *Solitude* with the fragrance of perhaps the bohemian cineast or film studies student researching that thesis, but was fooling no one.

Much to Brad's gleeful toldyouso-ness I had indeed found myself calling him up sporadically, suggesting perky halves or lumbering all-nighters in the Albert, and he had been initially more forthcoming, not having anything else more pressing than a couple of staff rotas and a repeat viewing of *Blade Runner*, (the surround sound director's cut, presumably). But even his usual voracious thirst for bad tidings had been overquenched after what was, let's face it, just the same hopeless story of boy meets girl, boy loses girl, boy takes up moping at Olympic level over girl told over and over again.

I wondered if retelling it in widescreen would perk him up.

Adrian in the meantime had wisely cried off most of these invitations with talk of the wife and the spare room which apparently wasn't even halfway ready and could do with a fresh lick.

The room, that is.

But when a crisp starched envelope dropped through my door one Wednesday morning, interrupting some serious kicking-of-skirting boards and forcing me to put on hold a real headsdown staring-into-an-empty-fridge session that I'd been planning, I threw myself towards Swiss Cottage for some much needed advice.

Adrian's roomy flat had the expectant tang of fresh paint and warm milk. Elizabeth was on the settee like a gargantuan scatter-cushion, all hot dressing-gowns and fluffy water bottles, her face glowing audibly — very tired, very sweaty, very very pregnant. Adrian clattered around the kitchen looking for clean coffee cups. I wasn't surprised he couldn't find any — the entire contents of their Swiss Cottage two-bedroom ground-floor conversion seemed to have been stuffed into the heaving blue holdall by the door. Blue deliberately, I reasoned, to stop Adrian mistaking its swelling bulges for his wife.

'Emergency bag,' Adrian explained. 'When those waters go, you don't want to be running about the place like a blue-arsed fly looking for dippers and jimmies.'

By which, I should point out, he meant slippers and pyjamas. From the moment one of Adrian's wriggling salty warriors had arrived at Elizabeth's womb, had a quick shifty round and decided to measure up for carpets, the pair of them had conversed solely in saccharine baby language. Going to sleep became 'Up the wooden hill to Bedfordshire', tasty food was 'Scrummy tum-tums'. You get the idea. After the first eavesdrop on this, I'd had to go and lie down. Or rather, *Visit snuggle-patch.*

In what appeared to be compensation for Elizabeth's permanent panting exhaustion, Adrian had a junkie feverishness about him. He ran one hand through his standard public-school centre parting and used the other to get milk all over the crowded worktop.

'Whoopsie, there we go. You sure you don't want one, Snimble-bun?' he called through to Elizabeth. She grunted in the negative.

Adrian and I leant against Formica and caught up on each other. Between scalding sips I learned that he and Elizabeth were both knackered, that Miriam Stoppard was an absolute godsend and Dulux do seventeen different blue matt finishes. I *of coursed, absolutelied* and *fuckin' 'elled* respectively. He seemed very relieved to have someone to talk to, someone who was neither dependent on him nor brandishing eerie X-rays.

Adrian is, under regular circumstances, what you might call a coper, my unrufflable feathered friend. The perfect desert island pal, not only does he own a humungous Swiss Army knife but he actually knows what each gadget is for. This being set in stone five or so years previous when he proved himself to be *the* absolutely must-have mate to have around when your finals are but days away and, oh for the love of bollocks I don't fuckin' believe it, I've left my cocking ringbinders on a National Express.

And, as Brad and I had back-slappingly assured him hundreds of times since last November, the perfect father-to-be. But that day, he seemed about ready to head shakily back to his corner for a spit, a rub, a pep talk and a bit of a sit down.

We took our coffees on a brief tour of the flat and I began to pour out a steaming mugful of my thoughts to match.

'I got a letter,' I began, wandering through to the spare room.

'Uh-huh?'

'Yep. From school.'

'And? *And?* C'mon, what did they say?'

'See for yourself,' and I tugged the crisp sheaf from my jacket, handing it over. Adrian put down his coffee and began to scan. I took the opportunity to throw my eyes over the room, which had far, far too much stencilling for my tastes and in all honesty, any of the other sixteen blues would have been preferable.

'Room looks good,' I offered.

'Fucking hell, Charlie.' Adrian looked up from the letter.

'Spectacularly well put.'

I'll spare you the details, but let's just say, reading between the *As a respected member of staffs* and *It comes with some regrets,* Charles Ellis BSc. (Ed) was now on the job market. Not fired, *per se*, but my resignation was expected return of post. I presumed Deborah had been dealt a matching hand. That's *presumed*, please note. Not hoped. I had no wish to see her hurt any more than she had been already. Deborah liked, perhaps even loved, her job. Far from seeing teaching as a cop-out, a handy safety-net for those so unsure of the colour of their parachute they had forgotten to pull the rip cord, Deborah saw teaching as an honourable, honest, valuable dedication. Another reason I had fallen for her.

'They're going to pay me until September,' I explained.

'Will you be able to find something else by then?'

'I don't know. Really mate, I've no idea.'

We slouched a while in the small spare room. Adrian opened the window to quicken the paint-drying process and an animal mobile began to twist and tinkle in the breeze. I watched yellow felt birds chase red felt lions chase blue felt antelopes, a soft candyfloss food-chain hypnotically turning.

Unemployed, my own place in the circle-of-life was slipping a little. I'd better grab what I could.

I steered Adrian back to the lounge where Elizabeth immediately snapped off the muted telly.

Now. A better man than me, a more polite, considerate modern man than me, would have left

Elizabeth alone – hushed Adrian back into the kitchen and let her get some rest. But that better man is currently unavailable. He's more than likely teaching pottery to handicapped ghetto kids or on a soup run through war-torn Chiswick or something.

So you'll have to make do with what I did.

'How are you then, Liz?' I opened.

'I am with child,' she groaned, flipping disinterestedly through *Which Rompersuit?*. 'My shoulders ache, my tits ache, my bum's sore and I haven't had a fag in nine months. Yourself?'

It was the hormones talking, I hoped. My plan didn't require wrestling through nine three-minute rounds with a black-belt in combat sarcasm. I was there to get some advice from my friends, problems shared and halved and all that homespun hogwank. And to pay back the favour by cheering them on or nodding with empathy, whatever they required. Obviously, that's why I was there.

Obviously.

'How's er . . . how's Deborah?' I threw in, with all the off-hand, heigh-ho, just making conversation-ness of a falling anvil.

Look, it was weeks since I'd last heard her voice and I needed to know. I had cold-turkeyed myself down to only two answerphone messages a day, messages that morphed between *Look I'm sorrys* and *Oh you're just being silly nows*, depending on my mood. But where the slow tick of time might have stopped me flicking through shoe boxes full of photographs and reading her horoscope, I was still a good five time zones away from not missing having her around or not instinctively reaching out to where her hair should be in the middle of the night.

'Still nothing?' Adrian queried with genuine surprise. 'What happened to going to go round to see her? You didn't bottle it?'

Ah, yes. Brad had bullied me into promising some sort of full-frontal, take no prisoners assault. *For god's sake*, he had pressed, *be a man. Get your flabby butt round there and sort it, goddammit.* And I had tried, really, really I had. As soon as I finish this chapter, I had promised myself one evening.

I had begun to reread some of my favourite books by way of a distraction, for some home comfort. For a bit of familiarness in what had become an unfamiliar landscape. But, as I'm sure you've found yourself, Donald Symon's 1979 blockbuster *Evolution of Human Sexuality*, especially the chapters concerning the indigenous culture of the Trobriand Islands in Melanesia, had just been a rollercoaster ride of fun and larks and I had never quite got round to ringing her doorbell.

Or getting out of bed.

Feeble, yes. But I find a packet of Hob-Nobs and an explanation of the findings of the anthropologist Bronislaw Malinowski far outweigh yelling through letter boxes and bouncing non-stick frying pans off my head. I'm old-fashioned like that.

Oh all right, just a big stubborn stupid fraidy-puss, suit yourself.

'Well,' I entirely failed to explain.

Elizabeth grunted into a more sitty-up position and let her magazine drop onto a teetering pile. She didn't deserve my pesterings. Adrian and Brad, well they were my friends. I could sob down the phone to them without feeling like a total manipulative shit. But Elizabeth, well she was just my friend's wife, there was no chummy history there. I'd never got her in a headlock or held her hand on New Year's Eve while she hiccuped and vommed on a grassy roundabout. I had never sat opposite her in an echoing Halls of residence, heavy male tears choking and crashing through soft stubble onto my flimsy t-shirt the night her dad died. My problems were my problems. However.

'I'm not meant to be talking to you,' she said curtly. 'But know this, young man –' My nervous innards grouped themselves into one mass of expectation and began a sprint towards the vaulting horse of hope. 'She wants you to give the phoning a rest and just leave her alone for a while.' I slipped on the springboard and collapsed with a squeaky thud into a heap on the gym floor, clutching my bruised bits.

'Oh. She . . . she said that?' This was not the news I had popped over to receive. 'When did you speak? Was this like two weeks ago or yesterday or what?' *Two weeks ago, please, say it was two weeks ago* I thought desperately. *The confused emotional wailings of a wronged woman. A woman who has since come to her senses and is willing to give the old boy another shot.*

'Yesterday,' Elizabeth said firmly. Then, as if catching herself, 'Look, Charlie, this is kind of difficult for me and in my state I don't need the aggro, you know?' and she rubbed her balloon-like middle softly. 'I mean, as an ex of a friend of mine, by all rights I shouldn't have even let you in the house.'

So, there it was.

Reconnaissance complete, head back to base for debriefing. *Ex.* Get that? *An ex of a friend of mine.* What more did I need to know?

Well, a fuck load more as it happens. I wanted it all. Deborah's personal diary, fully indexed and cross-referenced, bound in calfskin for my perusal, please. How did she sound? Was she bitter, resentful, optimistic, a new convert to dungareed lesbianism? What was she wearing? Had she had her hair cut (acceptably predictable split-up procedure), found someone else (totally unacceptable break-up procedure)? Speak, woman, tell me. I don't care what kind of bra-burning, all-girls-together solidarity you've cooked up. I want to know. I need to know.

The three of us sat in the little lounge for about six weeks before Adrian broke the silence.

'Time to move on, old friend. C'mon,' and he slapped my shoulder. 'Come and take a look at what I've done in the shed.' And with a local Parish Am-Dram Society sigh, we left Elizabeth alone. Adrian didn't want her getting worn out by delirious ravings of desperation and retribution. Which was fair enough. Though what did he think I was going to do? Tie her down, shine a lamp in her face and beat the facts out of her with the backs of some leather gloves? I mean, really.

Piano wire would be much more effective.

'What a fucking mess.'

'Yes yes all right, I haven't finished it yet,' Adrian nurgh-nurghed back irritably, pushing some MDF cut-offs up against the wall in a plume of dust.

'No, not this,' I developed, creeping into the dark mustiness of his shed, wet leaves scrabbling around the door. 'This is . . .'

Adrian snapped on the tiny bulb.

'. . . *oh cool.*'

Along one whole wall of the large shed, propped up on flimsy wooden legs at waist height, were huge flat planes of plywood. Upon these, half constructed amongst tacks and wiring, sprawled the biggest and most complicated Scalextric track in the history of juvenile homework-postponing entertainment.

'When the hell did you do this?' I squealed, running my hands across the warm, finely planed surface.

'Oh on and off over the last few weeks. It's for the baby. Y'know, when he grows up. Eventually.'

'Yeah right,' I smirked and we shared a conspiratorial giggle.

This was regression plain and simple. Many a Saturday morning or Thursday afternoon after games as kids, we'd pile round to Adrian's parents' house for a few hotly disputed laps, Brad's Murray Walker infamous amongst classmates.

Although being proud holders of the notorious Y chromosome, competition an innate part of our destinies months before we were born, it was in these young sugar-fuelled days that the instincts first raised their spotty heads over the parapet. Like little plastic cars, our hormones raced and jostled in irregular spurts, forever conscious of whoever crept up in the outside lane.

'I meant me,' I continued. 'This, this situation. It's a mess. I mean, I thought that if I was suspended for a term or demoted or they moved me to another form or something, at least Debs would be there with me, y'know? Or even if I *was* fired −'

'You *were* fired,' a voice corrected from under the woodwork. 'Pass me a screwdriver, would you?'

I handed him the necessary. 'Yes yes all right. But I

thought we'd be able to apply to new schools together, find somewhere we could both work, take a bit of the sting out of it, you know? But if Liz is right, then . . .' I let my voice tail off.

'Look, Charlie.' Adrian clambered up from his knees, examining a tiny fuse for a while before tossing it out of the window. 'Sorry. Look, what are you always saying? Be scientific. Look at it logically. This moping isn't helping anybody. You need to get back on the horse before you forget how to ride.'

'It's a bit bloody soon to be setting me up with other women, Ade. I only found out I was single five minutes ago.'

'Nonsense, now is exactly the best time to meet other women. While your sex life is still fresh, while you've still got some romance in your veins. Before your wardrobe and conversational skills go completely to pot. You don't want to turn into one of *those* guys.'

'What guys?'

'Single too long, comfortable with his own company, lots of hobbies and interests, the only woman I ever speak to is my mum type-guys.'

'A wanker.'

'Absolutely. So get yourself down the Albert to-night –'

'Oh look, Ade, I know you're trying to help and I appreciate it, really I do, but . . .'

'Shut the hell up. I'll get on the blower to Brad and

we'll find you some female company. Christ, you're the biologist, you should know this stuff. Stagnancy is . . . ?'

'Death.'

'A creature must learn to . . . ?'

'Adapt or die.'

'Good.'

'Thanks, Ade. I mean it. What with Debs gone I don't . . . well . . .'

'Shut up, I'm just looking after your interests. I'll get Liz to call around some single friends, we'll get you someone. No more miserable single Charlie. Evolve, my friend. Evolve.'

'You're taking the piss now, right?'

'You betcha. Now pass me that bit of track.'

So I moved on. I swallowed my pride, silenced my heart, mislaid my common sense and moved on.

I shouldn't have done. Obviously, I can see that now. I should have put things straight, reracked the balls for a fresh frame. *Oops, sorry ref, miscued there. Just warming up, let's have another go, thanks very much you're a gent.* Sure, things were bad. No future, no missus, no job, no possible chance of beating Adrian at Scalextric, but nothing was irreversible. I could have stopped things before they really got out of hand.

But I didn't, you see. So they did.

Dear Tell Me How,

I had Sunday in bed today and missed my friend Amanda's party because i had a dyorrear. Might some of my DNA come out? Is it in my tummy? Mum said it is all over my whole body but I don't see how I could fit that many recipe books in me. Mum has one and it is ginormous. Dad can just do fried eggs. Did my genes break and that is why i have to have lucozade?

Master Charles Ellis age 7

Ears-ears is grey but steve austin is brown with a white bit

Dear Charles,

Thank you for your letter and your lovely drawing. You certainly do look a little poorly. What a lovely bedspread you have. The spots match your pyjamas!

Your body is made up of cells which group up to form tissues, each one performing a different job. Some of these tissues group together to make your heart and lungs and other important bits. The cells are told what to do by things called genes that are made of DNA. Genes are arranged on tiny things called chromosomes which are inside a little box called a nucleus which is inside your cell! It's all very very small indeed! When you grow up you might want to study Biology – that is what it is called when you learn about how living things work!

Thanks for your letter. Keep reading!!!

Assist. Editor, Tell Me How

*'The fun of talk is to find out what a man really thinks,
and then contrast it with the enormous lies he has been
telling all dinner and perhaps, all his life.'*
Benjamin Disraeli

Now someone once said — once is funny, twice is silly, third time deserves a smack. Can't remember who. It was either Isaac Newton or my Aunty Iris. I get the two confused. But by jove it's undoubtedly a useful maxim, adhering itself as it does to most social situations without leaving a sticky residue. It can apply to everything from, ooh I don't know, letting your mates set you up with women to go out on dates with, to . . .

Well. Letting your mates set you up with women to go out on dates with, anyway.

Trust me.

I splashed a sinkful of water on my face, cursed the fixed blow-hand dryer and dripped back to the bar collecting a house red for her, another in a snaking line of large Bloody Marys for me, a bagful of ready salted nerves and a collection of funny looks as I went. I rejoined a young lady from Adrian's accounts department, billed as Katherine McCann.

Nice girl, Katherine McCann. And if you ever run into her, at a party or something, feel more than free to tell her I said so. You should have no trouble picking her out from among the Twiglets and compilation tapes – she'll be the tall sexy redhead in the corner regaling a cluster of whooping and tittering females with a story about how she once wasted a perfectly good Sunday lunchtime in a North London pub with a total wanker, I expect.

A wanker who managed to cheat on her without ever leaving the table.

I set her drink down among the greasy remains of our traditional English pub fare, sipped at mine, and foraged frantically for an all-purpose conversation re-opener. I expect Adrian had one on his Swiss Army knife.

'You were a while, are you all right?' she asked with a slightly crooked but by no means unappealing smile and a bedside manner that promised a future of crisp hospital corners and fluffed-up pillows. Like I say, nice girl.

'Hn? Oh yes yes. I'm sorry about that. I er . . . I'm fine,' I offered limply.

Which somehow managed to be, and you'll be impressed by this, both completely true and quite enormously false at the same time.

Which isn't that easy to do, when you think about it.

True because between the cold shivering facial dunk, the thought of another strong Bloody Mary awaiting me and the lengthy, steaming dark amber urination, I was beginning to feel a tiny bit more human.

And oh so very false because I'd just spent a panicky five minutes in the toilet unsuccessfully looking for the *OFF* button on a mobile phone belonging to Ronnie — a girl I'd been out with the night before.

'What?!' I had yelled back the night before. Saturday. A night that sensible people spend sitting quietly in the company of their loved ones, perhaps picking up the *Radio Times* every so often to say *Is there nothing else on?* But not me. Veronica Cousins leaned in and I stooped, my eyes stinging suddenly from the heady cloud of Ellnet firm-hold fixing spray and CK One that surrounded her.

'Can you hold on to *this* for me?' she hollered back, jabbing a purple mobile phone into my ribcage. I took it from her and explained eruditely, politely and totally pointlessly to the back of her head that I didn't think I would be staying long so it might be safer in the cloakroom. She turned back, having cloakroomed her furry Spitalfields Market jacket. 'Right then!' she beamy grinned, shoving a folded raffle ticket into a silver backpack about the size of a folded raffle ticket. 'I'll see you at the bar!' And she slipped through some very heavy double doors, the brassy disco of The Forum's *House of Fun 70s & 80s nite* swelling and subsiding as they swung shut behind her.

'Oh,' I said quietly to pretty much nobody. 'Righty-ho then.'

'Hoy, keep it movin', mate.' The cloakroom guy reached out an arm for my coat. A wirey, pale, studenty, Are-you-sure-you're-eating-properly arm that jangled with silver bangles. 'Just one, is it?' he bellowed.

'Yet again,' I sighed. This particular 'date' (and believe me those inverted commas do no justice to the spectacularly inverty-commaredness of the word use) with Ronnie, kindly set up by Brad for whom she worked once a week, had been limping along for about twelve minutes by this point. I can't for the life of me recall why I agreed to it, considering how roaringly awful my first blind date had gone only that afternoon with a friend of Liz's whose name I can't even remember.

*

'Dawn. Pleased to meet you.' (Oh yes, that was it.) And she stuck out a hand forthrightly like she was helping me onto a boat.

'Hi,' I said, 'Liz has told me all about you,' and I let her shake and pump my arm violently out of its socket. I allowed my eyes a quick flicker over the scenery. 'She did fail to mention, however,' I continued with a smile, 'that you look like a tent at the Reading Festival that's been blown over a fence into a haystack.'

Dawn took this remark astonishingly well. Had I said it out loud, however, I'm sure she would have swung her ethnic shoulder bag and knocked my white wine and me off the South Bank into the Thames. A bag that I would have proudly strutted into Ladbrokes and put twenty quid on containing a little purse with Hello Kitty characters on it.

We stood, a first-date's distance apart, outside the Royal Festival Hall among chatty groups grabbing a Saturday lunchtime vodka or two. Every time the heavy grey London clouds managed to shoulder-barge the sun off the touchline for a moment, a wet breeze reminded everyone of the dark green choppy Thames nearby and little summer cardies were pulled tighter.

'I got us tickets for this,' Dawn said, bringing out her purse. (Well okay, Miffy characters, it's near enough.) *Brief Encounter*. It's playing at the NFT. You haven't seen it, have you?'

Lightning decision.

'Hn? No no, I haven't. That's great,' I lied enthusiastically.

Well c'mon, you've got to. It was my first date in about five years and if there was one nugget of wisdom I had remembered from oh so long ago, it's that a little bit of fibbing to keep the atmos sweet is perfectly acceptable.

For example:

'You're literally the first woman I've even spoken to in, God, it must be six months.'

'No? Is that true?' Katherine rummaged in her combat slacks for some Marlboro Lights. (We're back in the pub, by the way – do try and keep up, 007.) 'Adrian never said. *Oh blesss*, you poor thing.'

But that's the thing about lies, they're like varnish. Slap it on once and you're so impressed with how everything comes up like new, you can't help wandering around the place looking for other stuff to gloss over and improve.

'I don't know what to say, I feel –' and she fiddled with her cigarettes nervously – 'well, privileged, I spose,' and she laughed.

I'd thought about telling Katherine about the clubbing fiasco with Ronnie the night before, really I had.

Yes yes, all right, and about the NFT trip with Dawn

the afternoon before that (what are you, my mother?). But, well, I didn't. Something told me knowing you were but *Girl In Pub#3* in the credits-role of a guy's social life would tarnish your view of him somewhat. And I liked Katherine, we were enjoying ourselves.

So much so that the following hypothesis that I had been mulling:

Sleeping with a stranger helps you get over your ex

was looking like it might get proved if I played my petri dishes right.

I wish I could tell you we were getting on because I had used up all the crappy dating clichés with Ronnie and Dawn and was finally being myself. But it was just because I'd learned which embellishments scored the most tricks. And, if you're taking notes, pose #3, *The Wounded Puppy*, is a dead cert.

'Well I'm glad I'm the first,' Katherine said, blushing softly.

See? It beats the macho pose for example. Ha! What a disaster that is.

'Are you gonna slouch like that all night? Come an' 'ave-a dance, you old moody pants.' Ronnie bounced from one stack-heeled leisure shoe to the next with pent-up energy in front of me as I handed her the drink I had waited ten minutes for.

'Do you want this?' I hollered over the music. Half

Ronnie's G&T splashed up my arm as thirsty boogiers all jockeyed for my vacated spot.

'Later, later!' she yelled back almost inaudibly, the club's sound system giving all conversation an underwater muffle. Then a piercing shriek of joy and she was consumed by the crowds as Dancing Queen's soaring piano and strings swept all the women dance-floorwards.

It took about two verses for all the guys left at the bar to individually come to the same decision that most men will eventually come to in these circumstances: Yes, real men don't dance. Brando wouldn't dance to this and nor would Dean, Eastwood, Wayne or Willis. Agreed, that guy over there in the V-necked t-shirt, giving it all slinky hips and poofy arm-waving, is a tosser.

However, we're here on our own and he's got a circle of very sexy girls waving their hips back at him.

Fuck it, here we go then.

By the time I located Ronnie, the DJ had slapped on 'Lovecats' and all the girls were grinding and oozing to and fro across the heaving sticky floor. Still holding both drinks and sort of jigging lamely from foot to foot like I had a septic verruca, I failed to catch her eyes, both of which were closed in tight sexual absorption of the rhythm. I considered moving in slowly and perhaps sneaking arms around her tiny waist, a move a lot of other men were considering and performing with varying levels of failure.

Fuck it, here we go then.

One two, one two, closer and closer. I could see warm sweat on her chest. First one hand, then the other. They clasped at the back.

Or rather they would have done, if I had remembered to put my drinks down. But I'd queued ten minutes for them. And five pounds eighty is five pounds eighty, after all.

"Everybodeeeeeeee!" the DJ yelled suddenly. "C'mon! It's Conga time!"

'Ow careful. *Shit.*'

'Oh for fuck's sake, Charlie.'

'Sorry sorry, here let me wipe –'

'*Leave it!*'

And as she bent and spun and I wiped and dusted, the dance floor made the unilateral decision that yes indeed it *was* in fact feeling hot hot hot and yanked us both Ow-that's my neck-ing and Do-you-mind-ing into a snaking conga.

'Well, when push comes to shove,' Dawn continued, 'give me a wet Monday afternoon, a tub of Häagen Dazs and an old black and white romance any day. They could make films in those days. They didn't need soppy car chases or a load of silly men pointing guns at each other. Just the music and those costumes . . .'

Dawn got a faraway look in her eyes and seemed for a moment to drift away to a smoky station platform and a manly silver-screen clinch, far far from the dark carpet and sprawling stuffy queue inside London's National Film Theatre. This remark was a dig at me, and not the first.

They do say that everyone has a soulmate – someone else on planet Earth instinctively in tune with one's tastes and preferences.

Well if that's true, I expect my soulmate would get as annoyed to shit by Dawn as I was.

'I never said I didn't like romantic films,' I defended, 'I just find a good car chase exciting, that's all. I've seen *While You Were Sleeping*,' I offered as a celluloid peace-pipe. 'That was all right.'

Dawn produced three double chins and a pair of raised eyebrows from her handbag. To express doubt, presumably.

'Yes. And I bet you went with a girl you wanted to sleep with and only agreed because Sandra Bullock had been in *Speed*. And the only good thing in it as well.' And she did a sort of half laugh, half shruggy cough. Which, combined with a parental shake of the head, succeeded in notching my annoyance up to eleven. 'Tch. Bloody men, all the same.'

'*Ahhhhh*. That's so *sweet*. You're so understanding, Charlie. It's so refreshing. And that's true? A different flower every day? She was a lucky girl, y'know that?'

'Well, y'know,' and I gave Katherine a stammery British shrug Copyright Hugh Grant 1995 All Rights Reserved. Look, I apologise. What can I say, it's a learning curve, the level of honesty you reach in a long-term relationship is simply not practical in the dating field. The *crikey-your-feet-stink* level, the *well-it's-not-mine-I-always-flush* level. I'd set off on that foot with Dawn and just managed to get her back up. Like I said, dating is going back to the little fibs, the tiny, almost imperceptible exaggerations that increase your stock worth.

'And she dumped you when you said you wanted to have a family? That's just heartbreaking, Charlie. *Really.*' And Katherine put her hand on top of mine.

"Let's go all the way! You Sly Fox!"

The DJ cranked up the synth drum intro march of the 1986 chart smash and the dance floor leaped and punched the air and fell over and sprayed hot sweat willy-nilly about the place. Struggling, I finally fell out to one side of the throng and my lungs fought for the little cold air that wallflowered around the edges of the dance floor. Sweat collected on the end of my nose and drip dripped huge tired salty drops at my freshly trampled feet and I mouthed a silent curse at Brad and his matchmaking skills. He had assured me I would have a good time. Punched me on the arm, tapped the side of his nose, winked and even made horsey gee-up noises. *Goowarrrrn, buddy, she's your kinda babe.*

'My kinda babe' was presently dancing about six couples away. The lager and vodka still a dark patch on her bum, a bum she wiggled at every guy but me.

So I took a breather and some wall space and watched everyone else shake their things.

The man next to me zipped his up and left, leaving me alone for a moment. The NFT gents' mirrors reflected a very sorry face back at me which I knew I couldn't entirely blame on the striplights. Dawn's and my stupid battle-of-the-sexes disagreement had escalated rapidly into waspy Wendy-house sniping and I'd retreated for a piss and a think.

'Charlie, my old mate,' I said aloud to the mirror as I washed my hands, 'calm the hell down. Blind dates never work, accept it. You're in this for a couple of hours, tops. You can manage. You're going clubbing with a mate of Brad's tonight and out for brunch on Sunday morning. If this one doesn't work out, then it doesn't work out. Now just' – I turned off the taps and shook my hands over to the towel – 'go out there, apologise and try and enjoy the movie.'

Back in the foyer, Dawn and the rest of the queue had disappeared inside. The film was about to start. Taking far too long explaining to the staff that I'd left my ticket with my girlfriend (well I mean my friend and she's a girl I mean it's a date really doesn't that sound old-fashioned you don't really hear it any more huh oh yes sorry she has the tickets can I go in please), I went through the doors and found my seat, just as the lights dimmed, the music faded out and the curtains began to close.

'I'm completely in the dark, honest,' I pleaded. Katherine furrowed her face. The shrill ring continued. Other Sunday lunchers began to tut and glare and audibly disapprove as I pulled out Ronnie's purple mobile phone.

'You don't know how it got in there?'

'Hmm? No. No I've no idea.' I placed it on the table in front of us. Its tinny ring continued. My smile failed to hit its mark. 'Do you fancy another drink? Take your mind off it?' Katherine rested her cigarette on her plate and picked up the phone.

'Oh answer it, for heaven's sake . . .'

Shit. It's going to be Ronnie asking for me. How do I explain her to Katherine? Katherine the, ahem, first girl I've spoken to in six months.

'Hey! Careful!'

'S-sorry. Let me.' I snatched it from her and jabbed the green flashing button. 'Er, hello?' A male voice.

'Where the fuck are you?'

'Where am I?' I shrugged at Katherine theatrically. 'Er, the Prince Albert pub, Prince Albert Road, London NW3. A table by the toilets. Who is this?'

'Prince Albert Road?'

'Yes. Sorry, who —?'

'Never fucking mind. Stay where you are, I'm coming over. And I know you're this Simon bloke. You and your roving dick are both in big fuckin' shit, mate.'

'Simon? N-never heard of him. I think you must have the wrong number.'

'This is Simon,' Ronnie hollered at me over Bananarama's 'Venus'. 'We go to the same college.' She turned to him and beamed with thinly disguised joy. 'You didn't say you were coming!' Through the sting of sweat and blinding strobe I noted three things. Firstly, this Simon character was quite revoltingly handsome. I mean, really offensively chiselled and toned. Secondly, Ronnie had her arm around his waist. And thirdly, fucking Ronnie fucking Cousins had her fucking arm around fucking Simon's fucking waist fucking.

Lemons don't go clubbing that often, being yellow citrus fruit, they have other interests. So as similies go, I don't know why, standing there, watching these two using their hips to try and create fire, I should have felt like one. But I did.

Simon's handsome palms (yes it is possible to have

handsome palms) ran and stumbled up and down Ronnie's hips and she threw her hair back into his face, gyrating her little silver backpack into his sixpack. There was just far too much pack going on from both sides for my liking.

'Venus' faded out and the DJ began to call out raffle numbers.

Ronnie rummaged and squealed with delight, the dancefloor applauded, Simon kissed her and she handed me a laminated bit of shiny cardboard.

'Oh, be a sweetheart and claim my prize for me.'

I opened my mouth to say why-don't-you-get-Mr-Muscle-here-to-get-your-fucking-prize when she unexpectedly planted a big sexy kiss on me. And, accident or not, I distinctly felt a bit of tongue.

'Will the winner make their way up here, please!' the DJ cheered.

Stagestruck? Hitchcock's *Stagestruck*? This couldn't be right, surely. Dawn had said *Brief Encounter*. Hadn't she? I leaned to my left, squeezed her lightly on the arm and whispered in the darkness.

'I'm a bit confused. I was looking forward to *Brief Encounter*.'

'Not with me you weren't, mate,' came a voice back. It didn't sound like Dawn. In fact the arm I was gripping didn't feel very Dawny either come to think of it.

The National Film Theatre in London is a repertory

cinema showing films both classic and contemporary.
Designed and built in the 1960s, it has two fucking screens
right bloody next to each other.

'Excuse me, sorry, sorry, coming through, whoops,
I'm sorry.'

'You don't have to apologise. You found a phone, put it
in your pocket and forgot about it. Don't look so
worried.' Katherine patted me lightly on the hand and
sat back. I smiled limply back at her and took a very
deep swig of Bloody Mary.

'Yes, yes you're right. I'm sorry,' I mumbled, wiping
my mouth. 'Y'know, as I said, I just found it in the
toilets just now and and and . . .'

'Yes, you said. It's fine, don't get so het up. You told
the guy where you were so he's going to come and get
it. We'll wait for him here. Just relax.'

Relax. Yeah right. Ronnie's boyfriend (yes, news to
me also), was now on his way to the pub. He had
phoned her mobile number and presumed I was Simon,
the college guy she'd obviously slept with.

The guy he thought was me.

Relax. Yes of course.

I was marching. I had a bottle of champagne in one hand,
a hardhat on my head and a big stick on moustache

hanging half off my face and I was marching. Next to me on the broad, bright stage of London's Forum, the *House of Fun* DJ grinned and clapped and cheered like a moron. *YMCA* pumped from every speaker and the two thousand sweaty young clubbers all stood at my feet, marching along and waving and laughing and pointing and spelling the chorus out at me through hysterical shrieks. I flung my arms about almost in time with the music like I was signalling an air crash. My eyes fixed on the back of the crowd.

Fixed on two people, one a short girl with a silver backpack whose prize I was clinging to. The other a tall handsome fellow with one hand up the back of her skirt.

'I'm trying to get in there, if this woman would let me.'

'You don't have a ticket, though, sir, my colleague informs me? Your girlfriend is in the cinema at the moment and has your ticket. Is that right?'

'Yes. Yes. Although she's not my girlfriend. My girlfriend, well my fiancée actually, we've kind of broken up. Well she's decided we've broken up, I didn't get much say in the matter to tell you the truth. I'm just seeing Dawn, that's her in the cinema, just kind of as friends. You know? Getting back on the horse before I forget how to ride. Er, so to speak.'

'Yes, sir, I see. But I can't let you in now the film has started you see, it's our policy. Might your, er, friend come out when she realises you're not there?'

'Er, no. Probably not. We had an argument about Sandra Bullock.'

'Of course. Well there's very little I can do, sir, I'm afraid. You're welcome to sit here and wait if you wish. *Brief Encounter* only runs for eighty-six minutes.'

'That's not very brief.'

'I'm sorry?'

'Damn, fuck and shit. Sorry. Nothing. Stupid joke, just a stupid joke.'

'I think it's funny, that's all,' Katherine said. 'My girlfriends and I spend all this time complaining there are no real men out there, no one with any sensitivity or integrity. I'm just about to hang up the old diaphragm and become a nun when you come along, some friend of Adrian's. Who'd have thought it.'

This overtly suggestive remark caused me to unclamp my eyes from the pub doors for a moment and focus across the table at a coy smile. *Did she just say what I thought she said? Am I, as it were, on?* All thoughts of having the shit kicked out of me were banished and I raised an eyebrow in the manner of Roger Moore. Or I tried to. I don't actually have eyebrows that do that. So I scratched my head as a cover-up and suggested we head back to her place for coffee. She smiled and grabbed her coat.

'I'm just going to pop to the bar, see if they'll look after this phone for us. And ask if they have any, er, any —'

'Champagne?' Ronnie said, as she came up for air. Simon brought his head up, his face scarlet, his mouth smeared with lipstick, his hair all over the shop but still incredibly fucking handsome. Like a genetic mutation of Brad Pitt and Robert Smith.

'Yes.' I dangled the bottle in front of her. 'Thanks very much I'd love some,' I continued, holding tightly on to Ronnie's prize as she reached for it unsuccessfully. I nodded at Simon and then at a nonplussed Ronnie and, bottle in hand, made my way through the pumping, pointing, jeering crowds, to find myself a cab. 'Bye then.'

'Is that it? Is that bloody *it*? That's all you're going to say? *Hello, how was the film*? You've got some nerve.' Dawn pulled on her jacket with huffs and mumbles. 'Wrong screen my eye! If you didn't want to see the film you could have just said something. Where's this nice guy that Liz told me about, that's what I'd like to know.'

'You need to head towards Regent's Park and then do a

left. I'll yell when we get near, mate. Awright?' The cab hurtled through the hot summer night. I flumped back into my seat, pressing the chilled champagne bottle against my sweaty cheek, enjoying the little shiver. I shouldn't really be doing this, finances being what they were. 'How much will it be, d'ya think, mate?'

'Eight quid? Eight quid?! I didn't even see the movie!'

'Well that's not my fault. Four pounds for your ticket and, if you're a gentleman, you'll pay for mine as well.'

'Okay here. Take it. Keep the change. Treat yourself. Buy yourself some . . . God I don't know. Some . . .'

'Condoms?'

'Yes. The machine in the bog is empty,' I half whispered over the din at the bar. A phone was ringing somewhere. 'You haven't, y'know, you haven't got any behind the bar, I suppose?'

'Nope. Sorry, mate. The guy comes and refills on a Tuesday. Can you hang on?'

'Not really.'

'Yes of course, hang on, I'll get him.'

'Huh? Oh, Katherine. I was just getting . . . oh, you've got the phone.'

She's got the phone.

Shit.

'It's someone called Ronnie for you. Last night did sound like fun. She says if her boyfriend finds out about it he'll kill you. Or something. Thought you'd better take it. Ta-ta.'

End of term report: SUMMER 2001
Charles Ellis: DATING

Although Charles applied himself initially to his coursework with some degree of enthusiasm, he still has.yet to grasp the basic knowledge required for a successful exam result. He might well be advised to consider alternative options come September.

Attendance: B+

Class Contribution: D

Overall Standard: C–

Dear Tell Me How,

Descendents are like grandad but he has gone away which is why nan smells of purfume and has eight cats. On my chart it takes human beings a long time to stand up properly. Is this because they slouch in front of the television in their caves and haven't sat up straight like a good boy at the table? I asked dad but he said the wrestling was on.

Master Charles Ellis age 7½

Steve Austin: likes to eat Wall's Vienetta but not the mint one.

Ears-ears got bitten by a cat today but he is all right.

Dear Charles,

Thank you very much for your letter and lovely drawing. I hope your father doesn't mind that Big Daddy has pulled his head off.

Yes you're right, humans took a long time to stand up straight. This was part of our 'evolution'. As more and more grown-ups walked around on two feet, looking for food and animals and things, the stronger our legs got. We also learned to use tools and make fire. This meant we could eat different things and work harder and run faster and keep warm at night. It was a jolly exciting time, I can assure you!

Thanks for your letter. Keep reading!!!

Assist. Editor, Tell Me How. (Look after that rabbit now!)

SEVEN

'At the top there we've got Dean from Cheshire, who's got an Etch-A-Sketch and wants some rollerboots'
Noel Edmunds

Jeremiah and I went, oooooh, way back. I had met him first, if my cheap Japanese memory wasn't going all flickery and in need of fresh batteries, back in the autumn of 1994. He was one of those salt-of-the-earth, friendly types – instantly likable, eager to please, a good egg. Someone who could, just by being around, make you relax and laugh and start humming 'What A Wonderful World' through a dopey grin. It was a combination of his contemplative silences that never made you feel awkward, his sad eyes which were a deep hazel and his gentlest of smiles. My primary school creative writing teacher would send me to the corner for this, but goddammit, he was just 'nice'.

Not that Jerry didn't have faults, it's just they were endearing faults, forgivable ones. He could be grouchy in the morning, like we all can; his personal hygiene was a little on the questionable side; he did stick his fingers up his arse and sniff them once in a while plus he had a tendency to shit himself.

But then, show me a silver-backed mountain gorilla that doesn't.

Alone in the Albert, I'd pulled up a stool —

(oo'er, missus. Sorry, biology teacher humour) —

and got myself outside another Bloody Mary. I sipped and ticked item #3 Maudlin Introspection off my things-to-do list and considered my next move.

Not in any kind of colossal Stalinist big-picture sort of way. It was more that with everything slowly slipping from my control, I should try and have optimum control of the little things: should I buy a packet of peanuts, should I wiggle my buttocks a bit to take the tingly cramp out of them, should I just fuck off home? That sort of thing.

No, I thought finally, grabbing my jacket. Enough of this. I left the purple mobile phone with the barman, trudged through the smell of old lager and damp crisps and out with a thump through the double doors into the

London Sunday sunshine.

I'd get some air in my lungs, clock up some healthy yards on my stroll-o-meter and make some decisions.

I jumped onto a 274 Routemaster and chugged through an overcast London summer. Alighting an incense-whiff's distance from Camden Town, I followed bleach-blonde Germans and double-buggied family outings up Parkway, the proud thoroughfare that spends a quarter of a mile brushing Camden's grimy dreads into the neatly parted respectability of Regent's Park. The Dr Marten shops become exclusive minimalist design studios and the bars a bit more Phil Collins and a little less Phil Spector.

It is but a futile respite, however, because, at the top of Parkway, where it meets Prince Albert Road, squats London Zoo. So just as you've cleared your lungs, the whole place gets all hairy and smelly again.

I negotiated the snaking queues of screaming infants and teeth-gritted parents with a surreptitious flash of my membership. Deborah had made me a member of Lifewatch and sponsored an animal under my name for a birthday present the year before – awwww, *bless* – and free visiting rights was a useful part of the package. Actually the only part of the package now, Deborah having sponsored a bird-eating spider who'd raised its eight hairy legs to heaven three weeks into the scheme.

But the thought was there and they'd let me keep the certificate.

Through the turnstile, the air was wet and musty, like a ground-sheet found in an old carrier bag three weeks after cub camp. Signs gestured eagerly to different attractions: Adventure Reef, Moonlight World, Disabled Toilets. The atmos was a little bit opening-of-Jurassic-Park and ever so slightly closing-of-Sainsburys'-car-park, what with the squawking of tropical birds above and the littery Cornetto wrapper tarmac below. But I headed on, past the echoey half-light that was the Reptile House, to the embrace of some old friends.

Every child educated in the capital is yanked over to London Zoo at some point. Along with the Natural History Museum and its younger, brighter and more streetwise sibling the Science Museum, it's your standard day trip, complete with worksheets, cheese & pickle sandwiches and a letter of consent off Mum. Actually, it's an all-day excursion to the gift shop for bookmarks and keyrings with a few elephants tossed in for scenery, but nobody seems to mind as long as the young 'uns are home for *Grange Hill* with the same number of limbs as they left with.

I would take classes to visit the tropical, primeval and exotic wonders of the Ice-Cream stall as often as I could.

It made me popular with the kids, giving them a day out of the classroom to run up and down tube carriages and smell elephant poo, and I got to revisit an old haunt with the accompanying sexy art teacher of my choice.

First time I'd done this, Deborah and I had to endure *Whooooh! Miss, Miss, he fancies you, miss, don't you, sir? Don't you? Whooooh!* all the way there and all round the enclosures. I had laughed and coughed and *oh look, that's interesting*-ed with my hands firmly in my chinos, face as red as a baboon's arse. I did fancy her of course, but I hadn't told her so she had absolutely no idea.

Yeah *right*, Charlie.

I approached the apes' enclosure. The huge cage was surrounded by tiny children, all standing precariously on the guard rails supported by encouraging dads. Liberally sprinkled among these were the German tourists I had followed, taunting the gorillas with Cheesy Wotsits and guffawing. I presume they were the same tourists. If they weren't, they certainly avoided the same fashion magazines.

Jeremiah wasn't to be seen among the straw, ropes and hexagons of chrome climbing-frame. His wife Diana was there, lolling to and fro on her leathery knuckles, occasionally hesitating to pick among the straw, nibble something, decide it could probably do with a garlic dip, fail to find a garlic dip and then resume her lolling with added vigour.

The children pointed and squealed and look-daddied with great glee, just as I had done when, on my sixth birthday, I had been brought here for the first of many visits. We had only managed to see about a third of the whole zoo, due to me reading aloud, with great care and mispronunciation, every information board on every cage we came to. I had loved it. Images I had only ever seen in books and on television, suddenly there in glorious 3D Stinkorama.

I suppose, in another life, across another galaxy, another Charles Ellis is now face down in a sludgy pit of mud and sweat, a burly, ginger-mustached Sergeant yelling at him – 'On your feet, you 'orrible little man!' and other supportive suggestions. Because in that world, Charles Ellis Mk II was taken, not to the zoo, but to the Imperial War Museum as an impressionable toddler. *Ooohing* and *Ahhhing* at guns instead of gnus, Tiger Moths instead of tigers and, well, moths. So he grew up a soldier, proud, lean, true. Instead of a biology teacher – proud, chubby and true-ish. Such are the decisions that govern our destinies. If such a mirror of me exists, I would love to meet him. He would undoubtedly despise me and my mannered, quiet, oops-sorry lifestyle, despise my unbrushed fringe and untoned stomach, not so much washboard as washing-maching. But I'd like to ask him a question. I'd like to know if, in his world, he ever met a short, dark-haired zookeeper and, if so, if he wouldn't mind helping me out of a tricky spot by telling me what the fuck her name was.

'Hello, stranger.' She smiled.

'Hi,' I responded with Linguaphone predicatableness. *Susan? Sandra? Simone?* Come *on*, brain, what do I pay you for?

'Remember me?' She cocked her head to one side. Around us, children scuffed and danced, tugging at the parental leash. 'We've met before,' she continued. 'You teach biology, bring classes. Charlie, isn't it?'

Sophie? I know this, I know this, don't tell me. Dark bob, green polo shirt, freckly forearms, brown trousers, clumpy boots, outdoorsy smell. *Come on come on.* Got it – Sarah. Thank you, thank you.

'It's Wendy,' she said.

Ooooh, shame. Let's see what you would have won.

'Wendy, hi, yes, sorry, of course. Charles, Charlie.' I offered a hand formally. 'How's it going?'

'Good, good.' She peered over my shoulder. 'On your own today?'

I peered over my shoulder instinctively like a moron, just to see if I hadn't accidentally brought thirty twelve year olds with me in my back pocket.

'Huh? Oh. Yes yes. Just killing some time. I was just at a kind of . . .' (careful here, Charles) 'a . . . thing, just now.'

Mental note. Appointment pronouns such as thing, whatsit and doo-dah instinctively make listeners think you are hiding something embarrassing, usually to do with clinics and genital warts. Don't hide, lie.

'A dentist thing,' and I gave myself a little rat-a-tat-tat on my canines.

Oh yes. And nobody goes to the dentist on a Sunday lunchtime, dolt.

Wendy picked some stray straw from her hair and motioned towards the rear of the ape cage.

'You want to say hello to Jeremiah while you're here?'

'Sure,' I bounced agreeably.

And off we went, two by two, into the ark.

Gorillas are one of the many offshoots of the African line of Old World monkeys, with which we humans share a descendant. They have all the standard features of your basic economy model – the sticky-out noses, the virtually useless furry, stumpy tails and, most importantly, the grippy hands with opposable thumbs.

Now lots has been made of this opposable-thumbness. It's one of those laboratory expressions that has made a courageous bid for freedom out onto the high street and into the pub – like ozone, chaos theory and that old chestnut about $1pc=3.26ly=204,265AU$. It's a little thing really. It just means that the tip of the thumb is able to touch the tips of the other digits on that hand.

Zowie, Cavey, strike a light, who gives a flying arse?

Well we may take this for granted, we have been able to do it for about 30 million years after all. But it's these tiny, almost unnoticeable, 'Hey! Look what young Ralph can do! There's a clever boy' advancements in our biology that mean, 30 million years later, we are still around – inventing D.I.Y. stencilling kits and sick-bags.

So how come we've got them? Well the most popular theory among your Darwinian Evolutionist is that of mutation. When little Ralph was born with his weirdy sticky-out finger, he probably got teased a lot to start with. *Oy, Cripply!* perhaps, or *Bendy Bones.* Or, if he went to my school, just *Freaky Wanker.* He was the last to be picked for games and sat on his own at lunch. But as Ralph grew up, he found his gammy hands gave him a slight advantage over his pals. He could pick up his Mr Men pencil case with more ease, grab his blazer firmly, thumb a lift into town. And being the most adept at hunting and gathering, not to mention being able to click his fingers Fonzy-style, made him an appealing and valuable mate. And so, bada-boom, bada-bing (scientifically speaking) he pulled himself a breeding partner and his type became prolific.

If we as humans hadn't evolved these multipurpose, Eez-E-Kleen, send-no-money-now gadgets, well? Well some other species would be pointing at us behind wire, trying to get us to eat cheese-flavoured corn snacks.

'There he is, old grumpy drawers,' Wendy sang, as we peered into the spacious glass anteroom that leads off from the main enclosure. Jeremiah sat, sulkily, on the edge of the concrete step, scratching himself dis-interestedly. His wise, dark eyes focused somewhere else, little ears twitching on the sides of his frankly enormous head.

'How is he?' I inquired, my nose inches from the toughened glass. He had been a resident here for years, it seemed, and I had become sort of fond.

'Oh he's pissed off,' Wendy said, matter-of-factly.

I gazed at the familiar dapply-green interior, the fraying yellow ropes, the urined floor and solitary tyre. Tidier than my place, certainly.

'Diana's on heat,' Wendy explained. 'You can tell by the swollen rear. Jerry's been sniffing about after her for days but she's having none of it. Now he's sulking. Aren't you, you old moody?'

Frighteningly familiar, I mused.

'In the wild, an alpha male of his age would have had access to numerous fertile females. Total access, more than likely.' She squatted down onto her haunches and I followed, surpressing the smile that Jeremiah encouraged. 'There would be other males in the group, but all younger. And the young tend to know their place. Old Jerry here would be the major stud. Wouldn't you. Hmm?'

Peck peck peck, I thought to myself.

Jeremiah looked up from his lap throwing a *Who me? Nahhh, get away* expression into Wendy's eyes and we both chuckled.

'Hey-up,' I said, 'he's off.'

The ape stood slowly. Not with any great purpose or urgency, just stretching his little legs. He loped over to his tyre, Wendy and I watching in captivated silence. The screaming kids and gawping tourists faded out of the soundtrack leaving just the three of us. His heavy movements seemed slowly so familiar. Not just because I had come to watch him as a student and on countless afternoons out with Deborah. His slow meanderings and sniffy, half-arsed curiosity as he hauled his mountainous, silver-backed hulk to and fro about his domain were floodingly familiar to me because. Well because?

Because he was me.

Watching Jeremiah that afternoon was akin to staring into a mirror in my flat any Saturday afternoon, coarse black body-hair aside. He sat, glassy eyed, staring off into space. Then abruptly he'd get up, for seemingly no reason, to wander over to his playthings. He'd touch them, perhaps pick something up. Put it down again. Scratch himself. Gaze at the wall. Lope back to his seat, all builder's bum and grumpy mood. Then just plonk himself back down, picking idly at some food and sniffing.

Add a slice of cold pizza and *Football Focus* and Deborah couldn't have told us apart.

We watched him lumber through the plastic slats, out of his cubicle and into the fresh air, head down, huge shoulders rolling. The crowd gave an excited squeal and camcorders whirred into life.

'Watch this,' Wendy half whispered with a nudge. 'He's going to try it on with Diana again.' And Jeremiah, with judged, cautious movements, knuckled it over to the centre of the cage, startling the young sparrows who'd been hanging out in his garden, *just getting our ball back, honest, mister.*

'How's your girlfriend?' Wendy inquired with innocent, friendly, getting-to-know-you curiosity, eyes still on the apes. 'She not with you today?'

Well really. How's a young man supposed to move on when he's constantly batting away such direct overarm balls, hmmm? Wendy had seen Debs and me together on numerous occasions, whether with school trips or just hand-in-hand, giggling, teasing, doing that playful, *Truly Madly Deeply* coupley larking. I'd hoped she wouldn't ask.

Fortunately, on the bus ride over, I'd rehearsed a short, bullet-pointed press release to deliver to my parents. I gave her a preview.

'Deborah and I are trying a short trial separation. Things haven't been going so well and we,' with big emphasis on *we*, 'are taking a breather for a while. Bit of space, sorting a few things out, you know. Still engaged but, well, just taking a breather. That's all.'

I turned to Wendy. She stared bewildered at me. I think she was just after a *She's fine.*

'Oh,' she said awkwardly. 'That's, er . . . nice.'

I made a mental note to call my primary school creative writing teacher and complain about a drop in standards.

'The female is very coy. She'll let the male get a good whiff before running off. It's all a big flirt. She needs to know she's wanted, so she'll make him chase her for hours.'

It took me half that sentence to realise Wendy wasn't talking about Deborah.

'Watch, watch. Here he goes.'

Jeremiah rolled his way across the damp straw. Tum-ti-tum, heigh-de-ho, don't mind me. Diana shifted suddenly in her seat, ears giving a spasm of curiosity. If she'd had a gin and tonic, she'd have stared into it. *This seat taken, darlin'?* Jerry questioned, edging up behind her.

The Germans gave a bar-room roar of libidinous encouragment.

'Doesn't Jerry get the hint?' I asked. Diana couldn't have seemed less up for it if, I dunno, if she was worried a load of school governors would walk in.

Or something.

'It's in her interest to keep him keen,' Wendy replied. 'Look, see how she lets him sniff her.'

And indeed, there was a whole lotta nosin' goin' on. Diana sat stock still, her deep eyes blinking, while Jeremiah nudged and butted her around the trades-man's entrance. Diana stared straight ahead, like you might do when you take the only vacant seat on a bus, only to realise the reason it's vacant is there's an insane shouty drunk Scotsman in the seat next to it who wants to tell you about the war.

'If she's too stand-offish,' Wendy continued, 'Jerry will think, blow this for a game of soldiers, and try elsewhere.'

Then suddenly, as if she'd been counting down from ten, Diana got to her feet. Jeremiah visibly thought *Aye-up, I'm in 'ere*, and lunged, face first for her puffy pink behind. The only thing missing from the next few moments was the theme to *The Benny Hill Show*.

Diana ran, or at least did the ape equivalent of running – a kind of bouncy, lopey trot – along the edge of the enclosure towards us, Jerry keeping up the rear, so to speak.

'Atta girl,' Wendy laughed. Personally, I couldn't help but side with Jeremiah as he lolled drunkenly behind. *Oy, oy, darlin', I only wanted to buy you a drink, honest. Hey, where ya goin?* Diana made a sharp left and scurried behind what seemed to be a gargantuan picnic basket in the centre of the cage. Jerry stopped.

'Will he follow?' I asked, rooting for the guy. All this effort, worth a snog at least.

'Watch,' Wendy said with a nod and accompanying knowing smile.

Jerry sat for a mo, weighing up his chances.

In the ape world, 'no' always means 'maybe'. Males Are From Mars, Females Are From Mars, every damn living thing is from Mars. It's a crowded little planet, by jingo, but a place of mutual understanding and good neighbourly cooperation, all encoded into their behaviour. They know what each other wants and they know how each other is going to get it.

They could write a book and live off *Ricki Lake* appearances for life.

Jerry rummaged for some leaves, which turned out to be celery. Placing it between his yellowing, twenty B&H-a-day canines, he crawled purposefully over to where Diana hid.

'Food for sex,' Wendy explained.

Now this I knew. Birds do it, bees do it, even educated chimpanzees do it. The trade up — gifts for rumpo. Female hanging flies, if you ever get caught in a bar with one, will insist on a dead insect to munch on during sex. Not after, not before. During. Crumbs in the bed clearly not a turn-off for your John Q. Hanging-Fly. In fact, if the female finishes her food before the male has finished his fuck, she'll happily buzz off, mid-bonk, for dessert. Bummer. Female chimps, also, are far far more likely to get a larger share of lunch if they flash their red swelly bits at the maître d'. Which may, or may not, come as a surprise.

Depends if you drink in the Albert on a Friday night, I suppose.

Jerry disappeared behind the straw basket out of view. The public on the other side of the cage could clearly see what was going on, as they pointed and giggled. One mother yanking her screeching little one off the railings with a look of *Well, really!* Diana appeared a moment later around the other side and clutched at a dangling rope. Jeremiah made a futile lunge but his missus had got wise. Arm over gangly arm, she scaled the rope with puffy urgency, those opposable thumbs showing themselves to be *the* must-have accessory for any modern woman, a cheer of delight from her captive audience. The crowds promptly began to break away, chattering and laughing, vacating their places for the 3 o'clock performance.

'Unlucky, buddy.' I shrugged, Jerry flumping down far beneath his wife's safety. 'Crashed and burned.'

'Don't worry.' Wendy smiled. 'He'll try it again in a half hour.'

EIGHT

'They say a reasonable amount o' fleas is good fer a dog
— keeps him from broodin' over bein' a dog, mebbe.'
Edward Noyes Westcott

'How's school?' Wendy asked.

Not having anything else planned for the rest of that Sunday, the following Monday or, now let me see . . . ah yes, the rest of my life, I decided to hang about in the zoo for the remainder of the afternoon. Home was a bit of a tip and I knew that once I returned, a mysterious force unexplainable to man would lead me protesting and procrastinating over to the Playstation and that would be the day gone.

Wendy left me kicking grit and scraffing tarmac by the crane pen. One stood, as angular as an upper case 'A', perfectly still on one leg. Every so often it gave itself a bit of a scratch and teetered, like it was on a *Generation Game* challenge. The whole place had a dark mossy smell with the tang of wet hay. Wendy returned with a couple of buckets of feed and then we made our way through the zoo.

'I don't think you'll be seeing too much of me any more, I'm afraid,' I said and began to explain my job situation.

But I only got about nine words in before I abruptly stopped explaining the situation, my self-esteem waving and gesturing frantically from the horizon — *Stay away, stay away, hazards ahead*. I coughed and *errr*-ed a bit and skipped forward a couple of tracks of my exposition.

'I just fancied a change. I didn't feel biology teacher was really me, y'know?' I threw the question back at her before she probed any deeper. 'What about you? You sticking with' — I gestured about the place as we passed the flappy clappy slapstick of the penguin pond — 'this lot?'

'Oh God yes, absolutely.'

'Didn't you ever want to do anything else?' I asked. We strolled under a canopy of birdsong, a constant hum and whirr with the odd screech thrown in. It was warm, the tarmac sticky under my clumpy Docs.

'Like what? Something better than spending all day outdoors in the company of animals?'

'Yeah. Like, I dunno, write an opera or become a pop star or anything?'

'Nope. Since I first dissected a frog at the age of thirteen, this is all I've ever wanted. Couldn't get enough of it. I stayed on at uni and got a teaching degree as well, like you. But it couldn't compete with up close, where you can touch it and smell it, that's for me. Getting home with dirt on your hands and that grassy smell on your clothes. Can't beat it.'

'You never wanted to change the world? You never look back and think – there must be more to life than this?'

'Er, *hello*? More to life than *this*?'

We reached the birdhouse, the air crowded and bursting with colour and noise. Cages ran the full length of one wall, divided up into square apartments for different breeds. Nervous frantic twittering and fluttering of the young gave way to the slow creaking squawks of the parents, the sight of Wendy's food bucket bringing them tanging and ringing their talons against the black bars, the larger birds biting and gnawing at the wire.

'Impressive bunch,' I said, a Benetton-bright Hyacinth Macaw (*Psittacformes*) spreading his blue wings with the pride and flourish of a matador. His eye was circled by the brightest yellow ring, a coordinated accessory to his vibrant yellow jaw.

'Yes, they are. Stunning, some of them. What's

literature or classical music got to compare with this?'

'Well,' I laughed, 'be fair. I think Shakespeare and Beethoven might have something to say about that. If they weren't dead, obviously.'

'Well yeah,' she conceded gallantly, 'but I mean . . . well look. You go to the Tate, right, and they've all those Rembrandts and Da Vincis — stuff to make you gasp and wonder and weep. Or maybe you sit in the Albert Hall,' she continued, scooping up cupfuls of grain and upending them with a whooshing rattle into feeders one by one. The macaw was joined by his twitchy partner who took off with a rustle from his heavy perch. 'All pomp and circumstance and stirring orchestras, really hairs on the back of the neck stuff. And English at school. It seemed to have all the fun — all the romance of Tennyson and Wordsworth.'

Wendy crunched back to the bucket, refilled her cup and looked me dead in the eyes.

'But the point is — they can't tell you *why* you feel this way.'

'I don't follow.'

Wendy dropped her cup into the bucket and stretched her arms wide.

'Biology is *everything*, it's not just lab rats and test-tubes,' she burst out. 'You must know that. Poetry is biology, music is biology, art is biology, everything. It's all physical responses, chemical reactions, synapses and endorphins. Why do we cry when we watch *E.T.*?

Because of the sounds vibrating our eardrums and images of light on our retinas. Books and paintings and films – these things are just the *what*. Biology is the *how and the why*. All these things happening deep inside us in the space of a pinprick at the speed of light. There's not a sonnet or a symphony that can even come close.' As if on cue, a white Moluccan cockatoo let out a piercing rape alarm of a call, hungry as it was, its crest flipping up like a magician's card flourish. 'Well, more or less.' Wendy smiled.

I said my see-ya-arounds and slipped away into the heart of the zoo. Pleasant girl. A little fanatical perhaps. I got the feeling this was a passionate diatribe that had been wheeled out for an airing once or twice before. She was right of course. The sciences were on their way to explaining pretty much all there was to be explained – gravity, big bangs, UFOs, ghosts – an entire travelling circus of superstition was debunked on almost a daily basis by smirking know-alls with lab coats over their *Red Dwarf* T-shirts. But Wendy was the plus side of such phenomena – a genuine wide-eyed wonder at nature and it's genius.

I did a fistful of thinking that afternoon, ambling among the cages and gardens, among otters and owls.

This, this was a place I could work. In all fairness to Brad and his more than generous suggestion of getting me in on the ground floor at his bookshop, I couldn't tell a credit-note slip from a Beatrix Potter bookmark. But I could tell Peter Rabbit from Peter Hare.

In fact could subset the entire *Peter Oryctolagus Cuniculus* family. A place like this had an almost magnetic draw. It took me back to my idealistic, rosy-futured student days. Days of ambition and wonder. Days before I'd lain down and let ordinariness carry me away. God I missed those times.

On that first school outing with Deborah those many years ago, I had shown off rather with my enthusiasm. Scooting about, naming all the creatures, many of them rather wankily, in Latin. I told her about breeding patterns and behavioural whatnots. And Deborah had been impressed. So she said. That is, she had agreed to go for a drink with me after we got back to school.

Or you could say, more aptly, I had offered her some prime meat in exchange for sex.

Now now, steady on, Charlie.

Because humans can't play that *8oz steak = rumpy-pumpy* equation. Not in our environment. It's all got more subtle over the millions of years that separate us from the oh-so-simple chimpanzees. Nobody seems to know why it had to get more complicated. But then nobody in their right mind hasn't noticed that deep, deep down, the same bartering exists.

You want sex with me? the female of our species will ask. *What do I get out of it?* Well, three Bernard Matthews Crispy Crumb Turkeyburgers ain't going to cut any ice, let's face it. But oooh, what about . . . ?

What about the opportunity of having a child with above average intelligence and a totally clean bill of health? Hmm? What's that worth?

Because that's what we're doing. With our sideburns, our fast cars, our broad shoulders. Or alternatively, our thumbed paperbacks, our sensitive horn-rimmed specs and our sonnets. Little signals, tiny hints that we've something to offer – be it money, health, brains.

Unconsciously, of course, I had presented Deborah with a potential father to her offspring. A father with intelligence, sensitivity, youthful energy and, in the shape of my teaching post, financial stability. And, one could say, her fancy was taken.

Sadly one could also say, if one was feeling particularly bitchy and clever-clever, it was the reinventing of myself as an impatient, lust-filled, thoughtless unemployed twat that caused her to look again at her investment and subsequently withdraw her funds.

Dear Tell Me How,

Thank you very much for my poster and my badge. Steve Austin has torn off one part of the poster and pooed on it so i do not know what we turn into after Neanderthal. I put my badge on my sleeping bag and my poster next to my map of London Zoo. Have you been there?

Please can you tell me what it means on the poster that chimpanzees have 98 humans living in them. Have they eaten the naughty people at the zoo who gave them crisps and got smack?

Master Charles Ellis age 7½

Dear Charles,

Many thanks for your letter and your lovely drawing. That is a lot of poo, isn't it! And what a funny colour! What has Steve Austin been eating?

What the poster means is 98% of a chimpanzees' DNA is identical to humans. This is quite complicated to explain. It means that a lot of the recipe that tells the cells inside a chimpanzee what to do is the same as the recipe inside you. Deep down inside, humans and chimps are very similar. That is because we share what we call a 'descendant' – which is like having the same grandad. But 30 million years ago! It will be on your chart I sent you. Can you see where we split away from the monkeys 6 million years ago?

Many thanks and keep reading!!!

Assist. Editor, Tell Me How

NINE

'It takes your enemy and your friend, working together,
to hurt you to the heart. The one to slander you and
the other to get the news to you.'

Mark Twain

Brad's place of work, or 'workplace' as he preferred to call it, goddammit, was one of those spacious, pine-fresh, well-lit West End book emporiums that smack far more of an IKEA show-home than a hushed seat of knowledge and literature. There were inviting, plump, bright pink sofas and slightly less inviting plump, bright pink staff, all snooty and graduated and, it seemed, freshly purchased from Gap in a variety of cuts and styles. They sighed and dismissed and oh-really-ed with so much higher-plane-ness that you just knew they all spent their lunch-hours writing screenplays and saying Tch! at the *Guardian*. I grabbed myself a *Petite Wet Coconut Latte*, the coffee shop staff having looked at me bewilderedly when I asked for *a cup of coffee*, and loitered my helpless self by the Self-Help section.

What was keeping him? I jittered.

I'd thrown myself round to Bradley's on the way home from the zoo for a bit of a chinwag about life and love and a bit of a fist-wag about this Ronnie Cousins and the mobile-phone/boyfriend incident. But he wasn't home. In fact, the fat wadded *Sunday Observer* which strained and wrestled at his letter box in a tattery flourette indicated he hadn't been home all night.

It was getting on for five o'clock. He was probably still blinking dozily at some young lady's bedroom ceiling, after an afternoon of munching toast and a few fresh mugs of sexual intercourse. God knows when the jammy bastard would be back.

Arse. I whipped the *Review* supplement out with a surreptitious deafening clatter and browsed it all the way home.

Thumping indoors, I was greeted by a spoilt eight year old's attention-grabbing whine. A pausette followed and then came the facts as a teutonic schoolmarm announced, with Orwellian authority, the state of my life.

You have two messages.

I threw my jacket onto two other jackets, under which I was pretty sure I had left an armchair and leant over the machine. The play button sat there, sandwiched between his two socially inept buddies – one very forward, the other very backward. *I know something you don't know*, it taunted. Another pausette. Two messages.

I went to the toilet.

Or rather, walked through to the lavatory and had a piss, I didn't wet myself with anticipation there and then in the living room. Urinating loudly, shaking hands with the recently redundant, so to speak, my brain raced with possibilities. Two messages. I'd been planning on coming home and sitting quietly for three hours, wondering quite how I'd managed to fuck up three dates with three women in the space of only 48 hours. But I had two messages.

Bleeeep. *Yo Chucky, whassup? You there?*

Brad. Fucky shitballs.

Guess not. How's the dating going? I gave you strict instructions to call me every hour on the hour with a progress report. But I haven't heard from you so you're probably still tied up, h-heyyy!

Sigh. I took a seat and let him monologue on, using the dull bits to take a gander at my humble home. The living room was a state. A neglected, poverty-ridden state where the mayor has embezzled all the funds and fucked off to Mexico with his mistress. Coffee and crumbs every-where, coffee mugs and plates everywhere else. Fast food wrappers, half-opened books, clothes. A pin had dropped out of Mr J. Fox causing him to bow reverently in my presence.

Aaaanyway.

Oops, pay attention.

Wotcha up to tomorrow? I thought lunch or something? Pop into the shop about one-ish. Otherwise, come over in the week maybe? I don't like the idea of you moping about on your own. We can go round to Ade's and I can whip your sorry butts at Scalextric.

Peck peck peck. Jesus, didn't he ever stop?

Or you can look at my new DVD player. It's fuckin' A. Perfect freeze-frame. Plus Basic Instinct widescreen. He-heyy, ideal for that fa –

I jabbed fast forward and play again. Brad was still rattling on about pixels and colour definition and iMac.

I skipped to the second message. The machine bleeped again. My heart climbed purposefully up my throat, thumping away like Lennox Lewis. My sphincter gave a game-show-host wink and the glamorous assistant in my stomach executed a graceless backflip. The machine whirred, there was the third pausette of the day.

Bleeep. . . . *You fucking pricks move . . .*

What the hell?

– every motherfucking last one of you . . .

Bloody Nora, I thought. I mean, I might be a bit late with my telephone bill, but *really*. And where did Busby learn language like that? It's that Maureen Lipman, I'll bet you.

A burst of surf guitar and it dawned on me. It was the beginning of that movie, that Tarantino thing . . .

Charlie? Charlie, are you there?

I'd known. Somehow I'd known. I went cold and hot simultaneously, the two fronts meeting at the base of my spine and my back began to rain.

If you're there, please pick up.

Her voice drowned out the music into a muffled rhythm. It was so good to hear her voice.

I guess you're out. I just wanted you to know . . . oh, just . . . sorry. Sorry, Charlie, I shouldn't have called. I can't do this on a machine. Forget it, just forget I called. Ask . . . ask Brad, he knows. Sorry, Charlie.

Time announcement is off spake Eva Braun. And I was alone again.

He approached lazily as I was draining the frothy dregs and wondering about Men being From Mars and Women being From Venus. This is only a paltry distance of 20 million miles. Surely, given our differences, women are more likely to be from Saturn? It would explain something about their obsession with elaborate rings.

'Awright?'

'Awright?'

And, pleasantries covered, we left for a McBite to eat.

'You having the usual?' Brad asked as we stood in the queue that snaked and snapped and collapsed into a swarming mess of hungry punters, all craning at the menus. 'This one's on me.' He held up a palm to silence my protestations. 'Just till you get yourself sorted.'

'Cheers, mate, that'd be grand.'

I had of course no intention of protesting whatsoever, my future finances being not so much projections, more just falling-off-the-table-onto-the-floors. Brad patted for his wallet, leaving me ample opportunity to fidget and twitch and exhale a held breath of anxiety.

So far, not even a reference to Deborah.

I'd called him immediately I'd heard her message the previous afternoon, letting the phone ring and ring, but he was still out and his phone had just rung and rung, leaving me no choice but to have a jittery Sunday night, all squirty with panic and possibility.

'So how's things?' he asked coolly.

'Well, you tell me.'

'Huh, I don't getcha? Oh, yes. Couple of Big Macs, a couple a fries, goin' large, two loads of nuggets and a couple of your apple pies, please, ma'am.'

'You've got some news for me, I understand?'

'News? About what? Oh, sorry. Two strawberry shakes as well, thanks. I'm not with ya, buddy?'

Was he taking the piss?

'You, er, you spoke to Deborah?'

I don't know if it's grammatically correct to say someone was suddenly doing something slowly. It doesn't sound right, does it? But anyway, with the blessing of Carol Vorderman or not, that's what happened. On these words, Brad quickly began to fuss with straws and napkins and counting out exact change. After three or four months, he turned and faced me, a lot of stuff going on behind his eyes. As if the guest of honour at a surprise party had rung the doorbell an hour early.

'I . . . I'm not with you. Deborah . . . ?'

Oh for heaven's sake.

'She said you'd spoken.'

'Oh. Oh that. Oh. Oh right. Well there's not a great deal to tell.'

Which was my first clue that all was, if not rotten in the state of Denmark, then at least bad enough to have people sniffing it and looking for the expiry date. What the hell was *not a great deal to tell*? Was he kidding? Brad knew I'd want to excavate and polish every phrase, every word, and slip it onto a glass slide for lengthy analysis. And as a mate, he knew it was his job, his duty, to spill the relevant gen.

*

'Honest, buddy, there's hardly anything to tell, we hardly even spoke. She just rapped about sorting herself out 'n' shit,' Brad explained, munching some limp fries. 'She's looking about for a new flat and some work. She just went on about taking some time and looking at shit 'n' shit.'

I wondered if there was something wrong with Deborah's lavatory.

'She's all right, y'know? I mean, she's well, she's okay. She's been hanging out with Liz a bit. Girly chats.' He took a gargantuan muffled chomp of burger. 'Hab you bird deyb hab ba bathey?'

What? I mean, sorry, *what*? This was all, very so slightly just a little bit of a fuck of a lot to take in. When did he find all this out? Was he going to let me know? Huh? And new flats? New jobs?

And *hab ba bathey*?

'The baby. Liz has had the baby,' he explained with a gulp. 'Ade's over the frickin' moon.'

Yes of course, the baby was due about now. I should go round and see them both.

Hmm, maybe Deborah will be there?

Oh for Christ sakes, Charlie. All my compassion was wrapped tightly in tissue paper and bustled out of reach by the overworked removal firm of Ego, Narcissist & Sons. I shook my head quickly, thoughts and questions clicking about inside like an aerosol.

'So, sorry, when did you find all this out?'

'Huh? Oh, a few, um, a while ago. I bumped into her

119

in town one day last week.' Brad shrugged and started, with expert origami skills, turning his drinking straw wrapper into a delicate scale model of a folded-in-half drinking straw wrapper.

'Bumped into her?'

'That's right.'

Well this was quite clearly *fiddlesticks and flap-doodle*, as the Nobel Prize winning Professor Yaffle used to say. I mean, nobody just bumps into anybody. Not in real life. Yes, in sitcoms they do. And in movies and crappy Ray Cooney farces with too many vicars and doors and exclamation marks. But not in a city of 8 million people.

'At the station. She was going the opposite way and we stopped to chat for a few minutes. And y'know, like I say — she seemed okay. I get the feeling she misses you.'

'Yeah?'

'Yeah. You know, having someone around. I mean, she's pretty much in your exact position.'

Except she's probably changed her sheets in the last month, I thought grimly.

'Out of work, on her own.'

Brad gave a McBurp and wiped milkshake on his sleeve.

'It's time, you know. She needs time.'

Sorry, you're confused. That should be *Time 'n' shit.*

'You didn't tell her about me seeing other women?'

'Uh-uh, no frickin' way. I thought that was best left out. How did that go anyway? Apparently Ronnie might have some kind of on–off boyfriend thing?'

I delivered Brad a detailed summary of my opinion of his matchmaking skills which, in a wonder of modern postal technology, fitted snugly into a handy two-syllable envelope.

'Charming. I was only trying to help,' he said.

'But, I mean, Deborah's not seeing anyone else though, right?'

Brad tossed aside two fresh white serviettes, wiped ketchupy digits on his chinos and stood up.

'C'mon, you miserable fuck, I'm going to get you a job.'

So I took that as a no.

I spent the rest of a long Monday afternoon trailing after Brad as he lauded it about his domain with alpha confidence. He left me alone every so often to deal with the life-or-death machinations of modern retailing – tills running out of paper, frothy spillages of cappuccino in the erotica section. At least I hope it was cappuccino. And I was left loitering, conspicuous hairy-knuckled store detectives visibly calculating their overtime at me.

Ambling thoughtfully through avenues of philosophy and psychology I felt a blanket of thermal 15-tog nostalgia gather about my shoulders. That rich smell of paper and wood tickled me with memories of the dusty, musty, sepia Sundays in second-hand backroom shoppes that Deborah and I used to enjoy. Of course, those Byronesque afternoons of bespectacled poetic lingering in Hampstead backstreets were just an elaborate pulling technique, as any young male graduate will testify. The attempt to appear sensitive and erudite, humming knowledgeably over first editions. The moment we'd slept together, we both resumed buying our John Grishams from WHSmith. But still. Such is the elaborate courtship of our simple species.

An hour flew by with O Level exam hall clock rapidity. I entertained myself, scouring the Not As Popular As You Might Think Science section for any new developments, any life-altering eurekas from my academic compadres. Next door, the slimmer and more slivery philosophy department peered over its half-moon specs at me, weighty with insight and condescension. It dawned on me, scanning the fat spines, how very few philosophers there were. A handful of major-league know-alls. One could probably get all the greatest thinkers of our time into one pub quiz team. Not that they'd be very good at the pop music questions. Or much good at anything really, besides looking unnervingly confident in a toga.

These dead guys in the Philosophy department (and they were all guys and all dead). Did they really think they had any real answers like they claimed? Plato, Kant, Socrates, Sartre, Beaky, Mick and Tich? Bickering as they did over marble tables and generations. I dragged a lazy finger over a millennium of debate. I, like many, had read *Sophie's World* looking for answers and found only questions. The main one being *I spent £16.99 on this?*

Frankly, their solutions to the world's mysteries were all too airy, too head-in-the-clouds for a boy brought up on *101 Facts to Amaze Your Friends*. No, give me the black or white, right or wrong measurable data of the laboratory.

'You all right there, Chucky?'

I jumped. Brad appeared at my side suddenly, struggling with an arm of shiny self-help and a fresh application form. 'Sorry about abandoning you, one of my part-timers has handed in his notice. Got to knuckle down to revise for his la-di-da psychology degree. But I got you this to fill out.'

I followed him over as he began to stack the books on a table, a table that teemed with gift ideas for the lonely alcoholic chain-smoking single overweight depressive in your life.

'So, get that filled in, I'll give you a reference. You'll get an interview, no probs. You can come and work here, it'd be kicks.'

'Look, I don't know . . .' I eased carefully.

'What? You're still looking for work, right?'

'Yes, well yes kind of.'

'Kind of?'

'Well yes all right. But, this . . .' I gestured at the stacks and shelves. 'I don't know. It's not really me.'

It wouldn't be 'kicks', I thought. It wouldn't. Surrounded by books, standing in the shadow of greatness, among the works and ideas of scientific geniuses. And *my* highly respected contribution to it all? Making sure they were in alphabetical order.

No, no I couldn't do it. I had decided. I'd turned my back on a meaningful future once. Held the coats while my peers rode the waltzer. There could have been a wild party awaiting me when I reached my thirties – of happiness and achievement and success. But no, I had chosen to sit upstairs in the warm, banging a broom handle on the floor instead, complaining about the noise.

There was as yet no Charles Ellis Award for Advancements in Science. No Charles Ellis Foundation for Biological Research. And the only plaque on my parents' house was where a satellite dish had once hung before I'd snapped it one evening, trying to find the porn channel.

And nothing was going to change if I allowed myself to take this job. Brad as my boss. No way.

Call it stupidity, call it stubborness, but this I could not do. It would be like putting up my hands and admitting I was a loser. One of a group of blokes who hung so much importance on status, on social positioning, on chart placing, accepting Brad as my boss?

'Then here, mate,' he said flatly. Not cross, not ecstatic, just words. And he handed me a book. 'Go, heal your life or something. I've got a shop to run.' I took it from him.

'Heyyy,' I changed tack with a chummy smile. I had hurt his feelings. It was one thing to get pissed on a Friday and argue about who had the worst job, but you didn't diss another man's career. 'Don't be stupid. I just want to try out a few things. See what's out there. We could never have worked together, we'd have gone mad!'

Brad shrugged. How to tell him that there had to be something out there for me beyond stacking M. Scott Pecks without it coming out like la-di-da psychology?

'Look, I'm sorry. I didn't mean it, I'm just a bit fucked up. It's losing Deborah and losing my job and everything. Howzabout I throw myself over tonight? I'll see what Ade's doing. Say, meet you outside at around six?'

Brad stopped piling and looked me in the eyes. A beat. Then he cracked.

'Yes. Yes all right.' Relief surrounded me in a Ready Brek glow.

Which Brad promptly threw a bucket of water on, producing billowing smokescreen.

'No! No don't meet me. Not tonight.' A sudden turn

and *The Road Less Travelled* suddenly forked off into twenty separate B-roads which opened up at our feet as his pile hit the stone floor with a slithery crash.

'Whoopsie,' and there was a sudden increase of elbows and knees and picking things up and saying sorry and here for a mo.

'Don't tell me, you're staying in and watching, I dunno, *Reservoir Dogs* again.' Brad had written to *Empire* magazine about the post-post-post-modern reference of the fact that Tim Roth, the spectator in the famous ear-severance scene, had previously played Van Gogh in a biopic. They hadn't published the letter.

Brad got up and began to straighten up his display.

'No. I did have a bit of a Quentin fest yesterday, though.'

'Again.'

'Yep. Got up early, read the papers and watched three in a row. Thirty-fourth time now. Fan-fucking-tastic.'

But then a feeling prickled the back of my neck surreptitiously.

'Sorry, you were at home *all* yesterday?' I asked. My bottom did something funny.

'Er, yep indeed. All day. Up at the crack, read the papers and kicked back with the old DVDs. Have I told you my Van Gogh theory?'

You know how sometimes you have a thought. And it's one of those thoughts that is so big, of such unrestrainable, forehead-slapping dimension, that it doesn't actually fit your head. So you have to let it out. And only then can you walk around it and poke it and kick it and see if it's got any substance?

Well that's the reason that, on the Jubilee Line train home, as it slid into Green Park with a sigh and the doors opened, I shouted '*Pulp fucking Fiction! You fuck!*' at a terrifying volume, causing a small child in a bobble hat to burst into tears.

Dear Tell Me How,

How do I become a scientist like you are and write about science? We study it in school. Today we blew up balloons and put them in washing up bowls to see if they floated. My bowl was yellow but I wanted the red one. If I go to big school and show them my poster will they let me dig for dinosaurs in the grassy bit behind Sainsburys? I think I saw a bone there once.

Master Charles Ellis age 8

I'm not to give Steve Austin any more Toblerone.

Ears-ears is still at the vet's house but I am being a big brave soldier.

Dear Charles,

Thank you for your letter and your lovely picture. What a handsome Brontosaurus! But remember they do not eat meat so your Nan would not taste nice to him.

There is always room for more scientists and we would love to have you working here when you are old enough. Perhaps one day you will find your own dinosaur and we could name it after you!!! Or maybe you could invent chocolate for rabbits to eat!!! Scientists can do anything!

Thanks for your letter, keep reading!!!

Assist. Editor, Tell Me How

TEN

'Don't get smart alecksy with the galaxy'
                                    E.Y. Harburg

The doorbell did what doorbells are prone to do when
you interrupt their silent Zen meditation by punching
them in the face. Stepping back down the steps onto
the leafy, white-pillared, detached, haven't-we-done-
wellness of Viller's Avenue, Swiss Cottage, and into the
morning sunshine, I sucked my finger maternally. It
still smarted like buggery from my yankage of Bruce
and his drawing pins from the lounge wall. It was now
Darwin's beardy mush that peered benignly down over
my daily rituals — a glossy A2 warden, keeping in line
my psyche and other animals. Not as sneery, macho,
balding or testosterony as Mr Willis, but a role model

definitely more suited to the new me, or at least one who would look as absurd in a greying vest as I would.

Not that we had much more than that in common at this stage, let's face it. Old Darwinipoos had pretty much scribbled a reminder *Must Get Married Someday* and fixed it to his fridge with a magnetic banana with no urgency whatsoever. Generally, his attitude to romance was as clinical and detached as his attitude to the embryological development of molluscs. If he had been a philosopher rather than a geologist, he might have taken a different slant on all things Cupidy. Perhaps arguing with his fiancée until dawn about whether a bed was still a bed if you weren't looking at it and hadn't we better go upstairs and make sure hint hint. Or alternatively, if he had become the doctor his father had wanted him to be, he could have passed his wooing off as a gynaecological after-care service plan.

But Uncle Charles was a man of science first and a man of flesh about twelfth. It is noted in his journals that, after returning from his five-year voyage, he drew up a pros and cons list of hypotheses regarding marriage and its potential consequences. It featured plusses such as *Charms of music and female chit-chat* and *Someone to take care of house*. And negatives such as *Loss of conversation with clever men* and *Quarrelling, fatness and idleness*. What a guy.

And yet. Think about it. Because, believe me, I'd been doing little else. There is a certain beauty, a certain elegant simplicity to Darwin's antiseptic pursuit of happiness. You can kind of admire his dedication, can't you.

Can't you?

Well all right, please yourself. I admired it. Better?

Here was a guy with belief, a man with faith. Science was his life, his spirit, his creed and motivation and he applied it to everything with unflinching resolution. He figured out on paper what he should want, what would be best for him, and set about getting it, and his emotions could go hang, goddammit. What he believed was right in his head, that was what mattered.

How many of us can say that?

'A-ha, morning, Ade.'

Adrian, resplendent in baggy-necked Gap Pocket Tee and boxers glanced down at a ribbed watchmark and failed successfully in stifling a yawn.

'Charlie, Jesus. What time is it?'

'Ten past eight.'

'Fuckin' 'ell, mate.' He chased an itch around his chest for a second. 'Are you —? I mean wha —. Er, come in, come in.'

'No ta, I'm taking you to breakfast. Come on, look lively, man.'

*

'You chose a great bloody time to make a reappearance. Nobody's seen you in fucking *weeks*. What you been up to?'

We sat at the window table of Café Rouge with our overpriced rolls and coffee. Or perhaps reasonably priced *croissant petit déjeuner et café au lait.* Who's to say. Around us, aproned staff swung and parried with empty trays, practising and perfecting the hoity air of irritable French waiters. Most of them had it down pat – the condescending sneer, the heavy sighs, the slow bored blink. Our waitress had smiled and joked with us but we forgave her, she was probably new. I stirred my twelfth sugar into my second coffee, the caffeine hit going about its panicky business – tidying the desk, sharpening pencils, opening the blinds.

'Ooh, keeping busy,' I explained. 'Getting on with things, sorting shit out, getting together my act.' I sipped my coffee. Yikes, needed more sugar. Adrian stretched out a wide cavernous yawn.

'Yes, likewise. No one ever tells you exactly how different everything is afterwards. Not for the father.'

'Did you know Charles Darwin was going to be a priest?'

'Huh?'

'Darwin. Priest.'

'I thought he was dead?'

'Well yes, he is. I mean before. He trained to be a priest. And a doctor. At Edinburgh University. I never knew that before.' Adrian paused, almond croissant hanging suspended 'twixt gob and fist.

'You're going to be a priest?' he asked fearfully.

'Hmm? No, no no no. I was just reading about it this morning. He didn't actually become a biologist proper till he was twenty-nine, when he was elected to the secretaryship of the Geological Society.'

'How marvellous for him,' Adrian said, distracted, not even pretending to be paying attention. He stared me in the eyes for a few seconds longer than is actually polite. Was I missing something? Should I have commented on his haircut? Had he had a nose ring? A tattoo? What?

'What?' I said finally. Sometimes you just have to ask. Adrian smiled. Somewhere, I heard somebody dropping a coin. Then I realised the somewhere was in my head and the coin was a penny.

'Jesus, I'm sorry. Congratulations.'

'Thanks, Charlie, thanks,' and we toasted with stained, off-white coffee mugs and coordinating stained, off-white grins.

'Well, details details.'

'Boy,' he said. 'George. And don't say it.' He smiled.

I smirked back and began to loudly not hum 'Karma Chameleon'.

'Seven pounds eight ounces,' he said and his smile was whisked hurriedly away from him half finished. Perhaps one of the waiters had it.

Like what's at number 1 in the charts, baby weights are one of those things that one is just supposed to know about. People throw random imperial measurements at you and you are required to grin stupidly at them. *Twelve stone nine!* they say, and you slap them on the back and offer them a Havana. I personally thought that seven pounds eight sounded just about right but Adrian went all quiet and started a load of fiddly business with his napkin.

'That's great. Right? I mean, that's about usual?'

'So the books say,' he mumbled, continuing his fumbling origami. 'But I mean, how can you be sure? How can you ever really know?'

'Well what did the hospital say?' I asked. But Adrian was lost in his own new-dad anxiety.

'I was seven pounds two when I was born. Liz was eight one. But I mean, we're a little nervous, obviously.'

Obviously?

'Miriam says . . .'

Oh gawd 'elp us, we're on first-name terms here. Oops, sorry, he's talking —

'. . . she says it's just fine. Almost the perfect average size. And all the doctors agreed.'

'Well then,' I said with a heartiness that would make Brian Blessed look like Beaker from *The Muppet Show*. But to no avail.

'But, well, we're taking him to a specialist because you can't be too careful, can you? Liz is looking into some kind of macrobiotic diet on the Internet. There's this woman in California . . .'

Oh Lordy, here we go. Cue a hundred weight of cotton-wool and a subscription to *Paranoid Parenting* magazine. Christ was this what fatherhood did to people? Turned level-headed, competent males into pale, shuffling wrecks?

'I mean, the labour was fine. No problems there. I held Liz's hand. She didn't scream as much as I'd expected, whole thing seemed to be over before it started, frankly. The nurses said it was the simplest and tidiest birth they'd ever seen.' Adrian stared off into the middle distance.

'Well there you go then, you've got nothing to worry about,' I said, attempting to shake him out of this a bit. 'I mean, it's natural to be overcautious with your first one.'

'But y'know,' Adrian continued, obliviously. 'That could be a bad sign in itself, couldn't it? Too easy. Maybe it's because he wasn't connected properly inside her, y'know?'

'Ade, look – '

'He might have got unplugged or something. Like when you're dusting the television and the arial comes out?'

Oh for heaven's sake. Enough of this. I clicked my conversational mouse on the fonts and chose something a little more friendly.

'So,' I began afresh. 'How come I'm the last to know, you old cunt?'

'Fuck you, you git, I left a message.'

'Up your arse you did, you tosser.'

'Bollocks, I phoned you twice and got your machine both times. Twat. Where you been?'

Well I mean. Where hadn't I been?

I'd spent the rest of the rattling stop-start of the Jubilee Line journey trying to pin point exactly on the tube map of my life where the major derailment had come.

Was it the Staffroom episode? Was it when Deborah stopped returning my calls? When Liz had told me Deborah and I were finished? Was it at the point the school fired me from my job?

Or maybe when I'd realised my closest friend had lied to me about where he was that weekend.

And about who he was with.

Well whenever it was, the last month had seen me going about the business of seriously going about my business. I had read and finished every book I had started reading and promptly given up on at college; had repeat viewings of Jeramiah in his unnatural habitat, watching him fail spectacularly in getting his hairy end away yet again; gone back and reread my books twice just in case I missed a good bit; three trips to the Natural History Museum; oh yes, and one whole lot of sitting at home reading.

Don't know if I mentioned that.

For times, oh yez, they were a-changin'. As I told Adrian a bit later over some grapefruit.

ELEVEN

*'The thing I notice is that I tend to look at things much
more logically than my colleagues'*
Margaret Thatcher

'So, sorry, what does all this have to do with you exactly?'
Adrian asked, spooning out his fruit cack-handedly.

'I'm just saying,' I explained. 'Darwin was nearly
thirty when he found his calling, what made him
happy. He tried the priest thing and medicine.
Although they were his dad's ideas really. And then he
got a job on the HMS *Beagle*, a 253-tonne Naval Sloop
Brig, and sailed around the Galápagos Islands. It took
him thirty years, but he found his purpose.'

'And in the Galápagos, too? Always the last place you
look.'

'Isn't it just.'

'So what are you getting at? You've been looking for a new direction, something like that?' Adrian furrowed himself quizzically.

'Yeah. Considering my options. Looking at things logically.'

'And what have you found? I mean, logically speaking, Captain.'

'Well, you've got to get up in the morning, right?' I began, shoving half a croissant into my face. 'I mean, you can't sit around all day moping.'

'This is what we've been trying to tell you, yes, you can't . . .'

'No matter what goes wrong, however things pan out, you've got to keep moving. Stagnancy is death, as we know.'

'As you say.'

'So everything moves forward and develops and changes. Lions go looking for antelopes and bees go looking for pollen and so on.'

'And fired teachers go looking for new schools to work in? This is what you're getting at?'

'No. Teaching I'm done with. Or it's done with me, anyway. That was one thing, that was like Darwin and the priesthood. He tried it for a while but it wasn't what drove him, it didn't get him leaping out of bed in the morning.'

Adrian finished his breakfast, wiped his chops and

tossed me a look of puzzlement. This was all very much news to him.

'But you're, y'know. You're a teacher. You're good at teaching. It made you happy.'

'Uh-uh, not really. Oh I wasn't shit at it. I could cut up a frog in an emergency or explain menstruation to a group of twelve-year-old boys without them laughing and saying *Urgh*.'

'You *could*?' Adrian said, impressed.

'Well no, obviously not. But you're missing the point. It paid well enough and kept me in oven chips but it was always a compromise. It never made me happy, not really. I mean c'mon, when we used to sit around your mum's dining table on Saturday evenings after *Knight Rider*, I never said I couldn't wait to grow up and grade year 10 biology papers, same as you never wanted to be crappy slogan-writing marketing whassit. It's just what happens when you're not looking.'

'S'pose,' Adrian admitted.

In our competitive trenches of sporadic fire, occupations were basic field equipment. They had taken over in a virtually smooth transition from the adolescent corridor bandinage of *You got a free period next oooh, you jammy git, I got double maths, oooh un-luck-ayyyyyy*. Who was now earning what for doing how much in the most hours kept many a back-from-the-movies walk fuelled with dead-arms and the word *bummer*. Current chart positions were as follows:

Adrian got highest earner; Brad got job security and opportunities to meet women; I got best holidays. Now I was unemployed of course, this meant relegation to the NatWest League of occupational rivalry. It was, like all our games, stupid and infantile and very male, with the goalposts continually on the move. I could score well with a well-timed Easter break but Brad could bring his defence forward with the offside trap of a free bar at a boozy book launch. Adrian was the head of the marketing department of a pharmaceutical house based in Barnet. Not the most sexy or glamorous occupation as he would admit. And about as far as you could get by foot from his teenage dream of forming a band with his brother and being the next Johnny Marr. But it was pretty much 9 to 5, no weekends and paid quite horrifyingly well.

Much to our annoyance.

'So what's going to get you leaping out of bed every morning?' Adrian asked.

'Well that's the trick, isn't it? What motivates you, what excites you. You and Liz have your kid, for Wendy it's the great outdoors . . .'

'Wendy?'

I explained about my new friend, Adrian getting ever so *I know what you're up to, my lad* with his eyebrows.

'Oh yes? Trying the old jealousy route, eh?'

I smiled but held his gaze with a long look, trying to

spot something going on in the face. Some twitch, some flicker. A blink, a rub of the nose, a glance away.

Anything.

I had deliberately not mentioned Deborah all morning. I was waiting, I didn't want to corrupt the data, so to speak. I had to know if Adrian was going to give anything away about her and Brad.

I figured he must know. I mean *surely*? I hadn't spoken to either of them for a fortnight, more out of a strange shell-shockedness if that isn't a word I just made up. Shell-Shockery? Whatever.

Brad had lied, this I knew. He hadn't been home that Sunday, he'd been with Deborah. And lying about it smacked of guilt. Adrian had obviously spoken to Brad recently, hence the *Nobody's seen you* remark. And even if, for some fathomless reason, they wanted to keep their affair from Adrian, Liz would have heard from her. *Surely?*

But here he was, beaming and whe-heyy-ing and saying *Corrr* in that rumbling Kenneth Connor way. Maybe Brad was lying to *him* as well?

'All I'm saying is it's happiness. Happiness, the pursuit of happiness, that's the prime human motivator. You find something that makes you happy, then you don't mind getting up in the morning. This, this is where I've been going wrong.'

'Okay, I'm with you. Sounds about right.' Adrian nodded. He leaned back on his chair and failed to catch our waitress's eye. She had obviously been reading the staff manual. 'You're going to find a job that makes you happy. But, that's just work. Y'know? I mean, there's more to life than work. Maybe it's not that we have to find jobs that make us happy. Maybe jobs are what we do so we can afford to be happy in other areas?'

'Like what?'

'Well, I don't know. Have a nice home, a family, a wife, holidays, your friends.'

This was all pure Adrian. He was a poster-boy for modern family values. His university walls had been all Audrey Hepburns and Cary Grants. It was only the lack of scented candles that told you the room belonged to a guy. 'Maybe that's where you should be looking for your happiness, let the work thing sort itself out?'

'Have you been reading Brad's self-help books?' I teased.

'Liz has a couple. She quotes them in bed.' He reached for his jacket and scraped back his chair. 'What are you reading at the moment?'

'I'm working my way through eight volumes of the 1985 edition of Charles Darwin's correspondence.'

'Obviously,' he sighed.

We sorted out the bill after two choruses of *Were we charged for bread?* and the middle eight – 'Pay That Funky Service Charge, White Boy,' and went our separate ways. Adrian was off to the hospital to see Liz and check on 'ickle Georgie'. And then presumably heading off to Harley Street to double-check with some expensive consultants that two arms and two legs was the absolute correct number for a child of George's age. *Sheesh.*

I took an uneventful stroll home. You can catch up with me there. There's somewhere to sit down now.

Honest, you won't recognise the place.

Home. Home, where it looked to all intents and purposes like the deer and antelope had stopped playing and had a good old chivvy round with the Bissel. The videos were back in their cases, likewise the CDs. The Playstation was unplugged and coiled up, back in its polystyrene. Mugs shone proudly away on their newly affixed hooks. And the books, or those I wasn't busy annotating or cross-referencing, stood upright, freshly alphabetized within genre, like children lining up in the playground at the end of playtime, all chin-up and vying for housepoints.

Michael J. Fox stared over at Darwin. He seemed somehow a little less anxious to jump into the Delorean and 88 miles-per-hour out of it since Bruce had been replaced. He was no doubt thinking that this bearded old crumbly might come in useful if his time-machine should land him back in the 1800s.

Flumping back into the armchair, my jacket hanging from its new hook on the back of the door (oh he's just showing off now) and a Bodum of freshly plunged coffee at my side, I sucked on the end of my Bic and flicked through the reams of notes I had been making over the last week. The fresh fruits of my new-found labour.

Adrian was right of course. You can't just rely on work to fulfill your life, not in any day-today, 9-to-5, fag breaks and grimy collared way. I saw people who put all their faith in their work. Strange people. At school they'd be the ones who stayed all hours, ticking every cork-board volunteer sheet – drama, sports day, orchestra. Which was okay for a while but if you trust your happiness to the 9-to-5, then every disaster, every rowdy classroom, failed inspection, missed promotion was a stinging slap in the mush.

I tore off a fresh page and made a list of areas happiness could be found. Scientifically, y'know?

Work

Money

Home

Family

Friends

Partner

All this anal and frankly absurdy nerdy wordy turdy list-making and chart-plotting was the sort of thing that us science types were good at. All the equations and posits, the subsequentlies and therefores – this was a language I loved and understood. A language I had recently reacquainted myself with.

Starting at the top, I'd see how I was doing.

Work. Well, I could cross that out for a start. I still didn't have any work. I hadn't applied for anything. I hadn't even taken the classic avoidance move of spending a few days tinkering with the old C.V. I'd tried to, obviously. Cleared the decks a few afternoons ago, got down to *Reasons I Left Previous Employment* and then sat rattling my biro between my teeth until it got dark.

I put a line through it and moved down one.

Ah. *Money*. Well, I had my cheques coming through from school as normal. But that was only for a couple more months. After that I could begin to expect brown envelopes to creep up to the door and demand attention, like zombies in *Night of the Living Dead*, each envelope the bearer of a window scarier than anything in the Amityville House (if you'll pardon the horror movie imagery).

With this sigh-inducing cloud of despair circling above me I put a line through the next on the list as well. My home was neat and clean but for what end? So the bailiffs would have a place to park their arses and enjoy a cuppa before tugging on the overalls and backing up the van?

Family? Well there was Mum and Dad. I had last seen them . . . ? Christ, was it Christmas? No, surely not. Surely not.

Or was it? We spoke on the phone once in a while of course. Or rather, she called me up once a month. And I let the answerphone take it.

Christ. This didn't leave much left.

Friends. I stared long at this one. Underlined it. I drew two arrows, marking one Brad, the other Adrian. Stared a bit more. Underlined them.

Fuck it. I left the coffee congealing into a primitive civilisation at the bottom of the plunger and went over to the shelves. Now where the hell was it? I pushed aside some well-thumbed books on chaos theory, each one thumbed to approximately halfway through the second chapter. The rest of the pages, it won't surprise you at all whatsoever in any way, remained neat, untouched and baffling as the day they were bound. Whoopsie, there we go, bottom shelf next to some of Deb's old school ringbinders. I tugged it out in a plume of dust and returned with an arthritic moan to the armchair.

Page one. Good God, look at that hair. Did people have no shame at all in those days? I don't care if it is remarkably mild for July – stop squinting, stand up straight, wipe round your mouth and get a bleedin' haircut. I mean, don't his parents have *any* idea? I mean *really*.

Why looking at my old photo album turns me into Tony Hancock I've never quite understood. But it always does, I expect you're the same.

I flipped quickly through some toddlers on rugs and some bleached-out shots of pet rabbits and beaches, pausing only to note how old-fashioned photographs look when they have rounded-off corners.

Now, there we go. That's got to be oooh, eight years ago? Maybe nine? Brad, Ade and myself. Ade, it seems, has foam antlers on his head, I think. Either that or he developed two very septic tumors in the first December at university and I'd forgotten all about it. No, definitely antlers. That would explain why Brad is wearing sunglasses with mistletoe hanging from the frames, I've got the intestinal stragglings of a spent party-popper in my hair and we look equally smug and pissed in that way that only first-year students can really pull off.

Equally smug, equally pissed and equally equal.

And today's keyword for those watching at home is *equal*.

Flicking through a bit further. The fire in the eyes, the barely suppressed beaming grins, the stubborn acne — we were the same people. Pissing about on a wet pebbly Brighton beach with a wind-caught frisbee, asleep in each other's halls on Sunday evenings, tuxed-up at the ball, shoulders back, cigars aloft. As the tight skin around jawlines began to lose its grip and slip slip slowly down into oblivion and we stumbled into our twenties, we were equal.

The snap-happy disposableness of those early years

clearly never lasted as I only have one photograph taken of us since we left university, all gurning and cheering up a stepladder in Brad's new kitchen a couple of years ago. I peeled back the sticky clear film with a crackling hiss and slid the image out, laying it gently with fingertips onto the page under my list.

These were my friends, my two shots at happiness. And we look like a fine bunch of backslapping, get-your-round-in pals. But of course, since this pic was taken, a lot had changed. Adrian was now a father, so every priority had shifted, a huge tectonic slide from blokes and booze and bonhomie to bonnets and breast-feeding and boarding-school. I knew I wouldn't be seeing as much of him as I used to from now on.

Especially as he and his wife were co-conspirators in the Brad & Deborah Affair.

With a sudden clench-toothed anger I carved a thick blue line through their names.

Which just left one source of happiness.

Or rather, ahem, didn't.

Now. After Darwin had finished his 'Marriage – pros & cons' list, he was able to draw some very specific conclusions:

'My God, it's intolerable to think of spending one's whole life as a neuter bee – working and working and nothing after all. No, no won't do. Imagine living one's day solitary in smoky dirty London house – only to picture yourself a nice soft wife on the sofa, with a good

fire and books and music perhaps. Marry Marry Marry.'

Well quite. Clearly to this great man of science, the pros far far outweighed the cons. It was logic and a matter of mathematical unambiguousness – married good, unmarried bad. So he married. End of experiment, hypothesis proved, congratulations.

That morning, in the comforting surroundings of my little home, I looked down at my scrappy amateur attempts at a similar assessment, for a conclusion, for a meaning. A man who has lived his whole life looking for and following instructions, weighing up measurements, he needs guidelines to follow. He likes a nice neat scientific answer, a tidy hospital-cornered signpost to nudge him in the right direction.

I stared down at the page. With a flash of inspiration I tore it away and wrote a new heading.

PEOPLE I KNOW WHO ARE COMPLETELY HAPPY.

I figured I'd see what they did, how they lived, everyone I'd ever met without a problem in the world.

Two hours later, the coffee now thick and cold, the list was complete.

You want to see it? Check to see if there's anyone there you recognise? Maybe see if you're on it yourself? Okay, well I include it here for your perusal.

Jeremiah the Gorilla.

Fuckfuckfuckfuckfuck.

Dear Tell Me How,

Ears-ears has been at the vet's house for a long time because he has to do experiments with rabbits that have been fighting with cats. Do you think that ears-ears might have baby rabbits when she gets home soon? I would like a white one and another white one and a spotty one and i would call them Keith, Noel and Maggie Philbin. Would one of them be brown like Steve Austin because they live in the same cage?

Mum said I would make a good scientist because I have neat handwriting. My dad likes Charlie's Angels *and* Nationwide.

Master Charles Ellis age 8

Dear Charles,

Thank you very much for your letter and the lovely drawing. I think if rabbits ever do go into space they would wear shoes just like that!

If your rabbit does have babies then it is very likely that they will be the same colour as their mummy and daddy. Colour is one of the things that is written in our recipe books (genes). If her babies have babies and those babies have babies then little Ears-ears' genetically coded information will live forever!

Thank you for your letter. Keep reading!!!

Assist. Editor, Tell Me How.

TWELVE

'Quistions questions quostions'
Spike Milligan

'Yes, a very good morning to you. Veronica, please.'

There was a shrill claxon of yelling and what sounded like a dog barking. Or possibly Ronnie had got a large chunk of Simon still caught in her throat. One or the other. I hung on the line and purposefully rearranged my highlighters so the blue was next to the green. Much prettier. So I did the same with my biros. And my fibertips. Lovely. The Sony earpiece was a loose fit, due to my grandfather's genetic predisposition for enormous ears which had been held back a generation for bad behaviour and restationed begrudgingly either side of his grandson.

A little genetic quirk eruditely explained in the eighteenth century by Gregor Mendel and an experiment with the breeding of garden peas.

If you're interested.

'Got it, Mum!' came a holler which sent the dictaphone equaliser leaping into the red. I twiddled the necessary.

'Hello, Veronica?'

'Who's this?'

'Charles Ellis.'

'Who?'

It took a few minutes for her to place me which she padded out with a variety of different-shaped *Errrs* and I wondered idly whether she voluntarily took total gits she'd never met before night-clubbing every week. Some sort of Sunshine Variety Bus charity work for the uncoordinated perhaps?

'God yes, the champagne thief,' Ronnie burst, finally.

Hmm. As much as I would have preferred *God yes, the sex machine* or even at a wide first-day-of-the-month pinch *God yes, the mysterious and enigmatic stranger*, I was in no real position to argue.

'Er, yes, that's the fellow. If it's any consolation, it wasn't much more than fizzy grape juice, to tell you the truth, you didn't miss much. I could get you another?' I offered, hesitating before the punchline. 'I dunno, you could send your boyfriend over for it, maybe?'

Ronnie audibly put two and two together with a clack of her mental abacus.

'Oh gosh, yes,' she flapped. 'I'm sorry about that, the phone mix-up and everything.' She began to explain hurriedly like I was a hard-shoulder traffic policeman. 'You see, he got the wrong idea in his head about where I'd spent the night and, well not strictly the *wrong* idea, but I'd hoped he –'

'No problem, no problem at all,' I interrupted. 'Couldn't matter less. I was just calling to ask you some questions, actually.'

'Questions?' she said. 'What are you, market research or something?'

I smiled, reset the tape counter to zero, clicked the top of my Parker and put a red tick next to *V. Cousins* on my list.

'Something like that yes. Anyway, if you've got a few minutes, can I just ask – when was the last time you laughed so hard it hurt?'

Silence from the receiver.

'Today, in the last seven days, in the last month or can't remember?'

Second call. Different colour biro. As a phone rang out for attention somewhere off the Kilburn High Road, London NW6, I shaded Veronica's boxes in two-colour cross-hatching. The results gleaned had held few real

153

surprises — lots of *Can't Remembers,* a handful of *Very Unlikelys* and two *Definitely Nots.*

Excellent.

Then somewhere off the Kilburn High Road, London NW6, a Ms K. McCann picked up.

'God, you've got some nerve.'

'Yes, yes, I do apologise for that,' I bluffed busily. 'I admit I didn't play entirely straight with you. I had seen another couple of women the day before you and I had lunch. I just didn't think you'd want to know about it.'

'Why? Why did you do that? Why do men *do* that?'

'Ha, well funnily enough, if you have a moment, I was just calling to see if you could help me answer that. In a roundabout sort of way.'

There was a Grand Canyon sized silence from London NW6, which I promptly unicycled over warily.

'On the premise that you inherited a million pounds, would you consider continuing to do your job, same responsibilities, same hours, just for the personal satisfaction of it?'

'What the *fuck* are you on about?'

The tape counter turned.

'Why d'ya ask, buddy?'

Still the mid-Atlantic twang. I ticked M.A.T. next to his name in red.

'Just – I need to know, that's all. You're not the only person I've talked to, don't worry.'

'Jezus, pal. I mean, for Chrissakes. You disappear off the face of the goddamn earth for, like, I don't know how long. You don't answer your phone, Ade and me never hear a word and now, bang. You're askin' about freakin' school fees for adopted children?'

'Stepchildren, not adopted children,' I corrected. *Freakin*? God, you leave him alone for two minutes. 'Would you pay to send a hypothetical child of your hypothetical wife's hypothetical first marriage to private school? I'm just asking.'

'I don't have a wife, hypothingybob or otherwise. Look.' An edge of gravity appeared in the voice, like a mid-morning television discussion show host when the subject of, Christ, I don't know, haemorrhoids comes up or something. 'What's all this about? Huh? I haven't seen you in God knows how long, then Ronnie tells me you came in the shop three Sundays ago and practically bought up the whole Popular Science section and left without even a hello. And now this? What're you doing, workin' on a thesis or something?'

I sighed. The tape counter turned slowly, like a Bond villain's nuke counter.

'In a manner of speaking, yes.'

'Well that's great. Terrific, really. You know you kinda went off the rails there for a bit, we were both worried but –'

He stopped suddenly, catching himself, as if he'd just realised he was telling an Englishman, Irishman, Scotsman joke to a load of men in balaclavas in a Belfast pub. The L.E.D. on the dictaphone vanished into blackness.

'Both, y'know, me and . . . me and Adrian −'

'It's okay, Brad. I know all about it. It's totally fine.'

Please note: for the required technical effect, dear reader, please stare into space for about an hour, then read the following response −

'Oh,' said Brad.

− and stare into space for another hour.

Done that? Marvellous. Your co-operation is appreci-ated.

'Deborah always liked you. You're a successful male, intelligent, educated, healthy, good prospects. You're a better provider than me. This is the way of things, it's perfect. Couldn't matter less.'

'Look, Chuck, don't get the wrong idea. I've only seen her, well . . .' Brad couldn't have been more thrown if he'd tried to wedgie Brian Jacks. 'She called me and . . .'

'I told you, it's okay, I understand. Now answer the question − stepchildren. Private school fees or not?'

As the Routemaster phlegmed and gristled its throaty way towards Regent's Park, I looked up from my folder for a moment, through the streaky grease of the window, into the afternoon crowds and counted smiles. This sort of summer Sunday put a slight bias in the data, as everyone in North London gets to play for an hour at living in Paris; the coffee bars spill onto the streets, painted toenails shine through strappy sandals and the odd salmon Vespa zips by like a chirpy wasp.

Still, I only counted four. And one of those was an infant in a buggy which, for the point of this experiment, didn't count.

I added this number in blue pen, lidded it, reached up and rang the bell.

'Charlie! What are you doing here?' Adrian hoisted an enormous blue bag onto his shoulder and slammed the cab door. As he fumbled and patted and have-you-got-change-for-a-tennered, Liz followed slowly behind, a tiny bundle in her arms that she smiled softly at, *Yesyouareahandsomeboyaren'tyou*-ing in a sing-song lilt.

'Charlie, a one-man welcome party. Good to see you. Have you been waiting long? We've been at my Mum's,' she said, looking up from the blankets. And yes, they were very handsome blankets. Very handsome indeed. Nothing really to sing about, though. So I put 3 million sperm, one egg and nine months together quickly in my head and came up with she must have the new one. 'How the devil are you?'

'Surviving,' I offered, groaning my way into an

upright bipedal stance on their front steps. Adrian graciously took up my offer of help with the huge bags and we oofed and crikeyed indoors for a cuppa that we all agreed *Ooooh, would be luverly*.

'Sorry, sorry.' I stumbled, reaching into my jacket for the tiny microphone as discreetly as I could, half a cup of tea later. 'Say that again — you don't *what*?'

'I said *don't start*,' Adrian repeated, wandering back in with a plate of much-more-expensive-biscuits-than-you'd-get-at-my-house. He looked absolutely shattered. If Jimmy Saville had suddenly appeared behind him, wrapped him in a big sheet of tinfoil, and given him a Mars bar it wouldn't have surprised me in the least. The centre parting was now a fringe and the shadow was way way past 5 o'clock. 'We're not first years any more and this isn't the S.U. bar on a Friday night.'

'God, I can just imagine it,' Liz chorused, following behind. 'I'm so glad I didn't know you then.' She eased herself down to carpet level next to a blue plastic baby carrier on a towel in which George dozed. She began to rock it gently. 'I can just imagine the three of you. *How do you know it's a pint? Yes but what is a pint? Maybe what you see as a pint I see as a paisley sheep, it's all subjective, prove it then, nurgh nurgh nurgh nurgh nurgh.* All to get out of buying a round. Utter tossers.'

'Precisely. It's like that one Brad rakes up every

Friday night about the last remaining volume of the complete works of Shakespeare and a ten-year-old orphan, both in a burning building. It's just stupid. I'm not eighteen any more. Now have a Hob-Nob.'

Humph. I had a Hob-Nob. I'd only asked, for heaven's sake. Your baby son and your baby brother are both drowning in a canal — who do you save? Simple enough question, surely. Ronnie, Katherine and Brad had answered it.

But then, oh shit whoops, Ronnie, Katherine and Brad hadn't all just given birth to a little baby boy. Concentrate, Charlie, concentrate, don't upset your friends.

'Sorry sorry, I wasn't thinking. How is little Georgie getting on?'

If they'd both gazed at the crib, then at each other and then at me, all would have been well in the world. Well, in Swiss Cottage anyway.

But they didn't.

They looked at *each other*, then at *me*, then at the crib. Which told me all I needed to know.

Even with my limited knowledge of children (and when I say limited, we're talking properly limited. Not limited like a Franklin Mint commemorative plate is limited) I could see that they were worrying over nothing. George was a fat pink squash of gummy joy who'd done nothing but smile and gurgle for the whole time I'd been there. It was all just over protective new-parent terror. To whit:

159

'Well he seems okay,' Liz said. 'The hospital gave him the all-clear immediately. But it's a few things that have got us a bit panicky. It's probably nothing but –' Liz looked back at Adrian in a *dare we tell him* sort of way. Adrian nodded and picked up the thread.

'It's his ka-ka.'

'I'm sorry?' I coughed, splattering Hob-Nob crumbs and tea onto the low table.

'It's coming out as a sort of greeny peanut-butter stuff.' He rummaged in a blue holdall and produced a small jam-jar. 'See?'

I stood up involuntarily with a Scooby Doo style *Yoikes* and excused myself hurriedly, disappearing into the toilet.

Without a jam-jar, you'll be pleased to know.

Jeans concertinered about my ankles, M&S pants likewise. Elbows on my knees, I took a mid-dump opportunity to flick through my notebook and ruminate on a couple of things.

The data collection was proceeding as expected and there were only three candidates left to question. In the interests of science, Ade's and Liz's answers would have proved especially fascinating, able as they were to give me first-hand parental insights.

But the pair of them were clearly mentally unstable and rapidly becoming shrieking paranoiacs so I figured the collection of their data was probably best left to a day less fraught with anxiety, stress, heartache and wetwipes.

Making a mental note of the next name on my list, I closed the notebook and dropped it to the floor, let out an echoing, resonant oily fart, turned the dictaphone off and promptly wished I'd done those last two in a different order.

Back in the lounge.

'I'm going to hit the road, I think.'

'Oh, righty-ho, then.' Adrian got to his feet quickly. Liz was sniffing the contents of the jar and peering quizzically at her gurgling infant.

'Can I get a phone number off you quickly?'

'Of course,' Liz said, tightening the lid again. 'Who is it you want?'

'Er, I have to give Dawn a bell later.'

'Dawn? Dawn, *my* Dawn?'

'Dawn I'm-going-to-hide-in-another-cinema-Dawn?' Adrian chuckled.

'Yes, that one. Do you have her number? I want to ask her something.'

Liz disappeared into the hall, returning with her address book.

'Asking her out again?'

'Hn? No no. I just want to know if she'd rather have sex with Stephen Hawking or Hulk Hogan.'

They exchanged looks. Well no, that's not quite

right. Liz passed her look over to Adrian, who then took it, folded it up and put it in his pocket to be dealt with after I'd left.

So off I biffed.

Down the steps with a bouncy new-shoes eagerness, the sound of coochycooing fading into a slam, past their big blue estate car, a thousand synapses started firing at once in recall.

'Hello there.'

'Wha . . . shitty cock lawks, hello,' was my chosen response, which I felt made up for in originality what it totally mislaid in pleasantness. 'I mean, well. I mean, shitty cock lawks, actually.'

'Yes. Yes, figured you might. How are you?'

'Hn? Oh well, you know.'

'No.'

'No. Right. I'm . . . not bad. Good. Great even.'

'Excellent.'

'Hn.' I began to jab spasmodically over my shoulder like a hitchhiker. 'You're going in?' A blue BabyGap bag was rattled in my face by way of an explanation.

'Thought I'd say hello. You just . . . ?'

'Yes yes, I just . . . yes.'

'Great.'

'Yes.'

Which, for the first conversation with Deborah in two months, I thought went pretty well. What do you reckon?

THIRTEEN

'I can't understand why people are frightened of new ideas. I'm frightened of the old ones.'

John Cage

I felt very small. Well, I am very small. Five foot eight or as near as makes no impression. And I was sitting down which didn't help. Sitting down with my elbows on my knees and my head somewhere within whispering distance of my laughably unfashionable trainers. Closed up tight, balled like a threatened hedgehog. The bench was dark and wet as all benches indoor and out somehow always are, as if they added a deep penetrating moistness at the factory. It caused me to squirm and fidget as if I had wet myself. Which I might well have done. I wasn't really paying much attention. This particular bench was inscribed *In Loving Memory of Jack, resident 1925–1938.* Never really understood the naming of benches thing. I suppose if you used to sit there a lot it might have particular resonance. But I'm pretty sure Jack didn't. Y'know, being a lion and everything.

If I try and tell you what was going on in my head you'll just get all cross and huffy and you'll probably find yourself saying *Oh for heaven's sake,* even if you'd normally require a two-zone Travelcard extension to get yourself near such a crap expression, so let's talk about something else for a bit.

It can wait. Really, it can wait. I'm in no hurry.

London Zoo is a very different place at ten thirty on a Monday morning. Like a rugby scrum-half at a christening, it's cleaner and fresher and tidied up and presentable and generally smelling less like old poo. I watched the keepers and sweepers doing their business with buckets and brushes, slowly, with an easy-going start the week *ahhh whatever.* The animals themselves seemed to be taking a much more yawny, lie-in-with-the-papers attitude as they sniffed and squinted against the September sun.

At that hour, other visitors were few. No doubt enjoying a glass of grapefruit juice and the *Daily Mail,* one of which is sour and indigestible and makes me wince.

A couple of chummy families ambled leisurely about, two or three fluorescent tourists. I had until lunchtime to enjoy the solitude. The soft whirring and chirruping of birds; the occasional irritable snuffly snort echoing from the elephant house's concrete hollow; the distinctive piercing cry of the native *Mummicus I've Dropped My Ice-Creamicum*.

'Wotcha.'

I looked up, startled. It was Wendy, all smiles and summer freckles.

'Oh hello. How's things?'

'Busy busy busy,' she said, swinging a heavy metal bucket awkwardly from her slim wrist. "What happened to you? Looks like you've lost a pound and found a penny.'

'Yes, could say that,' I sighed.

She tilted her head in a way that was far from incredibly unattractive. And on better days long long ago, I may have ignored the previous *Blow this for a game of soldiers* and the frankly nauseating *Found a penny* gambit and come on to her. But it really wasn't one of those days.

'Tell me about it?' she pressed gently. 'If you fancy the walk?'

Tell *her* about it? I haven't even told *you* about it.

Heigh – as I believe the expression goes – ho.

*

'I'm sorry if that's not what you wanted to hear,' Deborah said, 'but you did ask.'

'No no, you're right, you're right.' I nodded, palms up, fair-copping like I had the sheriff's silver six-shooter in my back. 'I asked. And if that's the truth then that's the truth.'

'It is.'

'Well, if you're sure.'

'I am.'

'Yes yes, you certainly seem to be.'

'I said I was.'

'Yes yes, so you say.'

We'd been pawing this conversational mouse between us for just that little bit too long and it was showing signs of giving up the pretence and throwing itself gallantly onto a claw, just so the world could move the fuck on.

Deborah and I had positioned ourselves in a Swiss cottage in Swiss Cottage. Which, now I say it, sounds a bit peculiar. And in fact, let's face it, it is a bit peculiar. The idea that a bit of London NW3 between Belsize Park and St. John's Wood called Swiss Cottage might actually be home to a Swiss cottage, all criss-crossed timbers and chalet windows. I don't know why exactly. It's just its obviousness, I suppose. It would be like climbing the steps out of the dust and tile of Waterloo station and finding three thousand dead Frenchmen lying sprawled and bloody across the Blackfriar's Road.

Once the becapped fellow selling the *Evening Standard* has clocked your baffled phizog and said '*Well it's effin Waterloo, innit. Whaddid ya expect, bleedin' elephants or summink?*' you have to shrug and nod and walk away beaten.

You're in Swiss bloody Cottage, it's a Swiss bloody cottage.

Thankfully for the punters, however, its Swissness is nothing more than an amateur dramatics plywood facade and it stops with a screech the moment you're inside. There are no complimentary army-knives in dishes on the bar and no lonely goatherds hogging the pool table.

'Why is it so impossible that I'm happy, Charlie?'

She looked different in a few flickering ways. Her parting had shifted over slightly, her hair had a just-cut straightness about it. In fact her whole body seemed to have more of a defined edge to it. The mouth was more linear, the jaw tighter, the back straighter — just a little bit more angular. It was as if the portrait of her that hung in the stark white gallery of my memory had once been a Monet but was now a more brittle Picasso.

Same face, different rendering.

She felt different too. That is, she felt different to me. I was pleased to see her, if not a little confused. And all that had changed between us meant that she wasn't exactly plucking my heart strings, just sort of giving them a couple of broad strums to see if I was in tune.

She fixed me dead on and her eyebrows flicked up and down. 'I mean I can kind of understand why you might not want me to be happy, but why are you so convinced I'm not?'

'Because . . . well it's just. It's not very likely, is it?' I said. 'I mean, I know a thing or two about happiness, more than most people know about happiness, I shouldn't wonder. And from what I know about happiness, happiness as a mental state happiness type happiness I mean, the chances of you currently being in the state of happiness are frankly rather slim.'

Sorry. It all went a bit *Two Ronnies* then, didn't it?

'Well, when did you become the expert?'

'I didn't say I was an expert as such, I just suggested that I might know more −'

'Yes fine right okay,' Deborah machine-gunned in, eyes tight shut. 'What makes you . . .'

She chewed some air in exasperation for a few moments. 'What makes you such an arbiter of other people's mental states?'

Debs was quietly but rather obviously losing her patience, which I was glad about. Not that I had shares in Adrian's pharmaceutical house and a vested financial interest in the sales of ulcer cream. It's just that Debs used to quietly but very obviously lose her patience with me when we were a couple and I was pleased she hadn't changed in the two long months since I'd last seen her. More evenings than I care to remember had ended with nowt but the rock and rattle of the last train home, Debs pulling out her paperback, me staring out of the greasy window in a mutterful sulk — an unfinished twenty-minute bicker about PMT or politics or Phil Collins hanging from the roof straps.

'I've done a bit of research into the subject,' I tossed out with a pool hustler's bait.

'You've researched happiness?'

'Uh-huh.'

There was a casual pause that ran into an easy silence that then kept running, through the tape, out of the stadium and into the car park.

'What, what kind of research? When? What are you talking about?' Deborah seemed somewhat apprehensive. 'Like at the library?'

'I've asked around. It's an interesting topic, once you get under the skin of it. But people never do, you see.' I swigged a mouthful of pub wine. Eyes down for a full house . . .

'People ask — how are you doing? And what do you say? Fine. Fine, not too bad, pretty good, can't complain, bearing up, never better, knee-jerk knee-jerk knee-jerk.'

'Yes, Charlie.' Deborah nodded slowly. I could see screaming behind her eyes the white-knuckle restraint of a YOU FUCKING SPAZMO DURRRR! pulling at its lead. 'We're British, that's what we say. People ask out of politeness. If you told people actually how you were every time they asked people would think you were mad or ill or, worse yet, American. It just fills the gaps after Hello.'

'Yes yes, you're right, that's exactly what I'm getting at. I'm not suggesting we all go and live in California.'

'What are you suggesting?'

'That we never really find out how people are because *How are you* is just a pleasantry. But as far as I can see, despite the response, very few people are actually, technically, fine. A more accurate standard knee-jerk response should be How are you? Miserable thanks, yourself?'

'I'm not miserable.'

'You're not?'

'No, no I'm fine. Quite happy as it goes.'

'About what?'

'Charrr-*leyyy*.'

'No I mean it, just think about it for a second. What are you actually happy about?'

'Well, y'know,' Deborah began to pitch her movie idea *A Shrug's Life* at me very enthusiastically, 'stuff. Same as everyone else, y'know? I've got a place to live, family, friends, bit of money, health.'

Damn. Health. Knew I'd leave one of them off the list.

She sighed through her nose. Which sounds a bit weird until you do it. No one says it for some reason. And it definitely was a sigh, rather than a heavy exhalation or a nostril-clearing snort.

How can I be sure? Because a sigh is exactly what you'd expect to hear before this:

'Look, Charlie, I'm sorry. I didn't mean for this Brad thing to cause such a problem.'

'What's the Brad thing?' Wendy asked as we ambled past the musty apes enclosure. The September afternoon toyed with the idea of getting a bit breezy and then procrastinated, deciding to let October look after that sort of thing, and the sun came out causing us both to scrunch up and squint.

'Oh yes, sorry. Deborah has replaced me with an old friend of mine. Brad, a guy I've known since school.'

'Already? Gosh that's . . . that must have come as a terrible shock.'

'Yes, you'd have thought so, wouldn't you?' I reached Jeremiah's cage and gazed into the dark glass room. He sat with his back to me, enormous shoulders hunched, motionless. I turned to look at Wendy, to find she had stopped walking a few yards ago.

'You were going to marry her and now she's sleeping with a friend of yours and you're not bothered?'

'Oh I didn't say I wasn't bothered.' I tapped on the glass, Jerry's ears gave a twitch. 'I'm just not shocked.'

Deborah was in the lavatory and I sat alone for a

moment, twirling the neck of my wine glass and having a bit of a think.

Up until this point, I'll be honest with you, I'd been holding out a little hope. Not a lot, the evidence from Brad and Adrian being pretty incontrovertible.

But holding out a little. That this *Brad thing* had been a figment of my imagination.

But as the saying goes, if you hold a little thing out, a bird will eventually swoop down and fly off with it. (Yes all right, sod off, it's bound to be a saying somewhere.)

But now I knew, and the kilo of molten lead that had been slooshing around in my insides for the past fortnight, keeping me awake and making me spend far too much time on the toilet, had hardened and cooled, leaving a heavy lump in my stomach.

I bet Jeremiah never had these problems.

Deborah returned to the table and picked up her bag.

'Oh, you off?' I said, scrabbling to my feet.

'I think so,' she said.

'You don't want another drink?' I wanted her to stay. I didn't know why. Our relationship was now about as over as it was ever going to be. Dead and buried. But something made me want to keep the wake going for as long as possible, topping up drinks and offering more limp sandwiches.

'I think I'd better get going.'

'Righto.' I shrugged.

'How are you then, Charlie?' Deborah asked after a long thoughtful silence. 'How's your happiness? You haven't really said what you've been doing. You keeping busy?'

'Me? Oh yes, yes. No problems. I'm fine.' I nodded. I felt like a teenager being interrogated by a well-meaning aunt.

'Given that Playstation the night off yet?'

'Once or twice,' I said and we shared our first proper smile in two months. 'I've been out and about. Museums, London Zoo, reading a lot . . .'

'The zoo?' she said, surprised. 'How's that monkey? He's not still there, is he?'

'Jeremiah? Yes he's fine. I told him about you, he sends his regards.'

Deborah nodded and fiddled with her jacket buttons. This had brought back a memory. Of lazy Sundays a long time ago. Ice-creams and white wine and the rich green smell of dry grass.

'Must be nice being a monkey,' she said. 'Such a simple life. No complications. If they could talk, maybe they could explain the secret of happiness for you.'

'Maybe,' I said.

'Oh excuse me! Jesus.' I said, stifling a gaping yawn.

'Haven't you slept?' Wendy asked.

'Er, no. No, not at all, actually. Not last night.'

173

'A lot on your mind, I guess.'

'Yes. Or rather, no. Not a lot. Just something Deborah said.' I peered through the bars into the empty cage. 'How many weeks?' I asked.

'Diana? Oh a couple, we think. Jerry caught up with her eventually.'

'Was it planned?' I pressed. 'I mean, don't you have a system or something for this?'

Wendy laughed.

'Oh we can try. We do our best. But it's nature. That's what gorillas do. In the wild, in captivity, you can't stop it. They're animals. If they don't reproduce, what *do* they do?'

We sat quietly for a while. A toddler appeared at my side, pointing and wailing. *Where's the monkey, Daddy, where's mister monkey?*

'What about you?' Wendy asked quietly, easing herself to her feet in a *must be getting on with things* sort of way. 'You got any plans?'

'Me?' I said. 'Plans?' I said. I stood up.

Oh yes.

FAO: The Editor
     Tell Me How Magazine

Dear Sir,

I do apologise for taking up your time this morning. I appreciate how busy you must be. My son loves your magazine and has been collecting all the parts with his pocket money. He has even made a little folder to keep them in out of cardboard, decorated with cavemen. I understand he has written to you once or twice and you have sent him some free gifts, which I thank you for.

However, I was wondering if, on this occasion, you might offer me some advice. Charlie is very upset at the death of a pet, quite uncommonly so considering the short time he has had it. He isn't eating and refuses to go to school. He seemed to have got it into his head that Ears-ears (one of our rabbits) had some kind of immortality. Rather worryingly, he seems obsessed by his 'Evolution of Man' poster and is asking questions I can't answer. Principally, and I don't know if this will make any sense to you, about why there can be suffering in the world when we have been trying to be happy for millions of years. I think you'd agree, an unusual turn of phrase for an eight year old and one that gives me no small cause for concern.

I wondered, as he dotes on your letters so passionately, if you had any words I could share with him?

Very many thanks, feel free to call me any time.

Dr Maureen Ellis

PART TWO

FOURTEEN

'It is always the best policy to speak the truth, unless of course you are an exceptionally good liar.'

Jerome K. Jerome

Extracts from the personal journal of Dr (*oh puh-leese, in your dreams, buddy*) Charles Ellis BSc.Ed

Date: Monday 25th September

Subjects #3&4:   Erica Hull/Stephanie Evans

Equipment: Three bipedal descendants of Austro-plithicus — one male, two female; adrenaline (9 million cubic litres approx); genitals — three sets, two female, one male (average dimensions, seasonal adjustments apply); ill-conceived prejudices (many, too numerous and colourful to measure without more complex and sophisticated equipment).

Location: Wembley Hill Road, Wembley, Middlesex, England.

Description of subject #3: Early thirties/5′ 4″ approx/10–11 stone/curly dark hair (dyed?)/ floppy woollen jumper with cat print on/ excessive beadage about neck and wrists/ leggings/inexpensive trainers/shoulder bag on sideboard capable of housing a large family of gypsies comfortably for six weeks/wide hips (good)/no noticeable shoulders to speak of (not that good)/large pear-shaped buttocks (not good at all, unless that's your thing. Which it isn't, by and large)/one gold tooth at front (either selective gum disease or fashion statement – never ascertained).

Initial comments: So far experiment proceeds as expected, if not as hoped. As with last two candidates (see earlier unpublished manuscript of transcription notes), made contact by telephone through personals column. Erica seems in full working order health-wise. Non-smoker, only two days off work in last fiscal year (migraines). Above average intelligence (2-1 in history at Sheffield University). Has worked for an employment agency in Paddington for three years and designs jewellery in spare time (of which, if her hand-crafted appendages are anything to go by, she has far far too much of). No children. Likes mid-period Abba, *Pretty Woman*, Aubrey Beardsley prints and, it would seem from the interior of the Wembley residence, anything at all with a cat on it — cups, plates, rugs, grinning porcelain figurines on tandems. Apart from jewellery sideline, no other hobbies or interests besides buying quite nice things that have been totally fucked up by having cats painted on them. Far from *Vogue* beautiful but *Woman's Own* pretty in a knitting-pattern-model-for-the-fuller-figure sort of way.

Sexual preference: Bisexual. Which would go about as far as one would need to go without a map to explain . . .

Subject #4:   Ah-ha, yes yes yes now that's definitely more like it. Stephanie is mid-thirties, taller, slimmer and generally a hell of a lot less like the bulky, *Viz* magazine dungareed image of her life-partner. Again, not *Vogue* cover material, but could quite happily slot inside in an advert for the *Next Directory* modelling strappy summer frocks and such. Dress sense is unrecordable as subject has only been seen in a towel with wet hair, but one guesses upper end of high street label market (Joseph, Kookai etc). Dark straight hair, big eyes (brown), long slender legs. As I say — much much more like it. Oh yes.

Sexual preference: Bi and large. That is to say, Erica.
        Fuckity fuckity fuck.

Transcription highlights follow:

ERICA: Well these medical certificates seem in order.
        You're not a smoker, are you?

CHARLES: Me? No never. Absolutely not.

ERICA: Very wise. And you said you were an architect,
        wasn't it? In Chelsea?

CHARLES: Hn? Er, y-yes that's right.

ERICA: With your own firm. That's great.

CHARLES: Yes, yes it is, it is. It's . . . lovely. Mmm.
    (enter Stephanie Oh I wish)

STEPH: This is for you.

CHARLES: Ooh nibbles? Lovely. Let me . . . oh.
        There's, er, there's nothing . . .

STEPH: It's for your sperm.

CHARLES: I'm . . . I'm sorry?

STEPH: Everything in order, hon?

ERICA: He seems fine. An architect.

STEPH: Architect? Ooh fancy-shmancy. Should
        guarantee some brains. Big cock?

ERICA: We haven't got that far.

CHARLES: Look look I'm sorry . . .

ERICA: What?

STEPH: I'll get the baster.
    (exit Stephanie)

CHARLES: I just, well. I thought we'd, well . . .

ERICA: You thought we'd what? You're not banging
    me, if that's what you had in mind.

CHARLES: God, fuck no no. Perish the thought. Oh
    sorry, not that you're not, well, y'know. It's just I
    thought we'd sort of, well, I dunno. Chat for a bit.
    Or something.

ERICA: Chat?

  (re-enter Stephanie)

STEPH: Do you want to use the bathroom? Or the
    toilet?

ERICA: I thought we'd stick him in the kitchen?

STEPH: Hm? Yeah, good idea. Keep it warm.

ERICA: Do you have a big cock?

CHARLES: Look, wait wait. Um. Ha. Let's not rush
    things. So, er, Stephanie. What do *you* do?

STEPH: What do I do? I'm a journalist. All the hours
    God sends. But we'll be sharing the rearing
    between us. She'll be in good hands. Or he.

CHARLES: Right right, I see. And you're both . . . well,
    partners, as it were. That's, er, that's . . . that's
    interesting.

ERICA: Interesting? How is that interesting?

CHARLES: Well, genetically. It's interesting. Homo-
    whassits. Er . . . lezzymajigs, you know. They pose
    difficult questions, biologically speaking.

ERICA: Like what?

STEPH: What *are* you talking about?

CHARLES: Hmm? Oh well. Your, er . . . well your

purpose on earth, in the scheme of things, the life cycle. Non-reproducers. It's just, well, interesting. That, er . . . that natural selection should still be producing such . . .

STEPH: Charming.

ERICA: We're not mutants Mr Ellis. We're just lesbians. Jesus, you're not a Christian, are you?

CHARLES: No no. Look, I'm sorry I didn't mean . . . I just meant that your, er . . . type, so to speak, are a fascinating case study. From a Darwinian point of view. He would have trouble slotting you into a category.

ERICA: Well that's his fucking problem.

STEPH: Exactly.

CHARLES: Yes, yes I suppose it is. Sorry, I didn't mean to . . . It's like ants, I suppose.

ERICA: Ants?

STEPH: Did he say ants?

ERICA: He said ants.

CHARLES: Mmm. Sterile worker ants. They caused Darwin to delay the publication of his theories because they didn't fit any rational pattern of evolution.

ERICA: Is bigotry hereditary?

CHARLES: Huh? No no, it's learnt. Knowledge or prejudice as such cannot be passed down genetically. They used to think so, though, even as recently as the seventeenth century. In fact it's quite interesting. The Greeks used to get their women, their pregnant women, to stare at beautiful vases and art and stuff, so the baby would inherit the good looks of its surroundings.

STEPH: Did you study the Greeks, then?

CHARLES: Yes, for a time. Greek thought and mathematics and . . . architecture. The Coliseum and . . . buildings like that.

STEPH: Right.

CHARLES: With columns.

ERICA: Well let's get on with it then, shall we? You can put your pants and stuff by the sink if you like. Though try not to get any on the floor, I only cleaned it this morning.

STEPH: Oh you did? Oh thanks, sweetheart, I was dreading that.

ERICA: Well, after you brought me breakfast I thought it only fair.

STEPH: Oh *blesssss*. What an angel. You couldn't ask for a better mother.

CHARLES: Oh. Are you? Oh. I thought.

STEPH: Erica will be conceiving, we decided. I can't afford the time off.

ERICA: So when you're ready?

CHARLES: Look look I'm sorry. I just thought you'd want to know a bit more about me. I thought we'd just sort of get to know each other first. You are considering bearing the product of my genes, after all.

ERICA: Oh you seem fine. Attitudes aside. I can tell very quickly about people. It was just your medical condition I wanted to be sure of. Anyway it's nurture, not nature. Little Leslie will have the best of everything.

CHARLES: Les-Leslie? You're going to call it Leslie?

ERICA: Yes, we thought so.

STEPH: Yes. No gender stereotypes. Boy or girl. Leslie.

CHARLES: Christ. Leslie Ellis.

STEPH: Leslie Hull-Evans.

CHARLES: Huh?

STEPH: Hull-Evans.

CHARLES: Right, yes yes of course. Look I'm sorry, I don't want to mess you about or anything . . .

ERICA: Oh for the love of God.

CHARLES: Yes I'm sorry. I just think we shouldn't rush things. This is all very new to me, I just didn't realise when we spoke on the phone you'd be quite so . . . well. So eager to, well, get stuck in, so to speak.

ERICA: There doesn't seem to be any reason to wait. I'm ovulating as we speak, you see. It has to be now.

CHARLES: As we speak?

STEPH: Oh for Chrissakes . . .

ERICA: That's why we got you here today. I'm not

waiting another bloody month, I've got a holiday booked.

CHARLES: Oh. Oh I see.

STEPH: So if you'd like to come through?

CHARLES: Come through what?

STEPH: To the kitchen?

CHARLES: Oh, oh right.

STEPH: Will you need any help? And you can take that look off your face for starters. I'm not wanking you off. I just mean visuals?

CHARLES: Visuals?

ERICA: Do you normally use a magazine or something? We don't have any, you see. But Steph is happy to strip for you. Y'know, if it'll help you get the old fella into action.

CHARLES: Lawks.

ERICA: Unless you'd prefer me to?

CHARLES: No! No sorry, er. Crikey. Um.

STEPH: Does this help? I haven't shaved my legs for a week or so, but the bikini line is fresh.

CHARLES: Hhwmlffgjjjbbbmnn.

STEPH: I beg your pardon?'

CHARLES: That's, er, that's very, er . . . nice. You have lovely, er. Things. Er, knees. Nice knees. The way they join there on your, er. Crikey. It's warm, isn't it?

STEPH: Not standing here like this it isn't no, my nips are like pygmy cocks.

187

ERICA: Very nice.

STEPH: Oh shush, you. Now, Mr Ellis. I'm not standing naked here all day. Are you coming or what?

(Tape ends)

FIFTEEN

'I have a cunning plan'

Baldrick

Er . . . okay look, I'll explain.

And before you get all excited and start adding the CSA to your speed-dial list, it's not what you think, just give me a minute to explain. Not that I *have* to. In fact one of the many shiny advantages of my new clean-lined, veneered, modern Danish outlook, is that this whole explaining myself lark has become very much a thing of the past. Shrugged off, balled up and rather niftily back-kicked into a bin bag awaiting disposal.

I've done that, you see. Explaining myself. Christ, have I done that.

Smiling on cue, curtseying to the royal box, nodding

away benignly like I had Gerry fucking Anderson at the controls. To my teachers, my parents, and then to heads of year and other people's parents. I've spent, if not the better part then certainly the intro and first two verses of a lifetime coughing, picking invisible fluff from jacket sleeves, staring at the floor and muttering 'S-sorry, I just thought . . .'

But, as I say, that was then. The *old* Charlie, a quaint, obsolete piece of software. Simple, slow, a bit clunky and prone to crashing when put under stress. This is very much *now*. The new must-have Charlie Version 5.1 for Windows. I'm clearer, sharper, more efficient – upgraded all round, really. But I do come with a rather weighty manual. So I'll do you the service of taking you through *Charles Ellis for Dummies* step by step.

Because, you see, I want you to *understand*, that's all. Just so you can keep up. I've too much at stake to have to loiter at each step while you click on the Help icon.

So. Pay attention.

The Meaning of Life. What is it?

Well it's two things. It's quite a big question, for one. In fact, let's face it, a question so phenomenal and teetering in its stature, nobody ever asks it. Not until ten minutes to closing anyway, on one of those Sunday nights. When we've all had two too many and the conversation has slowed right down to burping, long silences and the occasional sigh. When out-of-focus thoughts are on the fast-approaching Monday morning. Then someone will pipe up *Tch! Life eh, whassit all about?* and everyone will murmur and groan and someone will fart and coats will be pulled on.

In my experience, that's about as often as the subject gets raised.

Which, considering the fuck-off-ness of its magnitude, is a bit peculiar. You'd think it would be all we ever discussed. The reason for being, the point to (spread arms wide and flap your hands about the place) all of this (and relax).

And the other thing it is, is something which lonely, unemployed, single, depressive biology teachers tend to dwell on far far too much. They read too much and drink too much and generally annoy the rest of the world with nagging *Whys* and *How-comes* and *But-whats* like a three year old. Which isn't as peculiar.

Tedious, yes. Peculiar, no.

The really peculiar thing about the meaning of life, to me anyway, is that, after two thousand five hundred years of pondering and what-iffing and stroking of beardsing, through Socrates and Descartes, through Archimedes and Gallileo, when in 1859, the meaning of life was finally cracked and written down and published, it made virtually no difference to anything whatsoever.

Really. It didn't.

I mean, congratulations, whoop whoop, high five, awlraaaaaaat! The whole enchilada, sorted. You can go out and buy a copy of the meaning of life in any bookshop in the world.

And yet here we are, a hundred and forty-odd years later. Everyone still getting up in the morning, brushing their teeth, going to work, coming home, rowing with their partners, stirring pasta, filling out forms, playing Scalextric yadda yadda yadda.

Like, *doh?!*

Look, let me put it another way – have you ever stopped to wonder why we're always so keen to 'get away from it all'? I mean, isn't 'it all' what we've made for ourselves? Our lives, our homes, our jobs, our cars, our families? This is what we have, this is what we want, this is what we *do*. And yet we can't *wait* to stop. Any of us. Living for the weekend, dressing down on Fridays, saving up our holiday, packing paperbacks and *Rough Guides* and just fucking off out of it for a fortnight. I mean, for God's sake, us teachers only put up with all the shit and shouting because we get to spend twelve weeks a year not doing it.

Doesn't it seem a bit, I dunno, weird? No other life form seems so miserable, so frustrated and anxious that they need to take a break from themselves.

So the question I've reached is this – can we really be expected to believe this is a coincidence, can one really just put it down to chance? That human beings, *Homo sapiens*, wise man, the most intellectually advanced creatures ever to exist on this planet, are also the least content? I mean, what, you expect no one to put this little equation together and come up with a furrowed brow? C'mon, is it just me? Has no one else figured this one out? In everything I've ever read, everything I've ever seen, the smaller the brains get, the less complex the nervous system, the more limited the capacity for thought — all the things that make us humans so damn cocky — the happier the creature.

I mean, you never hear fish complain, do you?

Now okay okay, time out. (As Brad might say.)

(If he could take his tongue out of my fiancée for two fucking minutes, that is).

I realise, as arguments go, this one has both an air of fatuousness to it and a big fat cloud of *Oh fuck off, Charlie*-ness to it. The logic is about as cogent as the old joke my dad used to tell at teatime about carrots being good for your eyes because you never see a rabbit wearing glasses.

Yeah, good one, Pops.

Okay, I'll concede that one. But you have to admit that there's something in it.

Surely?

I mean, let's look at the human life cycle. Little baby George is only ever going to be three things: happy, sad or asleep. There is no stress or angst or depression or torment. Nothing. Just base animal instincts of hot and cold, energy and fatigue, hunger and satisfaction.

But then, as he grows, and his tiny mind expands, so will his capacity for emotion. He'll learn guilt, envy, hatred, despair, anger − all the horrible things that make us 'wise'. The cleverer he becomes, the more miserable he'll be able to be. The greater the understanding of the human condition, the greater the sorrow that rises from the understanding.

His simple smile, that blissful gaze, is just a look of happiness born of ignorance. George isn't sitting there, pleased as punch with the state of the world. He's happy because he is warm and fed and that's it. That is all he knows, that is all he wants and that is all he's got and that is why he smiles.

A dog is happy, it wags its tail. A dog is sad, it hangs its tail. Simple. And what is it that makes this dog's emotional state fluctuate? Politics? The environment? A lukewarm review of its latest poem? No. A dog knows nothing of these things. It is happy if it is warm and fed, and sad if it is cold and hungry. These other concerns do not exist for doggy-kind.

They are invented.

By us.

And we are no happier for it.

I can't say this all dawned on me in a flash, in some Archimedical bathtub eureka. (Which is a good thing really, because I shower. If I leap out with any astonishment I get a faceful of glass.) This was a notion that sort of just seeped in slowly, like a twenty-something's love of pop music.

As a teenager you wouldn't have caught me within body-popping distance of the Top 40. I was an *indie kid*. DMs and cardigans and a short back and sides. Brad and Ade were the same, it was part of our male glue. Classmates would chuck about shiny dog-eared copies of *Smash Hits* and *No. 1* magazine while we poured sensitively over *Q* and *NME*.

But now, at the age of twenty-seven, click a light fingernail over my CD racks and you'll be able to stop off at Madonna, Bananarama, *Now That's What I Call Music* and (ulp) Take That.

It wasn't the case that, one Sunday evening, the voice of Simon Mayo caused a moment of clarity and the scales fell from my eyes, taking my Wedding Present albums and my Cure posters with them. These noises, these tunes, just seeped in. One track takes you by surprise one summer afternoon, you're tapping your feet a little.

Although you just tell your mates *'This one isn't too shit, I s'pose. But it's, like, so commercial, y'know?'*

But then a few radio plays, a couple more singles at number one and you find yourself, five years later, picking up the *Singles Collection* in HMV and nodding to yourself.

*

That's how it was. A phrase in a book rang true, a trip to the zoo confirmed a suspicion. Another book, an idea, a documentary and slowly, seep seep. Cloudy notions and potions were stirred around the cloudy phial of my mind, each one dripping in slowly, all the while checking measurements and readings and watching them billow and swarm, fizz and dissolve. An adjustment to the bunsen burner and, slowly, the results began to crystallise.

And when they did, nothing was the same. The idea that we human beings, the very pinnacle of evolution (or so we would like to think), are the only creatures to know misery, stayed with me for days. Everywhere I looked I saw more examples proving my hypothesis. Giggling babies and purring kittens, screaming motorists and scowling commuters. Pigeons strutting, eating, fluttering, cooing. Lunchers queuing, jostling, pushing, munching, checking their watches and gulping their coffee.

And I wondered why. I wondered why we should all be struggling and fighting and worrying and working when other animals, the birds and beasts over which we rule, should potter about without a care in the world.

And then I realised. It was like Deborah had said, wouldn't it be simpler if we were like them sometimes?

But we can't be. Our evolution, of all things, holds us

back. We're just too clever for our own good. A chimpanzee's concerns are fairly simple to measure. Give or take a few, they are the concerns of the majority of mammals. Food, warmth and reproduction, that's about the size of it. And so they have the intelligence to match. To exist comfortably a chimp does not require a complex and sophisticated pattern of language. He doesn't need to understand chemistry or physics or mathematics or suchlike. Nor does he need to have the awareness to create art or music or drama or jazz or cinema. Their purpose and function, to exist solely to reproduce other chimps, is looked after by simple brains that, more or less successfully, get it to do so.

But us? Jeepers, the word overqualified scarcely begins to cover it.

We have minds that can compose symphonies, hands that can sculpt pyramids, tongues that can speak. And why? So we can reproduce and make other humans.

Are you following all this?

We seem gargantuanly overdeveloped, so unnecessarily complex machines, considering our purpose. And blow me if that isn't the reason for so much unhappiness. The legendary mind/body divide, the great split that is the human dilemma, the cerebral versus the physical. Why do monkeys not suffer this? Why do dolphins not suffer this? We have the exact same purpose in life as every other creature. Are there dolphin encounter groups? Is there dung beetle peer pressure? No. Because these creatures have not the consciousness, not the self-awareness to be in need of such things. Only we are. It is the reason our software and hardware keep breaking down. Our hardware is just too complicated.

I mean, look at it this way — if you were on *The Great Egg Race* or *Robot Wars* or one of those *Engineering can be fun, kids!* BBC2 shows, and you had to create a machine that cut out, I don't know, pastry shapes or something, ad infinitum, it would be simple. A big pastry-shaped knife on a hinge going up down up down. You wouldn't bother fitting it with carburettors and fuel injections and plush leatherette finish and catalytic converters and a radio alarm and a clock. Too much stuff.

Too much stuff to *go wrong*.

But it seems that somewhere along our evolution, our purpose got a bit skew-whiff. We had to develop self-awareness in order to survive in this environment, but this self-awareness is just too damn good. We rage against our machine. We choose to defy our instincts. On a daily basis. We're hungry, but we wait until teatime. We're thirsty, but I'll just get this letter typed out before I put the kettle on. I'm cold but I won't grow my hair long because it's soooo 1970s.

You think a bumble bee, old *bombus terrestris,* worries about hoops making him look overweight? No (in case you're wondering), he doesn't.

And when we discovered this purpose, when Charles Darwin published *The Origin of Species* back in 1859, showing the world where man did come from, what changed? Well there was outcry, certainly, initially. A few religious types got their cassocks in a twist, had a Valium and two days off work, what then?

Nothing. Nothing, that's what. Everyone continued to live exactly as they had been doing. Same jobs, same lives, same headaches, same stresses and complaints. And when Richard Dawkins published *The Selfish Gene* in 1976, which explained eruditely and with great intelligence, the whole reason for human existence, was there a news flash? Did all the great leaders of the world release statements saying, 'The world's top scientists, after two thousand five hundred years of study, have deciphered the meaning of life. It is, to whit, reproduction. That's it, no more no less. We apologise to the religious, the poetic, the artistic. We apologise also to the impotent and the infertile. You are a waste of valuable air. The international pairing process will begin at 0600 hrs. Those without a breeding partner, please report to your local municipal Coupling-Booth?'

No they didn't. A few prizes and medals were dished out, a few pats on heads, a couple of gold stars stuck on the bottom of a couple of pages, and then everyone promptly went about their business of designing trousers and washing up and mowing lawns and setting video recorders.

Oh yes, and getting drunk on a Sunday night and wondering what their purpose in life was.

I've said it before and I'll say it again. Like, *dur*?

Not that I'm anything special. I can't claim to have discovered any of these things, and up until now, have been as totally blind to their day-to-day significance as the rest. I mean, for heaven's sake, I was teaching biology for four years. And it still never really dawned on me how important what I was teaching really was. And I know my students certainly didn't care. As I trotted out corpuscles and aortas and chromosomes and genomes and nerves and bones, it just didn't feel important, not really important. Not as vital as English or mathematics. But it was the way Wendy put it those few weeks ago, with her fervour and passion.

Biology, what are other subjects without biology?

Because we are but gene machines. Our purpose nothing more than survival and reproduction. Everything else you can imagine – philosophy, religion, art. All window dressing, all garnish.

You don't believe me? It's okay, I don't blame you. Come into my bedroom, I'll show you something (and you can take that filthy look off your face for a start).

The wardrobe itself is an oh-so-stylish black-ash affair, the one piece of furniture I stole from my parents' house when I moved out. The door on the right sticks a bit but if you give it a *yank* – ah, there we are.

Well no real surprises here if you've ever seen a twenty-something's clothes en mass before. It smells a bit musty because it always takes me two days to take wet clothes out of the washing machine.

Deborah was always much better at that kind of shit.

Top shelf, the obligatory tumbling mess of jumpers, greens and navy blues. All crew-necked. I dunno, V-neck has always been a bit school-outfitterish to me.

Down one side, shelves with my socks (mostly black, mostly M&S, mostly pairs); pants (mostly button-ups, a few boxers hanging on); jeans (six pairs, although I only ever wear one).

Hanging up on wirey cheap hangers, my two work suits. Both Next, neither of them cost me more than £150 (which included a free shirt and tie set. Mmm, *nice*). A row of pale blue cotton shirts. Then, apart from the bottom which has one pair of what my mum would call 'good shoes' and three pairs of Nikes in varying states of falling-to-bits-ness, the rest is t-shirts.

Like most men, out of the Christ knows how many I've accumulated and refused to throw away, I only wear about six of them on a rotational basis. These are all smarter, ribbed, GAP style. All more than fifteen quid, all grey marl.

All bought by Deborah.

Which will go as far as we need to go to explain how shit the other few hundred are. Indie bands, television comedians, foreign holidays, comic-book characters, album sleeves, tour dates. My chest has been a 100% cotton, baggy-necked, unironed, untucked billboard for the better part of twenty years.

Okay, point made, we're done in here. Just give the right-hand door a slam and leave the other one, the hinge has gone. I'll put the kettle on.

T-shirts serve two functions. One is to cover the upper torso and protect against the elements.

The other is to get the wearer laid.

The colour, the fit, the slogan, the label – the t-shirt is an advertisement for sexual reproduction. I mean obviously, *all* clothes are. And all jewellery. And all haircuts and accents and possessions and an entire catalogue of items. Everything we have on Earth, from the tiniest paper clip to the Natwest Tower that holds it – a device to, eventually, keep us alive and get us laid.

The t-shirt is a particularly brilliant example, though. Brilliant because it is so blatant, so obvious. And yet is so acceptable in polite society. The t-shirt is the peacock's tail, it's the gorilla's chest, it's the stag's antlers.

It's the dog's bollocks, let's face it.

We buy and wear t-shirts to make us look good (correct fit, right length, contemporary cut, fashionable brand – whatever) illustrating our physical condition to the opposite sex. And then, in a masterstroke of biological urgency, we slap an image or a slogan on it as further shaggability information.

It would be like a female baboon having the words 'I can also cook' tattooed on her arse.

Yes, it all seems very unlikely, I know. That we should be so basic, so simple, so animal like. The idea that most well-known architects and painters and composers are men because, basically, we're the biggest show-offs. That I should choose to wear a Level 42 tour shirt, not just because I like a bit of fancy bass-guitar, but because I think a female Level 42 fan would be the most suitable mating partner for my offspring.

But there you go. That's why. Everything we do, from the time we get up to the time we go to bed, nappy to headstone, is for survival and reproduction. Our one, our only, purpose in life.

Which is why my every instinct stops me chopping off my knob and throwing myself under a bus.

Our unhappiness, in all its myriad forms, it seems to me, is born of our denial of this fact. Our snooty Victorian presumption that we are so much more advanced, that we are so much more intelligent than the simple fishes and birds — that we have a higher purpose. The classic human struggle of heart and mind, of instinct and intelligence, is only a struggle because of their incompatibility. The mind of a haddock and the body of a haddock are in perfect harmony — they both just want to make more haddock. Which is why they don't smoke dope or need Woody Allen movies. But our bodies want one thing and our heads, for some reason, want something else. Hence angst and torment.

If we could only get the two to agree.

If we could only stop railing against our bodies' desires and just please them.

All human misery, surely, would disappear.

SIXTEEN

*'My first rule of travel is never go to a place that sounds
like a medical condition.'*

Bill Bryson

Now, as I said, I don't want you to think I arrived at this
life-altering decision lightly. I am well aware that there
are light years between a twenty-something male
smuggling home a copy of *The Best of Rick Astley* in a
slithery HMV bag — and a twenty-something male
deciding to make the successful continuation of his
genetic line the sole purpose of his existence. I know
that. (Which one is more *embarrassing*? Well the jury's
still out on that.) But what I'm saying is, this was a plan
that had had a number of false starts before it appeared
fully formed.

Just ask Julie, she'll tell you.

'Yes, good morning, sir, take a seat. How can I help you?'

'Uhm, yes yes, good morning. The, er, Trobriand Islands. Do you have anything?'

'I'm sorry, which islands are those? The Troh . . . ?'

'Trobriand. They're in Melanesia. Papua New Guinea, I wondered if there were any flights.'

'Well let's have a bit of a look-see, shall we?'

Having bid farewell to Wendy, my first stop on the way back from the zoo that Monday morning was the branch of Thomas Cook on Camden High Street. It's an odd place to find such a thing, surrounded as it is on all sides by leather jacket shops, incense boutiques and Hash Marts. It sits there like the posh kid from the suburbs trying to blend in with the lads off the estate, its red facia a blush of awkwardness against the trendy black scowl of its neighbours. But even scruffy herberts in beaten-up suede jackets must need somewhere handy to book their trips of self-discovery to India, Morocco and Amsterdam, I guess. So there it is, would you mind not smoking that in here, sir, how can I help you?

'Hmm, right,' the assistant said (badge – Julie, apparently *Happy To Help)* after a few shift-return-F1 manoeuvers on her PC. 'Not a lot, I'm afraid. When were you thinking of travelling?'

'When? Oh. Gosh. I don't know. I guess immediately.

Right now. Well, not now now — it's ten o'clock on a Monday morning. But soon. Asap.Y'know?'

'Hmmm right,' she said again. 'The islands have one airport as far as I can see. Let me just find out . . .' and she began to jab at the keys, her tongue poking out of the side of her mouth in concentration.

'Yes, Port Moresby,' I finished for her, helpfully. 'South coast of Papua New Guinea.' However, Julie began another one of her now famous *Hmmms* that she managed to extend, in a self-indulgent lengthy one-note drone worthy of Laurie Anderson, through a handful of screens before she allowed herself to agree with me.

'H-Hmm! Port Moresby. Yes,' and she flashed me a smile lifted direct from a thirty-minute videotape on customer-service standards. 'You're very well informed. Have you been before?'

'No, no never. But I have read a little bit about it.'

'Hmm?' She nodded. Tippy tap-tap.

'Yes, Bronislaw Malinowski wrote a fascinating book in 1929 – *The Sexual Life of Savages in North West Melanesia.*'

'Ah.' Julie nodded without a blink. 'I'm reading *Cujo* at the moment myself.' Tippity tappity beep. 'Here we go then. There's nothing direct, I'm afraid. We have a flight that stops off at Singapore and then picks up again to Port Moresby.'

'And the cost of that one?'

'One thousand and five pounds return.'

'A thousand pounds?' I spat.

'And five pounds.' She smiled. 'Return.'

'Lawks.'

'Yes, not cheap that part of the world.'

'And if I wasn't returning? If I decided it was what I was looking for and just, well, stayed there? How much for that?'

'A single?'

'That's the fellah.'

Tippy tappy tip beep.

'Another five hundred pounds on top of that.'

'A-ha, hmm right I see.'

Which is of course the correct response. No-one who ever launched into the HOW THE FUCK CAN YOU CHARGE ME MORE TO ONLY GO HALF THE COCKING WAY?! response has ever got a satisfactory answer. One nods and smiles and *Uh-huhs* as if this is obvious and durrr, silly of me to ask really. Really, it's the easiest thing.

'The return ticket is valid for a year, though. Were you planning on staying longer?'

'Than a year? That depends really. I don't know how long it will take to do . . . ah, what I have to do. It may take a while, what with development and such. I haven't read anything more up to date.'

'Right.' Julie nodded cautiously.

'You don't know much about the place, I s'pose?'

'Not really, sir. Unusual place for a holiday. It's not really very resorty. Have you thought about Northern

Australia? Or Fiji?'

'Er, no, no not really. What are the women like there?'

'The *women*, sir?'

'Yes. Well no, no I'm not going over there just for the women, obviously.'

'No.'

'No. The whole place has, well, just more the culture I'm looking for.'

'And what's that?'

'Very, uhm, how can I put it . . .'

'I'm not sure I really understand the sort of holiday you're after, sir.'

'Yes, ha. It is a little difficult to explain.'

Which I foolishly thought would cover it. As if Julie would nod shiftily, tap the side of her nose and slide me a brown envelope under the desk full of plane tickets and traveller's cheques.

No, she was a professional and she wanted an answer. Tippy tappy beep.

'Fiji is becoming more and more popular all the time. Would you like a brochure you could take home with you?' And she planted her palms on the desk in a *let's stand up now, shall we* gesture.

'Uh, oh, okay.'

I was beginning to realise this was a mistake. It had seemed the right thing to do at the time, really it had. Striking while the iron was hot, and so forth.

We edged around the queue of would-be holiday-makers, each one with that look in their eye. *Happiness is somewhere else. Out there, somewhere, is the answer to my problems. That'll sort me out, two weeks lying down on a towel near water.*

None of them got it.

Julie was handing me brochures.

'These are all for that part of the world, we have flights to all these. Plus Northern Australia . . .' she burbled on happily.

'Look, Julie,' I said. 'I'll be honest. These aren't really what I had in mind.' I flashed a look at the glossy slipperiness of brochures in my arms. A lot of tanned flesh, a lot of tiny swimwear, a lot of healthy white smiles. 'Although,' I changed tack, 'will these women be at these resorts? I'd like to meet these women here.'

'I'm sorry?'

Oh for goodness sake, what was I saying? Somebody stop him, please! But no, it kept on coming.

'You want to go on holiday to meet women, is that right?'

'Well yes. But not so much *meet* as *have lots of sex with*. Although meeting is obviously part of it.'

'Yes.'

'Difficult to have sex with someone you haven't met.'

'Yes.' Julie's eyes flashed nervously in every direction but mine, as if she were scanning for Lancaster bombers.

'Not that easy to have sex with someone you have met, actually.'

'No.'

I can't give you an excuse. I could try but . . .

Oh dear.

The floodgates were bursting. My theories and plans were boiling over, plumes of billowing smoke and bubbling green liquid in trembling phials – my head was a mad-scientist's lab. Enormous steel balls fizzed and sparked, dials spun crazily, Hammer Horror style. I needed the intrepid team of investigators to break the door down and flick the huge, wall-mounted switch and stop me in my tracks. But it was all going too fast. I suddenly saw myself, shock of white hair, lab coat, drinking down the foaming serum and disappearing, coughing and gagging, behind my workbench. A flash of lightning, some descending organ chords, a green clawed hand appears above the table, a ghoulish laugh echoes about the castle walls.

'But in Melanesia, that's not a problem.'

'Hmm, I see. Anyway, let me check availability for you,' and Julie began to steer me back to the desk.

'By the time they're thirteen or so, they're at it like rabbits. The tribal elders actively encourage it. Of course, its beauty is in the simplicity of the transaction. They just meet up and ask directly, Fancy a shag? And they either do or they don't. It's quite brilliant.'

'It sounds very . . . interesting. I'm not sure, however,

211

that the hotels actually will offer that service to the guests.'

'Hm, no no of course.'

'You might get a kettle in your room. With some sachets of coffee and such.'

'Well it's a start.'

Now seated behind the barricaded safety of her red Formica, Julie stared at me for a moment, no doubt a little unsure whether she should reserve me a ticket, forward my details to Singapore Airlines or just go ahead and make out a docket to head office ordering more staplers, a desk tidy and a large truncheon. An awkward silence. I sat on the very edge of my chair, unshaved and unwashed, one foot jigging maniacally. I should go, really. This needed more thought. The pause stretched on, which for reasons best known to somebody else, I decided to fill with –

'But what Malinowski found interesting was that the male was required to present a gift to the female, much in the manner of fruit flies and chimps, before the transaction could take place.'

'Okay then, that's great. If you decide you want to book a seat,' Julie began to make a note on a business card hurriedly, 'call any of our branches on this number, or Singapore Airlines direct.'

'But the extraordinary thing is, even in this culture of open exchange, female coyness is still important. Can you believe that?'

'Today, sir, nothing would surprise me.'

'No-one wants a girl who has been around too much. The idea of the men as pursuers and the women as the pursued exists in every culture, no matter how base or sophisticated.'

'Oh-hokay! Who's next, please?'

'I could lend you the book if you're interested?'

'Can someone call the manager?'

Oops.

But a false start, just a false start. I'd been a bit keen, that's all. The trial and error method of scientific procedure allowed for a few messy wheel spins before tearing off down the right road. I knew what I wanted, I just had to choose my route a bit more carefully, that's all. A head full of ideas and paperwork, a cranium full of pie-charts and Venn diagrams. I should have just taken a bit of time to colour-coordinate my ring-binders. That's all. No harm done, no harm done.

Back home, a pot of coffee on, I cleared a space at my desk and composed a letter of intent to the world with which I could mark out my future. I include it here for your perusal.

> Architect, handsome *27, seeks intelligent partner, athletic, healthy, non-smoking, professional, 21–30 GSOH, for companionship and affection. Box 975*

And it's that simple. There are other ways, of course. Other ways as colourful and varied as there are blues on the Dulux colour chart: phone-chat lines for the wealthy and disfigured; singles bars and dating agencies, all sweaty, rather urgent places called things like *Sweet-Meets* and *Heart-Search* and *Mate-Match* and other bile-inducing wank.

But such things take time (lots of it), money (even more of it) and at least one very good suit. And of these I had none. What I did have, however, was a mission. And like all good missions, there was groundwork, preparation and a new pack of biros to be sorted before D-Day could commence successfully.

I plumped for *Architect* for a fistful of reasons. I wanted my ad at the top of the page alphabetically speaking, and it implies brains and creativity. I imagine it pays pretty well and it's easier to bluff in casual conversation than *Astronaut* or *Aardvark Salesman*.

While I was weighing up the value of falsehoods in the world of the lonely heart, I was tempted to lie about my age as well. But I'm one of those twenty-seven year olds who looks, well, twenty-seven.

The rest, all that *intelligent, athletic, healthy, non-smoking professional* and *GSOH* stuff? That was all necessary in the interests of science.

Handsome was just a lie.

Oh, and while we're at it, that *companionship* and *affection*, that was a lie as well.

As was *partner*, now I think about it.

And porky whopper number six was my specified age-limit preferential. But we'll get a stiff drink inside us before I unveil that particular one.

See, it was important that whoever was to join me in this little experiment had to be fit as a fiddle. Fitter in fact. As fit as a fiddle in leg-warmers who's just finished the *Flight of the Bumble Bee* without pausing to catch her breath. And have an acceptable sense of humour (that is, Robin Williams no, Robin Asquith yes). And be brainy. Not nerdy, no friends, sellotape on the glasses brainy. More the glamourpuss with her hair up in a bun, remove specs, *Why, Miss Perkins, you're beautiful* type.

You know the sort.

I could be direct about that, ballsy and upfront, the other ads covered it without blushing. It was the whole age thing that gave me trouble.

21–30. Twenty-one to thirty. Born somewhere between *The Graduate* and *The Omen*, that's what I wanted.

Apparently.

But I'm not at all afraid to say (no more apologetic little Charlie), that someone born between, say, *Clash of the Titans* and (er . . .) *Back to the Future* would have been . . . how can I put it . . . well, more, er . . .

Well, would have perhaps been a little more . . . as it were . . .

Well, Malinowski would understand.

But it can't be done. Charles Ellis would no more be accepted by the indigenous population of the Trobriand Islands as a potential father for their females' offspring than a ravenous timber wolf could apply for a baby-sitting job. Before you could say *Get your pasty western clams off my youngest, you little tyke,* I'd be chased out of the tribe with not so much a flea in my ear as an eight-foot spear.

And plus, of course, I didn't have £1,005.

So this is why my plan B required looking a little closer to home.

SEVENTEEN

'The lion and the calf will lie down together but the calf won't get much sleep.'

Woody Allen

There are certain female fireflies in the genus *Photuris* that are able to do a not-too-shabby impersonation of the mating flash of females in the genus *Photinus*. So consequently, the male *Photeni* mistakenly comes a-calling. Enabling the *Photuris* female to eat him.

How cunning.

And there are butterfly pupae that, in a certain light, bare a distinct resemblance to the head of a snake. And, should a predator get too close, they can start giving it some shaky-snakey vibes to put them off.

Cunning again.

There is also an orchid that looks like a female wasp. I mean, not breathtakingly so, unless of course we're talking about one tremendously ugly wasp, with green stalks and leaves and such. But the resemblance is enough to fool male wasps. So they approach and end up involuntarily spreading the orchid's pollen.

Cunningness aboundeth.

Because organisms may present themselves as whatever it is in their genetic interest to appear like.

What one must remember, however, is that this bare-faced deceit game is just as suitable for two players as it is one.

Date: Saturday 30th September
Subject: Miss Jennifer Tyler
Location: St. Mark's Gate, London NW1

'S'cuse me.'

I felt a firm squeeze on my upper arm and glanced down quickly. I'd been lost for a moment reading the sturdy iron map of Regent's Park that marks the entrance to the gate. A female hand held my arm gently. A slim, manicured female hand. A little tanned, with a heavy silver ring on the index finger. Well kept, but not a young hand. The hand lived at the bottom end of a well-appointed wrist which the owner had adorned with a glittery expensive watch. A watch that looked so expensive, in fact, that it can only have cost about three quid. As I turned, the arm ran away from me, disappearing into a sleeveless blouse, the neckline of which had taken a plunge that would induce aquaphobia in Captain Nemo. After a month of talks and sanction agreements I finally persuaded my eyes to give up their weapons, surrender and make their way from the cleavage area and up to the face and I took the first look at whomever it was wanted me to *s'cuse* them.

Sunglasses. Big sunglasses, I mean, for September it was a sunny day but these would be considered over cautious by Julia Roberts' dentist. And, framing these bug-like specs, a huge tumbling tousle of bleach-blonde hair. The officially registered owner of all of the above plucked her cigarette from her lips.

'You teach my Stuart, dontcha?'

Oh Christ.

I mumbled something about not thinking so and having one of those faces and gazed intently at the pink wet blossoms that dappled the pavement but I couldn't get out of it, my panicky heartbeat audible to pretty much the entire population of NW3.

'Yeah Ellis, innit? Mister Ellis? Science? Well I never. I didn't recognise it as you on the phone.'

'Biology,' I sighed with a *you-win* resignation, looking into her eyes for the first time. Or where I presumed her eyes were, hidden by their huge 78s.

'And whassit,' she read aloud from my advertisement

on the torn corner of grubby newsprint, 'architect too it says 'ere? Man of many talents.'

Oh Christ.

Jennifer Tyler (Ms), mother of Stuart, (year 10) tossed her cigarette to the floor, ground it to nothing with a strappy sandal and slipped her arm through mine.

'This *is* a turn-up. C'mon, you can buy me an ice-cream and tell me *all* about it.'

We crossed the small footbridge over the soft lapping and idle fishermen of Regent's Canal, the traffic's hum disappearing almost immediately, and we made our way up Regent's Park's inner circle to the zoo.

Much the same as I had with Stephanie, Erica and the others too embarrassing to mention, Mrs Tyler and I had initially made contact through a tennis set of phone-mail messages. Jenny (as she had called herself) had made it clear she was willing to start with a quick meeting, somewhere public, somewhere central — just like the safety tips printed at the bottom of the newspaper suggested. Having fallen for her husky B&H telephone manner, I'd suggested Regent's Park. I could use it to my advantage and show off a bit if the conversation ran dry.

Also the zoo was bereft of any interesting buildings so I wouldn't be asked what obscure pieces of architecture might be called.

And most importantly, I knew I could surreptitiously arrange to have Adrian loitering around the penguins at two o'clock as a safety net if it all went horribly wrong.

Jenny had laughed and said she hadn't been to the zoo in years. But a date had been made and as we strolled along the wide street through the sunshine, her hair specking and flashing in and out of the shade and heels clicking beside me, I crossed my fingers that this, this face from the past, might be the woman with which I could begin my experiment.

'He used to love your lessons, our Stu. Come home talking all about this and that, cuttin' up worms in the garden. Science was his favourite.'

'Oh, I didn't know that. He didn't exactly make it clear.'

'Oh yes.' Jennifer pushed her sunglasses up on top of her head. 'Mister Ellis this and Mister Ellis that he'd go on and on. Made us buy a chemistry set thing one year. Went on and on about it. Cost us a fortune.'

We walked slowly up the steps into the cool darkness of the rhino house, a sting of ammonia causing us to pinch and wince a little.

'He only wanted to blow things up of course. But it was an interest.' She sighed with a half smile of resignation. 'Didn't even stick at that, though.'

Inside the dusty interior, the floor wet with urine and water, the smell was quite a smack in the chops at first and we shared a grimace but it quickly levelled off into a dull brown pong. All the stalls were empty bar one and we clicked and scuffed over, sitting on the damp concrete steps. The rhinoceros, Rosie, snorted and snuffled to and fro. A little bit one way, a little bit the other. A family settled in next to us, the children leaning over barriers and enjoying their echoing voices in the half-light. We watched them in silence for a moment.

Jennifer had been happy to natter on for the better part of an hour, mostly about other people at the zoo and what the bleedin' 'ell they thought they were doin' lettin' their kids be'ave like that. Other people's families seemed so much more fascinating to her than the animals themselves, I thought. We probably could have had just as interesting a time wandering around Brent Cross. I had managed to puffily back-hand any questions regarding building design and set squares but fortunately for me, Jennifer, it seemed, knew even less about architecture than I did.

Which is extraordinary if you think about it.

'Used up all the glass whatnots in two days and then he was back kickin' his football against the garage door.' She chuckled. 'Here, grab hold of this, will ya,' she said, handing me her dripping ice-lolly, 'I'm havin' a fag,' and she rummaged in her bag for her lighter. I took this discreet opportunity to allow my eyes a quick refresher course over her painted toes, shapely legs and cleavage.

'Look at the horn!' one of the children squealed jumping up and down, two hands on the wet barrier. 'That's the biggest horny horn in the world!'

Well quite.

This past hour, as I'm sure you don't need me to tell you, had been a bit on the bloody weird side. In all my many, varied and *18 Rated* Mrs Tyler fantasies, I hadn't once conjured up this scene. Darkness? Yes. Wetness? Occasionally. The overpowering stench of fresh shit? Well . . . okay, maybe once. But sitting down in the dusky pongfest of the rhino house listening to her talk about her son?

'I didn't realise I'd been so popular with Stuart,' I said.

'Oh yes,' she said, shaking her Bic and flicking it into a spitting flame. 'You were his favourite. Says you picked on him a bit for messin' about.'

'Well . . .'

'Oh don't worry about it. He says everyone picks on him. They probably do an' all but he does himself no favours.' Jennifer reached up and tugged her sunglasses from her dirty blond hair and began to play with them idly, flicking them by the arm. 'So,' she said, standing up and brushing dust from her skirt. 'What's a clever fella like you, architect an' all, doing teaching my kid?'

Well, lying like fuck, obviously. But I didn't think that was the response she was looking for.

I'd foolishly not even dreamed my prefabricated back-story would come under anything but the mildest scrutiny. I had constructed this phoney outer shell like a chameleon disappears into the bark of a tree – a subtle untruth to aid the survival of the genetic line. I hadn't prepared for a predator to come and jab me with a stick.

'I, uhm, I was . . . just . . . using it to study . . . school buildings.'

Well come on, what was I meant to say?

'Their construction and . . . things,' I said standing and we walked with a squint back out through a cloud of dancing midges into the blinky daylight. 'I've been commissioned to design a large school and I thought that if I did some research into the teaching environment, it would, uhm . . .'

Jennifer nodded slowly throughout this feeble fumbling, stretching her face against the sun.

'. . . well. That kind of thing,' I closed with a whimper.

''S'funny,' Jennifer said eventually. We took a seat under a Britvic umbrella at a scattering of green plastic tables and chairs, the air wet from the nearby fountain. Above, the low sky burst with the shrill whirr of the macaws. Families all about us at other tables bickered over cellophane sandwiches and cartons of orange drink. 'That's not at all the idea I had when I read your ad.' She rested her cigarette with a precarious dangle from her lips and fished out the tatty scrap of paper from her bag. I blushed audibly.

'No? What did you think?' I asked gingerly, craning my neck around to read the ad.

As if, God, I dunno. As if I'd forgotten what bleedin' job I'd apparently studied for seven years.

'I thought you were lying to make yourself sound interesting.'

She took a long drag on her cigarette and fixed me with a look which cracked suddenly into a warm smile and she laughed a cackley but infectious laugh.

'It's all right. Don't make any difference to me. I've been out with so many fellas since Stu's dad left I can spot a liar at ten paces. I'm just as bad of course. Didn't exactly play straight with you neither, did I?' she said.

I thought back to her voice mail message. Straight? No, not exactly. She had claimed to be Jenny (possibly even a Jenni), a fun-loving twenty-something single girl. Which is quite a crooked way from cigarette-loving divorced forty-something single parent.

I fetched us some drinks and she let her past out of its box for a bit of a wander among other wild animals.

She was finding difficulty snaring a partner, a step-dad for young Stuart.

Well, of course she was.

The kid was a scowling mass of scuffy hormones and

rage – all skateboards and combat trews. But even if Jennifer had been mother to a gleaming, side-parted, bespectacled chess prodigy, there were never going to be men queuing up to help.

'They're just not interested. But they don't even come out and say it, do they? Oh no, that'd be too easy. They start goin' on about it being *too soon* for them or they have a *problem with responsibility* or they *like Stuart really they do* and then bang. Wake up next morning and there's not even a note on the fridge.'

'We can't all be that bad. I mean, some guys are looking for a family, surely?'

I know I was. Or rather, I know I thought I was.

Jennifer laughed.

'Yeah, I can just see blokes queuing up to get involved with a middle-aged, divorced single parent. I'd have to take on a part-time job to help pay for the thousands of nights out with eligible men. I'm knackered enough as it is.' She shook her head and stretched her legs out with a dry chuckle.

'Well, you never know unless you try? Maybe some nice guy . . .' My voice trailed off.

'Oh I tried it,' she picked up. 'At the start, after Stuart's dad left. All those bars and evening classes. Lord, they were depressing places. I put in an ad that I thought would wow fellas with its honesty.' She cleared her throat theatrically. *'Young at heart single mother, early forties, would like to meet solvent male with an interest in country music, nights out and a genuine love of children. Smokers welcome, London.'*

'You remember it that well?'

'God yes,' she said with a shake of her head. 'At one time you couldn't pick up a magazine within the M25 without finding it.'

'But no luck?'

'Nothing. C'mon, let's keep going.' And we got to our feet with a weary groan, causing pigeons to strut and scatter. Heading past the burning sausage campfire smell of the café, we trailed a lazy route towards the big cats.

'No, I tell a lie. There were a few. Weirdos most of them. I guess they could smell the desperation on the page.' She stared off for a moment, her mind elsewhere. 'Not a good time for Stuart.' She took a puff of her cigarette. 'Pretty shit time all round really.'

We passed the macaws, still screeching and flapping away.

'So now I leave him out. Early forties has become mid-twenties, I've ditched the country music.'

'Yeah?'

'If I was dragged out line dancing one more time . . .' and we shared a laugh.

I was having great trouble reconciling these two women. The Mrs Tyler from my grubby small-hours imagination – all blonde pouting and *oooh big-boy*. And this one in front of me. The other side of forty, tired, cynical, funny but not beaten. She looked older than my imagination let her look. There was time and there was sadness in her face. The jaw tight through too many knocks and disappointments. The eyes firm from having to see through so much male bullshit. The hands wrinkled from clutching compromises too tightly. My head was having difficulty processing these incompatible pieces of data.

And my knob didn't know if it was coming or going. So to speak.

'So what's your story?' she asked. We had come to a stop by the lions. A popular attraction, a couple of families had their faces pressed to the circle of thick glass.

'Me?'

'Yeah. What's all this architect bollocks all about? You're no more an architect than I am.'

'Oh. Ha, yes. It was, well . . .'

I felt very suddenly very stupid. In the harsh illumination of my little desk-lamp at home it had all seemed very sensible and rational and logical. A mere exaggeration, an embellishment no more unnatural than the peacock's tail or baboon's arse. But when she put it like this?

'I mean, *I've* got to jazz it up a bit,' she said. 'What with Stuey and that. But you?'

The families pushed off and we stepped into their spot. A lion, of the Asian *Panthera leo persica* variety

228

(in case you wondered) paced to and fro across the dry bark floor of his geometrical home, marking out the same few feet of flat dust. His tiny amber eyes blinked slowly beneath quizzical eyebrows. His paws, huge flat and grey, had never needed to kill, never needed to hunt. He looked sad. A white beard, a little dangling saliva from a black lip, too tired and bored to lick it away in this confined heat.

'Oh I don't know, it just sounded better than over-weight, overdrawn, unemployed biology teacher, I suppose.'

'Oh hey now, don't be so rough on yourself,' Jenny said and she reached out and touched my upper arm, rubbing it softly like behind a cat's ear.

Heh-heyy.

Oh Charlie, for God's sake.

What? I couldn't help it. You have to understand, even at this point, middle-aged single parent or not, Jennifer was a remarkably sexy lady. Sexy in a rather clumsy and obvious way perhaps. In a way that really tends to annoy plain, intelligent women when their men go all dopey. As if responding to the obvious signals (legs, breasts, big eyes, blonde hair etc) was a sign of idiocy or ignorance.

In fact while we're on the subject let me just put this one to rest. Sexual tastes, what rings our bell, lights our fire, double-clicks our mouse, whatever – is in no way linked to general intelligence. It isn't. Okay? If a man finds whopping great jugs, an invisible waist, long eyelashes, pouty red lips and long shapely legs a turn-on, this does not make him stupid. He might become a drooling loon when exposed to two or more of these attributes, but it doesn't mean he's an idiot. These are signals developed over hundreds of thousands of years to illustrate youth and fertility. They work and we exist because guys like them. What can I say — Einstein used to write for *Playboy*. I rest my case.

Well all right, he didn't. But he could have if he'd wanted to. Look, we're getting off the point.

Standing there with Jennifer by the lions that afternoon did put a few things in perspective. When it comes to surrogacy, human males are pretty bad news. Now as bad news goes, we're not as shocking as the banner tabloid headline behaviour of, say, these Asian lions. But we're somewhere on page six with an artist's reconstruction of the courtroom scene.

A lion, such as this specimen in front of us, when entering a new territory that it wishes to stake as its own, and faced with the young cubs of others, will often kill them. Simple as that. Lions are not at all interested in working and feeding and slaving 9 to 5 over a hot antelope carcass, just to keep some other lion's kids in square meals. No, if there are young ones to be looked after, they want them to be their own. So they won't think twice about killing and even eating another lion's young and getting the female pregnant all over again.

Nature, red in tooth and claw. Thoroughly despicable, *yeah yeah yeah*.

It makes perfect sense for them to do this of course. An animal that invests time and energy in another's young is an animal whose genes aren't going to get very far. Surrogate parents have no blood link, no genetic ties to their kids — which is why children in their charge are in such danger.

And why Jennifer is having so many bad dates.

She had her neck craned over the sign on the wall by the glass. A little map with a shaded area told her where these particular beasts were from, her eyebrows knitted slightly with interest.

'Apparently, unlike the African lions, these ones only really socialise to mate.' She nodded to herself.

She was great. Good company, very attractive. And she had that fight to her that had appealed to me so much that afternoon in Douglas's office.

But downside, she had nature sitting on top of her, pinning her soft freckled shoulders to the canvas, shouting *Men, please return to your homes, nothing to see here, please, nothing to see here.* Her little Stuart was screening all calls.

From fairy stories to true-crime reconstructions — stepfathers and stepmothers are wicked. Wicked to an extent that natural parents could never dream. They might as well have *fee-fi-foe-fum* written on the backs of their jackets.

Because the nature that governs the behaviour of the lion has the same interests, the same ends in mind for us.

She turned to me and smiled. She knew this wasn't going anywhere. She knew she'd end up chalking this harmless afternoon, another harmless afternoon, up to experience. I was another in a long queue of guys who had no desire or urge to waste valuable hunter-gatherer time rearing another man's child. She would have to battle on without my help.

As, it dawned on me slowly, all women would.

Of course.

For what was this plan of mine but a single-minded tunnel vision attempt to create a legion of Jennifer Tylers? Hundreds of single parents, each one wooed into submission by a heady cocktail of cheap wine and some fancy talk of architectural prowess. Only to be deserted, left wandering shopping centres and dusty playgrounds with little ones. I mean, yes they'd be mine, every one of them. A tiny package of Charles Ellis, ready to grow up and spread his tiny genes and fly away.

But who would take care of him? A single mother? What if she went looking for support in the lonely hearts columns? The evidence was standing next to me in a denim miniskirt. This wasn't right. I'd had a lucky escape.

I needed a new tack.

And I needed Adrian to appear and get me out of this one.

I checked my watch. Almost two o'clock.

'So, Jen.' I said. 'You want to keep going? We could go and see if the penguins are about?'

EIGHTEEN

'How does that poem go?
They tuck you up, your mum and dad.'

Hugh Laurie

There they were, a family so nuclear they'd have to be buried in a lead-lined mausoleum and dumped at the bottom of the ocean. They stood among the clustering crowds at the penguin pool. A large flat Bauhausian structure, it banked and swooped with German precision as penguins slapped and jumped and splashed. Every dive and slip a cheer from the crowd.

Adrian stood, the proudest of proud fathers, all Barbour jacket and Timberlands; Liz in (shiver) the same and, in a three-wheeled pushalong buggy straight out of Brands Hatch, tiny George, cocooned in polythene, dozing contentedly.

'Hey up!' Adrian hollered with a wave, 'look who it isn't. Uncle Charlie, fancy that.'

He and Liz flashed a quick look at each other. A glitch in an otherwise Oscarworthy performance. Adrian had been told two o'clock sharp. I hadn't explained why. But as I approached with Jenny, I could see him feverishly scribble various equations on his mental blackboard. Plus entirely fail in unclamping his eyes from Jenny's legs.

'Gosh kids, what a surprise! What're you doing here?' Perhaps not De Niro, but at least *Man in Shop #3* from *The Bill*. Jenny seemed none the wiser anyway. We came to a stop and circled the buggy. Children were pointing and whooping as a beardy keeper tossed out stinking fish from a green bucket and the penguins dived into the rippling turquoise.

'Oh just getting out of the house,' Liz explained, brushing a fringe from her eyes. 'You all right? Haven't been over for a while.'

'Yes yes, I'm grand. Never better. How's the little one?' and I motioned to the squidgy bundle of clothes, blankets and milky sweetness. A small circle of mist expanded and retracted on the inside of the plastic hood as George breathed his hot baby breath.

'Oh he couldn't be better,' Adrian said. 'Still early days of course and we're not counting our chickens. Apparently it's okay that he wasn't able to make a comment about his

235

bedroom. The Harley Street specialist said we were probably hoping for a bit too much there.'

'We're not out of the woods, though,' Liz said firmly, the tiniest hint of a scowl twitching behind an eye. 'I mean, we've sent a nappy sample to Middlesex University to see if they can tell us anything about the smell and they've said it will be a good six months before they'll have time to look at it.'

'They were a bit sarcastic about the whole thing to tell you the truth, weren't they, hon?' Adrian said, slipping an arm around Liz with a soft squeeze.

'We're taking each day at a time.'

'Right, right.' I nodded. Christ, it was getting worse by the day. I mean, parents are meant to have strong protective instincts but y'know. There's such a thing as *too far*.

Adrian looked over at Jennifer and smiled with a half nod. Liz did likewise.

'Sorry,' she said eventually. 'He has no manners. I'm Liz.'

There was a few seconds of hand pumping and general hi-how-are-you-ing.

'S-sorry, this is Jennifer.'

'Jenny,' she corrected, hoisting her bag up onto her shoulder self-consciously.

'Jenny. Right yes. We're, er . . .' She looked at me.

Well I mean really, what's the standard term here, hmm? We're what? Friends? Well Liz will ping down that particular tin duck in a pecosecond. If I'd known a girl called Jenny for longer than an hour, Adrian would have met her, Brad would have asked her what she thought of *Under Siege 2* and Liz would have taken her discreetly to one side during coffee and apologized to her for the three of us. So really, I had only one choice.

I would have to tell them the truth, that she was a woman I had met through the personals columns of Thursday's *Evening Standard*. Charlie Ellis, International Man of Methodicalness.

'We, er, Jenny is . . . we're kind of . . .'

Time began to pass a little more slowly than it had been doing up until this point.

'. . . like-minded individuals.'

Best I could do. Sorry.

Fortunately, Jenny laughed unattractively causing me to carefully examine a Toffee Crisp wrapper on the floor for about six weeks, face burning wildly.

'We're kind of on a date thing,' she said.

Why didn't I think of that?

Ade and Liz nodded, throwing two pairs of conspiratorial eyebrows at me to look after.

'How's Brad?' I asked, tossing the eyebrows back with an extra pair for them to juggle. 'Seen him recently? Or . . . anyone?'

I don't know why I was asking, I didn't expect the truth. I'd pictured the four of them together, over and over. An opulent dining room lit by tall white candles.

Ade pouring expensive wine into huge glasses, Liz dishing out something creative with pesto, Brad finishing some hilarious anecdote and Deborah laughing — throwing her head back and revealing a slim white throat. Probably placing a hand on Brad's thigh to show just how fucking funny he was.

I don't know why I took time to think these things. Easier than nailing spikes into my eyes, I suppose.

'No.' Adrian said. 'Not for a bit. He's coming to dinner tomorrow night. Maybe,' Adrian covered carefully.

How marvellous.

'Oh,' Liz said, surprised. 'Are they back?'

'Back?' I said and the earth stopped with a screeching lurch, causing ideas, posits, feelings and rationality to tumble from the luggage racks and spill out all over the floor.

'He went to, er . . .' Adrian began, '. . . some film convention.'

Which was (phew!) fine and I exhaled. Or rather would have done if, simultaneously, Liz hadn't said 'They went to her parents'.'

During the pause that followed this revelation, a number of things must have occurred. Behind me, away from my field of vision, a small BBC Outside Broadcast crew, cameras, booms, dollies etc. must have wandered past holding open auditions for *Playschool* presenters.

Because Liz went —

238

'Doh lickle Georgie a bit of a sleepy patch, den? Dawww, so coot. Shall we go and find da ponies? Shall we? Shall we then? Yeeeeees!'

— all of a sudden.

'You want to come for a walk, Jenny? Leave these two for a bit?'

'Nahh, I'd better be headin' off myself. Go and see what kind of state Stuey's left the house in.' She turned and gave me a dry peck. I tried to contain the white-hot explosive pressure that Liz's slip had caused behind my eyes which now smouldered from magma to smoking igneous rock. But apparently not very well.

'I'll walk wiv' you, though,' Jenny said with a nervous smile, and the pair of them fucked off sharpish.

So. They'd reached the *bringing home to mummy* stage?

Okay fine. There's no law against it. They're both single, they're both over twenty-one, or over sixteen or past nine p.m. or whatever the fuck you have to be in this country. She was taking the moving-on process very seriously. Wasn't I trying to do just that? What was Jenny, chopped liver?

No, fuck it, I wouldn't get annoyed. I wouldn't let myself get annoyed. If anything, I should be pleased for her. She's doing what she's told; she's obeying her

instincts. She might not know she is. In fact, thinking
back, she probably wouldn't even care that she was:

Turn the light out, hon.

H-huh! That's amazing!

What?

This, this book.

What are you reading now?

The Origin of Virtue. *Matt Ridley.*

Again?

Yeah. Listen. The queen ant . . .

I'm trying to sleep, hon.

Sorry. I just think it's interesting, that's all.

Uhgnn.

Don't you think?

Zzzzzzz.

Are you asleep?

Zzzzzzz.

Deborah?

Shut the fuck up!

and so on.

But obeying her instincts she is. She's twenty-nine.
Twenty-nine and childless. Twenty-nine and childless
isn't that worrying, not really, not unless you're
planning on breaking the British Record for reproduction (forty-two, in case you were wondering).
Twenty-nine and childless is just dandy in a Bridget
Jonesy Ally McBeally kind of way. But if you're
genuinely concerned about the continuation of your

genetic lineage, you wouldn't want to be twenty-nine, childless and *single*. Ooh no, that's a whole other womb game.

Ade and I stood watching the birds for a while (the penguins, I mean) as they slipped and waddled about their stark enclosure. They gathered, chatting around the feeding bucket like eager children at an ice-cream van, their excitable quacks slapping an echo against the wet tiles.

'She seems like a . . . like-minded individual,' Adrian said. And then laughed inappropriately for about a year.

'Fuck off,' I reposted, making a mental note to stick a bookmark in my E.O. Wilson and read some Oscar Wilde when I got home.

I explained in detail how we met, leaving out the *why* entirely.

'And I was your escape plan? Glad to be of service.'

'So how *is* Brad?'

'Hn?' Adrian grunted absently.

Which was a giveaway the size of the British Library because Adrian has an auricular cavity to rival a vampire bat.

Which sounds rude, but isn't.

'What's happened? Him and Deborah, what's happened?'

'Hn?' he said again, panic flashing across his eyes like

241

it was a new soft drink being advertised on Piccadilly Circus.

'Tell me!' I yelled. Loudly enough for a load of *Psittaciformes*, sensing a domestic, to squawk off with a coarse flap like someone giving the tent from the garage a good shake out.

'Look, don't beat yourself up over this, there's nothing going on. Don't be thick.'

Well he would say that, wouldn't he?

'Well you would say that wouldn't you?'

'Yes,' he said, turning to face me and shoving his hands deep into his jacket pockets. 'I would say that. Because I'm your mate and it's true. Now stop being such an arse and let's go and get a drink or something,' and he began to wander off.

'Do you want to find Liz? Tell her where we are?'

He grabbed at some long grass by the ducks as he walked away, snapping off a handful idly. 'Oh she'll find us,' and he disappeared behind the trees.

'God, there you are,' Liz called, pushing and bouncing the buggy across the hot tarmac in front of her, her face a little flushed, fringe in her eyes. 'What have I told you two about wandering off?'

'Sorry, Mum,' Adrian and I chanted together, sharing a surreptitious smirk.

We were back under the Britvics. I sipped a warm

242

Coke, Adrian slouched, his boot up on another chair, tearing up scraps of his BLT and tossing them at the skittering pigeons at our feet.

He'd been wanting to say something. But being a guy, he wasn't going to serve it up immediately. So he made me munch through a dull starter about how his shed was looking. He'd just got to the point of clearing away the conversational plates and looking up in a *But what I really wanted to say was* way when Liz had rattled over.

She dragged over another plastic chair from an adjacent table while Adrian began unclipping, clicking and snapping the web of belts and braces and straps that pinned tiny George to his chariot of sire.

'How's the job-hunting going?' he asked. 'Know what you're going to do with your life yet?' He lifted the almost weightless bundle which Liz instinctively held out her arms for.

'He's all right,' he protested. 'I was just going to . . .'

'Give him to me. You finish your drink.'

And so he was passed to his mother for sheltering and cradling.

'I've got some ideas,' I said.

'Still looking for happiness?' he smirked.

'As much as the next man.'

'Hmmm. The next man normally doesn't feel the need to do a twenty-page survey on the subject.'

'Maybe that's why the next man is so unhappy?'

'Maybe that's why you're a smug git?'

'Up your bum.'

'Your mother.'

'Would you two stop it?'

Ade and I shared a grin laden with male status context. Mine managed to hum, 'Under Your Thumb' by Godley & Creme; Adrian's subtly hinted that, if Liz wasn't around, he'd whip my sorry 'ass' with some filthy parental-based cursing.

Liz looked up from George.

'Hon, have you got the wipes?' There was a brief fuss as Adrian fished around for a tube of moistened towels to dab a microscopic piece of spit from George's mouth with the care of a microsurgeon.

'Jenny seemed very nice,' she said, balling up her tissue. 'Said you taught her son or something?'

I nodded.

'He was a disruptive little fucker. But no, you're right. She's not bad.'

'Said you probably wouldn't see each other again, though?'

Oh. Had she? Well that saved me a tricky phone call, I suppose. She'd either picked up on my vibes and sensed I wasn't interested in the long haul.

. . . or she just didn't fancy me . . .

Whichever it was, it left me at a loose end, dangling awkwardly. My new plan of stripping away life down to the biological basics had hit a definite snagola if I was going to get all antsy over the plight of the single mother. There must be a solution, though.

'Probably for the best,' Adrian said. Liz was rocking George cautiously to and fro, touching noses. Little bubbles appeared at his mouth. 'Kids are a handful at any age.' And he flashed me a look.

'Have you got his Tigger there?' Liz asked suddenly.

'Oh, er . . .' He patted down his jacket pockets. 'Shit.'

'Oh Adrian *really*.' Liz explained to me. 'He likes his Tigger at lunchtime . . .'

'Yes yes, I see,' I lied.

'It's all right, he's in the car. I'll get him,' and Adrian stood up quickly.

'I'll come with you, mate.' I stood up and put a hand on Liz's shoulder. 'Best be off.'

'See you, Charlie. Don't be long now, hon',' Liz said over our shoulders as we walked past the spraying fountain towards the car park. I just caught a murmur from behind. 'Isn't Daddy a dopey-head, eh? Yes he is! A silly Jilly! Forgetting Mister Tigger Wigger!' she explained to the little one.

'Left him in the carky-parky, Adey-Wadey?' I asked, receiving a thumpy-wumpy on the army-warmy for my troubley-woubley.

NINETEEN

$$\text{`}\omega\Delta z = Cov\ (\omega,z) = \beta_w z_{vz}\text{'}$$

George Price (1923–1974)

Heading car-park-wards, Adrian and I followed a rather splendid set of buttocks for a minute or two in silence.

Guys will do this. Drift off independently of each other, eyes and groin drawn by a revealing cleavage or an appealing thigh. Conversation will halt and a warm electric silence will descend. Sometimes, after the object of desire has swum from their purview, they may be moved to share a comment, a brief artistic appreciation along the lines of a sliced-meat *Mmmmm*. Or perhaps the more sophisticated *Hubba hubba*. And then, like as not, the world will start up once again slowly and they will return to their discussion of Ford Mondeos without another word.

This particular distraction pulled out in front of us near the reptile house and we both spent an idle few moments watching it. A petite figure, a nimble little sashay, a blue denim jacket and a short summery frock. Until the owner, and simultaneously her buttocks, stopped suddenly and turned round. Adrian quickly craned his neck up to the sky in embarrassed self-consciousness to examine a particularly gripping cumulonimbus, while I ran through forty-six confusing emotions at once.

'Wendy?'

'Hello, Charlie.' She smiled and the sun came out. And I can't at this stage say these two things were totally unrelated. 'I thought I heard your voice, how are you?'

'I-I'm good. Good.' I nodded. Crikey she scrubbed up a treat. She had obviously just finished for the day and shed her outer layer of grubby work gear. But despite losing the polo shirt and the Doc Martens, she still had an appealing earthy outdoor freshness to her. I wondered for a second what fabric conditioner she might use. 'Sorry, this is an old school-friend of mine. Adrian, this is Wendy.'

Adrian nodded a hello and we stood in silence for a second.

'Great frock,' Adrian said quickly, causing Wendy to

pull at it a little bit like an awkward bridesmaid and flash a nervous smile.

'Yes,' I leapt in. 'You look very . . .'

Wendy met my gaze.

'. . . very, er, you look very different.'

Feeble, I know.

'Oh. Thank you,' she said, smiling again, brushing hair from her eyes. 'You walking this way?' She jestured towards the exit.

'Mm!' Adrian nodded and, yanking me errant-adolescent-style by the elbow, we followed her bouncily out towards the turnstiles. Stupid of me, I know. I should have asked her to hold on, of course. Just to give us five minutes so we could pop to the gift shop. That way I could have purchased some bold, primary coloured flash-cards for Adrian to use. You know the sort. With words like CAT and ELEPHANT and OVER-FUCKING-DOING-IT and ER-HELLO?-SUBTLTY? on them.

Just a thought.

'So, Wendy, you off to see your boyfriend?' Adrian began, bouncing along like he was Davina McCall after twelve particularly sugary doughnuts. 'Or your husband or something?'

'No no,' Wendy said with a, er, gentle grin. Or beam. Or . . . something.

(Oh look, while I've got you here I might as well explain. My thesaurus and I are eventually going to run out of ways of saying *she said with a smile* so here's a thought. Just take it from me that Wendy is the rare but incredibly attractive type of person who is innocently surprised and pleasantly amused by the world around her and never really does anything but look enormously happy. All the time. Okay? Great, I appreciate it. It'll be better in the long run, trust me.)

'I'm meeting some girlfriends a bit later, that's all. Actually,' and we stopped on the street, 'what time have you got?' She pulled back her denim jacket sleeve and revealed a loose Swatch that hung from her slim wrist. A couple of fair hairs curled affectionately around the strap.

'About three thirty-ish,' Adrian offered. Wendy *hmmed*. 'Why? Are you late?'

'Early,' she said.

I threw myself suddenly stumbling forward into her, spasmodically, like Norman Wisdom. Or so she thought anyway.

'Ade?' I hissed, pushing his hand from my back, 'what are you trying –'

'Charlie'll keep you company. He's sod all to do now he's single, have you, mate?'

I looked at Wendy and sighed, trying to show *Tch! Cor dear, friends eh? Really. Just ignore him. Tch!* with my left eyebrow. And *Although I s'pose technically I don't have anything to do and that really is a nice dress and with your hair up like that, well, go on, what've you got to lose?* with the right one. A mite ambitious for eyebrows, some may say.

'Well.' Wendy straightened herself in her dress a little (with a smile, don't forget). 'If you don't mind. . . ?'

Just call me, dan da-daaaaah – Captain Eyebrows.

'What are you reading?' I asked.

Wendy stopped rummaging for a purse and tugged the paperback from her bag that was getting in the way and placed it on the pub trestle-top where we were perched. I gave it the once-over eagerly, it looking not only right up my street, but up my drive, indoors and putting its feet up with a cuppa.

'I haven't seen this one,' I said, flipping it over to read the back.

'I've only just started it,' Wendy said, re-emerging from her bag with a plain leather purse. 'Now, what are you having?'

She disappeared inside to get us some drinks and I flicked through briefly to where a crumpled postcard marked a page near the front. The card was from Kenya, from someone called Chris who was apparently having a 'bonkers' time and 'missing her like crazy'. It was unclear from the handwriting whether the 'bonkers' Chris was missing Wendy in a flatmatey way, or in a dangly-toilet-bits way. I closed the book and took a deep breath and concentrated on who my heart was hoping this guy was. I thought about him watching telly with Wendy in a small London flat, him in an armchair, her on the sofa flicking through a magazine. That seemed fine. No increase in blood pressure. So I contrasted this by trying to picture Wendy perhaps naked. Perhaps with this bloke nearby.

I felt my brow furrow involuntarily. Oooh no. Didn't like that at all. I tried the same picture with a more 'bonkers' male. Nope. Deely-boppers or not, it made me uncomfortable.

A bottle of beer appeared in front of me so I concentrated on that instead.

'Cheers,' she said, sitting down. We drank.

'Looks good,' I said, closing the book and placing it down. It was *The Darwin Wars* by Andrew Brown and had a picture of the old beardy genius himself gracing the dog-eared cover. 'What's the gist?'

'Oh I don't know really,' she said picking it up. 'I just liked the look of it. The beginning's good, though. About this biologist guy, George Price,' and she bent back the spine to her postcard. 'He killed himself. And on my birthday of all days.'

'Wasn't there any cake left?'

'No, my mum caught him fidgeting at musical statues and he took it very badly,' Wendy countered without missing a beat. We shared dopcy smirks. 'In 1974. He was living in a one-room squat sort of thing. Not far from here actually. Euston way. He was doing this theoretical research into human behaviour.'

'Uh-huh?' I liked the guy already.

'He came up with this equation — here look,' and Wendy turned the book around. There was a confusing mess o'algebra splashed across the page like Eddie Izzard was trying to play Scrabble during an earthquake. I nodded. Don't know why, made fuck all sense as far as I was concerned. I guess I wanted to make the new teacher feel welcome.

'It means, apparently,' and she picked up the book again, 'hold on it's here somewhere . . .'

I watched her flick through with enthusiasm. I caught myself hoping that bonkers Chris was her brother.

'Here we go. This apparently proves that good behaviour — kind, generous actions — does occur between animals. But, and this was his point, there is nothing to be gained by it. Only by egotistical, selfish, self-serving behaviour that gets ones genes into the next generation.'

This all sounded familiar.

'Which means that kindness in human beings is ultimately limited. And our *evil* side if you like, our selfish cruel side will always be with us. You can't get rid of it.'

'I can see why you invited him to your party. He sounds like heaps of laughs.'

'Well,' she said. 'Interesting, though, don't you think?' and she closed the book and, apparently, the subject, and slid them both to one side. She sipped her beer and we sat in the afternoon quiet for a while. The while lasted a beat too long for the pair of us and we both started talking at once. I let her go first.

'Sorry, I was just going to ask how you were bearing up?' Wendy eased herself out of her denim jacket revealing two sun ripened shoulders, causing the Chris Bonkers of my imagination to fall down a mine-shaft to a horrible death.

'Bearing up?'

'You said your girlfriend and your best friend . . . ? Sorry.' She pinked slightly. 'If you'd rather not . . .'

'No no, that's fine. I'm, well . . .' I got a bit shruggy and sighed. 'I'm doing okay. Getting back out there, meeting people, y'know? Just easing myself back in.'

'Have you heard from her? Has she called or anything?'

'No,' I said. 'Not a peep.' Wendy tilted her head a little, thoughtfully, and nodded.

'And how are you finding the game?'

'The *game*?' I queried.

'Being back out there. *Dating*, if you want to call it that. Are you enjoying it?'

I thought back to my lonely-hearts experiences.

'It's been an education. You could say I'm learning a lot.'

'I can imagine.'

And an edgy silence descended once again. This was becoming something of a motif, these quiet bits. They weren't comfy Sunday silences. Not easy late-night bedside-lamp reading silences. These were heavy pauses loaded with apprehension and nerves. They were, if I wasn't too much mistaken, firsty-datey sort of silences. We shared another in a short queue of quick smiles and examined our drinks a bit.

'What were you going to say?' Wendy started. 'Before?'

'Hn? Oh, I was uhm, I was just going to say that whassisname, George Price. In your book. How would his theory explain, oh I don't know. Say . . . that,' and I flicked the corner of Wendy's bookmark with a thwup. 'Postcards seem like pretty altruistic acts to me. No-one ever postcarded their way into anyone's knickers, as far as I know.'

Yes I know this was a painfully transparent way of finding out who this Chris character was, while also bringing the conversation around to graze awhile on a safer turf. But I had a feeling. That's all. And perhaps a small hope.

'Well quite,' Wendy said. 'It is a pretty bleak outlook on life. And yes, I suppose it doesn't take these things into account. Postcards and birthday presents and things like that. He's just a nice person, I suppose.'

'Yeah, right exactly.' I nodded, egging her on a little. I took a swig of beer and hoped she'd want to fill the pause.

'I mean, Chris and I, oh that's the guy who sent me the card . . .'

Bingo.

'. . . we've always just kept in touch. We kind of have, or had, an on-off thing for a while. It's a bit complicated –'

Arse.

'We're going to try and just be friends. But that's just like him. He's got no ulterior motives. He's just being nice.'

The sun came out again and I got a bit cross with nature for her misjudged symbolism-for-the-hard-of-hearing routine. So this guy was a long-term crush. Which meant what exactly? I mean, come on, what the hell was I getting so jumpy and cross about? What did I think this was? Where did I think this was going? This wasn't a date, Wendy wasn't on my list, not on my battle plan at all in fact. And yet.

She was quite something. And I'm afraid I can't get much more specific than that. Not without 15ccs of sodium pentathol and a magnifying glass, anyway. Even though I hadn't factored her into any of my equations, Wendy's romantic revelation was encouraging vaguely adolescent behaviour in my heart. It was misbehaving noisily behind my ribs, passing dirty notes to my stomach and generally disrupting the class.

'You must have friends like that, though?' Wendy asked. 'Everyone does. Not in it for anything, I mean. Just nice people.'

'Well I thought I did,' I said.

'Oh,' Wendy said. 'I'm sorry. Gosh I'm putting my foot in it, I didn't mean to bring it up . . .'

'It's fine really.' I held up my hand and let it drop. It landed on hers lightly and she pulled her hand away quickly. And then realised she'd done it a little too quickly and put it back on the trestle top. Near mine.

'Do you miss her?' she asked.

Lordy, where the hell was this going?

'Uhm,' I said dopily and thought about it. It probably looked a bit calculating and blokey to Wendy — as if I was working on a response. As if I was analyzing the handy-touchy moment and measuring what the best thing to say would be to get a repeat of this tactility. And that was why she probably thought I wasn't just immediately nodding.

But that wasn't the truth.

'I don't know,' I said finally. 'I . . .' and I trailed off a bit.

'Sorry,' she said again and touched my fingertips. Leaving her hand just resting there. A small hand. Pale. There was a little bit of the zoo under her fingernail.

'This is going to sound terrible but I haven't thought about her that much. Not in the last few weeks anyway. I mean, obviously from time to time. But,' and I let out a deep breath. 'But yes.' Something large got caught in my throat and I swallowed hard to no difference whatsoever. 'Yes I do miss her.'

And it was true. For all my talk of masochistic

dinner-party pesto fantasies. And even learning of Debs and Brad at her parents' house. She wasn't part of my consciousness like she used to be. My mind had simply been focusing on other things. But sitting there in the sunshine with Wendy, her hand on mine, I let Deborah back in for a wander around the stark gallery of my head once again. Walking among the theorems and equations.

'You know what I miss? I miss *missing her*. If that makes any sense.'

Wendy closed her eyes and nodded with what looked like familiarity.

'I spent weeks thinking about her, after she left. Weeks with that dull ache, staring at photos and forgetting to eat. And then slowly that went away. And now, sitting here, I'm not sure if I'm pining for her, or if I'm just missing those feelings. Missing feelings that intense. Because I don't feel anything much. Not like I used to.'

'And seeing other people hasn't helped?'

'Erm.' I thought about it. 'No. No not really. I don't think so.'

'Maybe it's too soon,' Wendy said. 'You probably don't want to hear this. But . . . but maybe she's still the one, still a huge part of you. And forcing her out is just making things worse. I don't know. Maybe you should be trying to think of her more, rather than less. Maybe.'

Memories and thoughts began crashing around my

ears. Wendy had a point there. Maybe I was missing something. Maybe this was the answer.

'I saw you both that first time. When you came on that school trip. I figured you were on a first date.'

'Yeah?'

'You could just tell. The way you were together. But it was confusing. I thought . . . oh listen to me, forget it,' and she shook her head.

'No, go on.'

'It's the lunchtime beer. It's just,' and she took her hand away and gripped her beer bottle, focusing hard on it like a magician's volunteer making sure it didn't vanish. 'I kept seeing you over and over, coming to visit Jeremiah, and I didn't understand it. Because every time you turned up, it was like your first date. You both talked and laughed and cuddled and I couldn't get the dynamic. It was as if those early flushes weren't wearing off like they do for everyone else. Like Chris and mine did.'

I thought about this.

'I was quite jealous to tell you the truth. I imagined the pair of you clucking over your first baby like a couple of proud . . . oh I don't know. Don't listen to me.'

But I was listening to her.

Very closely. I was.

TWENTY

'People are interested in birds only inasmuch as they exhibit human behaviour'

Douglas Coupland

Now monogamy, there's a dirty word. Or so we have been led to believe. Although, surprisingly, it doesn't actually appear in my Dictionary of Profanity. *Mooning* and *Motherfucker* are happily affianced without a pair-bonding term betwixt them.

But you'd think, in the land of Darwin, survival of the fittest, adaptation, mutation, nature red in tooth and claw and so on, there wouldn't be much call for standin' by your woman (once you've stopped lyin' underneath her, I mean). Surely, mathematically, you want to be moving on. Sowing the seed of love, so to speak. Not sitting at home wasting valuable todger time watching the Teletubbies and hanging Maisy Mouse mobiles above cots. You might think that nature frowneth upon the strangely Catholic idea of pair-bonding for life.

Well it's not that simple. There are advantages to that too, it turns out, as I discovered that very afternoon.

Wendy had drained her beer and left to go and meet her friends. She gave me a peck on the cheek and a hand squeeze and left me sitting alone on the bench with my thoughts.

I liked her a lot. I liked her hair, her clothes, her smell. She did something to me, to my insides. Something I liked. Her and Chris Bonkers would work something out. They were bound to. She was just too darn nice to stay single for any length of time. He'd come back, they'd meet at the airport and she'd be making post-sex toast and Marmite in a My-Boyfriend-Went-To-Kenya-And-All-He-Got-Me-Was-This-Lousy-T-shirt T-shirt before the autumn was out.

As for me, I drained my drink and headed west. Wendy had given me an idea.

There are two types of library in the world, and Marylebone public library on Porchester Road, London

W2, is definitely one of them. Not for the residents of Paddington the shiny chrome Philip Starck look. Computers and other such technology are present but, like the rickety wire spinner with the VIDEOS AVAILABLE ON REQUEST sign, handwritten with venom and spite, they feel rather tacked on. There's a dark respectful creak as the oak doors are pushed open and, what with the polished floor and stained glass, they've no need for QUIET PLEASE signs — it's just an automatic reverence like you're in church or an art-house cinema foyer.

The building itself is actually said to be haunted. Every seventy-five years, a spectral white-haired figure is said to float silently among the shelves and tables, her face a deathly pallor, her eyes blank and hollow.

Fortunately when I arrived, they'd given her a job on the information desk.

'Sorry, excuse me.'

She lifted her head slowly and looked me up and down.

'Yes, er, hi. Natural History?'

After two hours in the company of some weighty encyclopedias, I had my answers.

Out, across the road and left, up to Royal Oak tube station. Eastbound Hammersmith and City Line to Baker Street. As the train rattled and swung through the brittle landscapes of palettes and industrial estates that lean against each other to make up Paddington and Edgware Road, I thought about our friends the macaws. Their mating instincts are the mirror opposite of that of chimps and bonobos. Where old PG Tips Face would be happy to wander about the place, poking his nose and other pokable appendages into females' business, going for quantity rather than quality, so to speak, your male bird takes a different view. Once he's mated, the deed is done and the eggs are laid, he sticks to her like an old cornflake to porcelain. He ain't goin' nowhere.

And why? Well look at this lot.

Stepping off the train at Baker Street, into that Victorian half-light of the Circle Line platforms, a young mother was struggling with her double buggy. She panted a harassed set of thankyous through an unbrushed fringe as I helped her off. Two children, barely eight months old, were strapped slightly into the chairs – as if at any moment Houston might finish the countdown and fire them off into the stratosphere. And, causing most of the trouble, a young girl pulled and strained, finally breaking free to twirl and spin with glee on the crowded platform.

Your tropical bird would be halfway through a rather stiff letter to Esther Rantzen if he caught a glimpsette of this lot, believe me.

You see, a tropical bird's young, either in handy to-go egg form or as your cheepy fluffy kind, are your basic foodstuff of a number of predators. One-parent families simply don't stand a chance in hell. The mother (let's presume for the sake of avoiding a tedious sixth-form debate) has to nick off and find some worms. But when she does, like as not, there will be nowt but a nest of shattered shell and yokey nastiness upon her return. Which is very bad news for the mother and father, genes-wise.

Obviously also not that great a revelation for the chick who, presumably, would rather have had the chance to develop into something rather than a 'McMuffin', but that's by-the-by.

So Daddy stays. Does the gathering of worms and such, leaving Mummy to stay home and play house. And indeed vice versa. Yeah, right-on.

Point is, newborn children are very fragile indeed.

And this little one, all pink party-shoes and bunches, was going to end up under a train if her mother wasn't too careful. She spun dizzily and bumped into me.

'Whoopsie, there we go. Shall we go and find Mummy?' I said.

'The twins are getting haircuts,' she said forth-rightly, as if this answered all the questions in the universe. Well, it probably answered all the questions in hers.

'That's marvellous,' I said. 'Not you, though?'

'Dad drank my 'effing haircut,' she said, twirly twirly twirl twirl, and back to her mother, narrowly missing, oblivious to the world's heart-seizing terror, being liquidised by an eastbound Circle Line train and spread generously between here and King's Cross.

When your young are this much at risk, that is to say, when your whole potential genetic lineage hangs in such a fragile balance, your species either develops a nurturing instinct sharpish or it doesn't get many invitations to grandsons' birthday parties. It's that simple.

Little human types weren't always in such jeopardy. But one of the downsides of our evolution was that as we developed and advanced, walking more and more erect, the female's pelvis naturally narrowed over time. Thus slimming down the birth canal. But this, combined with babies' heads getting larger, meant that a full pregnancy term was going to cause some major tailbacks uterus-wise. Which goes some way to explain why human babies are born much more prematurely than your other primates. Premature and, to all intents and purposes, just warm, pink, wriggly lunch-to-go for your Savannah predator.

So the genes that encouraged the stronger parental instinct flourished.

Which is why I decided to try another tack.

TWENTY-ONE

*'I never speak behind people's backs. If I've anything
nasty to say — I pop it on a postcard.'*

Victoria Wood

Up and out into the fresh air of Swiss Cottage once
again, I kept my head down in case George Lazenby
should come skiing over the pub roof pursued by
balaclava'd machine-gun-toting meanies.

Fortunately Blofeld must have had them all in mufti,
hollowing out a volcano somewhere in the Pacific, so I
just nipped over Northway's Parade, into W. H. Smith's
and the colourful rhyming grin of the greetings cards.

Every possible anniversary and celebration has been
covered, it would seem. From the vibrant primarys of
Birthdays and Good Lucks to the crisp white solemnity

of the Communions and Christenings. Between which sits the watercolour wishy-washyness of numerous woodland folk hoping I'll be happy in my new job. And one or two hilarious ones which invited me to poke a finger through only to find out that from the inside, (dohhhh! Slap-forehead) it looks ever so slightly . . . nothing like a penis.

How clever.

But neither weeping hedgehogs with waggly genitalia nor Thomas the Tank Engine magnets seemed to convey the message I was looking for. Surely it wouldn't take Purple Ronnie long . . . ?

*Sometimes in staffrooms after school the teachers get
    quite flirty
They rub each other's squidgy bits and tummies go
    all squirty.
If they get caught their cheeks go red and suddenly
    they're single.
Why can't they hold hands tight again and make
    each other tingle?*

Or along those lines anyway.

In desperation I fought my way past the crowd of students all flailing and drowning in irony as they tried to work out whether Tamsin was Little Miss Naughty or Wonder Woman, grabbed something fine-arty and got out of there.

*

I perched myself on the waffle-buttock lattice seating of the bus stop outside and sucked my biro.

Tricky.

I wanted Deborah back. Plain and simple. I wanted to go out with her again and to be her boyfriend and to fill a warm triple-chubbed, double-glazed house with hundreds of children.

See, I knew that my initial lonely-hearts plan wasn't going to work. Advertising my services, spreading myself about a bit — doing the bonobo thing; it was just too risky. Once my genes were out there, running free, jumping off climbing frames and scaling oak trees with Blytonesque topping larks, it was all out of my hands. The valuable nurturing and educating would have to be left to the mother. And by its very definition, the sort of insane, chunky-knitted, cat-loving hormonal loon who wanted to have a child by a total stranger in the first place.

I stared thoughtfully into the busy traffic for a moment, a stabbing panic at a future vision of what-could-have-been if I'd seen my first plan through: grubby, barefoot, jostick-ridden communes, sprouting up all over London as mothers – all called Womb Maiden and Soil Gusset — sat around burning tyres and singing. All united by the fact that each of their filthy Dickensian offspring had a podgy, middle-class biology teacher for a father.

Not that I would ever see this vision manifested of

course. Because I would have the CSA staking out my flat with an armoured tank division, shining in searchlights and lobbing grenades and heavily annotated copies of *The 60-Minute Father* over the fence.

A juggernaut rumbled past with Mothercare printed in three-foot letters on the side, the glass of the bus stop juddering around me, snapping me back to planet Earth.

No. New plan.

Genetic success would have to see me doing as the birds do. Finding a mate, producing the goods and staying around to make sure the infant grew up sexy, sturdy, strong and true.

So I had to get back with Deborah.

Whether she would have me back, of course, was another story.

To be honest, I was banking on Brad being rebound material, just Debs seeking solace in the arms of another. This little union wouldn't take much battering before its foundations collapsed. It just took the right attack, that's all.

I sucked my biro a bit more.

Dear Debs, I began.

Hi, it's me. Good good. Chatty informal. Presumptuous? Just *It's me*? Her graphology skills were never extraordinary.

Charlie, I added. Excellent. Then stuck some brackets around it, attempting to come over a bit (h-huh! Remember me?!) And then immediately wished I hadn't. Ah well.

Right now, where to go from here? Do I credit her with intelligence enough to know what the hell this is all about? Or is it worth dancing about the place with linguistic smokescreens about the weather and did-you-see-*EastEnders*-last-night-cor-dear-what-was-Pauline-wearing stuff? I mean, the moment she clocks the handwriting she's going to pick up the whiff of reconciliation. Maybe I should just do the honourable thing and come out with it.

Yes.

I miss you very much and want you back.

No. Fucky shit wank. I tore it in half and popped back into Smith's.

Another £1.49 and I was back on the bench.

Dear Deborah, hi. It's me, Charlie. No brackets this time.

I rattled the pen between my teeth for a while, running a few phrases past my internal editing team to see which ones got the red ink.

I hear you and Brad are no no no no no arsey arsey cunt toss.

The girl behind the counter at Smith's made a *'H-huh! Back again?'* face which I acknowledged with a shrug and I was back on the bench before the seat had time to cool.

Right. This time, last time, and no fannying about.

Dear Deborah, hi. It's me, Charlie. Call me.

Which was just about right. I looked it over a couple of times. Nope, pretty good. I sealed it in the envelope.

But not before I had completely fucked it up by adding *if you want to* in brackets at the bottom.

This time, I queued up and paid at the video section. I mean to say, I didn't want anyone thinking I was some kind of wierdo.

I was thinking about you the other day

Good, good. Nice and cool.

and I wondered if you wanted to get together for a chat.

Yeah, liked that. Not too pushy, not too blasé — clearly Charles has something on his mind that he wants to share.

Bit easy to ignore, though. Not exactly a great deal of urgency to it. I mean, I want her to feel wanted, for heaven's sake. I want her to know I want her back — I don't just want to get together and divide up the crockery.

Adrian told me you're seeing Brad. Hmmm, like it like it. Bit of guilt there. *Hope you know what you're doing.* Oooh yessssssss. Sow the seed of doubt. Not perfect. But enough to have her stuffing the card under a cushion if he walks in and looking at him in a slightly different light.

Splendid. Enough to be going on with.

Give me a call, your friend Cx.

*

I headed south and took a right opposite the shiny Odeon, down Hilgrove Road, past the low blocks that make up the estates' landscape where kids screeched and tore their BMXs over municipal London greenery, dead spider-plants and wheeless bikes jammed up the second-floor balconies. I swung a right at the bottom of the hill and I was at her door.

In the three-storied house, Deborah had the fourth storey. It was more like a wide shelf than a floor and had clearly come about through the original builders bringing nine-too-many bricks and not wanting to be stuck with them. It was a wide cream-coloured structure with black iron gates and steps up to the broad front door, each one sticky and spot varnished from the sap that leaked from the huge overhanging trees.

The rusty intercom with its crooked facia and cobwebby grill grinned out at me. Next to the buzzers, four names were sellotaped up, and there, at the top, was Deborah's.

The label was new. Printed out neatly on yellow paper from her mum's word-processor. Which meant one of three things. She wanted me banished from her life with such completeness that my handwriting wasn't even allowed to remain. (*Lordy, I hope not.*)

b) She had moved out, torn the label off, stayed with her mum, and then moved back in again. (*Lordy, I very much hope not.*)

Or finally, c) a council from the Tate Modern had

camped out on her doorstep for three weeks until the offending article, with its nasty sloping ascenders and scruffy unintelligible 'S's had been replaced with something more aesthetic.

Well, you see. Could be any of those, let's face it.

I was banking heavily on number three. As numbers one and two meant she was taking our break-up a little more seriously than I had first imagined.

I slammed the card through the brass spring-loaded rottweiler that doubles as a letter box, donating two fingertips to the *Feed the Doormat* campaign and mooched back down the crumbling white steps, down the path, round the fence and back onto the street.

And then immediately stepped back past the fence and back onto the path, grabbing at a shrub for support.

Because Deborah was coming down the street with Brad.

Shitty cock wank. I was trapped. I'm going to presume you're familiar with the phrase *fight or flight*. It's the reason your body suddenly runneth over with adrenaline in dangerous situations. A preservation mechanism. *Shit shit shit, we're under attack, energy levels increase now now now goddammit,* and everything in your body notches up to eleven and runs about – reflexes, heart rate, senses, blood. It stops you standing stock-still like a bewildered mannequin when a bus is aiming at your head or a lion is pouncing on your children. It's one of our species most valuable new refinements.

That's what it says in my book, anyhow. And I'm going to presume the book is now out of print, or at least a very very old edition. Because it makes no mention of what to do when a) *flight* is impossible due to, whoopsie, having fallen over a wheely bin; and b) *fight*, or a half-arsed attempt at it, is just going to get you arrested for unprovoked assault. Maybe the revised edition covers it. Must remember to look it up when I get home.

There was nowhere to hide in the front garden. I crouched behind the family of oily wheely bins, scuffing and scabbing about on my knees in panic. Their voices were becoming audible. They were laughing about something.

'I only told you to blow the bloody doors off,' I heard Brad reiterate for the too-manyeth-time and Deborah laughed like she'd never fucking heard it be-fucking-fore in her whole life, which was nonsense.

I said it about eight hundred times a day when we were going out.

But then she was happy to sit in her jogging bottoms, picking her feet and eating Coco Pops when we were going out too. And from what I could see through the hedge of her and Brad's cosy shopping soirée, neither Tony the Tiger, Honey Monster or any other character-based cereal was going to be featured on their table any time soon.

Harts the Grocers. French sticks. I mean, for God's sake, who do they think they are?

I backed further away into the shrubbery as they túrned into the driveway and up the path to the door, grinning like they were both chewing a radiator grill from a 1954 Chevy.

Don't turn round, I pleaded internally through every pore. *Don't turn round.*

'Well it's up to you, but I think it might help,' Brad continued.

'I don't know. Maybe you're right,' Deborah said, her keys jingling as she tried not to drop her bag of, oh I don't know, croissants and fucking strawberries or something.

'Say you'll think about it?' They pushed the door open and began to rustle through. 'My parents wouldn't mind another guest.'

What? I almost fell out of the bush as they disappeared inside.

'I don't want you to spend the holiday season withou— hey-up' — Brad crouched down — 'you've got a card here . . .'

Slam.

Arse.

Picking myself up, I hightailed it out of the bushes, managing to leave at least a bit of the bristling shrub behind, and nipped off sharpish back towards the station.

Holiday season? That's fucking Christmas in Britain, you Yankie-verballing titwit. Christmas? Debs round at

Brad's folks' for Christmas? She'll think about it?

Well, that settles it. Two alpha males. One female. Status battle for rights to her eggs.

There's only one thing for it.

TWENTY-TWO

'You can always count on a murderer for a fancy prose style.'

Vladimir Nabokov

Now there's a rather pendulous moral question that hangs precariously over that crazy little thing called murder.

At some very recent point in our development, here in the West, a lot of behatted gentlemen with handsome sideboards sat around in a room, surrounded by slightly smaller handsome sideboards, and decreed it so. Many of these fellows penned books on the very subject, books which are to be found padding out and stuffing Brad's Philosophy section. Anyone caught with their hand on the blunter end of a knife while the sharper, business end punctures valuable living equipment is a very naughty boy indeed and to be locked away for a long time. Likewise anyone with the non-risky end of a gun, rope, lead pipe and other such Cluedo ephemera.

Murder, a very bad thing indeed – pretty much a universal opinion.

However.

It goes on. On a quite biblical scale, on an hourly basis, murder is being committed by an incalculable number of species all over the globe. Whales kill plankton, lions kill antelope, owls kill mice, sparrows kill worms, spiders kill flies, flies kill . . . well, really titchy stuff. And not a flag is waved, not a petition signed, not a rally rallied. This is but the circle of life, Walt Disney tells us. This is but a fragile ecosystem, David Attenborough whispers. And we nod and smile and eat some more pasta and say 'He really has got a lovely voice', content and satisfied.

That is, one rule for them, and another for us.

I returned to my flat for about three p.m. and tried to open my front door. A few moments of teeth-gritted shoving and puffing and oh-for-heaven's-sake-ing, the loose knocker banging wildly, and I fell indoors in an angry fume. The anger, however, was quickly replaced by bewilderment, as I racked my head for the memory of ordering a small mail-order mountain. Did I come home drunk one evening, flop open a copy of *The Himalations Catalogue* and tick the *Please rush me my quarter-scale model of the Kilimanjiro* box?

A closer inspection. No. It's amazing how quickly final demands build up when you're not looking.

I took the armfuls of angry brown envelopes on a brief tour of the hall and deposited them on the desk in the lounge, cracking a random one open with a release of that synthetic fishpaste smell.

Dear Mr Ellis,

Yadda yadda yadda standing orders yadda yadda loan repayments yadda yadda overdraft yadda hereby ten days yadda yadda final notice bada-boom bada-bing, yours, give-us-our-freakin'-money-back,

Mr Barclays Bank esq.

Which is the downside to losing your job, I suppose. Like a shopping basket so full of baked bean tins that there's no room for the tin-opener, my head bulged and burst with ideas and theorems, pushing more mundane stuff aside. It needed sorting, of course. I needed some kind of income to sort me out. But it had waited this long, it could wait a bit longer. The school owed me one more cheque which I confidently knew I could eek out for a couple of months if I didn't eat. So I swept the unopened remains that ranged from black to red and all the vibrant variety of financial purples in between into a neat pile, ordered them efficiently by size, colour and postmark and dropped them into the bin.

Holiday season? I don't want you to spend the holiday season without . . . ? Without *what?*

Without *him*, right?

I pottered about in the kitchen a while, clicking on the kettle and staring hopefully into empty cupboards. Sadly, burglars hadn't jimmied their way in and prepared a lasagne while I was out. While the kettle billowed and bubbled I wandered idly back into the lounge, tossed a few *Scientific American*s into the bin (oo'er, yes yes, let's all just grow up a bit, shall we), plumped up a cushion and stared about the place.

There was still a good deal of crap about. Since my refocusing of priorities and restructuring of goals, I had been trying, bit by bit, to pare down the flat, like my life, to the essentials. I wasn't exactly going for monkish dry-bricked poverty — bare feet on cold concrete and itchy all-in-one. Just a plainer, more functional environment. So far this hadn't gone well, most of my juvenile knick-knacks and novelties making it to the not-sure pile, only to be back on the mantelpiece ten minutes later in a fit of nostalgia and sentimentality.

I'll start properly in the bathroom, I thought.

I took my tea through and placed it on the side of the bath, picked Deborah's toothbrush out of the mug on the sink, lowered the lid of the toilet, sat down and turned it slowly in my hands.

Let's look at things logically here.

The female (Deborah) has deserted her long-term

pair-bonding partner (me) and set up with another (Brad).

Why?

Well, clearly, she didn't have enough invested in me to demand fidelity. I wasn't her only source of food or warmth and she wasn't carrying my child. In purely biological terms, there wasn't a great deal holding us together in the first place. She had, however, invested a great deal of time in me. Which is never to be underestimated.

I stood up, dropped the toothbrush into the bin and swung open the doors of the bathroom cabinet to see what bottles could be persuaded to take an eviction notice.

Considering how long Deborah and, in my experience, most women spend in the bathroom, you'd be forgiven for thinking time wasn't much of an issue for the female. Their relaxed and luxuriating baths with a whole cauldron of exotic spices and aromatic lotions. Their . . . what was this one? Dewberry 5 Oils Moisturising Lotion. Jesus. It dropped into the bin with a fat thud. But it's men, of course, who have the time. At any point, from the age of thirteen to sixty, a man can drop his trousers and father a child. And I do mean at any point. Half past six in the morning on a layby up the M6 on a wet Bank Holiday Monday? As long as he can find a willing female with a spacious womb to rent, he's in business. And at six forty-five, after he's had a fag and a bit of a read of the paper, he can do it all over again with someone else. Time just isn't one of our worries.

Which might explain why we tend to be the crapper of the genders at things like anniversaries. Whether it's been ten years or ten days, what's the difference?

Whereas females? Tick-tock tick-tock tick-tock. It's our two-week anniversary, it's our three-month anniversary, it's been 72 hours since we last had a bit of a hug, where's my card? *Jesus Christ, woman, calm down. Fuckin' 'ell, there you go, there's your card. Stick your finger through there and waggle it. Ha! Brilliant eh?*

I gave up reading the backs of these identical white tubes with their inexplicable ingredients and just began to sweep shelves of the things into the bathroom bin. I was left with a can of shaving foam, an empty packet of razor blades, a razor, a broken electric shaver and a bottle of Oxy 10 spot cream which had remained not quite empty since I was fourteen. I spread them out a bit like five commuters taking up an empty tube train but they just looked more feeble so I took them all out and dumped them with a crash into the sink, lifted the cabinet off the wall and dumped it by the kitchen bin.

Much better.

See, Deborah had invested five years of her reproductive life in me. That's about a sixth. A hefty amount of time. Five years of training, five years of improvements, five years of me getting used to her quirks, her getting used to mine. It's a common complaint by women who have been upgraded to a newer and sleeker model – they've put in all the hours teaching him how to dress, how to cook, how to behave.

The right pants to wear, perhaps.

Only for some other dame to reap the benefits of all her tutelage. I will admit that in the early days I was ever so slightly Eliza Doolittley to Deborah's Henry Higgins. Just for the little things, you know. About not wearing trainers all the time, about rinsing around this sink after shaving, I remembered suddenly, skooshing on the cold tap and rubbing the porcelain with squeaky vigour.

But she chose to cut her losses, throw those five years away and start afresh. So there has to be something she needs from her new partner that she is unable to get from her old.

I returned to the bathroom and peered at my reflection in the mirror. What did Brad have that I didn't?

When a new male enters the pride and asserts himself the females are very quick to gather round and suss him out. During the lengthy sparring for territory that will go on between the males, it is worth the females' while keeping their eyes on the victor. Because whoever steps out of the ring is going to be coming a-calling and dropping something substantial in their laps.

And it ain't gonna be his gum-shield.

It doesn't do your females any good to be hanging about with the losing team. Standing by, polishing the bronze medal and feeding them spurious hogwank about the best thing being the taking part – no points for that, I'm afraid. It's all change, all change, all fertile females to the winner's enclosure, please ensure you have all your vagina with you when you leave the train.

Of course, you're free to backhand this one firmly across the net with a sweaty grunt. That's absurd, you're free to say. If that was the case, what did Deborah ever see in your pasty-packed phizog? The only men with wives surely would be cigar-chomping captains of industry and the odd billionaire movie star.

To which I say a-ha!

Because I'm feeling a bit annoying like that.

I snapped off the bathroom light with a stringy twang and mooched back into the lounge.

A-ha, I say. If planet Earth was one big tribe where everyone knew everyone else by name and all lived together in one expansive clearing, all competing for the same piece of food, the same sheltering tree, then yes – that's exactly what would happen.

I flumped into the armchair, fishing the remote from behind a cushion, and winked on the telly. The BBC balloon globe floated high above the city.

We have colonised every part of this planet – literally spread our tiny knees and run away. We now live in tighter-knit social peer groups of fives and sixes. Which is why, while they will still fantasise harmlessly about movie stars and pop icons, women still cross their fingers hoping their fellas get that promotion and setting their sights on the most generally successful male in their peer group.

Flashy flashy peacock taily.

And why Deborah has chosen to sleep with Brad.

It was so obvious. Once I had lost my job, and by extension caused Deborah to lose hers, she's bound to be looking for some way, however subconsciously, to re-raise her status.

Question is, could I compete?

Toughie.

Leaving the television flickering away quietly in the corner, I rummaged through the sheaves of notes on my desk until I yanked out my notepad. There, sellotaped down on the front page, was that photograph – the gang of us decorating Brad's place. Peeling it off, I went and sat down again. I gazed at it a while, my eyes boring into the three grinning mushes.

It reminded me of something but it took me a good few minutes to place it. That old *Frost Report* sketch with the two Ronnies and John Cleese. You remember the one? You must, Dennis Norden drags it out screaming every year in Great Comedy tribute shows. They stand in line, three different heights, three different outfits, three different accents. *I'm upper class, I look down on him, I'm middle class, I look up to him* and so on and so on.

Status personified, rather like this photograph.

Liz is the only one out of shot so she must be behind the camera. The walls of his kitchen are half blue. The rest of the paint is divided up equally between the brush in my hand and the hair on my head. I'm at the base of the ladder, Adrian at the top, roller in hand. And perched between us, halfway up, like the Grand Old Duke of York, is Bradley, beaming away. Deborah is the other side of the ladder, holding a spattered dust-sheet over her head.

Never one for a photo op', our Debs.

I don't know what it was exactly that made me uncomfortable with this snapshot. The painting party was relatively fun and larks, as I recall. Budweiser and Pepperoni at lunchtime, groaning and stretching and fuckinellmyarmsareaching by six o'clock. But all in good humour.

But it still left me with a bad taste in my mouth that I couldn't put down to cold sweetcorn and turps.

It's just a smugness about Brad's face and, as I thought more about it, his whole mood that day. He'd been all proud ownership and *mind my paintwork* and *where's my ladder*. He hadn't got this through a joint income like Ade and Liz. And nor was he locked up in the Rental Asylum like Debs and myself. He'd invited us over to help, yes. But also to watch him spray his scent all over his new patch of Savannah, chest out, tail spread, blood rushing to swell and brighten his colours.

He was the success, the young single homeowner with staff beneath him, a car in the drive, Jigsaw carrier bags in the wardrobe and a lounge full of remote controls.

This, this is what I was up against.

That smug face. That smug chiselled face which was, I checked my watch quickly, probably at this very moment being gazed into lovingly by my ex, all the while his mouth going ten to the dozen. Like a Ronco Woo-Matic, *more coffee, sweetheart? I've got a nice wine in the fridge if you like I love what you've done to your hair I've got us tickets for this no no let me pick you up my treat mmm you smell gorgeous c'mere.* All the arms in his olive-green romantic arsenal deployed. The Oozing 9mm, the Surface to Hair complimenting missile.

This is what I was up against.

I threw the photograph across the room with a card-sharp's wrist flick.

And then promptly tutted, got up and fetched it from behind the telly, still murmuring away to itself. Because I could whine and stamp the floor and beat my fists and thcream and thcream and thcream until I wath thick about it not being fair.

But had I learned nothing?

It's not meant to be fair. Natural selection never

claimed to be an equal opportunities employer. If you're not born with the right spikes or antlers or stripes or venom or perfect teeth or prominent cheekbones or any of the standard advantages, then you've got to get off your swollen red behind and make your own.

But of course, I thought, dropping with a huff onto my haunches and fanning my irritable face with the photograph, I had nothing on Brad. Not really. He had a very nice home, his own car, a very good job, big blue eyes, long dark lashes, a clean bill of health. He was alpha male numero uno.

Which brings us back to murder.

I'm not going to tell you I didn't consider it, albeit for one fleeting shiver of a moment. Because I did. And I don't mean that hot fury that burns the cheeks and stings the eyes after a scolding from the headmaster or a public dressing-down in front of the area manager. Where you imagine them dead and you wish them dead and you plan their meticulous torture all the way down the corridor with silently spat curses, fingernails biting your palms – only to have calmed down by the time you reach your desk.

When I say I thought about it, I mean I thought about it. Possibilities, pros and cons, reasoned value judgement.

And decided – no. Murder will not solve this problem. Not now, not here, not at this stage in our evolution. Yes if I could plot the curve, pluck the courage, pump the adrenaline and do the deed, he'd be out of the way (bar the shovelling, bin-bagging and frantic-relaying-of-patio-ing) but would it make Deborah any more mine?

No, of course it wouldn't. Because she would be inconsolable and I would be in prison — for the better, worse, richer and poorer part of a lifetime. And I don't want to go to prison. They all seem to be having jolly boysy larks in re-runs of *Porridge* it's true — *oy, you nurk, where's my naffin' snaaat, MacKay?* etc. But they never show Slade after dark, when Fletch — big butch sweaty Fletch — with his tree truck arms exposed in a white cotton vest, leans over the bunk to the wide-eyed naive Godber and whispers, *I miss my wife.*

I know I said that I wanted sex with many varied partners, but I'm sure sex in prison would hurt. Which would be horrible. And then it wouldn't hurt.

Which would be worse.

I gave my head a shake and focused for the first time on the television in front of me, the answer to my problem appearing there like a vision at Lourdes.

Striding across the screen, a wet toothless grin, disposable nappy gripping the chubby waist and squidgy thighs. Then rolling playfully on a fluffy white towel.

God, did Brad hate children. He hated children with a venomous passion, in a way that only someone who has spent upwards of six hundred quid on a DVD player only to have it jammed full of Marmite soldiers by his niece can really understand. As far as he was concerned, it was like some twisted Orwellian statement – 2' bad, 6' good. Kids were just pests. When they weren't bawling through movies at the cinema they were destroying his stock of picture books at work.

Which was my only weapon left in the rack with any firepower, the last costume in the dressing-up box. That of the simpering, kid-loving, new-mannish dad figure.

I couldn't outearn him, I couldn't outfight him, I couldn't out anything him.

But.

If Deborah had any sort of cluckiness forming about her gills, I could appeal to that side of her. It wouldn't be easy. What with this whole Christmas time thing, Brad had clearly got his claws in pretty deep. But that pink talcum powder smell, that milky skin, those tiny fingers.

It was my only hope.

Up and over to the phone, I dialled quickly and hung on for her to pick up. They would be home by now, bound to be.

Click, 'hello?'

'Liz? Hi, it's Charlie. Oh fine, fine, how's ickle Georgie? Yeah? I was thinking, you must be knackered. You could do with a break, I bet.'

TWENTY-THREE

'You see a limo go by, you know it's some rich jerk or fifty prom kids with a dollar seventy five each.'

Jerry Seinfeld

'Charlie? Charlie, is that you?'

'Hn? Bloody hell, Debs. Shit, what're you . . .? I mean, hi. Shit, what're you doing here?'

'Me? This is where I work now.'

'What? Here? You're teaching here? This school?'

'Yes, since the start of term. What're you . . . ?'

'Oh just out for a walk, getting some of this autumn air in my lungs.'

'Gosh, what a coincidence. What are the chances of that?!'

Well, since she's asking, the odds are very favourable

indeed and ones that would get the manager of any self-respecting Ladbrokes scuttling off to phone head office. The insider info that tips the odds in this favour being that a) Liz told me where Deborah was working; b) I'd been staking out the aforementioned primary school for a week; and c) I'd been standing on the opposite side of the road for the better part of an hour waiting for her to appear.

The Norland Place First & Middle School sits quietly, tidily, hair-brushed, always puts its hand up and never shouts out in Holland Park, London W14, on the corner where Holland Park Avenue meets Addison Avenue and the two roads politely doff their toppers before going about their business. Their business seems to be providing ideal locations for Georgians to throw up four-storey, white-pillared residences and for current leaseholders of said homes to lean a whole Kerplunk's load of scaffolding outside them before pissing off to Provence for the weekend.

Considering Holland Park is the swanky West End's last cocktail before the woozy headaches and melancholy of Shepherd's Bush and Hammersmith set in, it is a surprisingly pukka part of town. From what I glimpsed in one of the estate agent's windows as I kicked my heels waiting for Debs to appear, anyone who can afford to live there is very comfortable indeed. And anyone who can also afford to send their little Charlotte or Emily skipping gaily every morning to Norland Place, buffed leather satchel and cello case compulsory, is in serious danger of becoming so comfortable that they slip into a coma. Everything about the place is attractive and appealing. The gleaming gold plaque on the ironwork gate, the chequered tiled steps that lead from the wide street up to the heavy doors.

Even the new art teacher they've got is absolutely lovely.

'So you've been here since September? Gosh, that's great. How are you, y'know, how are you finding it?'

'It's another world,' Deborah said, flicking some hair out of her eyes that the wind rather wanted to play with. She looked well. Her hair was a little shorter, framing her soft features with a gentle vanilla scoop. She looked like life was beginning to be a little kinder to her. This early autumn wind had put a smudge of pink on her cheekbones and a dot on the end of her nose, the sharp wind a little mist in her eyes and her pink scarf and white woollen gloves softened the whole scene into a pastelly Tony Hart. 'The children are very different.'

'*Children?*' I said. 'They must be. They were *fucking kids* not so long ago.'

She smiled. 'Yes, don't remind me.'

The children in question played and skipped through the protective doors out onto the street, all pleats and straw hats. Played and skipped like any local comprehensive kids would, but slower somehow. Without that heads-down, sugar-fuelled insanity that my pupils used to demonstrate.

These were children brought up on violin lessons and sushi, their whole world turned at a more civilised pace.

The street, covered with a light film of pale brick dust from all the surrounding renovations, bustled and coughed with people-carriers and hulking 4x4s, as nannies and au pairs and other by-the-hour surrogates fetched and crouched.

'And they're looking after you here? I mean, you're settling in okay?'

'Yeah, yeah they're a good bunch of people. I feel happy.'

She felt happy. She'd cracked it.

And hats off to her. Deborah had definitely landed on her feet with this one. Gently guiding the larval droppings of the rich and shameless into the heady world of finger-painting and potato prints with a firm hand, a sweet smile and a not inconsiderable donation to her bank balance on a monthly basis.

This cushy new position, combined with Brad at home buying surprise tickets to the opera and hot buttered Sunday papers, was going to be a difficult one to crack, no question. I knew I couldn't compete there.

But I was quietly confident that afternoon.

Because had the Emotional Deviousness division of the Morality Police pulled up in a van, I would have been arrested immediately for going very heavily equipped indeed.

'Aw, and how's lickle Georgie here?' Deborah said with a syrupy voice, peering into the front-mounted carry-pouch I had strung about my chest. 'You got him for the day?'

I nodded.

'Uh-huh. We've been having lots of fun, haven't we, you liddle rascal?' I goo-gooed, jigging him up and down gently.

'I got your card,' Deborah said, avoiding my look.

'Oh,' I said. And decided to stop jigging. Difficult enough to pull this one off convincingly without looking like I desperately needed a piss.

'Thanks.'

'That's okay, really. I just wanted . . .'

What? I just wanted what? Fuck I don't know, my insides turned to wet lead, my armpits suddenly hot and prickly. I couldn't even remember what I'd put in the card. Something about saying hello and something childish about Brad. That he had pooey pants or a bogie bum or the lurgi or some such, I expect. I immediately began to regret every word.

'I was going to call,' she said, fiddling with her gloves, gloves that as far as I could see didn't need any fiddling done with them at all. 'But y'know,' and she shrugged.

'Mm,' I said.

Understanding, caring, sensitive, new dad.

'So what's with all this?' Deborah shifted gear, stroking George softly across the head.

'Oh I'm giving Ade and Liz the day off.'

'That's sweet,' Deborah said.

'It's a total pleasure.'

'Yeah?'

'Absolutely. He's a great kid,' I bonded.

Deborah smiled.

Lies lies lies.

No, I'm not lying about the fact she smiled. She did. A warm, slightly hesitant smile revealing incisors, canines and premolars that caused a minor seratonin surge through my cortex.

It's just George isn't a great kid, taking him out wasn't anything like a pleasure, total or otherwise, and I wasn't so much giving Adrian and Liz the day off as a pair of stomach ulcers each.

'You want to what?' Liz said. I was sitting in their lounge. A lounge in which everything that didn't smell of warm sweet sick smelled of the pungent citrus bleach that they'd clearly used to remove warm sweet sick. I drank tea and breathed through my mouth.

Which is a fucking difficult thing to do if you think about it.

'I thought it would help, give you two some time to yourself.'

'Thanks, Charlie, that's, y'know, very thoughtful but, well but y'know . . .' Adrian made a bluffety attempt to dissuade me as he perched on the arm of the sofa. Was it me or did he smell of sick as well?

'He's still so young and everything,' Liz started, 'and the, the doctors er uh erm urrghnn –' and her face, clearly unable to contain this amount of tact and etiquette behind it, collapsed into a squidgy mess. I turned to try Adrian, who was nodding sensitively at his wife.

'I thought the hospital said he is perfectly healthy? Couldn't be better, you said?'

'He is, he is,' Adrian said. 'I mean, he's a real fighter. The guy, the consultant fella, he said he couldn't see any problems and he said, didn't he, hon, he said he didn't think we had anything to worry about.'

This was good. I was banking on Adrian's male pride. He didn't want to look like some weedy, watery-spermed Charles Hawtrey figure in front of me so he was playing up the positive. He reminded me suddenly of Spike, the big dog in the Tom & Jerry cartoons, patting his diminutive nephew on the head firmly with a gruff *That's-a-ma-boy*.

It was Liz who was going to be the stumbling

building block here. I tried an emotional gambit. Cue shruggy shoulders, a sigh in the voice and a couple of limp gestures. Okay here we go: Shruggy limp sigh . . .

'So it's just that you don't trust me then?'

Ooooh, refer*ee*!

The pair of them visibly crumpled at this and opened their mouths, about to boost me up, but I hammered on, the wounded party. 'No no, I understand. Maybe I'm not the best person to look after your boy for an hour or two. Lost my girlfriend, lost my job — I s'pose I must look pretty irresponsible . . .'

'Charlie, Charlie, don't be silly . . .'

'We don't think that, c'mon, don't be so . . .'

'I just wanted to help, y'know? I'm feeling pretty' — frustrated pause — 'pretty fucking useless these days'. They flinched at that one — 'I just wanted to' — study the carpet, two, three, four — sigh — okay now the big one. Stand up quickly — 'I should go . . .'

'And Liz is happy to leave him with you?' Deborah asked.

'Absolutely,' I said as we strolled up the overtly wide, overtly leafy and generally a bit too Mary Poppinsy avenue. The huge trees bowed overhead casting shade from the afternoon sun onto the endless line of cafes and dry-cleaners and rug shops.

Yes, rug shops. *Jesus.*

'They wanted some time to themselves and needed someone who was good with children. They couldn't find a child-minder they trusted so they said I was their natural choice.'

'Liz didn't mention it to me.' Deborah furrowed and we kept walking. As we approached the polished stone mustard arch of Holland Park tube, next to the red newspaper kiosk with *Hello!* plastered all over it, she slowed down and began to rummage in her bag.

'This is me,' she said. 'It was good to see you, Charlie.'

Huh? No, wait. Shit. This wasn't enough. I wasn't likely to wow her back into my life with an open mind, open arms and open knees (oh Je-*sus*, Charlie) if she buggered off now. I was meant to be proving myself a perfect father figure. As it was I'd merely suggested I was an ex-boyfriend with a big helpful streak.

Or that might just be baby puke.

'Oh, we're going this way too,' I blustered.

'I thought you had shopping to do?'

'Hn? Yeah. In 'um . . . ' I ran the red east–west slash of the Central Line through my head. 'I do, we're off to that shop. Gap, er, thing. Junior. Junior Gap.'

'Gapkids.'

'Yes. On Oxford Street.'

'You'd be better off on a bus probably.'

'Ooh no no, Georgie wants to see da trains, don't you, lickle one? Come see da puff puffs wiv aunty Debby Doos?' I jigged up and down with a bit more vigour, causing his head to nod comically. 'See? He can't wait.'

'Careful, Charlie, he'll be sick.'

'Nooo, he's all right, aren't ya, little fella? Eh? Eh? Oh fuck no shit don't oh bollocks.'

'So how's Brad?' I asked. The train rolled and rattled eastwards towards town.

'You've still got a load on your jacket.'

'It's just a speck, don't worry about it.'

'People are staring, come here,' and Deborah began to fumble about in one of the eighty-seven holdalls I had strung about my person, looking for the wetwipes.

You know those little blue signs that are thoughtfully pasted up above sporadic seats on public transport, the ones that pre-empt chivalry by suggesting one gives up one's seat to those carrying children? I always presumed this was because children were deceptively cumbersome and weighty. This is just so much arse. Children, with a modern harness, are easier and lighter to carry than your average sports holdall. The only reason those with babies should be given access to a seat is so they have somewhere to dump all the bollocks that goes with them.

'Where are the wipes?'

'They're in the blue bag, I think.'

'Which one?'

'Huh? Oh, er . . . I dunno. One of those two. Or

perhaps that one.' Deborah rummaged some more. 'So you were saying . . . ?'

'What?'

'Brad. How is he?'

'Have you not spoken?'

Oooh she's a cool one.

'Not for a while no.'

'Oh he's fine, he's fine. What the hell is all this stuff?' Tumbling from the seventeenth blue holdall, although actually, it could have been the forty-sixth now I think about it, spilled a mound of coloured fluffy plushness – Simba, Tinky-Winky, Goofy and Tigger all made their bid for freedom across the floor of the carriage. 'How much have you got in here?' Deborah protested, finally emerging with the wipes.

'Liz just gave me the bags – she said it was the essentials.'

As Deborah wiped and rubbed at the yellow throw-faster stripe on my coat, two friendly commuters rescued the soft toy menagerie and handed them back to me.

A young woman, all square-framed specs and black suit, waggled a plush Goofy.

'Here you go. He's a sweetheart, what's his name?'

Er hello? Public transport? I positioned myself to pull the emergency handle and have the guard come and explain to this dame that strangers do not, under any cir-cumstances, open up conversations and that she should

300

get her nose back in her Marion Keyes, when she smiled at me.

Now women on trains don't tend to smile at me. In fact, thinking about it, I don't think a woman on a train has ever smiled at me, no matter what those Dateline *Have you ever wondered what might have been?* posters might suggest. But smiling, plus making conversation? It must have been my new fragrance.

Which of course it was. Paternity by Calvin Klein.

I took the toys with a shy smile.

'Thanks. His name's George.'

'He's lovely,' she said and her eyes went all twinkly and a dopey grin spread across her by no means incredibly unattractive face.

Lawks. This fatherhood lark works a treat. I glanced over the other faces in the carriage. All the women, no matter what age, gazed over at tiny George, flicking admiring glances in my direction like TVR headlamps.

A bloke next to me waved my Tinky Winky at me (oo'er), wafting away the misty romantic clouds from my eyes with a gruff snarl.

'Oy, mate,' he said, handing it over with fingertips like it was radioactive waste.

I was getting less than adoring vibes off this fella, which was understandable. To Mr Wall Street here, in his Next suit, battered brogues and burgundy briefcase, lapful of spreadsheets and highlighter at the ready, I was competition. There he was, working all the hours God sends, loosening his tie, using Gillette shaving products and pulling down 40k by the seat of his ass goddammit – status status status, peck peck peck – and I was getting the attention. Not playing by the laws of his forest, a newcomer, and I had all the females lining up.

I don't blame him for hating me at all.

'There,' Deborah said, balling up the towlette.

'Thanks, thanks. So how far are you going?'

'Bond Street.'

'Straight home?'

'No I'm meeting someone. What are you getting for George?'

'Getting for him?'

'From Gapkids?'

'God, I dunno. I-I mean, I'll see what they've got, you know. Browse for a bit.'

'Well you don't want to keep him out too long at this age. It's getting dark, he'll get cold.'

'Well I'll buy him a coat or something,' I said a little too quickly. The train pulled into Lancaster Gate, leaving me only two stops to make a better impression.

Or, at least, a better impression than Brad.

'I love spending time with George. Don't you? I mean, just playing with him, watching him. And that newborn smell. It's lovely.' I jigged him up and down on my lap a little. 'I mean, look at that little face, that smile.'

'He's a sweetie, no doubt,' Deborah said, tugging off a glove and touching his bottom lip tenderly.

'Brad's not really a child-lover, is he?

'Brad?' Deborah said.

'Yeah. I mean, he likes his gadgets and his technology and shit. Not really one for the nappy-changing.'

'Well it's just priorities, isn't it?'

'Priorities?'

'Yeah. I mean, why would he need to change a nappy now? He wouldn't have time. Not now he's moved jobs.'

'Is he not at the shop?'

'Don't you two ever talk? No, he got a better offer. Some friends of his at another chain. More responsibility, bigger site. And of course, a lot more money.'

'I-I didn't know.'

'Yes.'

'Well, congratulate him for me, won't you?'

'Yes of course. How's the job hunt going with you?'

'Oh wonderfully. I'm just choosing what to go for really. A lot of avenues, you know.'

'That's excellent. You still with teaching?'

'Hn? No no. I'm in, er — finance.'

'Finance? What are you talking about?'

Yes, Charlie, good point. What are you talking about?

'It's this, er, City thing. Big business, you know. Big bucks. It's a lot of work, long hours. Deals, trading, that kind of thing.'

303

The train burst into Bond Street station and Deborah reached for her case.

'How on earth did you get into that?'

'Just helping out a mate and one thing led to another. I'll stick at it for a few years, make a bit of cash you know. Then take early retirement, I expect.'

Deborah got up, another tired commuter edging into her seat expertly.

'That's, that's excellent, Charlie. Really. You're certainly full of surprises.'

'Yep, it's the new me, I've got it all planned. Furnish the nest and then make time for one of these,' and I waved George's hand at Deborah. 'Byeee, Aunty Debby Doo.'

'Cheerio,' she said and with a hesitant thought, she left the crowded train, the doors sliding behind her.

The train glided out of the station into the dark tunnel and braked suddenly with a lurch, causing Wall Street man to spill a hot coffee on my lap.

'Hoy careful!' I snapped, turning to face him. Realising too late into this stand-off that the hot dark liquid spreading across my lap was coming, not from a Starbucks cup, but a towelling Mothercare baby-gro. There was a pinched groan from those nearby and newspapers covered noses.

'I expect with your *big, new City job*,' Mr Wall Street said with a snakey smirk, 'you'll be able to afford to get some new trousers.'

TWENTY-FOUR

'The primitive man in the wolf pelt was not keeping dry;
he was saying:
"Look what I killed. Aren't I the best?"'
Katherine Hamnett

I swear W. H. Smith gets shinier every time I go in.

All their wares laid out, shimmering and sparkling under the striplights with a smooth oh-so-shiny shiny sheen of pristine newness. Spotless perspex shelving tightly holds varnished magazines in slippy cellophane and we are transfixed. Well, we're meant to be. For shiny is clean and clean is new and new is young and young is fertile. We pace slowly, mouths hanging open just slightly as if we slammed them in a hurry and broke the catch. And we gaze and pace and flick and thumb. All of us, looking for a friend, someone as enthusiastic as we are about fishing or guitar solos or icing sugar or wedding dresses. A friend that we can purchase and bring home and spend two hours in the company of so we needn't feel like outsiders any more. So we can belong.

Personally, I gaped at the large section marked Lifestyle.

Lifestyle, it promised. You have a life, that's not under debate. You have a life – otherwise you'd be over in the Model Railway section or the Amateur Photography section. No, you have a *life*.

You just have no *style*.

I left after half an hour, the weight of my purchases turning the carrier bag handles to cheese wire as I walked with them banging and bruising my knees in the September wind.

With a ting, a tiny bell signalled my creep into the barber's, but nobody looked up. I sat myself down on the torn leatherette bench, my trainers squeaky on the black lino feathered with locks and tufts. A radio played somewhere in the back, inconsequentially. There was a quiet, civilised clip snip swip, a slow brown clock ticked above the mirrors opposite, the air slightly old and wet with that WWII oily tonic dad smell.

I clicked and gurgled myself a scaldsome vending

coffee from the brown machine by the door and slipped my magazines out onto the low Formica table with a flap ferlap serlap blap thud.

Esquire, FHM, Vogue, Cosmopolitan and *Marie Claire.*

By some miracle, the magazines still retained some of their shininess. Not as glossy or appealing as they had been twenty minutes ago when they had pouted and winked at me from the shelves, but then what is? Through a cloud of piped music and the harsh fingerpointing of striplights – everything looks better in the shops. I laid them out next to each other, sipped my coffee-style drink and thought for a bit.

Yes, these would do it.

My reasoning being, if you're going to lie, *lie big.*

It's Adolph Hitler who is famous for saying that people will believe any lie as long as it's big enough. He's famous for a few other things as well of course, one of them being the destruction of a lot of people he didn't consider up to the job, resulting in the word *Darwinism* causing much tutting and well-reallying around ill-informed dinner tables.

But Adolph was as bang-on about fibbing as he was well-offside about eugenics. Lies, fibs, whoppers, porkies – call them what you like, for once size really is what matters. When you're late for work for example, don't jog in red-faced, puffing apologies. Do a bit of shopping, saunter in at lunchtime with talk of a fire at

Waterloo and utter chaos and a derailment and two ambulances colliding on the Edgware Road didn't you hear about it on the radio. Something so implausible, so spectacular in its unlikeliness, no one would dream of making it up.

Something as unbelievable as, say, that man's chin.

Jesus, where do magazines *get* these guys?

If a male of a species is going to woo a female, then it does him the world of good to know what the females are currently considering woo-worthy. Certain species find certain traits or features attractive – a peahen getting all flushed at the peacock's tail, a doe getting all, well, doe-eyed at the stag's antlers etc. And these are not interchangeable. Let's face it, a peacock, new in town, having a strut about the ladies with a pair of three-foot antlers sticking awkwardly out of his face isn't going to get very far, shag-wise.

Fortunately, of course, animal courtship being infinitely more simple than human, these signals rarely change. A group of female giraffes, clustered about the beauty-parlour muttering, *Well I don't know, Doris. Long necks just seem so last season to me,* are a species in trouble. Natural selection doesn't work that fast in the animal kingdom, so as a basic rule, males can pretty much trust their ancestors' advice. If it got him laid, chances are it'll get me laid.

Which sadly doesn't tend to work for us.

I glanced up at the hall of shame that hung in a line

along one wall of the barber's, above the shelves of bottles and jars. Black and white headshots of another time. Those bouffants, those beards, those mustaches and flattops. Why do barbers never feel the need to update the decor? I don't mean video screens and coffee shops. Just a few headshots that might suggest the staff had had a customer since 1972. But someone must have fancied these guys *once*, presumably? And if I chose to model myself on these guys, my ancestors, if I climbed into the swivelley chair and pointed to the Brylcreem Boy above – where would that put me status-wise with a modern female?

And can instruments even measure that low?

Because us *Homo sapiens* in our wisdom have a little thing called fashion. And just as a fish with a swollen red arse would get no girlfriends and a baboon with shimmering scales would get no girlfriends, a human male looking for a partner must at least know whether the vogue is big tails or big antlers.

And if you don't know, then you have to find out.

'All right, ma' fren'? Is okay for you?'

'Hn? Yes yes, good. Fine.' The barber, all short sleeves and hairy arms and combs in jars, flapped a shiny bib about my neck.

'What we do, today, ma' fren'?'

Fuck, I don't know, I thought. I was very nervous, I

needed more research time. I'd only managed to flick quickly through *Esquire* and *FHM* when I was called up to the chair. As far as I could see from these mags, men had two choices, style-wise:

Male #1: *Tall; Black or white; clean hair, clipped at the back; no facial hair; clear skin around a tight jawline; broad-ish shoulders (but not circus strongman); big hands and feet (size ten); dark single-breasted suit and dark tie (shirt either white or black); cigarette (white filterless), unlit – hence white teeth (lots, all very shiny – displayed in a head thrown back manly smile).*

The image insofar as it is known, is this.

And this, I presumed from his type's voluminous appearance throughout the mag, was what males at the start of the third millennium should look like – *Homo Dappien* (man the well groomed). Used to sell everything from shaving gel to fountain pens. And this was *Esquire*, for heaven's sake, not some new fly-by-night glossy with a bikinied TV presenter on the cover. I mean, it's been around forever, it's an opinion to trust, surely. Men have read it for years.

I flicked a look upwards. A one-time *Esquire* reader from 1983 stared down at me from his photograph, through his layered blond wedge.

'You whan' me to tidy up, yeah? Make smart?' the barber said, fiddling expertly with clippers and attachments like a Bond villain with a detachable hand.

'Er . . .' I said, my feet clanging nervously against the

foot rest. A hair-dryer burst into life next to me, making me jump, a pastel Bakelite jet engine whirring away. 'Shorter, I think. At the front a bit,' and I tugged feebly at my fringe.

Or maybe I should be going for Male #2? *Homo Gappien* (man the wearer of utility gear)?

Shorter; wavier hair (cleanish, tousled and loose, getting in eyes a bit) or very very short (bogbrush, in secondary-modern parlance); facial hair (grubby goatee or clipped stubble); stringier wiry build; the same big hands and feet (booted and trainered, not a half-brogue in sight); denim, combats, plaid, fleeces, leather (real outdoorsy types); no cigarette but obligatory pint of ale accessory hence raucous blurry pub shot with miniskirted pool-playing waif in tow.

In one way or another, men have always fallen into these two categories – Clark Gable vs James Dean, Kenneth Williams vs Sid James, Sidney Poitier vs Mr T. And really, guys, you're one or the other – it's a rare beast who can put a boot in both camps without suffering considerable groin-strain. Ask any 18 stone rugby player who's had to itch and strain in a shiny suit for a TV appearance. Or, for that matter, any oily middle manager who's been forced to clomp out of the changing room in combats in the name of team-building.

They are enduring roles, of course, displaying as they do the valuable traits of brains and strength. The question was, which one would Deborah find the most attractive? Antlers or feathers? Boots or suits? Short or long? Parted or spiked? Up or down? Brushed or tousled? The barber snapped on his clippers and they began to buzz angrily like a spiteful wasp.

I had literally seconds to decide my fate, for the haircut decision would dictate the whole bodily look. Oh crikey, my stomach flipped over and bubbled slightly with anxious gas.

The barber smiled.

'You like a number two, ma' fren'?'

Half an hour and nine quid later, I was out on the street, pacing quickly with that just cropped itchy twitch. Every shop window was a cloudy mirror as I passed, my free hand constantly straying up to the back of my neck where the wind seemed suddenly colder.

The next stop was to rid myself of this aging outer skin.

'Afternoon, sir, welcome to Gap.'

'Oh, thank you. Thank you very much.'

In all the years Deborah and I were together, she never really made clear what it was she specifically saw in me and, therefore, by extension, what she liked in men in general. I didn't wow her into bed with a duelling scar and a Harley Davidson. But then neither did I send her knicks plunging earthwards with sonnets and silk. We were just about the same age, had the same background, similar goals, both grown up listening to the same bands and watching the same cartoons. Except for a certain weekday when she had had piano lessons so never really discovered *Captain Caveman*, our upbringings were almost identical.

We had just got on. A few staff meetings, a couple of Friday evening drinks and a week with year ten in the Brecon Beacons and we clicked.

Of course all the clicking now was with Bradley and to all intents and purposes they were at it like rheumatic tap-dancing Rubik's Cube salesmen.

I scanned the store guide and took the stairs two at a time to the Menswear section. A lot of yellow pine, a lot of white cotton and a lot of beige. Coloured polo shirts circled like synchronised swimmers, walls cushioned with denim. There must be something here for me.

Brad wasn't really a classic poster boy for *dappien* or *gappien* males, but given the choice, he was nearer the goatee and combats than the cufflinks and cravats. Friday nights used to see him in Levi's and a crisply ironed (but untucked) Ben Sherman. The trendy scruff. Not making an effort but quietly aware of the importance of quality in leisurewear. And it suited him, I thought as I strummed a pile of plaid button-down shirts. He knew his shape, he knew his style and he dressed relatively well. Not so well as to be labelled a homosexual, but with an informed confidence.

I don't think I could really say the same. And that was my problem. I needed to find my shape, find my style and make the most of it. Choose to fight with the weapons I'd been given.

'All right there, mate?'

I turned. A tall, tanned Australian fellow with a gleaming white shirt beamed at me. Whoever sold him the shirt would have got salesman of the month because they'd also persuaded him to accessorise it with a set of matching teeth.

'Er . . . I was just looking,' I fobbed, replacing a denim shirt with its family on the table.

'What sort of thing are you after?'

'Hn? Oh Lord, I don't know. A look, y'know? Something modern, something . . .' The Rolodex in my head riffled through my objectives. This guy looked good, he looked right. Maybe this was the help I needed, a little one to one. I pointed to my hair.

'You got anything that'll go with this?'

'With . . . with your hair?'

'Uh-huh. Look, I'll be honest with you. I'm looking for a new look. This stuff' – I plucked apologetically at my attire – 'wouldn't impress a blind nymphomaniac. I'm looking for something that says, *Hey I'm a man, I'm a man with style*. But not like in a poncey two-hours-in-the-bathroom-each-morning way.'

'Obviously.' The assistant nodded cautiously.

'*I'm a man who's a success, I'm a man who knows*

where it's at. As it were. *A chancer, a risk taker, adventurous yet reliable, dependable and a good solid father figure.'*

There was a pause as he took all this in.

'Have you thought about easy-fit khakis?'

'Lead on, good man, lead on.'

TWENTY-FIVE

'Anybody seen in a bus over the age of 30 has been a
failure in life.'
Loelia, Duchess of Westminster

'Please stop crying, please stop crying, please stop crying, please stop please please please for the love of fuck just stop for two fucking . . . HOY!' A cyclist whisked past on the inside like a silverfish, slamming a riding-gloved hand down hard on the red paintwork. 'Watch it!' I yelled. His unfeasibly tight squeeze-me squeeze-me buns, sheathed in black lycra, swayed and beat away from me like a metronome arm as the cycle slipped silently away into the traffic ahead.

Behind me, in what was laughably referred to as a *backseat* – and I suppose was one as long as you ignored all laws of Newtonian physics – strapped in tight, George continued to bawl like an air-raid.

'Please, Georgie, be a lickle ookums for unkie Charles and put a fucking corky-worky in it, would you? This is difficult enough as it is.'

In front, visibility was excellent. Which is to say, I could excellently see the huge white van blocking the view and excellently see that I had no idea what was going on up in the road ahead.

I drummed my fingers on the wheel for a moment. 'You want some moozik, Georgie? Is that it?' I cooed. 'A few tuney tunes for singalong?' I clicked the stereo on and jabbed at the presets until the velvet West Coast waft of Brian Wilson & Co washed through the speakers. 'H-hey, that's better. All together now, *Gotta keep a those a-love Good, Vibrations a-happenin' with her*...' George failed to either drop in with the descant part or wave his Zippo about, preferring to sustain a monotone wail throughout the middle eight and chorus reprise. I punched the *Vol* + button over and over until George became but a Munch-like silent gawp and the Beach Boys a close harmony shark attack.

Suddenly a dull thunk snapped me alert and threw my heart out of its chest as a silvery can bounced off the bonnet.

'Turn it down!' a voice yelled as another cyclist slipped past and his half-full drink began to glug isotonic glucose refreshment into the car's fresh dimple.

'Hoy! Fuck off!' I bellowed back eruditely. 'Look what you've done! You fuckin' . . .' I writhed and strained against the seatbelt with gritted teeth as the can rolled and clunked to the tarmac.

'Perhaps,' Mr Morley, the Porsche dealer, interjected with a polite cough from the passenger seat, turning the music down slowly, 'we'll try with the roof *up*, shall we?'

The Porsche 911 Cabriolet is capable of 231 bhp, has a rear-mounted air-cooled boxer engine and a 3164 cc capacity. It does 20.8 miles per gallon, has a galvanised steel bodyshell and a belt-driven single overhead cam gear system. It is 168.9″ long and 64.96″ wide.

And, of course, totally out of my league in every way − affordable only to successful, confident, wealthy alpha males.

'Right then, just a signature there and there, sir. And that's your credit card there, thank you. It was a week, you said. Is that right?'

'Yes yes, that should do it.'

'Excellent. Do you want me to show you how the roof catch works one more time, sir?'

'Ha, no no. I think I've got it. Thank you.' I scooped the keys up, grabbed the carry-cot and bounced through the doors onto the forecourt and into the chilly morning.

As far as the guise was going, the car was the final part, the flame on the candles on the icing on the cake. I had *uhmmed* and *ahhed* over which model for a while – the low slung, laid-back bloodstain of the Lamborghini through to the uptight, upright beep beep what-ho of the vintage Rolls. But I finally settled on the 911 because, well, you can stretch believability just so far.

And I was asking Deborah to believe I had changed. And *changed* doesn't even begin to cover it. The old Charles Ellis was now gone and in his place, well, something very different indeed.

This new Charlie would never leave the marking of year ten's mocks to eleven p.m. on a Sunday night. This new Charlie would never spend 4 consecutive summer afternoons indoors, curtains shut, hunched squintily down in front of the Playstation trying to get to Level sodding 6 of *Driver*. And he definitely wouldn't buy Deborah the *Back to the Future* box set for an anniversary present (once, okay? *Once*. She'd hinted about it often enough. I didn't know that anniversaries are meant to be more, well . . . oh forget it).

No, this new Charlie was a mover and/or shaker in every sense. Every part of him that was in any way movable or shakable was being moved and shook, repeatedly in mixed company. Oh yes indeedy-doo. I mean, come on. How could it fail?

I began to hook and clip and snap the baby seat out

of the back and into the front, George gurgling happily in his cot all the while.

'There there, little fella, we're back to Mummy and Daddy now. And not a word to them about the car, eh? That's right.'

'Oh my giddy aunt, what do you look like? Liz, come and have a look at this, Action Man's at the door.'

'Yes all right,' I said, stepping indoors.

'Let's have a go of your Eagle-Eyes.'

'Yes yes, fuck off.'

'Hoy! Language in front of this one.' Adrian took the carry-cot from me, handing it to Liz who had come to gawp at my new . . . er, look. I rubbed my fingers, chaffed by the heavy straps, while I got the thrice-over. Liz gave a little whistle which could be read as a)very sarcastic; or b) see a).

'Whe-heyy, what happened to you, soldier man? Mister Seh-heeexy! Get that crop,' and she stepped forward to scruff the front like I was a pet-shop puppy.

'All right, good one. I'm just trying something a bit different.'

'Very nice,' she chuckled. 'How was he today?' she said into the carry-cot in a tender and concerned tone. 'He looks exhausted, poor lambkin.'

'Quiet as a mouse,' I lied with a reassuring smile. Liz

wandered away back into the lounge, chatting animatedly to the dozing infant.

'Time for a cuppa?' Adrian offered.

'Absolutely. Those boots are fucking agony.'

'So,' Adrian said, all smuggety eyebrows and smirkity smile, wafting his mug at me. We sat at his dining table, liberally layered with newspaperings and supplements. Two tomato-smeared plates were piled by the sink, crusts of bread on top.

'So? So . . . what?'

'What's all this about?'

'This what?'

Quite rightly, Adrian was having absolutely none of this innocence lark.

'You. That haircut, those trousers, those boots,' and he kicked me sharply under the table.

'What's going on?'

'What?' I said again, incredulously. 'Cor, dear, you can't do anything different around here without everyone taking the piss.'

'You can, Charles my old mate. You can do a lot of things differently. You just can't come around here looking like something out of *GQ* without everyone taking the piss. Subtle difference.'

We stared at each other for a moment.

'She won't go for it, you know,' he said finally.

321

'Who won't?'

Adrian let out a scream of frustration and balled up the newspapers in frantic white fists.

'Stop bloody pretending you don't understand. Jesus fucking Christ!' he hollered, raining tatters and strips of Saturday's *Guardian* upon me.

'Hoy, language in there,' a voice drifted in from next door.

'Sorry, hon, I couldn't help it. Charlie's being a twat,' he called through. 'He thinks that dressing up like a gay model will make Deborah take him back.'

'Wha . . . ?' I coughed, looking down at myself as if for the first time. Down at my ribbed V-neck, fitted, grey-marl tee, my olive-green waistcoaty thing and the voluminous multi-pocketed black combat trousers that bunched up acres of heavy spare fabric above my chunky mountain boots. 'I . . . I hadn't even thought . . .'

Adrian sprung up, sending his coffee sprawling out all over the papers in a spidery splash, lunging at me and getting my head into what Dickie Davies would have called a half-nelson. I began to struggle and choke, beating him across the forearm. He brought his mouth down close to my ear, his breath sweet and vinegary. Two glasses of white wine with lunch, I guessed.

'Admit it,' he rasped with a little laugh. 'Admit it's for Deborah to win her back. Admit it or die here now, you saddy old saddo. Admit it!'

'Bughkirkgh, bughkirkgh!' I explained. Which is pretty much what *okay okay* sounds like when you have a combined radius, ulna and humerus cutting off oxygen to your oesophagus.

'Why? Why won't she go for it? Hn? Why shouldn't she?' I asked, as Adrian began to mop and swab up the coffee from the mushy surface. 'Give me one good reason.'

'Because, dear friend, she's not stupid. For heaven's sake, how long did you go out with her? Five years? Give her some credit. You think she's going to see the new you in some designer baggy trousers and believe you just happened to pick this point in your life to try something new? You reek of desperation and she'll smell it a mile off. C'mon, Charlie, ten out of ten for trying but you've gotta let this one go.'

'Well,' I said petulantly, gazing at the floor, kicking the table leg idly with a heavy boot, 'it's all right for you.'

'And what's that supposed to mean? What's all right for me?'

'This,' I said, waving my arm over the kitchen. 'Everything.'

'What about it?'

'Well you've done it, haven't you? You've got them all nailed.' I rattled off my list mechanically. 'You've got your job, cash, this place, your mates. Tick them off, you did it. You're a happy guy.'

'What're you getting at?'

'And of course,' I pressed on, 'little Georgie – you have gone forth and multiplied. Sown your seed upon fallow turf, a womb to call your own. Your genetic lineage is secured. Your immortality is written, all that . . . cobblers, you know.'

'I have a son. That's what you're trying to say? It's all right for me, I must be perfectly happy because I have a son?'

'Duh!' I said. Rather cleverly, I thought.

We sat staring at each other for a moment. I wanted to say something, and I sensed Adrian did too. But I hadn't the foggiest idea what I wanted to say and 10 to 2 he didn't either. Something needed saying though, that much was sure. Fortunately the spell was broken as Liz wandered in carrying the baby.

'What are you two yelling . . . Oh who spilled their coffee everywhere? God, you two, you're worse than him. Aren't they, Gee-Gee? Daddy mess monster? Yes dat's right.' She tore off some kitchen towel and tottered off back to the lounge leaving the room in silence once again.

You're not going anywhere until someone owns up. I can wait all lunch break if I have to.

'I never wanted him, you know,' Adrian said finally.

Uh-uh, hold up, wait a second. What the hell was this?

'C'mon, let's go. I'll tell you about it outside.'

*

324

'So what are you saying? You didn't want a kid . . . a son, an heir? You didn't want one?'

'Nope. I told Liz – Not yet. Not till I'm ready.'

Adrian snapped on the bulb and yanked off a dustsheet with a flourish.

'Oh cool,' I drooled, running my fingers across the now completed Scalextric track, all gleaming and slithering with chicanes and bridges and snaking bends.

'Work is a load of toss at the moment,' he continued. 'I've got this close to just walking out, like, fifty times. It's driving me crazy, they've got a new management structure, I never know what I'm doing. I'm reporting to, like, four people on the same job, they're all shaving deadlines.'

He clicked on a couple of wall plugs and produced a shoe-box from underneath the desk.

'You want to be Schumacher or Hill?'

'Schumacher.'

'Sod off, you can be Hill,' and he clicked the plastic cars into their grooves.

'We'd talked about kids before. Or rather Liz had. Not until I'm settled. I should be branching out on my own, setting up my own consultancy. You're the blue one.'

'Huh?'

He passed me a plastic handset. It fitted snugly and I pumped the thumb-control with retro-excitement.

'So what happened?'

'Duh!' he said. I guess it was his turn. 'I'm sitting at my desk working on some repackaging of a soluble ibuprofen –'

'Glamorous stuff.'

'Absolutely. Ready?'

'Er, yeah yeah,' I said, giving my palms a quick wipe on my shirt.

'Three two one, GO,' and we jammed our thumbs down urgently, the two cars haring off down the straight with a high-pitched buzz.

'So reception calls me to say my wife is here. So I shit my pants, right, because she should be at work and she never comes to the office – oops, mind that corner. So I figure her mum's died or there's been an accident, right? So I leg it round and she's standing there crying with a dopey grin on her face and she says, *Guess what?*'

'In your reception? In front of the telephone girl?' I said, my eyes fixed on the whizzing toys, my sweaty thumb white with excitement.

'Oh not only all four telephone girls, but about eighty people from the accounts department all back from their Christmas drink.'

'Cocking hell.'

'Well quite.' The cars zipped past, neck-and-neck on their fourth lap. 'So what should have ended up a bit of a sit-down, a stiff drink and a very serious talk indeed turned into a load of shrieking hugs and party poppers and for he's a jolly bloody good bloody fellow.'

'But what about when you got home? I mean afterwards, didn't you talk about it? About your plans and . . . I dunno, about . . . stuff?'

I'll be honest with you, I wasn't taking this at all well. Not at all well. George was a mistake? Not part of the great plan? Here I was, taking my life, my health, my savings and my no-claims bonus in my hands for that purpose and that purpose only – to pass the genes on, to finally find contentment in my basic animal reproductive urges. And here was a guy who accidentally stumbled upon it, like kicking the kitchen bin in the night whilst going for a glass of water. And it looked like he was about to spend the rest of his life hopping about in his pyjamas cursing his rotten luck.

'Truth is,' he said matter of factly, 'truth is it never came up.'

'Never came up?!' I took a corner too quickly and came spinning off the track. 'Put me back on, put me back on!'

'Fuck off, put yourself on.'

'Bastard,' I spat and dodged behind him, scrabbling Damon Hill back into position, now over a lap behind.

'You'll never catch me up. Anyway, that's what I said – it never came up. Once Liz fell pregnant, that was it. We were, dan-da-da-daaa – having baby. I mean, it wasn't as if we said we never wanted kids. It was just sooner than I would have liked, that's ALL! YESSS! That's one-nil. A stirling performance from the young

327

German!' and he lifted Michael Schumacher's car and gave the light plastic bonnet a fond peck. Damon zipped past a few seconds later, rather feebly.

'Best of three?' I asked, whipping off my waistcoat and setting my car up again.

'I'll beat you one more time if you like, sure.'

Three two one and we were off again.

'So you don't, y'know, you don't, like, regret having him or anything?'

Adrian said nothing, he just watched his car slip past for a couple of laps. Which told me everything. This, this is what he'd been getting at at the zoo that afternoon. My heart dropped two feet. Which was clumsy and dangerous because Michael Schumacher promptly ran over it.

'Of course I regret it,' Adrian said. 'I never wanted him at all. I just said I did to Liz.'

'Why?'

'Because you do, don't you? You have those conversations about names and little school uniforms and you watch Disney movies and you sigh and she stops outside BabyGap and points and you have to stop too otherwise you're being rude and it's all just, I dunno, just presumed. You're married – you have a family. Bang, end of story. But no, I never wanted it.'

'But, but why not? I mean, it's as you say. You're married, you have a family, it's presumed. But of course it is. It's what we do, we meet and mate and . . .'

I had no idea what to say. You think you know someone and then with a twitch back of the curtain, the wizard is revealed for what he really is.

'If you didn't want kids, what did you get married for? Why didn't you just live together like before. I thought kids were the only reason our generation got married?'

'I don't know, mate.'

'You don't know why you got married?' I spat. 'Ade, mate, I . . . I . . .'

Truth is I was beginning to feel a bit sick. Whether it was watching these cars spin round and round or the fact that my entire belief system was being trashed by my only friend, I'm not sure.

A bit of both, I expect.

My head swam. This was a feeling I hadn't had since the end of *The Usual Suspects*. In fact I would have been less surprised if Adrian had told me he was, in fact, Keyser Soze.

'No no no,' I rattled, tearing off some verbal bandages quickly, 'that can't be right.' I was scrabbling around now, trying to make sense of the picture, sifting and recounting the dish of change at the end of a meal, trying to magic together the missing eight quid. 'George, he might have been a mistake. Right, fine, that I concede. Split condom, missed pill, punctured diaphragm, coil got, I dunno, accidentally straightened or whatever. But you can't accidentally get married.

What are you saying? That Liz turned up at your office in a white frock, ring in one hand, vicar in the other?'

'No, nothing like that. I was drunk and I didn't expect her to say yes.'

'Ah.'

'Ta-da! Two—nil to me. You're feeble. I dread to see you behind the wheel of a real sports car.'

I dropped the controller down and cracked my stiff fingers with a groan.

'So what are you going to do?' I asked eventually.

'Do?' Adrian said, clicking off the plugs. 'Do about what?'

'Er, durrr.' (I figured duh! was getting a little passé.) 'About the fact you're married to a woman you never wanted to marry and you're father to a kid kid kid er kid kid Jensen.'

'What?'

'Kid Jensen, that Canadian fuckwit. When's he going to drop that absurd tag? The Kid. He's eighty if he's a day. Kid. Git. Tch!'

'Why are you discussing crappy drivetime DJ's?' Liz interjected, leaning in the doorway. Fortunately for Adrian, I'd seen her pass the window and just caught myself.

'Hey you.' I smiled. 'How's little 'un?'

'Asleep, thank the Lord. I'm taking a breather. You kids want coffee?'

'Mmm,' we agreed together and Liz disappeared again.

'That's all we get these days,' Adrian murmured into his chest sullenly. 'Breathers, quick respites. The odd break while he sleeps. The rest of the time we're on twenty-four-hour fucking sentry duty. Non-stop till his eighteenth birthday. I mean, I know we're being over-protective. I know. But you can't help worrying.' He shut off the light and we stepped out into the sunlight. 'He's fine, of course he is. He's the healthiest baby on the planet. But we still can't just leave him. I mean, we've got our anniversary on the thirteenth, right?'

'Shit yes, of course.'

'I wanted to take Liz away somewhere nice, for the whole weekend, right? But we've got to think of the baby and everything. It's just, I could – we could – do with a break, y'know? A bit of rest. It's wearing me out.'

'Well.' I smiled, sending a pally arm around his shoulder. 'Next weekend? I might be able to help you there.'

TWENTY-SIX

'*I have often wished I had time to cultivate modesty . . .
but I am too busy thinking about myself.*'
Edith Sitwell

'I done a bit of a sorty out in here,' the old fellow began, 'and this is all her doings and nubbins and that. Now in here – and you got to bear in mind she couldn't stick viscose – we've got her gowns and smalls.'

'Well this is lovely, sir,' I said in a polite but firm shouldn't-you-be-getting-off-home-now manner. Irene, the woman who ran this Oxfam in Kilburn, had warned me when I started. *A lot of folks will pop in for a natter and if you give them an inch they'll keep you chin-wagging till doomsday. Get the bags off them, a brisk thank you very kindly and cut 'em dead.*

'In this one, oof that's a weight. In this one it's her woollies. There's a cardie in there that'd suit a young 'un and the Millets bag is her oojamathings, her bits and bobs.'

I placed the bags behind the counter and scrawled their contents on the outsides with a marker pen. When I stood up, he was still standing there.

'Sorry, sir, was there anything else?'

'Well she had a stairlift but I couldn't get the blasted thing apart.'

I felt my will to live stirring uncomfortably in its pen.

'Are you interested, though? Cos young Keith's gotta van. Well more of a scooter really. Since Maureen's hysterectomy the boot-sales have gone for a Burton.'

My will to live had woken in a grouchy mood and was looking about for its coat.

'No no, sir,' I said, 'I meant was there anything more I could do for you?'

He gazed at me, slack-jawed for a moment. Actually it must have been quite a considerable moment because my jaw began to throb quite spectacularly, fixed as it was in a patronising simper.

Then finally –

'Well I'm not here for my health, young fella, how much'll you give me for the doo-dahs? You could get a couple of bob for that lot up the boot sale.'

Despite my gritted teeth, my will to live managed to

burst forth out onto the counter and I reached forward and grabbed him by the scarf, yanking it down towards the counter. Snatching up a heavy paperweight, I pinned him down with it and began to cover his gurning face with my pricing gun, screaming, *You insane old codger, your time here is done! You are no longer useful as a) a reproductive unit or b) a guardian or teacher of the young. Nature has given you a built-in obsolescence for this very reason! Now take your senility and your burden on this planet's resources and stop wasting my time!*

Or rather that's what I planned on doing, when there was a light angel-wing ting from the door and a very familiar figure wandered in with a couple of bulging carrier bags.

'Oh shitty fuck arse,' I cursed in a frantic half-whisper. The old gent rocked visibly backwards on his Blakeys.

'I beg your pardon, young man? Really, you ask a civil question! My sainted aunt, I've never been so . . .'

'Yes yes you're right,' I shushed rapidly, prodding and pushing him towards the clothing rails. 'Take whatever you like as payment, really whatever you like, thank you so much you're very kind it's just this way whoopsie come on come on keep up.' I crouched, head down across the floor, pulling him behind me like a sandbag shielding machine-gun fire. Finally I got within lunging distance of the old orangey curtain that separated the shop floor from the stockroom and dived through it with a clatter of pottery and bric a brac.

Shit shit shit, I wanted to be ready by now. I brushed clouds of asthmatic dust from my knees. If that old codger hadn't kept me talking . . . Still, can't be helped. I rummaged around in my rucksack and tugged out a T-shirt. Tossing it onto a large understuffed cuddly panda that sat forlornly in a corner, I fumbled at my shirt buttons.

'Who's on tillpoint, Charlie?' came a voice from around the corner.

'Huh? Oh I'm just grabbing some more price stickers, Irene, the shop's empty at the mo.'

'Righty-ho!' she called back cheerily. Good sort, Irene. In a dinnerlady-the-sensitive-kids-would-hold-hands-with-at-playtime sort of a way.

I got a mouthful of faded cotton pulling my T-shirt over my head and ran a sweaty hand through my brush of hair. Checking the reflection in the cubicle, I quickly ran through three different variations on an expression that said *Gosh what a lovely surprise!* and then held the most convincing one firmly as I clicked the little radio's presets from Heart FM to Radio 4 and pushed back the curtain onto the shop floor.

'Charlie!'

'Huh? Gosh, Debs! What a pleasant surprise, how the devil are you?'

'Well I-I'm fine, I'm fine. Wha-why-ho-?' Deborah looked genuinely flummoxed and flabbergasted, her eyebrows knitting and purling and generally dropping stitches all over the place. She opened and shut her mouth about sixteen times, as if the scene her eyes and ears were being asked to process was so beyond comprehension she'd had to enlist her taste buds to try and help. 'What are you . . . Why are you . . . How . . . ?'

I gave her a grin. I was quite enjoying this, to tell you the truth.

'I'm a volunteer here,' I eventually explained. For everybody's benefit. If her rapid jaw movement and hyperventilating got any worse she'd suck all the air out of the building and leave nowt but five dead pensioners.

Which is two more than the daily shop allowance will permit without a docket from head office.

'I just do the odd weekend,' I explained, clearing some coat-hangers from the floor and popping back behind the desk. 'Oh, cheerio then, Dora!' I called out with a wave. Deborah spun around to see an elderly lady puff and struggle with the door and her wheelie basket, eventually wandering out into the sunshine. 'That's Dora. Lovely lady. Husband killed at the Somme. Pops in for a cup of tea and a chat some afternoons. Never buys anything but, well, y'know, she likes a bit of company.'

'Really?' Deborah said distantly.

No, I thought to myself. Not really. Not at all, in fact.

Tell you the truth, I've never seen her before in my life. It was a guise, a screen, a facade.

And it wasn't the only one.

'You look different,' Deborah said. 'Your hair's shorter. It's nice. And that's new, isn't it?' She motioned at my T-shirt.

'Hn?' I grunted, feigning ignorance. 'This old thing? Naaah, you must have seen it before.'

'I don't think so.'

'Sure sure, I've been a member of Amnesty International for years.'

'You kept it very quiet.'

'Well, you know.' I waved bashfully. 'I didn't want to make a fuss. It's only a hundred quid a month, I'm not Bob Geldof. Whatcha got in the bags?'

'Huh? Oh just a few things, having a bit of a clearout, you know how it is.' She shook her head with a light laugh. 'I can't believe you work here now. How long have you been . . . cos y'know, I pop in every . . . well, on the odd y'know . . .'

Yes I know you do. You pop in every Saturday morning at about eleven to flick through the paperbacks, I thought. *I've seen you do it.*

'It's odd I haven't seen you, I've been doing this for a few months. Oh, but I went away for a while.'

'Holiday?'

'Er, kind of, if was more of a . . . well . . .'

'What?'

Bingo. Got her curiosity here. Carefully does it.

'I'd rather not say actually. It's kind of a well. . . . another time.'

I left a couple of beats for her mind to paint pictures before I threw a bucket of turps at her.

Metaphorically speaking.

'How's school?'

'Oh it's great, I'm really enjoying it. Yourself? How's the world of finance?'

'Couldn't be better,' I said. 'The futures market is stabilising for the first time this fiscal quarter and Tokyo are playing hardball over the Krugerrand but the mergers acquisitions are uhm . . .'

Fuck it, I knew this yesterday.

'They're uhm . . .'

Deborah stared. And the lady queuing behind her stared. And I expect most of north-west London were staring as well but, to be honest, I was a little too flustered to check.

'The Nikkei Dow Jones thing has, uhm, crashed.'

'Gosh,' Deborah said. 'Crashed? That sounds serious. I didn't know, I haven't seen a newspaper.'

'Well, a-ha, not crashed as such. But financially it's, ahhh, dented a bit. The prices. Of . . . shares and . . . things. They're a bit . . . broken.'

Rehearse, Charlie boy, rehearse. What did I tell you this morning?

'So, ha, anyway, what're all these clothes? You going

338

for a change of wardrobe?' I tugged and yanked out a handful of girly items.

'It's just a few things I don't wear any more.'

'What's this? You're getting rid of the polycotton halterneck with the contrasting darts? And your Agnes B bias-cut skirt?' I pulled more and more items from the bag, including a heavy pair of boots. 'And not your half-length stack-heeled Kurt Geigers, surely?'

Deborah stood agape. *Men aren't meant to know any of this shit*, she was thinking. But there was no stopping me. Onto her second bag – slashes, turtles, maxis, pedals, pencils and Prada.

I tell you, fellas, you read enough *Cosmo* this stuff just seeps in, what do you want me to say?

And then I stopped mid-grab. This item I knew well. Very well.

A matching bra and brief set. Size 12 briefs, 34C bra in a blue and white lace-edged gingham. A cotton and lycra mix. M&S, I think. Yes, definitely. The labels and price tag still attached, they both swung loosely from the original black plastic hanger. I held them up. Deborah's face went from *What are you doing?* to *Oh shit*. Surprisingly slowly.

But then her face had had to pop in via *I suddenly remember who bought me those*.

'These look familiar,' I said.

'Shit, Charlie, I'm sorry, I didn't expect you to, well . . . I didn't think you'd be . . .'

'It doesn't matter.' I smiled good-naturedly. 'You didn't like them?'

She shook her head after a beat with a little half shrug, a little colour in her cheeks.

She was embarrassed. Embarrassed, not so much that I'd found her out after all these years. More that the memory had clearly taken us both back to a distinctly awkward place neither of us wanted to go.

It was suddenly one July morning. The sunshine sending the bedroom into a drowsy soft-focus haze. Radio 1 humming a chirpy Huey Lewis number quietly. Deborah was naked, a brushed cotton sheet about her hips, the salty smell of fresh sex hanging at waist level in the air. There were lilies in a blue glass vase on her dressing table – a last day of term gift. A small green and gold plastic bag empty on the bed. I was just out of the shower, towelling and patting my hairless chest softly. Deborah held up the underwear, just out of the bag and smelling of new cotton. She gushed thank yous and they're lovelies and it seemed to dawn on us both simultaneously we had six glorious summer weeks ahead and we fell into love-making once again.

That's where I was, standing in the dusty Oxfam in Kilburn among damp and chintz. And by her expression, and the way she gripped her gloves tightly in white knuckles, I figured Deborah was there too. Briefly, for a fleeting second perhaps, but it showed.

She blinked hard, rapidly, trying to shake it off like a bathroom shiver on a cold morning and began rattling around in another bag.

'I've, er . . . there's also some, er . . .' She brought out some tatty paperbacks and began to stack them on the counter absently, her mind still otherwhere. 'Most of these are old and and . . .'

I lightened everything up briskly.

'Let's see what all this is. *Not a Penny More, The Stud, A Time to Kill, Polo.* These are going back a bit, you could restock a small airport with this lot.'

'It's just some old paperbacks from long ago.'

'And what's in here?' I said finally, tugging out a final book from the bottom of the tatty bag.

'That's . . . oh shit, Charlie, I'm sorry,' Deborah gasped as the book fell onto the counter. 'I don't know how that got in there. Really, Charlie, Brad must've . . .'

'Brad?'

She'd said his name and he was here suddenly. Between us.

'Yes, he gave me a hand bagging this lot up.'

'Right, right.' I picked up my copy of *The Naked Ape* from the countertop and riffled it. A bus ticket was tucked in halfway through, five months old, I noticed.

'That should have gone in the *keep* pile. He's mixed up the bags.' Deborah peered into the last carrier at her feet. 'Oh bloody hell, I'm going to have to take all these back again.' I held the book out.

'That's fine, don't worry about it. You want to take this? Finish it? You're only up to the chapter on fighting.'

'No,' she said. 'You'd better take it,' and she gave a small smile. 'I know how you get withdrawal symptoms. I mean, you can't have reread this one for a few hours now.'

'I have no idea what you mean.' I smirked with mock aloofness.

She thwacked me on the arm with her tiny gloved hand. Firmly, in a way that seemed to say *I miss this*. But then, come on, who are we kidding here? I've never been that great at reading her signals so you might not want to —

'I miss this,' she said.

Oh. My signal-reading had obviously improved somewhat.

And then came the tears.

They burst forth suddenly, unexpectedly, in a wail of unhappiness and distress. A long drawn-out cry that caused all the octogenarian browsers and dawdlers to look up from their browsing and dawdling. A cry that became hiccuping sobs and coughs and sniffs.

'What the hell was that?' Deborah asked.

'Oh that's George,' I said, motioning over my shoulder to the orange curtain. 'Irene's got him, he's probably just woken up. Liz and Ade are away —'

'Their anniversary, of course . . .'

'So I'm doing the whole daddy thing. I tell you what, you have a quick rummage through this lot, make sure there's nothing else in here that Brad has – well – that might have got in by mistake, and I'll tend to the little one.'

I left Deborah rummaging and disappeared out the back.

Beautiful, I mused with a tight smug grin, couldn't have planned it better. First the haircut, then the T-shirt. Then an unexpected double-hitter with the underwear and the Desmond Morris.

'Hey, Irene, whassup with this little fella, hmm?'

Irene had run this Oxfam for years and was as trust-worthy a part of the fittings as the severed polystyrene heads in the window displaying the faded hats. She was also a mother of three grown-up boys which is why I'd felt safe leaving George with her while I built the scenery.

'Oh he's just grizzling,' she chuckled from the staffroom, where she had laid him out on a towel on the table. He gurgled a little and kicked as she counted and recounted and triple-checked his quantity of *lickle tiny toesy-woesies.*

Still ten, it seemed. Adrian would be pleased. Which reminded me, I should check when they were due back.

That could wait.

'I'm going to bring him out front in his buggy, Irene, if that's okay. It's a little less stuffy.'

343

'Yes yes that's fine. We've had our lunchy, haven't we, Georgie? Haven't we? Daww, dat's right!' and she blew a raspberry on his round tummy. 'Just keep the buggy from under people's feet, will you, love? I'm sticking the kettle on, you want one?'

'Absolutely. C'mon, little fella.' I gathered him up and strapped him writhing into his McClaren single seater. 'Now,' I whispered, tightening the numerous and frankly paranoid number of tightenable bits, 'don't you let me down. I want adoring and cute, okay? Remember, like we discussed in the car? Adoring and cute.'

Back in the shop. Deborah was stuffing bits and bobs into one split carrier bag from another equally split carrier bag.

'Here he is!' I called.

'Brad's managed to put a whole pile of my things in the wrong . . . Ohhh look who it is! Hello there, little one, hello there! Gosh he's getting big.'

'Isn't he?' I said, parking the buggy neatly to one side. 'Say hello then. Say hello, c'mon, wave.'

Deborah waved and her face crumpled into a warm, softening smile.

'You two are seeing a lot of each other.'

'We are,' I agreed, 'we get on famously, don't we, you, hmm?'

Deborah crouched down to eye level with the buggy, touching the baby oh so very tenderly on his plump red cheeks.

I figured this was as good a time as I was ever going to get. The warm smell of cotton and skin, the Desmond Morris on the counter, her irritation with Brad still floating on the surface like pond scum. I held my breath and counted down from three.

'Can I come and see you soon?'

Her brain processed this information quickly, visibly. She looked up, her fingers still on George's face and, most importantly, the smile still on hers.

'You know' — and she looked away — 'I have been meaning to call.'

'Can I then?' I pressed. After all this set-up, all this preparation and preamble — the job, clothes, baby — I was getting a firm date right now godammit.

'Come over tonight,' she said finally.

Whoopsie, whoah easy there hold you horses. I mean, I'm keen, I know but . . .

Fuckin' 'ell.

'About seven thirty, eight? I'll make some dinner or something. We can talk in peace. Okay?' She stood up, meeting my eyes for the first time, the tiniest tiniest hint of sadness swimming behind them, all but imperceptible to anyone who hadn't known her a long long time.

'Er, okay. Sure, I mean if, y'know, if you want.' A thought struck me suddenly. 'Actually if I'm coming over, I could bring these bags of stuff for you. Save you dragging them all over NW6.'

'No no no don't be silly, you can't manage all this lot. I mean thanks, but it's fine really.'

'It's okay,' I said, waving her off, taking the bags and trying to suppress a grin.

'I've got the car.'

'Bloody hell, whose is this?' Deborah gasped, her eyebrows floating above her head like French punctuation. The Cabriolet glinted and winked in the city's autumn sunshine.

'Hn? Oh this is mine.'

'Yours?' She flapped with disbelief.

'Yeah.' I shrugged as casually as my frantically overexcited limbs would let me without an internal haemorrhage. I longed for nothing more than to skip about the street, throwing car keys from hand to hand chanting, *See? This is what you missed, ha!* etc.

But I didn't.

'I know it's a terrible extravagance in London but it's just a nippy little thing to get me from A to B. Kind of a bonus from the firm cos I'm doing so well – blue chip gilt client portfolio base and . . . stuff. I'm off to, uhm, Stuttgart next month so it'll come in handy on the autobahn . . . things. Y'know?' I walked around to the back of the car.

'So what's up with it?'

'Up with *her*?' I queried, stressing the gender, rather

poncily now I think about it. 'What do you mean? She purrs like a kitten.' I unlocked the gleaming red boot and lifted the bags to place them inside, stopping suddenly as I peered in. 'But, er, ha, I like to give her a quick, er, polish before setting, er, off.'

Shitty shit fuck. Rear-cocking-mounted engine. What a crappy Krauty idea.

I wiped the cylinders ineffectually for a second and fiddled with the cables just to double-check that, hmmm yep, they were still cables, shut the boot and lugged the bags round to the front. I loaded the car and slammed the hood with a macho *Top Gun* cockiness.

'So I'll see you tonight?'

'Huh? Oh. Oh y-yes,' Deborah stuttered, snapping back to life. The car, the job — I was, granted, laying it on a bit thick. But this was a one-shot deal. I was attempting a leapfrog in the food chain, a step up the evolutionary ladder. The kind of mutation required to bring about this huge change, this path-skewing paradigm shift, was never going to be brought about by just ironing a shirt.

Deborah, rooted to the pavement for a second, gave a tiny hesitant wave and wandered into the crowd.

Was it a quick walk? An urgent walk? Was it a slow thoughtful amble? I tried to gauge her feelings as she disappeared amongst the noise and bodies of the Saturday shoppers.

Fucking hell, what am I doing standing here? I checked my watch. I've got work to do.

'Charlie, I've got your tea here, d'you want . . . ? Charlie, where are you going? Leaving? What headache? But Mrs Fearnely isn't due in until three. Can't you hang on until three, Charlie? Charlie . . . ?'

TWENTY-SEVEN

'Success is a science. If you have the conditions you get the result.'

Oscar Wilde

Okay, right. C'mon, settle down, settle down. Hoy, you there, are you chewing? I see, well did you bring enough for everybody? No, sir, well then swallow it. Now let's have a bit of hush, shall we? Come on, it's your own time you're wasting. Right, good. As promised last lesson, we're having a test today . . . there's no point oh sirrrr-ing me, you've known about this for 60 billion years.

So chop chop, books away, question one.

If a twenty-seven-year-old man is standing in the centre of a room 12 feet by 16 feet, and a woman of the

349

same age is in the adjacent kitchen, 12 feet by 8 feet —
should the man offer to help with the meal?

No, don't put your hand up. Write it down.

'D'you want to put some music on or something?' Deborah calls through from the kitchen.

'Sure, no problem,' I respond in an offhand and relaxed, but not unconfident, manner. Putting my vodka and tonic down (cool but not too cool) I hop lightly over to the stereo.

Deborah is clattering pots and plates. I offered to help half an hour ago upon my arrival but she shunted me into the lounge with a friendly peck and we've been yelling non-sequiturs to each other through thin walls and long pauses every so often since then.

Like my choice of Porsche over Rolls-Royce, I figure suddenly becoming a cordon bleu chef in the three months since we last shared a meal would be stretching the whole thing just that bit too far which I don't want to do.

But as I kneel down in front of the stereo, the one thing I wish I had stretched a bit further was these trousers.

I've plumped for the black loafers tonight. They're new and crunchy and feel a bit weird after the boots but they go better with this dark grey Paul Smith suit, which I've lightened up (which *FHM* informed me I was perfectly within my rights to do) with a white ribbed T-shirt.

The cost of this ensemble? Don't even ask. Suffice to say if you're quick, you might be able to nip down to a second-hand shop in Notting Hill and pick up a video, TV, stereo and Playstation – one careless owner.

The whole thing has a prickly newness to it and it feels like I've left the hangar in the trousers. Squirming and itching, I reach round the back, my armpits prickly with nervousness, and with a sharp snap, I pull the scratchy price tag out of the tee.

'Just stick on whatever,' Deborah calls out.

I eject the little CD tray with a whirr and peer at the contents. It's nine minutes past eight.

Okay, all done? Well hurry up. Right, question two is a multiple choice. A male wishes to appear impressive, educated, stylish and high in status in front of a female as a precursor to reproduction. Greatest success will occur by use of a) Marvin Gaye b) Frank Sinatra c) Chris Isaac or d) whatever she wants?

I lift the silver disk out nimbly. It looks to be *Viva Hate*, Morrissey's first solo album. A quick squinty scan down the silvery surface, pop pickers, reveals such gems as 'Late Night Maudlin Street', 'Bengali in Platforms' and the upbeat bounce-along boogie fest which isn't 'Margaret on the Guillotine'.

No no no, this will never do, I think, and snap it into its case.

And then with a jolt, I twang it out of its case and drop it with a click back into the tray. Because I don't want this to look like I'm setting it up.

But of course, we know different. I can't leave this, my stab at happiness, my lunge at immortality, down to chance, can I?

So I whisk Morrissey out and flick rapidly through her CD rack. Tricky, tricky . . .

Sexy music is divisible into two clear categories, which we'll call *a & b*, because there are knife and fork sounds coming from the kitchen and I haven't time to argue. You've got a) – music you slap on when you and your partner are both, absolutely, no question, deffo for sure, up for a 'bit'. And it's an *I'm gonna pop to the bogs, why don't you stick some music on or something, don't start without me* situation. Usually slow stuff, maybe sixties-ish, Motowny.

Nothing by Rolf Harris, anyway.

Type b we will call groundwork music – tunes put on as a scene setter, to put the other person in the 'mood'. A more subtle kettle of minims.

You see the trouble with choosing music on an occasion such as this one is that what you really want, ideally, are two different tunes happening at once. The first to illustrate how clever and modern sophisticated and all-together groovy one is — a bit of obscure jazz perhaps, a rare piece of Charlie Parker vinyl. Or maybe something classical and sensitive — a Schubert string quartet or similar fiddly business.

But of course the downside to these is that no one in the history of audibleness has ever got off with anyone during a freeform bee-bop progression. And nor has a feel been anywhere near copped while four begowned spinsters fannied about with cellos.

Which is why, simultaneously, you need something more obviously bedroomy, which to my mind, and to the mind of a very helpful article in *Q Magazine* this month, has always been the home of the lone crooner.

The only ones I can find nestling here are Sinatra's seminal 1956 classic *Songs for Swingin' Lovers* and *Wicked Game* by Chris Isaac.

If this whole evening hadn't been sprung on me at such short notice I might have had time to bring a couple of Walkmans with me.

But my eye falls suddenly on just the thing and I scrabble about, catching my nail on the case. A *Now that's What I Call the Best Soul Album in the World . . . Ever Volume II.* I slip it in with fragile haste like it was a porcelain condom and a smirk smirks back at me in the stereo's reflective black plastic finish.

Because Marvin Gaye's 'Sexual Healing', which was playing on the radio that wonderful first night, five years ago, is track twelve. Which gives me until about nine p.m. to lay the groundwork.

Excellent.

'God, I haven't heard this for ages,' floats in a voice behind me. In a panic, I spin around. No, phew, Deborah's still in the kitchen. I have precious seconds to prepare the room properly.

'Er, yeah, yeah,' I call back. 'I've, y'know, been getting into this sort of stuff recently.' Lionel Richie seems to be bragging about how he can go *all night long*. At his age, he probably means *to the toilet*. I dart nimbly about the room, crouching and hunching in the corners, like a wrestling referee, trying to get all the views I can. Over by the door – hmmm, it's all a bit bright. I try with the light off. No, too dark. Now what about . . . ? I flick on the table lamp. A-ha, that's better. Still not quite right, though.

'Dinner's up!' she calls from the kitchen. 'Can you give me a hand with the wine?'

Shitty shit shit. The lamp would work better over by the television. Have I got time to grab the extension cord from the cupboard under the sink?

'You might want to give the glasses a rinse.' The voice is nearer. There's a click and the hall light goes off. I spot just the thing on the mantelpiece.

'I hope you're hungry . . .'

Shit shit shit come on come on come on come on, light, you waxy fuck, light.

'There's a bottle opener in . . . oooh you've lit the candles.'

I turn, shaking the match out, squeezing the box into the pocket of my new flat-fronted Paul Smith trews, to see Deborah framed in the doorway, a tray held out in front of her with two huge white plates of something sort of pastary and tomatoey and peppery. The smell billows through the room in a garlicky plume.

All right, settle down. Question three. What's that? No I haven't, you should have brought a spare one. Question three, if you can all see the board. We have here a picture of a young woman. She is dressed in a white tape yarn vest, a tie waist full-length skirt in beige silk and a pair of brown wedge crossover suede mules. What? Well you should have revised a bit harder, this really is Book One *stuff. Question is, is this woman showing any interest in pursuing sexual intercourse?*

She looks beautiful. I snap forward and start wrestling with a set of nesting tables as she bends lightly to lay out the plates. The rich smell of the food is trying its darndest to overpower her feminine just-bathed perfume but it can't and I get a woozy headrush of it.

Deborah has tied back her hair and piled a bit of it in spiky hedgehog clumps on the top of her head, a few stray strands waterfalling over her face. This looks suspiciously like it's designed to appear casual and *Oh this? I've hardly had a moment to do anything with it.*

I should know, I have half a stinky green tub of Superdrug gel trying to pull off the same act on my unruly crop.

But something is different about her hair. It's longer or shorter or lighter or something. Something that makes me want to touch it softly, anyway. The strands lead the eye to the face, a face which, again, has had a lot of time spent on it to give the effect of no time at all.

As she lays out condiments on the table, chatting away inconsequentially about herbs or something, she reveals two clean armpits, pink and pimply from a fresh shave.

That's got to mean something.

'I'll sort out the drinks,' I say quickly and nip into the kitchen where I take the opportunity to wipe my sweaty hands on a Brecon Beacons tea-towel and have a bit of a pace and a think.

While making loud clattery corkscrew-hunting noises, obviously.

The hair. The hair and the vest and the armpits and the little peepy-toed shoes. This isn't exactly slumming-round-the-house stuff. This is Diana, sitting in the corner of the cage. This is Diana, positioning herself to hide a potentially swollen rear. Possibly. Too early to say. And is Jeremiah going to try and sniff her or not?

She can't tell yet. But some effort has gone into this, I'm pleased to say, and not all from my side.

Let's face it, this could go either way.

'Can you bring a cloth through?' she calls out.

'No problem,' I holler back, which, as dialogue goes, is about as raunchy as it's got so far. We've spent this half hour circling each other. Wary, but not timid. The communication has been simple, practical, fraternal. Storage and napkins and telly. I mean, I knew I wouldn't be beating her off with the blunt end of her Dyson but she's playing it cool, no doubt there.

Back into the lounge, Deborah takes the cloth to wipe up a splash of tomato sauce. She stands and hands the cloth back and I take it and our hands touch slightly and we share a tiny smile.

'This looks great,' I say with harmless bouncy enthusiasm. Just strolling round the cage now.

'I think I may have overdone it with the green peppers but . . .'

'Oh no, I'm sure it's fine. Here,' and I pour a healthy glug of Merlot. The male will traditionally offer refreshment.

Deborah takes the sofa which means I back away, unthreateningly, into the opposite armchair. Which, incidentally, isn't out of any awareness of feng shui. I'm merely planning ahead. If, three glasses of wine in, she begins to look a bit tearful (because as I say, this evening could go either way), the soft *Hey hey, what is it?* has much greater impact if it's combined with a move from *fig #1 – Opposite* to *fig #2 – Next-to*.

So we sit. And we eat. And we drink. And we *mmmm* and we *that's better* and we *oooh, what a day*. Or rather, Deborah does. Between gulping mouthfuls of wine, I grunt out a response or two and nod wherever nodding is required. But I can't concentrate. My mind is busy on sixteen hundred other subjects. One of which is Stevie Wonder, who's swaying all over 'Misstra Know It All' (rather aptly, I think to myself). Which is track five. Giving me about half an hour. Everything else on my mind comes under the general heading of BRAD.

'How was your food?' Deborah is asking, snapping me back suddenly.

'Hmm? Oh it's good, very good.' I nod, twirling up the last strands of spaghetti awkwardly.

She smiles and munches for a bit. 'Yes, I thought you'd like it. I did it especially.'

I grin and scoop up my wine glass again.

There isn't a single trace of Brad anywhere. I mean, I presumed that, being a thoughtful sort, Deborah would have removed any overly gratuitous memorabilia – large oil paintings of them both outside a country mansion, *B 4 D* spelt out in chunky plastic letters on the fridge, suitcases full of sex toys. But there's not a photo, not a borrowed book, not a video cassette box, not even a beer can in the bin. It's like he's never been here.

'It's good to see you, Charlie,' Deborah says.

I look up. Her plate is on the floor, along with her shoes. She's swept herself up onto the sofa and she's smoothing the excesses of her skirt over her legs quickly. I get a flash of pink thigh through the slit and it's gone.

'It's been too long, don't you think?'

'Yes, yes it has,' I say.

Hey-up, where the hell is this going? This wasn't in the book?

'I'm glad you could make it. I've been thinking about you – well about us – I've been thinking about us a lot.'

Oh Christ, no. What's coming? I've timed this to the second. I have a few probing questions, a couple of impressive lies and, bada-bing, on the first beat of Marvin, I move in. What's she trying to pull? She's been thinking about us a lot?

Shit.

This is going to be how we're better apart than together, presumably. How we should stay in touch. How she wants me to stay friends. That's got to be it.

'We were good together, weren't we? We were happy.'

Were. You get that, viewers? We *were* good together. Not 'we *are* good together'. Fuck. This is all I need. I can feel sperm deep within me groan and stick the gears into reverse.

'But I really needed this time apart. You know?'

I fix her a look. Her head is tilted slightly, her mouth open the tiniest part. Hair falls across one eye but she doesn't brush it away. She just looks at me. One hand holding the balloon-like wine glass, the other stroking her bare ankles beneath her.

It's obvious I'm not going to say anything. I'm waiting for my fears to be founded. My light autumn suit suddenly seems weighty and a feel a bead of sweat run into my armpit. This isn't going to be good. She and Brad are obviously more serious than I thought. Maybe they're moving in together? No, no surely not.

But that would explain why none of his stuff is here . . .

'And I know I should have called. I know. But I knew that if we spoke then I'd just get all confused and I needed a good bit of time completely without you to make sure what I felt was for real. Because this is a big step for me, Charlie. A very big step.'

Oh Christ. Here we go.

'I asked you round because I want to get married . . .' she begins and a roar of panic mugs my insides, sending my brain smashing into the front of my skull. The music is Macy Gray, something about 'Why Didn't You Call Me?' Track six. It's eight thirty-seven. Oh fuck.

'Charlie?' Deborah says. I haven't heard anything else, the blood screaming in my ears. My one chance at happiness, my absolute focus, and she's asking my permission to marry Brad. Mister Alpha himself. All

the posing, all the posturing, the car and the clothes —
all too late.

I get up.

'Charlie, say something . . .' Deborah says with a
break of urgency in her voice.

'I'm just getting some water,' I say and head
stumbling into the kitchen.

*Right then, moving on. Question four. Two males, who
appear to be of equal status, engage in battle for the rights
to a lone female. One male, the trespasser, strikes an
almost fatal blow. Bearing in mind what is at stake, how
much should the second male risk in a counter-attack?
Score between 1 and 10 — 1 for retreat, 10 for kamikaze
charge.*

In the kitchen. Oh God, what am I *doing*? Pace pace
pace. This is what she invited me over for? To tell me
about her and Brad. To break this news to me. That's
why she's all bathed and clean, all wine and candles.
The atmosphere's as comfortable and pleasant as she
can make it, all pasta and *put some music on* because
she's delivering bad news, the worst news. Oh Christ,
what have I done? My head's going like a roulette
wheel and I pace back and forth, back and forth, giving
the countertops a slap at every turn. What to do what to
do, slap turn pace, what to do what to do, slap turn pace.

'Are you all right, Charlie?' Deborah's voice floats in.

'Yes yes fine, just, er, just give me a second,' I yell back, stammering.

A third slap turn pace. Well I'm not giving up. Absolutely not. She may have staked a claim on the male but the visiting intruder doesn't have to skulk back into the forest. She's seen the suit, the hair, the car, the job. I can come up with one more trick, surely? One more display.

I gulp down some water straight from the tap, wiping the dribbling run off from my chin on my new suit sleeves, and shut off the tap firmly. I can hear Aretha Franklin belting out how much she really feels like something. A natural woman, an early night, a bit of sit-down. One of those. That's track ten. It's seven minutes to nine.

Here we go.

'Charlie.' Deborah stands up as I walk in. 'Are you okay? Look, this has all come as a shock, I suppose, but don't you see . . .' and she walks towards me with her arms out and a soft smile, her face a warm glow through the wine and candlelight.

'Deborah,' I say firmly, my hand held up like I'm dancing to 'YMCA'.

(Trust me, I'd know.)

'Deborah, just listen.'

She stops where she is and drops her hands to her sides.

362

'I want to talk to you, I want . . . well I want you to listen to me.'

'What is it?'

'Just . . . just come and sit down.'

She returns to her place on the sofa and I squeeze in next to her among the cushions, our knees touching.

'Look.'

No turning back now, old fella.

'You know when I saw you this afternoon, in Oxfam?'

'Yes.'

'And I told you I'd been working there a few weeks. And I told you I'd also been away on holiday.'

'I remember,' and she smirks a little for some reason.

'What? What's funny?' I ask.

'Nothing, nothing,' she says with a clearance of throat and a shakance of her head. 'Go on.'

I don't know what she's grinning at. Have I got tomato round my mouth? A bit of pepper on my chin? I glance around for a reflective surface quickly. Nothing. But I haven't time to worry, Aretha's fading out.

'Well, I have to apologise to you.'

'You do?'

'Yes, yes I do. Because I wasn't exactly telling you the truth there.'

'Ah,' she says. And the little smile is back. But I'm on a tight schedule here so I press on.

'I actually . . .'

'Yes?' She stretches out slowly.

'I've actually been in Mozambique. I was there for a month, on famine relief work with orphaned children.'

'Oh Charlie, for the love of *God* . . .' she says, taking her head in her hands.

'No please let me explain.'

'Charlie . . .'

'It's something I had to do.' I stand up and turn my back on her. Which is a bit of a soap-opera move but I need all the help I can get. 'I was based out in the capital Nampula where the suffering is worst,' I explain to her window, all the while cursing myself for not thinking of this sooner. Maybe I could have arranged for a postcard to be sent or something. Or at least to have the *Observer* article I'm quoting from blown up and stuck to her curtains. 'I didn't tell anyone I was going because I didn't want a fuss made. The office gave me a month's paid leave and I caught a flight out on a *CAFOD* Aid Relief plane. That's why I never called you, that's why the phone messages stopped. I thought about you all the time I was there, looking into the eyes of the starving children and . . . and . . .'

I spin around and look at Deborah, earnestness written all over my face in block capitals. She's still sitting on the sofa in silence.

'And I thought, if only all men could see this. Not just men like me – successful, wealthy, in good health, with prospects and a good set of wheels, but all men. Then the world . . . well, the world . . . What's so funny?'

Deborah pulls a cushion over her face and squeezes it. After a second or two she looks up, flushed, her hair tumbling around her face, beaming.

'That's where you've been, is it?' she says.

'Th-that's right. I'm glad you're pleased for me.'

'So you haven't spent the last month, say, seeing other women and moping about at home?'

'No, no absolutely not.' I race forward and sit next to her again. Track eleven — Al Green's 'Let's Stay Together', is halfway through. 'I know that's the sort of thing most guys do, regular guys do. So I don't blame you if that's what you imagined.'

'And the car out there,' she says, brushing her hair out of her eyes and picking up her wine glass. 'Remind me, you were given that by your new work . . . Where was it?'

'In the City.'

'In the City, right.' Deborah nods to herself.

I let a pause run while I try and work out what that smirk is all about. I can't recall a single theory about females finding males' courtship amusing. There's no reason for it, absolutely none. This stuff shouldn't be making her feel happy. She invites me round to cook me dinner and explain it's all over between us — and now this smiling lark? I am very confused.

But the clock on the mantelpiece says two minutes to nine. I haven't time to worry.

'Don't you see?' I say. 'I've changed. I'm not the same person you left in that staffroom in July.'

'I know that, Charlie. The old you never would have gone to all the trouble of pretending –'

'Pretending I was over you,' I interrupt quickly, 'I know, I know. But I want us to start again, really I do.'

'Start again.'

'Yes. Start again properly,' and I take her wine glass from her and hold her hands.

'Okay.'

'Because I think I'm ready now. I'm ready to provide for you, I'm ready to take care of you. I can offer you what you want.'

'Okay, Charlie.'

'Food, shelter, warmth, status . . .'

'Charlie, what are you –'

'Health, hygiene, essential needs . . .'

'*Charlie.*'

'Sorry, yes?'

The room goes quiet. We look at each other. Marvin has begun his slow groove across the floor of the lounge to where we sit. Together.

'Let me ask you something.'

'Sure, sure,' I say, giving her hands a squeeze.

She's going to apologise about going off with Brad. She's going to ask me to forgive her. She's going to ask if all three of us can be friends one day. She's going to ask me to stick the kettle on then pop to the bathroom cabinet to make sure there are plenty of condoms while she phones Brad to cancel their wedding. She's going to ask me if I'll agree to shut the fuck up and not say another word all night . . .

'What?'

'Not another word. No fibs, no boasts, not a word, not a word all night. Not until the morning.'

I open my mouth to complain and then I get it and crack a grin.

I'm still going to be here in the morning.

'No problem,' I say, miming a zip across my lips. Although hold on, what does she mean by fibs? I open my mouth but Deborah quickly leans forward and kisses me.

Which comes as quite a surprise.

I think we kiss for about four weeks, I'm not entirely sure. I know that the CD has clicked itself off by the time I open my eyes and come up for air.

Deborah opens her eyes slowly, smiles, her mouth pale and smudged where lipstick used to be.

'Too much wine,' she says. 'I'm going to the bathroom.'

And with that she puts her hand on my shoulder with a squeeze and leaves the room, her skirt rustling and whispering as she disappears.

Fan-fucking-tastic.

I can't suppress a huge smug grin and I take a big swig of wine. Relationship back, marriage back, children a mere formality.

And Brad? Well the best man won, no question there. *Although.*

I stand up and pop nimbly out into the hall to where the bathroom door is locked.

'Deborah,' I say to the stripped pine with a little knock.

'I'm on the loo,' she says. 'And I said no talking.'

'Yes, sorry. I just have one question.'

'Oh all right, go on.'

'There's no chance . . . well there's no chance Brad will come back, is there?'

'Back? Back where?'

'Back here, I mean. Cos if he comes in and finds me, well, having sex with his girlfriend, y'know. There could be problems.'

'Sex with his *girlfriend*? What the hell are you on about?'

'Considering you and he have been at it for a few months now, and he thinks he's going to marry you, he might take it badly to find me here. Filling in for him. So to speak.'

Silence from the bathroom.

'Deborah?' I call out. 'Are you okay? I mean, I can put the latch on the front door if you like. So he can't come in. Did he take a key . . . ?'

'What the fucking hell are you on about?' she yells from inside, her voice loud against the tiles.

'I . . . I just thought, to be careful . . .'

'What the hell has he *told* you?!'

I open my mouth to the shrill burst of a ringing phone.

Which, before you contact a speech therapist, is coming from the lounge.

'I'll get that, stay where you are,' I shout and jog back through.

'Charlie!' Deborah yells.

As I approach the little white handset, tucked behind a lamp on a small table by the sofa, I shiver. I sit. The curtains are closed and motionless, there is no breeze. But I shiver.

Because somehow I know. Somehow I know this will be him. This will be him and he'll be surprised at my voice. And then he'll want to know what I'm doing here.

I need an excuse. I need a plan, a preparation, a speech. But all the time I'm thinking, *What can I say? What can I say? What can I say?* My hand is reaching for the phone.

'Hello?'

There is a pause. The mute roar of distant traffic. It's a phone box. Or a mobile.

'Charlie, is that you?'

'Yep, hi. How are you?'

'Good, good. Thought you might be there. How's my baby?'

'Hn? Oh shit . . .'

The voice on the other end of the line is suddenly a lot of things. It's shocked, horrified and furious. It cracks and wavers. 'What the fuck do you mean?! Haven't you got him?! Where the fuck is he?!' it yells.

The voice is not happy.

And it's not Brad.

'Where the hell is my fucking son, you thoughtless bastard?! Oy! Answer me! What the fuck have you done with my son?'

TWENTY-EIGHT

'When this baby hits 88 miles per hour, you're gonna see some serious shit.'

Dr Emmett Brown

The Porsche 911 Cabriolet, as we have already discussed, is capable of 231 bhp, has 3164 cc capacity and does 20.8 miles per gallon. I can't recall if I mentioned it can throw itself forward at a quite staggering 0–60 mph in only 5.5 seconds.

But it can. Boy, it really can.

Less than two minutes ago I'd dropped the telephone handset with a sharp yelp as if I'd stuck my nose in a gas ring. I'd imagine. My shoes were suddenly glued to

Deborah's rug by the thick adhesive of panicky indecision.

Where was the baby, where had I left the baby?

I gritted my teeth and pressed the heels of my hands to my forehead, hard, as if the answers were the last drops of soapy water in a kitchen sponge. The room about me was dark, the candles having snuffed themselves out. Their white smoke smooched and wiggled upwards, illuminated only by the yellow street-light glow from behind the curtains. I couldn't focus, too much going on. Deborah in the bathroom, sex on the agenda, the horrific screams of Liz punctuating Adrian's measured fury.

I'd had him in the shop. Yes, yes that's right. I began to slow my breathing. And then after Oxfam I'd gone . . . straight home. Home to change for tonight.

Home.

One hand on the back of the sofa, I vaulted the nesting tables with the athletic grace of a professional plate-kicker, the stringy spaghetti remains splashing and crashing against the hard floor, deafening in the dark silence. I banged my way off walls down the hall towards the door, stopping with a squeaky screech at the bathroom.

'Charlie? What the hell's going on out there?!' Deborah yelled from inside. I could hear the rustle of a skirt being straightened. A toilet flushed.

I ran.

Bounding the stairs two at a time with heart-lurching terror, past the calm white doors of the other flats, I thudded down the hall and threw myself sweating into the chill September night.

The car tore through the darkness of north-west London, heading south, down Loudon Road towards the Wellington Hospital, the freezing city air roaring through the open windows turning my fear-filled sweat to ice. I stuck to the leafier side streets, dodging parked cars with lurching swerves. My heart, after about two minutes, decided it was safer elsewhere, leapt out of my mouth and strapped itself into the passenger seat. I had a fuzzy red-wine headache which the constant engine roar was doing its best to aggravate.

Shooting through an amber light to the blare of car horns at Grove End Road towards Lord's Cricket Ground, the whole world had the loud, white-knuckle phoniness of a Playstation game. The halogen lights throwing two white ellipses ahead, the surrounding trees and houses smudging into one dark stripe. The engine, which I struggled to control through my pounding head and slippy wet palms, fighting the tiny steering wheel. Every time I swerved past slower cars and shifted up a gear I expected a little bleepy fanfare in my head and my new score to appear floating in front of me, bright neon in the road.

Five hair-raising minutes later, I spun into my road with a real *Starsky & Hutch* squeal of rubber and whooshed past the dotted stripe of parked cars looking for the usual space outside my flat.

The usual space that was now home to a large blue estate.

Easing off, slowing the engine, I spotted another space a little further along and slipped the Porsche in untidily, shutting it off with a German, precision-made click. The dashboard lights dimmed like dying stars and the engine began immediately to tick and cool.

I listened to myself breathe a while.

I didn't want to get out, but I suppose you'd figured that out yourself. I wanted to secure the roof even tighter and sit in here with all the guy stuff. Warm, expensive, contoured and reassuring guy stuff. I clicked on the interior light and took a moment to run my fingers over the smooth lines. The CD player, the panelling, the gadgets and bucket seats. The specs, the power. Safe. Because out there, in the darkness, the unknown, was a lot of female stuff. Stuff which, despite my studious research, suddenly seemed very frightening.

Nothing in my books had covered this particular situation very comprehensively, I thought. What exactly to do, what the expected form was. There was bound to be something, though. Somewhere on my creaking shelves, somewhere in my reams and ring-binders. I'm sure if I spent a day cross-referencing through indexes and bibliographies there would be some research available.

Hmm. I tapped my fingers on the sticky steering wheel, clammy from my sweaty grip. I wonder if they'd let me pop inside for a minute and make some notes? Nothing too definitive, of course. Just enough to be able to rebut some of the inevitable charges. Perhaps I could put together a slick Powerpoint presentation and invite everyone over tomorrow night for white wine and nibbles to really put my point –

'Hoy!'

My heart jumped out of the passenger seat into the ashtray and sat there quivering and I turned to see a pale fist squash and squelch against the driver-side window as it hammered. The owner of the fist yelled again. 'Charlie, get out of this fucking car! Now!'

Oops.

Another voice came from behind me, muffled through distance and tears as I struggled with the seatbelt clips.

'Is that him? Adrian? Has he got George? Has he got him? Adrian?!'

I took a couple of days to finally undo the safety belt and make sure it was fully taken up into the galvanised steel frame where I wouldn't trip on it. I spent another fortnight rechecking the ignition key, ensuring I had definitely turned the car off. And then, and only then, did I stop to take six months examining the precision German stitching where the wheel met the steering column.

'Charlie!' Adrian yelled again with a burst of hammerings-on-windowings as accompaniment.

I decided to get out because they both seemed to want me to so much and it sounded like Adrian was not too far from whipping out his Swiss Army knife and slashing the roof open. Slamming the door, I straightened up, my shirt heavy and cold with sweat in the night air.

'Where is he? Huh? What the fuck have you done with my son?'

I looked up at Adrian. He looked, well, he looked out of it in a big way. He had a thick checked shirt pulled over a fancy evening-dress waistcoat, untied scuffy Timberlands finished off his black tuxedo trousers, his old leather coat bunched in his tight fist and Polo by Ralph Lauren on the breeze.

His face? Well that of a man who's had a bit of a night to say the least. Likewise Liz, a few yards away on the pavement outside my flat in a cocktail dress and trainers, a heavy sweater pulled over the top, hugging herself in a long black coat.

'Well? Come on!' Adrian spat and with a shove, sent me tripping back against the car.

'He . . . he . . . he's in the house.'

Liz turned and ran back towards the front door and Adrian and I marched in head-down serious silence after her, shivering against the cold blue street.

Well, Adrian marched. I sort of jogged along

behind like a bad puppy who was worried that his mess on the carpet would mean he wouldn't get his Pedigree Chum.

At the door, Liz crouched, calling cooing sympathetic noises desperately through the letter box. She stood up as we joined her on the step. He face was cold, the evening make-up streaked, her nose red from tears.

'I can hear him inside,' she said to Adrian. She didn't look at me. She couldn't look at me. Adrian turned.

'Open the door,' he said flatly through clenched everything. Teeth, fists. I even think he'd clenched his ears.

'Look, Ade –' I began.

'Later, Charlie. Now just' – he let out a long breath, 'just open the door and let me get my son back.'

I reached down to my tight trouser pockets for the door-keys but remembered how I didn't want the line ruined and had put them instead in my new Hugo Boss overcoat pocket: I tried reaching for that but couldn't quite manage it, hanging up as it was in Deborah's hall.

'I don't have the keys, I . . . I've left them . . .' My voice trailed off and Liz exploded.

'Oh Charlie, you thoughtless, thoughtless . . .' she sobbed and she began to rain down tight fists and hot tears on my chest. An upstairs light clicked on from another flat. *She's going to bring the whole of NW4 out of their houses at this rate*, I thought. Selfishly, just as a change.

But her tears didn't disturb anyone else you'll be glad to know.

No, everyone else was disturbed by the loud crack of Adrian kicking my front door off its hinges. I cried out in complaint as Liz threw herself indoors in a frenzy.

'You!' Adrian blazed, turning to face me, his nose inches from mine, wild fury in his eyes. 'You don't say a fucking word.' And, holding this tableau frozen on the gravelly doorstep for a sharp moment like some photo-story, he broke away and vanished through the door offering a soothing male *It's okay it's okay* to his terrified family.

I sat down on the step with a sigh and scratched my itching scalp. Some dry gel gathered up under my finger-nails and I picked at them idly. The cold September wind blew about my ankles. Somewhere a dog barked, a black cab hissed past the house and all was night-time quiet again.

An honest mistake, I thought to myself. Really, just an honest forgetful mistake. My mind was on so many other things when I'd got back from Oxfam that evening, plotting what to wear, what to say. I'd parked George, sleeping silently in his foldaway pushchair, in the kitchen while I grabbed a quick shower and then, well . . .

Just an honest mistake.

No, no, Charlie, not this time. I shook my head and began to rub my hands together for warmth. I was so used to justifying every little nuance of my behaviour with technical data, I was having trouble fighting off the internal spin doctors.

I stood up quickly and began to pace around the pavement, stamping my feet and kicking the gravel. Whether this was an attempt to fight the cold or to see off nagging thoughts I can't be sure. Which ever one it was, however, neither was going anywhere.

'Adrian!' I shouted, making myself jump in the silence. I didn't like being left out here alone with my inner voice. I couldn't trust it. I stepped up into the door-frame. Should I go in? Should I leave them to it? Are they cursing me for standing out here like a coward or glad I'm not showing my face?

Then, with a thud and a clatter and a dark, hateful *Ex-cuse me,* they appeared, pushing past me. Adrian had a giggling gurgling George held tightly to his chest, oblivious to the distress and drama of the evening. Liz carried the foldaway pushchair, collapsed in one hand, the other she used to wipe her eyes hard. Wiping relief and exhaustion away into the night.

'Oh, th-there you are,' I bluffed and blustered. 'I was . . .'

'What?!' Adrian snarled. 'Worried? Were you worried? Huh?' His voice was deep and loud and flat against the suburban silence.

'No no,' I said, backing away. 'Look, Adrian, I . . . I don't know what to say. I . . . I . . .' But nothing came, just a tightening around the throat. Because, really, I didn't know what to say.

'Do you have any idea how angry I am? Do you? Huh? Where the hell were you? Of course, at Deborah's. And what if we hadn't come home early? You'd still be out trying to get your leg over and George would be lying in there, lying in there . . .' He began to shake, full tilt and I knew I had to let him get it out.

'As long as Charlie's okay, isn't that it? Nothing else matters. Charlie and his little experiments with everyone else's lives. You've done nothing but think of yourself since Deborah left. How can I get her back, how can I be happy again, *nurgh nurgh nurgh*, you're like a spoilt fucking child.'

He stood glaring at me for a few seconds, my mouth opening and closing but saying nothing.

'Ade, let's just go,' Liz pleaded from beside the car. 'Let's get him back home in the warm.'

Adrian spun and walked over to the large estate car, handing George to a tearful Liz who began to climb into the passenger seat while I stood, the motionless spectator. Adrian slammed the car door but turned and came marching back to me, stopping only when our toes almost touched.

'What the hell's wrong with you, huh?'

I looked down, my face burning despite the cold. I tensed for the further reproach, for the final battering. It didn't come. I looked up at Adrian again. He wiped his eye hard with the heel of his hand.

'Huh?' he said. 'What the hell's wrong with you?'

He actually wanted me to answer him, to explain myself.

I could have told him it wasn't my fault, that I was doing the selfish thing, like I'm supposed to. That if he wanted to be cross at someone, he should rail against natural selection who designed me this way.

I could have told him that modern evolutionary psychology would be on my side. Explained about surrogate parents, how they will never be careful enough, how we're designed only to favour our own. I could have asked him why he was getting so upset about a child he apparently didn't want. I had all these things to say, all these things on my side.

I just had to choose the right words.

'I'm sorry,' I said.

He stared at me. He turned and he left.

Because he didn't give a damn about any of that.

And for the first time in far too long, with the tears stinging in my eyes, neither did I.

TWENTY-NINE

'Howabout "Planet of the Dopes"?'

Billy Crystal

My first sensation is that I'm swimming. Which can't be right. Because prior to this I can distinctly recall a mattress and a duvet and a blanket of confusion coupled with regret and a headache.

But now I've moved on to swimming. The pool I'm in is long. Long in a can't-see-the-end-of-it sort of a way and smells of chlorine and urine mixed with the echoing slap of shouts against the tiles which reminds me of Thursday afternoons at the school baths.

And I'm naked. And I'm swimming.

Or rather I'm trying to swim, desperately, but my ankles have been strapped tightly together in what is either a perverse punishment for forgetting to bring my trunks, or a very controversial new addition to the Bronze Life Savers Award.

In a gulping, coughing panic, I check my fellow swimmers to see if one might stop and untie me. But I'm either swimming in the most highly polished, well-kept, no petting-in-the-shallow-end municipal pool in London, gleaming mirrors all around or I'm swimming against five thousand identical copies of myself in a pool even more infinitely wide than it is infinitely long. I'm not entirely sure what it is I'm swimming towards, but it is all of a sudden vitally important to me that I get to the other side of the pool before, well, before my other selves do. I'm not in the lead, I'm aware of that. Aware because I can see another Charles Ellis about three strokes in front churning the stinging chemical water to foam, his tail (his *tail*?) whipping fizzing whiteness in my face.

His *tail*?

And also there is Jeremiah, nattily decked out in Reeboks, baseball cap and a yellow singlet, pacing the edge of the pool with a whistle and stopwatch, yelling at me to put my back into it, his gravelly voice echoing over and over in waves against the wet walls.

So I keep swimming.

But the more I struggle, the more I strain and yearn and thrash in the pool, the more the other Charleses (*Charli*?) whip away from me, their slim white tails (yes, *tails*) flicking through the choppy blue until my vision is crowded and knotted with myself. Jeremiah begins calling out positions.

Ellis, you're number ten sixteen, Ellis, you're number ten sixteen, Ellis you're number ten seventeen.

And I keep swimming.

But then my arms, overcome with exhaustion, stinging and buzzing with the effort, simply stop.

So I wake up.

It was an unfamiliar bedroom, bitingly cold. The digital clock on the table read 10:17 a.m. I blinked away the night-time glue and sniffed a bit. A very unfamiliar bedroom indeed. The lumpy creaking mattress, the black-ash wardrobe, the picked-off wood-chip – they were all mine. The gritty greying sheet that I sprawled and dribbled over, fully dressed in a crumpled suit, was definitely mine. But this wasn't my bedroom.

This bedroom came equipped with a piping hot mug of PG Tips and a plate of hot buttered toast on its bedside, the tea's rich steam dancing towards the peeling ceiling in the morning sunlight.

I couldn't recall the last time I'd awoken to toast and a hot cuppa. It must have been years ago. It's a snug, comforty feeling.

Or rather, it is if you live with someone. If you live

alone it's the cause of not a small bit of concern. Maybe I was still dreaming? Freud always claimed dreams were wish fulfilment. Did I wish there was someone around to bring me breakfast and tuck me in?

Yep, pretty much.

I sat up with a creak and a groan, my clothes sticky on my body, and took a hot sip of tea.

Nope, definitely not dreaming. My subconscious has strict instructions regarding the admittance of cups of tea that aren't wearing the proper sugar.

'You up?' came a voice that caused me to yelp. Out of shock mostly, that living alone thing again. But also out of slooshing-boiling-water-down-my-shirt-ness.

'I'll take that as a yes,' the voice said and Brad pushed open the bedroom door, munching a blackened corner of toast. 'I would have knocked, buddy,' he said with a crispy chomp, 'but there's no front door.'

As Brad banged around in the kitchen, I gulped back sweet milky toast and buttery slivers of tea (not the greatest chef, Brad) and sat up a bit. I chewed my lip, it tasting fractionally nicer than the toast, and tried to rub some life back into my face, massage a bit of sense out of the scenery.

It was too soon for panic. I had panic jotted down as a definite *to-do* for that morning. But it was running second on the agenda to head-spinning bewilderment. We were doing things alphabetically, presumably.

What the hell was Brad doing here? Apart from, if the sounds were anything to go by, constructing an armoured car in my kitchen? Had he spoken to Adrian? Did he know about my George fiasco? More importantly, had he spoken to Deborah? Shit, did he know about us? Did he know he had been overthrown in the duvet-sharing stakes?

I listened out for a moment with a cold shock of panic. Bewilderment stood up and shook my hand and was asked to send in the next candidate on the list. Because yes, Brad was definitely constructing an armoured car in the kitchen.

I gave my head a quick scratch to speed up the thought processes, rolled out of bed and decided I was best getting out of this fancy babe-magnet clobber. Facing Brad was going to be difficult enough, I thought, tugging frantically at a trouser button – I didn't want to damage my case by appearing in front of the judge in a hooped jersey and with a swag bag over my shoulder.

Breathless and sweaty with nerves, I eased my head round the door and found him in the kitchen, the radio on, trying to do something ill-advised with an egg. Of course, I'd been trying to do the same thing twelve hours ago with Deborah, but by Brad's chirpy singing-along and rustling-up, I could only figure he didn't know this.

Yet.

I stood and watched him for a few moments, trying to gauge which way the explosion was going to throw me in.

'Hey, there you are, pal. Do you want this?' he offered, waving a pan at me. I peered in.

'Is that, er, is that scrambled or fried?' I asked cautiously.

'Oh, it's boiled actually.'

'Then absolutely, I'm starving.'

We ate a while in the lounge, plates on laps, mugs on the floor, every so often exchanging shrugs and eyebrows. He hadn't given away a thing.

I had to say something, the silence was stabbing me in the side and twisting the blade maliciously with every mouthful of breakfast.

'So,' I said.

Yes, not great, I'll admit. But I hadn't been up long, bewilderment was still wandering around the building looking for the exit and I was still letting the sunlight between my ears.

'So,' Brad repeated, nodding.

He obviously didn't want to give too much away either.

A slow realisation seeped in, like an upstairs bath left running, as we munched and gulped noisily. And that was, if Brad didn't know Deborah and I were back together, then he had no reason to think he wasn't still going out with her.

So what in the name of pair-bonding theory was he doing here?

The world in which I lived gave a low Richter of anxiousness which rattled all the crockery.

'So, er, what brings you here?' I asked tentatively.

'Cos I haven't seen you in ages,' he said, spraying toast crumbs onto the sofa, 'and you're a mate and I thought it about time we had a pow-wow. Y'know?'

'Oh,' I said. 'Oh right, right yes. Probably a good idea.'

'Reckon so.'

'Mm.'

This make any sense to you?

We sat in silence again. A silence that threatened to go on for ever if one of us didn't just bloody well do the decent thing and cough up onto the slide whatever it was we had on our chests. The deafening hush got the better of Brad first. Thank Christ. I guess it's because he works in sales, he likes to keep the patter going.

'Tch, would you look at all this shit,' he said, rising out of his seat and wandering over to the cluttered desk. 'You been shopping then?' Huge paper carrier bags sat squarely on the desk top, Jigsaw, Gap, Reiss, Paul Smith, tissue paper spilling over onto the floor like generous cappuccino. The surface was reams deep in receipts and

388

notes and diagrams feverishly scribbled. Mostly, upon closer inspection, about Deborah and Brad. Maps, strategies, back-up plans. Ring-binders, splayed open face down like prefab roofing, Post-Its upon Post-It upon walls and lamps, books in teetering piles on the squeaky office chair. I clenched my buttocks tightly hoping he wouldn't probe too deeply.

At the desk, that is. Not my buttocks.

'Fuck, this is going back a bit,' he said and he plucked the Blu-Tacked photo of himself, Ade and I off the wall with a sticky thup. 'God, look at us,' and he laughed.

That second, it dawned on me, any stranger peering in through the curtains at this scene would be enjoying an American sitcom moment. The autumn sun grinning through the window, the smell of eggs and toast floating in from the kitchen, two old friends chuckling over shared nostalgia. We looked like we were about to grab a bagel and go and shoot some hoops in the yard or take our freckly kids to *li'l league* or some such bollocks.

What this live studio audience would be missing, though, would be that, sitting perched on the sofa, watching Brad pore over the snapshot, I was pretty much about to shit my pants.

I couldn't get the gibbering panicky paranoia from off my shoulders, even though I wriggled and beat at it like cobwebs. This was all too weird. As far as he was concerned, he'd slept with my fiancée, the ex-fiancée he knew for a *fact* I wanted to get back together with, while my side of the bed was still warm and he'd lied about it for months. And here he was, all cups of tea and, what had he said? — *you're a mate*. If I didn't get an explanation soon I was going to burst. A bulging water balloon hurled by a year ten lad, last day of term, that was me.

'What's this?' he said, turning over the photo and holding up the white side, covered with scribbles, for me to see. 'Maths?'

I peered at it. 'Huh? Oh, er, equations,' I said.

'What's it mean?'

'It's about, um, friendship.'

'Yeah?' he said, reading it again.

'Yeah, it's nothing. I just copied it down. A guy called George Price came up with it.' I was wittering, keep the mood light. *Easy there, eeeeeasy*. 'Kind of a way of measuring goodwill.'

'Charitable fella?'

'Er, yes, yes sort of.' I thought about the equation, the conclusion he'd drawn. The empathy I'd shared.

'Give him a call then, buddy,' Brad said, flipping the photo onto the desk and walking towards the door. He gave me a slap on the leg and disappeared. 'He can help us fix this door. C'mon.'

I followed him gingerly out into the squinty sunlight, half expecting it to be a trap. A circle of police cars, helicopters droning above. Head down, back of the van, off to adultery jail. But outside was just a quiet suburban Sunday. September had stripped the trees of their greenery, the sun dappling the wet floor of leaves. I helped Brad heave the door up and we leant it against the outside of the house. We stood for a while, hands on our hips like two old dads, every so often Brad leaning forward, picking a splinter of wood from the hinges and blowing on it, meaninglessly.

'No tool kit, I s'pose?' Brad asked, peering at the tattered frame.

'Er . . . no, no nothing,' I said. 'No drills or crowbars or axes or anything like that anywhere in the place. At all. Nothing you could hit anything with.'

Brad stepped back, hands back on hips, sucking in air through his teeth noisily like an expert. 'I could really do with a nice big heavy hammer . . .'

'Look, Brad,' I shouted suddenly, the water balloon bursting loud and flat and messy on the playground floor. My heart pounding violently against my ribs. 'What . . . what's this about? What do you want?'

I had to know. I couldn't play any more. For Chrissakes, I had a busy day planned. Deborah was bound to phone at some point to scream and holler and cry and curse me for running out on her. I had to be home for that. Plus I was expecting Adrian and Liz to turn up with revenge and a cricket bat at any moment and I hadn't even got a cake in.

'Well,' he said, squatting down and picking up a bent

screw from the ground calmly. 'I had a very shaky Adrian on the phone to me last night.'

'Oh, did you?'

'You really screwed up there. The kid's fine of course. He was never in any danger. Built like a fuckin' tank that one.'

'Right, right.' I nodded.

Shit that was a weight off. I don't know what I would have done if George had come to any harm. I mean, think about it, it was Adrian's *son*. All that talk last weekend about not wanting kids, about how he'd been a mistake. And then that look of fear, that white smack in the face of uncontrollable terror last night. He'd held his future, his very *self*, in his arms and felt that tiny heartbeat. That tiny pulse he'd almost had torn away from him.

I knew for the rest of that tiny child's life, he'd have the best dad in the whole world.

'Plus,' Brad said, and he stood up to face me, 'Deborah gave me a call.'

My whole world lurched in a Richter of fear, incomparable to the first, the ground cracking open wide.

Oh no, my mistake. It was Brad's grin.

I stepped back, away, instinctively. *What? What? Cannot compute, system error.*

'Congratulations, buddy,' and he threw his arms around me in a tight bearhug. 'Congratulations. It's fantastic, frickin' fantastic. Just say I'm still your best man.'

'You're, er . . . you're still . . .' I coughed and swelled as my ribcage was crushed. 'You're still the best man.'

'Grand!' And he released me with a groan. He stepped back, hands on my shoulders like a proud parent on Graduation Day.

'Any booze in the place?'

'Er . . . no, no none.'

'Better sort that out then, hadn't we, Mr Groom. C'mon.'

'B-but the door . . . ?' I said, still reeling, my mind on a thousand other things, clicking together a *Krypton Factor* puzzle of times and dates and conclusions slowly, its tongue poked out with concentration.

'You got anything worth nicking?'

'Huh? What?'

'TV, stereo, microwave, video – what have you got?'

'Oh, er . . .' I thought back to my recent trade-ins. 'Nothing.'

'Nothing?'

'No, no I got rid of it all.'

'Why d'ya do that?'

'Erm. Y'know I'm not entirely sure.'

'Well it doesn't matter then,' and he bounced up and down on the spot excitedly like a boy on Christmas morning. 'And we're taking your car so move.'

*

'Can I ask a question?' I said.

'Oooh, I've got to get myself one of these,' Brad oozed, paying me no attention, lost in the guy world, lost in a bucket seat and a leather trim and a wide smooth corner. He had insisted on driving the Porsche to the shops. And insisted on driving a very long-winded show-offy route indeed. We passed a sign for Leeds at one point with a worryingly small number of miles next to it. And of course, he had the roof down. I had whined and whinnied about insurance liabilities but after he'd playfully punched my arm fifty or sixty thousand times, each one with a matching *Gooowarrrrn*, I'd tossed him the keys resignedly.

Using my less fractured arm, naturally.

'Where d'you get her from?'

'Hn? Oh some hire place off the Edgware Road. It goes back tomorrow.'

'Another part of the act, eh?' and I caught him smile in the rear-view mirror.

I shrugged.

Brad had figured the whole thing out. I mean, just because he's stupid, doesn't mean he's stupid. They'd all figured it out. The City job, the car, the clothes. This absurd haircut I'd stuffed under a baseball cap. Between Ade and Liz reporting back, and Deborah on the phone every night, they'd all managed to draw up a pretty accurate picture of the culprit. My motives, my alibis, my *modus* as it were *operandi*. They'd found the whole thing faintly hilarious.

'Suit me, one of these,' he said, having a bit of a wiggle in the seat like it was a new pair of Levi's. 'I've got the flat looking good, I've got the job. I've turned the spare room into a home cinema. One of these babies on the front? I'd have them queuing up.'

'Brad,' I opened again, swallowing hard twice. 'Did you sleep with Deborah?'

'Ha!' he barked. 'Absolutely not.'

'She wasn't interested?'

'No of course she wasn't, you dope. Why should she be?'

'Well, because . . .' I took a few sets of traffic lights to mull this over.

A week ago, even 24 hours ago, if you'd asked me, I could have come up with thirty-six reasons, sixteen case studies, ten annotated lithographs and a bibliography.

Today? Everything was the same and totally different.

'Coz you're a success, y'know? Look at you. Like you say – your flat, your job and everything. You're a winner, you've done well. Women are meant to want guys like you. Not guys like me.'

'Yeah? I haven't had a date in fourteen months. Who are these women?'

'Well . . . you know.'

'Nope.'

'That's what females find attractive,' I said.

'Listen to you. It doesn't work like that. For someone so clever you can be mighty dumb. Women want this, men want that. Science says this, science proves that. What kind of world are you living in?'

I opened my mouth and said nothing.

'Okay fine, look at it your way. The world is a terrible lonely place, interstellar bleakness and all that sixth-form drivel. But you seem to think that means we should all be horrible to each other, whereas, I dunno, I prefer to think maybe knowing this means we should all just try and be a bit nicer to each other.'

'But for what purpose? To what end?'

'*To what end?* To try and be happy, you knob. If everything is as you say, it's all we have.'

'And are you happy?'

'Me?' Brad thought for a while, staring into the winter sunshine. 'Yes. yes I am. Work's okay, the flat looks all right, Adrian's calmed down about George a bit. It's a sunny day, I'm sitting in a freakin' Porsche, listening to . . . oh.' He flicked on the radio and a roaring saxaphone burst around us. 'H-heyyy, listening to Springsteen –'

'The Boss,' we said in unison.

'I've got my mate by my side, we're going to head back to his pad and get hammered. So yes. Happy is what I am.' Brad swung the car round through a gap in the traffic and pulled up with Teutonic grace outside a corner newsagent. 'And you? Happy now?'

'Happy? No, not especially. I think I've fucked a lot of things up.'

'Deborah, you mean?'

I sighed.

He shut off the engine, unclipped his seatbelt and turned to face me, perching his fake Raybans on his head.

'Listen,' he said, squinting in the lunchtime sun. 'Two months. Two damn months I spent listening to Deborah talk about you. Phoning, dropping round, crashing on the sofa. Two months of sitting in her flat listening to her talk, watching her flick through photo albums, letting her cry.'

I sat silently through this, open-mouthed, catching grit and dirt and flies and other nutritious ingredients that make inner London air such an ideal brunchy treat. My ears were taking delivery of the words and running about the loading bay, confused, no record of any purchase order.

Was he *serious*?

'She was upset and needed someone to talk to who knew both sides. It should have been Liz but she's had other things on her mind.'

'Hmm.' I nodded. Then, 'Shit,' the memory of last night so pin-sharp it drew blood.

'She didn't want you to know about it so she insisted, *insisted*, all of us keep shtum. She wanted to figure all the shit out on her own and didn't need you on her doorstep every night putting pressure on her and fucking with her head. She just wanted a few weeks over the summer to find another job and sort herself out. And to assure herself, old buddy' – and he slapped me on the leg, clambering out of the low car with a slam – 'to assure herself that the stupid selfish thicky dope she'd chosen to marry was absolutely and incontrovertibly the right stupid selfish thicky dope for her. Won't be a sec,' and he jogged off into the shop.

Alone at last. Alone with my head for the first time that morning. As I sat there, deep in both bucket seats, and thought, the rest of the world wandered past about their Sunday morning business. Buying newspapers, milk, bread. Occasionally a male would loiter over the car, peering at the body-work, pouting at the curves. And on any other day in my life I would have luxuriated in the spectacle, in the status. Sat back, turned up the radio, pecking away the competition, claiming the seed for myself.

But that day I just sat. Sat and thought about Deborah, about Adrian, about George. About happiness, evolution. About men and cars, about women and wine.

About a lot of things.

Brad was taking his time. I glanced over at the shop, a standard North London newsagent. Cards advertising discreet massages in the window, a faded bubblegum machine on the pavement. Shops that seem to survive on the curiously disparate stock of hardcore porn and cat litter.

Brad appeared with a wave, holding a carrier bag aloft.

Oh, make that porn, cat litter and the odd dusty bottle of champagne.

He tossed a newspaper onto my lap and climbed in.

'Thought that might interest you.'

I scanned the headlines, my eyes fixing on a photograph. There in full colour at the bottom smiled a friendly face. Three friendly faces in fact. A family. The child was a day old and was the dead spit of his dad. The tiny ears, the gentle smile. His eyes were wider, keener. Full of wonder and excitement. I failed to suppress a goofy smile.

Jeremiah, Diana and their new son Ralph smiled back. Happily.

'And what if she'd wanted your kids?' I blurted out, throwing the paper on the table.

We were in my kitchen. It was about ten to twelve. Brad clomped about, slamming cupboards, looking for champagne glasses.

'What, if Debs had come on to me?' he said, peering under the sink.

'Yeah.' It was just something I needed putting straight, something I needed planing down and chamfering off and knocking flush to the rest of the world. 'You'd have stepped in, wouldn't you?'

'She did.'

'She did?' My palms went cold suddenly, my face prickly. 'She did?'

I knew it. I fucking knew it. Well it was all going to come out now. I hoisted myself up and perched on the worktop, drumming my heels against the cupboard doors.

Bring it on, I can take it.

'The day before you came to see me at work, that weekend I set you up with Ronnie.'

He closed the cupboard door and lifted the bottle from the flimsy candy-striped bag with a rustle.

'I was at Deborah's. We'd had some dinner, it was late. She'd had too much wine and we got onto talking about families and children and you, and she started to cry. Wouldn't stop. Big tears. I mean, she was just drunk and upset about everything, she asked for a hug and I gave her a hug and she tries to kiss me.'

'Serious?'

'Serious. But I stand up and go and make some coffee and when I get back she's sniffing and she says sorry and don't go and I spend the night on her sofa.'

'You didn't . . . I mean, she offered and you could've . . . but you didn't . . .'

'No I didn't, of course I didn't.' He was genuinely hurt. Because I'd genuinely hurt him. 'How long have we known each other? Mates don't do that shit.' He tore off the foil, uncranked the wire and began to ease the bottle round in his arms, loose but firm. 'I can't believe you have to ask. Mates, I think you'll find, don't screw around with other people's wives. Even wives-to-be. They don't go behind your back just to get laid. I mean I'm desperate . . .'

There was a loud Pop Clang Whe-*heyy!* as the cork ricocheted off the hood of the oven and frothing bubbles arced onto the grubby lino.

'. . . but I'm not an animal. Here.' I took the bottle from his fizzy fingers. 'Here's to the wedding.'

An hour later I stood in the shower, letting cold water shiver and burn me out of that oily, slept-in-your-clothes feeling. I had Brad next door in the lounge making phone calls, I had a half-empty champagne bottle on the kitchen draining board, I had an overdraft in the bank and George Price on my mind.

His equation, the one Brad had found scrawled on the back of the photograph, was a turning point in the world of theoretical biology. Alone in that Euston garret, nothing but a bare bulb and an academic mind, he had figured out what he thought was a way to mathematically measure human nature. Applied his rigorous scientific thinking to the human spirit. Whether it paid, in the long run, to be good guy or a bad guy. Superman or Lex Luthor.

Look out for your friends, help the aged, bob-a-job.

Or mean-spirited, self-serving, *nurgh nurgh nurgh* egotism.

'I'm fixin' a cup of Joe, you fancy one, buddy?' Brad rapped on the bathroom door.

'Sure,' I yelled out over the roar of the icy water. I lathered up some shampoo. Well, some Fairy Liquid actually, the shampoos and conditioners having been binned along with other non-essentials.

There had been a perfectly sound socio-biological reason for that if you recall.

But it escaped me for the moment.

Of course as Wendy had explained that afternoon, George Price discovered that looking after number one, following your instincts and screwing over the other guy actually won more tricks in the end. And George, after double-checking the maths with his calculator, another calculator and his spare abacus, finally opened his mind to this realisation, but not before he opened his wrists to the walls of his tiny room.

I gave the shower button a jab and stood there, dripping onto the porcelain.

I thought about Jeremiah.

Together with his partner and his son. How had the article put it? *We've never seen them happier.*

And why? Because they're simple. They're gene machines. Pastry cutters. Designed for one thing.

And us? Well we're more complicated than that. We have mortgages and jobs and regrets. Bills to pay, CVs to send out and shower nozzles to descale. We have disagreements, misunderstandings and tears.

But we're all going through it, every one of our simple species. And we can help each other. We can listen and lend, fix each other's doors and paint each other's kitchens.

See, nature isn't interested in our happiness. Not at all. It cares only for our numbers. So if you're going to obey it, bow down and worship — don't expect many smiles. We came up with happiness and friendship and love on our own.

And once you accept that nature won't lend a hand, you either do what George Price did . . .

. . . or you say fuck it, I'll find it on my own.

The smell of coffee slipped under the door, shaking me awake, and I stepped out of the shower. I bunged a threadbare towel about my flabby middle and padded into the lounge. My coffee sat steaming on the desktop, a desktop Brad had cleared of rubbish and straightened up neatly. He was on the phone again. I gave him a matey nod of thanks and took my coffee through to the bedroom.

I yanked open the wardrobe.

Science doesn't believe in friendship, it can't find a

reason for it. We only do good to those who can repay the favour, it says. Reciprocal altruism, it's called. I could lend you a book on it if you're interested. I've got about a dozen. You won't have to worry about returning it either. I've also books that say that your mates are inclined to nick your girlfriend if they can. You can help yourself to those, too.

They believe that, in all species, there is no reward for doing the right thing, no reward for being decent.

I grabbed a clean pair of jeans and began to dress.

There was a light knock and Brad stuck his head round the door.

'You decent?'

I allowed myself a smile.

'That was Deborah. I told her I'd drop you round there when you're ready.'

'Is she furious?' I asked, pulling on my trainers.

'No no, I explained what happened. But she says if you're just going to come over and pretend to have been elected the President of the United States or something you shouldn't bother.'

I laughed.

'I really thought I'd blown it, that she'd be livid.'

'No. Adrian's livid. I spoke to him just now.'

I sat up quickly, my hands cold and prickly suddenly.

'R-really?'

Brad grinned.

'Yep. Debs was round there this morning and she and

Liz discussed wedding dresses and flowers all morning. He's gonna kill you when he sees you. Which is tonight at eight if you're not out at Oxfam or Wall Street or whatever.'

'No, I'm not doing anything like that any more.'

'Good, now get a move on.'

I stood up and reached for a shirt.

Which to choose? The plain grey – classic and stylish? The black V-neck – a bit more dangerous, a bit more glamorous?

I grabbed one at random from the yellowing pile at the bottom of the wardrobe.

It was faded, baggy-necked, creased, smelled musty and damp. It made me look exactly like the dozy, unemployed, thoughtless fool that I was.

It felt great.

Dear Tell Me How,

My mummy says thank-you for having me to your office to see the people who make the magazine is made. It was a very nice day and I missed school but not much. There were so many desks and my favourite was the drawings. The man did a picture of Ears-ears for me to have at home and I did put it in the hutch so Steve Austin can remember his friend. He is missing her a lot.

We went to the shop and I got a lolly and a new rabbit today. She is called Jamie Summers because they are in love. Mum said it is true that animals are like people and get lonely without their friends so Steve Austin should be happy now.

Also because I gave him some Toblerone but don't tell.

Master Charles Ellis aged 8

Here is a picture I done of the wedding of rabbits. Jamie Summers is the one doing a poo.

ACKNOWLEDGEMENTS

I have done my very best to get all the science right. But I probably haven't. So any glaring inaccuracies are completely my fault and I apologise for them.

For a much more well-rounded and grown-up take on evolutionary psychology, human behaviour and science in general, I would recommend getting yourself outside *The Moral Animal* by the extraordinarily lucid Robert Wright, *Unweaving the Rainbow* by the labcoated powerhouse who is Richard Dawkins, *Why Nothing Can Travel Faster Than Light* by David and Barry Zimmerman, and *Darwin for Beginners* by Jonathan Miller and Boris van Loon. Very clever men whose bunsen-burners I am not fit to buff up, and I thank them for making my research such fun.

Also thanks to all those who didn't punch me when I forced early drafts upon them (they know who they are) and to my family for their encouragement.

Thank you to Elizabeth Wright and the Darley

Anderson team, plus of course Andy McKillop and all at Random House for their tremendous support.

And finally thank you to Helen for letting me borrow her fine word processor and even finer female insight.

And Neal — who knows, more than most, at two in the morning, what isn't funny.